MUSHROOM SATORI *the cult diary*

a novel by
Joseph Szimhart

D0899692

Aperture Press

ISBN: 978-0-9850026-9-5
Library of Congress Control Number: 2012937737

This is a work of fiction. Names, characters, places, and incidents are either the product of the author's imagination or are used fictitiously, and any resemblance to actual persons, living or dead, business establishments, events, or locales is entirely coincidental.

First Edition, 2013

Cover and interior designed by Jere Stamm
Set in Adobe Garamond

Acknowledgements

My Appreciation goes to all who encouraged and critiqued this novel after reading early and later stages, especially Robyn Arielli and Rick Larsen (author of *Cult Encounter*) in Western Australia, Mark Laxer (author of *Take Me For a Ride* and *The Monkey Bible*), Kenneth Paolini (co-author of *400 Years of Imaginary Friends* and father of Christopher Paolini of *Eragon* fame), J. Paul Lennon (former priest and author of *"Fr. Maciel" who art in bed*), and my eccentric old friend John Snell in New Mexico who often believed in me more than I believed in myself—the lights of inspiration cast shadows of discouragement during the creative process. Inspiration for this story came from many hundreds of current and former "cult" members and their families that I've encountered, confronted, and, when I could, assisted during the past decades. Key sequences in the story were derived from the behavioral health clinics and state institutions that have employed me, especially *Pennhurst State School and Hospital* (closed by 1987) and *Montgomery County Emergency Services* on the grounds of *Norristown State Hospital* in Pennsylvania. I would also like to acknowledge the *International Cultic Studies Association* for the opportunity to submit my book reviews and articles for their journals and for the challenges as a writer and speaker at their annual conferences for the past two decades plus.

Motivation came from my three wonderful daughters Nadia, Ana, and Lani who had no idea I was working on this story that addresses the transitional period a young adult faces after leaving home.

And special thanks to the staff at Aperture Press, to Sharon Wagner, Steve Wagner, and especially to editor Jere Stamm for his encouragement, diligence, suggestions, and his sensitivity for the theme behind the story.

Finally, I dedicate this novel to my dear wife, Becky, who was not so surprised that the mushroom emerged as a key theme in the story. She can add this one to her collection!

Was ist Aufklärung?

—Immanuel Kant

Prologue

"Hello. Please come in. You must be Jake's mother. Neal and I just got off the phone," he said, indicating that he spoke with her husband. "Please, have a seat."

Monica shook his hand and entered a small, neatly cluttered office. She removed her green scarf and long tan overcoat. Her host hung the coat and scarf on a wooden door peg. She was dressed in dark green slacks with matching jacket and a white blouse. Her graying hair was tied back in a bun. She was slim with distinct Northern Italian features.

The man she met was around fifty-eight, a few years younger than her husband who referred her. He was thin, even wiry and well over six feet tall. He was clean shaven with a thick shock of parted and nearly white hair that slid over his right eye when he leaned forward. He indicated a seat, an old oak arm chair where Monica could sit next to his equally old oak desk.

Neal knew him from their college years when both were working on dissertations. While Neal concentrated on cognitive therapy, John Xavier focused on group behavior through social psychology. He compared and contrasted the behaviors of two groups: A Chicago street gang with a small, Evangelical church that had an authoritarian preacher. He found a host of similarities partially based on W.R. Bion's analysis of how neurotic groups tend to align with pathological leaders. In mid career, he developed an interest in Eastern religion, especially the non-dualist Hindu tradition, and vegetarianism. It was for these latter reasons, not to mention his knowledge of radical group behavior, that Neal felt his step-son might benefit from meeting him.

Books and documents filled a wall of shelves that extended to the ceiling. Monica noticed a number of statues and other objects along the top shelf. There was a bronze *Ganesha* or elephant-headed oddity with four arms, a stately Egyptian cat carved out of dark stone, a meditative wooden Buddha, a variety of metal bells, a standing framed family photo of four children seated on a stone wall, an old baseball with a signature, and a fifteen inch tall cast metal reproduction of the modernist

Walking Man by Giacometti. There was also a white porcelain statue of the *Woman Crowned with Twelve Stars* or the *Mary*, Mother of God as described in the *Book of Revelation*. Monica noticed each object in turn as she removed her coat. She had an urge to bless herself when she saw *Mary* but she repressed it.

"Well, Monica, tell me what's on your mind," John said as they both took their seats.

"Thank you for your time," Monica said as she set her soft leather bag next to her seat on the floor, but not before she pulled a few photos out of it. "Neal told you about Jacob, my son, who was involved with a Buddhist commune. I won't repeat the story unless you have some questions. Since he returned last year—you know about what happened the first two weeks—he has mostly kept to himself about it, at least around family. We're concerned that…"

"Yes, Neal told me about Jake spending a few days in a hospital. Rough start for him! But he seems to be doing well enough after that. I understand he held down a job since?"

"Yes, mainly in construction. He went back to the commune for a short visit some months ago and that worried me. He said he was helping someone with research. I don't know. Maybe I am overreacting, but I'm wondering if you could offer an opinion. Could he slip back into it? I heard that people that leave cults could benefit from a *deprogramming*."

"Well, I would not use that word—perhaps *debriefing* might be better. But most defectors work things out fine through re-socialization which is a more natural process, I think. It depends on the individual experience and the nature of the group. In any case, I'm not a deprogrammer or a cult recovery therapist, but I know one in the area," Xavier said as he grabbed a pencil and paper.

"It's hard, you know—we do not want to appear like meddling parents. He's an adult. He's always been private about his feelings with me. Introverted, maybe? Anyway, if you think he could use a debriefing by a professional, will you let him know? We want this to be his choice."

Xavier laid his pencil down. "Okay. Let me meet with him first. I'll be discreet.

This will be more like a friendly chat. We will see where it goes."

Monica spread out her photos on his desk.

"Here are some pictures to give you some idea. This one of Jacob was taken in 1997." Her son appeared with a bushy head of hair. In another, taken five years later, he was bald. "That young, bald man next to him is his good friend, Usagi— that was his cult name. I think his real name is Waylon. He is an Apache Indian," she said as she pointed to the Indian. "And this last one I took two weeks ago." Her son appeared smiling, nearly clean shaven, and with very short hair. "That is his older brother Harry with him," she said. Harry was a larger man but there was no mistaking that they were brothers standing arm in arm. "I'm relieved that he agreed to meet you. You can send us the bill."

"Not necessary," he said. "I told Neal this session is on me. I'm curious to pick his brain about his experience anyway. It's been a while since I studied fringe groups."

"What do you do, by the way?" Monica asked as if she suddenly felt ignorant. Neal only told her that his friend John could be a good resource for her son.

John Xavier laughed. "I'm semi-retired. I was a social studies teacher at a private high school until last year. Now I consult with several firms doing various things that involve staff harmony and productivity."

"I'm curious. Are you religious? Neal said you were a vegetarian. My son started eating meat again but sparingly after he left the commune."

"I do not attend a church or follow a group, if that's what you mean," he said with a hint of defensiveness. "I have a preference for an aspect of Hindu philosophy. It comes from a saint that lived in India over ten centuries ago. Oh, what else did you say about a vegetarian?"

"Are you a vegetarian?"

"Not strictly. I still eat fish now and then."

"My son will probably find you interesting then. He's not doctrinaire about anything these days, if you know what I mean. Jacob was raised Catholic. I think he's confused about religion now."

Xavier merely smiled and nodded.

One week later after a major snowstorm Jake drove his beat up, white Jeep Wrangler to the *Manayunk Café* in a Philadelphia suburb. He arrived fifteen minutes late. He noticed Xavier immediately, just as Monica described him, as the tall man with white hair wearing a blue and white Nordic sweater. He was seated and reading a book in his booth. Jake wiped his feet before approaching him.

"Hi."

Xavier looked up at a hooded young man in khaki pants. He removed his glasses. "Oh. Hello!"

"Sorry, I had trouble with parking. There's snow piled up everywhere. Where did you park?" Jake asked not bothering to introduce himself. He unzipped and removed his insulated denim hoodie, throwing it on the bench.

"I took a cab," Xavier said with a laugh as he leaned out to shake hands with his client. "No problem. I always bring a book," he said as he hesitated to grab Jake's bandaged right hand, but Jake shook hands readily anyway.

"Banged up my knuckles yesterday moving rocks," he said. "No worries. Nothing broken. What are you reading?" Jake wondered with half-interest as he took an opposite seat in the booth.

"A curious book I've had in my collection: *The Guru Papers*. It seemed appropriate for our conversation. I was going to give it to you."

Jake glanced at the gray paperback cover. He ignored the offer but he felt immediately comfortable with Xavier. They ordered black tea and desserts. The diner was nearly empty that winter morning. Many businesses were closed in the area.

"Thanks for meeting with me," Jake said flatly. "I want you to know I'm doing this as much for myself as I am for my mom. Neal told me something of your background. So, where would you like to start?"

"From the beginning, I suppose. What got you started on this quest?"

"Nietzsche."

Xavier was surprised by the direct and simple answer. "Nietzsche? How so?"

"He got me thinking. I wanted to take charge of my life rather than merely follow a pattern, you know, of the herd, as he would put it."

"Your mother seemed concerned that you rejected your Catholic faith. Did you?"

"That started before Nietzsche, when I was thirteen, a year after my dad died. And I was reading all that stuff about deviant priests in college. I lost interest in the whole bit. I'm still not convinced that the churches are what Jesus had in mind."

"And what about Buddhism?"

"What about it?" Jake took a sip of his tea. He stirred in more sugar.

"You must have come to some position after ten years in the commune."

"No, not really. I mean, I was not raised in a Buddhist culture. I realize now that much of the subtlety was lost on me."

"That's quite an admission. Let me run something by you that I presented in my dissertation…"

The two men engaged each other for several hours. Jake identified with Xavier's description of how easily the charisma around a psychopath can fool otherwise intelligent people. Xavier found him intriguing, quite normal in many ways, yet with an edge that he described as numinous to Monica. John saw no reason for Jake to seek further therapy.

A week after they met, Jake dropped off a stack of black and white marble notebooks at Xavier's office. They contained over ten years of his diary entries—most of them dated. He left a note saying, "Do whatever you want with them, as long as you do not reveal my identity."

After looking through the notebooks, Xavier called Jake. "My colleague, the recovery specialist I mentioned, might want to look these over, if that's okay with you."

"That's fine, but let him know that I am not interested in talking to him or anyone else about the contents."

Six months later, John Xavier returned the stack of notebooks to Jake in person. He also handed him a twenty-page proposal for a manuscript. "Look this over. The specialist sketched out a story based on your notes. He's thinking of basing a novel on it. What do you think?" Jake skimmed over the chapter briefs for a few minutes and smiled.

"Okay," he said. "Let him go for it."

Do you presume yourself to be free?
If so, then I want you to tell me what is your ruling idea,
and not that you have broken free of some fetter.
Are you the kind of man who ought to be unfettered?
For there are many who cast off their final value
when they cast away their chains.

—Friedrich Nietzsche, *Thus Spoke Zarathustra*

1   Panic

Lose the expense, loser. Fifty dollars and change will get you home from the airport with some left over if you are lucky. Mom is going to pity you. Neal will avoid asking why. Neal never mentions what an idiot he thinks you are. Now you can prove it to him. It took you ten years—6 October 2007

An anxious Jake stood in the line with his flight ticket for Minneapolis in hand. He had been waiting to board for a half hour. The delay occurred due to a minor malfunction with the carrier's food service at the Colorado Springs airport. It was early morning. Jake could hear a short Asian man behind him talking in Japanese into a mobile device. The man said, "tadaima," an expression that Jake understood to mean, 'at home'. The man's chatter triggered two-year-old memories of his Zen teacher's funeral in 2005.

"I should have left the old man's place back then," he thought with some irritation.

Images of years gone by and good friends left behind, a mere day before, flooded his mind. He began to feel uncomfortably warm as his mind reeled out more and more vivid memories. He snapped out of his disturbing trance when the flight attendant announced that boarding was about to begin. Then the surface beneath him began to quake.

Jake stared at the trembling ticket in his left hand. He clutched it with his right hand and drew it to his chest. He felt eerily odd and short of breath. He gasped several times. Dizziness nearly overcame him. He shuffled his way over a tilting floor to the nearest empty seats. He dropped his blue backpack and army green shoulder bag onto the blurry gray carpet as he clumsily collapsed onto a padded seat. As he sat leaning forward, he gasped for air and then lowered his head to his knees.

An alert, young flight attendant at the desk noticed him struggling. She quickly walked to his side, deftly squatting in her dark skirt next him, and calmly addressing him as her hand laid gently on his shoulder. "Sir, are you okay?"

Her soft touch and whispered words startled him. He lifted his head with his mouth wide open while gulping air. He tried to compose himself with eyes fixed on her dark stocking-covered knees.

"I just felt dizzy. I don't know what—I think I'll be okay," he blurted as he continued to struggle.

She kept her hand on his shoulder, her eyes locked on his face. She felt him trembling.

"Do you have a heart condition? Are you on medication for anything? Doing any drugs? Do you have a fear of flying?"

"No, ma'am, no, none of that. Never happened to me before..," Jake replied as his words trailed off. He glanced into her blue eyes and immediately felt ashamed to be falling apart in front of such a pretty woman. He lowered his eyes again.

A few minutes passed with the flight attendant continuing to sooth him with her calm attention until he lifted his head. "I feel better now," he said. After inhaling deeply and exhaling, he began to breathe normally. His fingers tingled. He rubbed his hands together. "Thanks."

"You look pale. Maybe you should lie down," she suggested. "We called for a medic," she said. "Here, come with me."

Jake took her free hand as she gripped him under his arm to help him rise. A large male passenger stepped up to assist. They half carried, half moved him to an open set of seats with no armrests where he could stretch out. The flight attendant asked a pilot behind the boarding counter to get some water. The passenger assisting her retrieved the bottle from the pilot and brought it to Jake who took two, uneasy sips. An observant female passenger grabbed his bags and brought them to him. The attendant recapped and set the clear plastic bottle down on the carpet.

"I think it best you change your flight. I can arrange something for you," she said. Jake nodded. He handed over his boarding pass.

As she explained the options, a chubby, bald man appeared with a stethoscope draped over his shoulder and a blood pressure cuff in hand. He introduced himself as a registered nurse. He asked Jake to sit up for a minute. Jake pushed his torso upright with effort. The nurse took Jake's pulse and he looked him over carefully, checking his eyes and skin, and then questioned him about his general health. Satisfied that Jake was basically fit, the nurse stood up.

"Seems you've had an anxiety reaction—that is my guess. Does flying bother you?"

Jake shook his head slightly to indicate it did not.

"Maybe you should rest a bit before you fly anywhere. You okay with that?"

"Yeah," Jake said while breathing methodically.

"Listen, fella," the nurse said, "I have to get back to my office; I can hang out here a few more minutes. Okay?"

"Okay. Thanks."

The flight attendant rescheduled Jake for an afternoon flight. "You can board at this gate in seven hours," she said. "Here is your ticket, Mister, uh, Jacob. Sorry, I can't pronounce your last name."

"Thassokay," Jake said, sounding apologetic. "It's a hard name to pronounce, if you're not a Polak! Americans usually say *Ger-zib*"

The impatient nurse was satisfied that Jake was breathing normally and his color had returned. "Have them call if you need me," he said as he walked away.

"Okay. Thanks." Jake stretched out on his back. Despite, or perhaps because of the din of background noises and occasional announcements over the intercom, he dozed off with his head propped on his backpack. Within a few minutes he was snoring. The snores caused a little girl nearby to laugh. Jake remained in that position for fifteen minutes until he grunted loudly. He sat up waving his left hand at something in the air. He appeared disoriented. Something had startled him.

The young, dark-skinned woman in tight jeans seated across from him looked away. Her hand was over her mouth to hide her reaction. Her five-year-old daughter was not so subtle. "Mommy, that man shouted," she said as she pointed to Jake. "He's funny, isn't he, mommy?" The little girl placed her hand over her mouth imitating her mother. Jake noticed their mirth and he knew he caused it.

17

"Uh, excuse me. Sorry," he said with a confused look. He slowly maneuvered his body into a sitting position. He glanced around. No one but the little girl and her mother acted like they noticed him. He nodded and smiled to the little girl who kept staring, hands still over her mouth. "I'm okay now," he told her. Jake picked up his things and relocated to a less occupied area across the aisle. He took out his notebook and recorded the dream.

One minute you are watching a large-eyed, green bug peacefully eating an insect in a sun-drenched meadow. The next minute, after the green bug spots you, you watch its face morph into a red-eyed snarling demon. It leaps large disappearing into the thicket next to you. You know it is about to spring. You try to run but your legs move miserably. You fall. You are not going to get away.—6 October 2007

He felt emptied but not in a good way, the way you feel after you empty a trash can into a dumpster. It was like someone who had just lost a job or a best friend. He caught himself in another daydream about friends he left behind at the commune and felt a dull pain in his gut. Jake forced himself to stop thinking about the place by focusing on his surroundings. He picked up his bags and began to walk about the terminal for the next hour. By eleven o'clock, he felt hungry. Stopping at a deli stand he ordered a tuna fish salad sandwich on rye, and a coffee with no milk, no sugar. The disposable platter came with potato chips and a large, green pickle. He stared at the pickle for some time before deciding to eat it. He recalled that someone at the commune, someone who was a kind of nutritionist, proclaimed that pickles were indigestible. The nutritionist said everyone should avoid them.

What do you know about pickles? You know that cucumbers are soaked in vinegar. Cucumbers are good for you. Vinegar has a long history. Mom always served pickles to cut down the effects of greasy foods. She told you that was why she served pickles. Pickles made your mouth water, thus increasing saliva and digestion. So what is bad about pickles? You believed that self-righteous food guru at the old man's commune and you did not eat a pickle for five years. Jiro believed the diet quack Dr. Herb what's his name who died miserably of Parkinson's. It took you five f'n years to finally look up the facts. Even then, you hesitated to eat one until now.

You know, come to think of it, over the years the old man attracted a lot of weirdoes.

How many good pickles did you avoid?—6 October 2007

His flight would be leaving in two hours. Jake finished his sandwich and he savored the entire pickle feeling fully satiated. Gathering up his bags again and with his remaining coffee in hand, he wandered over to a magazine kiosk. He purchased a weekly news magazine and was tempted to buy a beer in the adjoining tavern, but thought better of it. Something was off, not right with him. He wanted to cause no more scenes at the airport.

Jake walked to a gate next to the one assigned on his ticket because the area was relatively empty of people. He sat alone facing out toward the window overlooking a loading dock. The sky remained overcast from the storm system he drove through the day before. He sat down after gently balancing his half-empty coffee cup on the next seat and casually turned the pages of his magazine to scan the contents. Profiles of presidential hopefuls grabbed his attention. He read about Hillary Clinton's privileged life and how John McCain survived five years of suffering and torture as a prisoner of war. He pulled out his notebook.

McCain as a POW for so long survived and thrived—hell, he can handle running for president. There's hope for you yet. You can get through this.

After reading nearly half of the campaign article, he turned to a title about Neanderthals. "New evidence from an ancient culture discovered in France, revealed that 100,000 years ago Neanderthals ate one another." After reading the article twice, Jake retrieved his notebook again.

With brains as large as ours, they apparently cared for their sick, made simple jewelry and buried their dead—perhaps in quasi-religious ceremonials.

Did they sit and meditate? You believe this question suffers from cynicism.

Why would the great hunters waste their time? Maybe they practiced a form of Zen tranquility while patiently waiting for game to cross their path. Tranquil patience favored the hunter who could become one with his surroundings and control his breathing at crucial moments. And then there is this: "According to a report in last week's Science, at least some Neanderthals butchered, ate and disposed of their kin as if they were so much slaughtered game."

Or did they sacrifice and eat the body of a hero?—6 October 2007

Jake read a few more magazine articles. He sipped his coffee that had gone cold then stood up to stretch his legs and realized he was still hungry. It had been six hours since his breakfast as an unexpected guest at Tom's house. He thought about Tom and his wife, and he smiled. Jake walked over to the deli where he refilled his coffee cup and purchased a jelly donut. After eating it at a stand-up counter, he decided to stroll around. He abandoned his magazine on a seat and dropped the nearly full coffee cup in the trash.

After a half-hour of strolling, he entered a men's room. Inside, he set his things on the floor, relieved himself, and then walked to the row of washbasins. He was alone except for one fellow in a toilet stall. Jake placed his hands palm up under the faucet triggering the automatic flow of warm water. He splashed water on his face twice, rubbed some over his head and then he peered into the mirror. Before him was a man with a wet face the reverse of his own.

The world in the mirror opposed him simultaneously in every way.

"Is the man looking at the past or the future or nothing at all?" he asked in thought. He let the warm water run over his hands again for a few seconds. Anxiety rushed back into his body. His hands trembled again. His chest tightened up. The room tilted sideways. Jake leaned forward with his wet hands flat on the counter to steady himself. He locked his elbows to push himself upward, almost lifting his body weight off the floor. He kept that pose and tried to breathe slowly and deeply until his arms hurt. The physical strain helped. He relaxed, lowering slowly onto his heels. A slight dizziness lingered, and then subsided. His fingertips tingled again. He rubbed his hands on his hip pockets to dry them. He looked up at the man in the mirror again and saw a man who now appeared alien.

What did you expect to see anyway? Several days ago you were clean-shaven and bald and a good imitation of a monk. Now stubble shades your scalp and face. You could be a male model for a new line of cologne, or you could be a bum. A shapeless and faded flannel shirt frames your neck. Your hollow eyes…what are you trying to write here? What do you know about hollow eyes?

The Neanderthal hunter did not have to know what was real. He was real. His life was real. Survival was real. He did not shave.—6 October 2007

Over the intercom, a female voice announced that Flight 1230 to Minneapolis was ready to board. Jake boarded without an incident. He was happy to have a window seat. There was a delay for almost an hour on the runway due to a passing storm. He did not mind. He felt slightly dazed but pleasantly so. He was asleep when the plane taxied into position. The take-off woke him up but this time he was calm. No dreams.

Jake concentrated on a crossword puzzle in the free NWA World Traveler for the entire flight while he was awake. He avoided communication with the woman next to him. She was all business anyway, checking her Blackberry messages before takeoff and was on her laptop during flight. She was clearly a frequent flyer dressed for meetings with important people, he figured. The flight seemed to go by quickly and smoothly. He dozed off twice.

People in the forward rows were already exiting when he awoke the second time. He followed the businesswoman out of the airplane and up the exit ramp. Jake felt a certain comfort in her presence. She seemed so self-contained, so steady in her gait. He noticed her well-developed calves tinted by dark nylons. Her gray skirt swayed below the bend in her knees. He detected a delicate hint of rose cologne that seemed to emanate from her wavy, auburn hair.

"Some kind of expensive shampoo," he thought. He thought about how well she fit into society, a woman in charge of her fate, smooth, in a flow. She lost him when she entered a ladies' room. Jake left the magazine with his unsolved crossword puzzle on the airplane.

Switching flights in Minneapolis went well for him despite the tight connection to Flight 680. He was happy to be rushing through things. The intensity kept him focused on the moment and not thinking about his warped past or obscure future. This time on the plane he watched the scene on the tarmac below from his window seat as the plane rolled away from the gate. Two men in bright orange vests were laughing, no doubt sharing a good joke. Jake eyed them jealously.

He was alone in his row of three seats. He retrieved a pillow from the storage above after the plane leveled off into a smooth flight. Jake watched the farm fields and rural towns drift by. He imagined a bird soaring silently, far above the tallest trees, a bird with two squirming grubs in its beak, returning to its chirping brood. Within minutes he was asleep with his mouth slightly open. He slept through the beverage and snack offering. An attendant roused him to bring his seat forward prior to landing. She startled him as he was dreaming. He pulled out his notebook.

Cows wandered with you along the slopes of Mt. Wheeler. Marga guided you along a narrow trail. The old man was high up on a ridge laughing at both of you. Marga smiled at his antics. You felt outrage. You picked up a rock to hurl. Marga gently pushed you to a seating position. She joined you in meditation. A cow waited patiently chewing cud behind you on the trail. Her breath smelled like roses. You began to float slightly in the air. Then Marga shook you. You opened your eyes. Marga looked like a flight attendant—6 October 2007

The late evening sun struck golden highlights on the new Comcast tower and other Philadelphia skyscrapers. Jake watched the familiar cityscape pass by from the back seat of a taxi cab that took him up I-95. Along the way, he passed bridges named Walt Whitman, Ben Franklin, and Betsy Ross. By the time the driver pulled off Route 95 onto an exit, Jake was asleep again. A gruff announcement startled him.

"Yo, fella! You awake? I think this your stop."

Jake paid the Russian driver's fee and added a five-dollar tip. The driver appeared anxious to move on to his next fare. He made a hasty three point turn with tires squealing and drove away. "I guess I didn't tip him enough," Jake muttered to himself. He turned around to assess his next move, as he faced his old home. He stood there alone under a street lamp, staring across the yard at the front door. This was the house where he grew up near New Hope. The great white oak in the front yard was gone. In its place was an ornamental Japanese maple that was ridiculously tiny by comparison. "Shit, it had to be a Japanese maple," he said under his breath.

The cab driver left his two bags on the sidewalk. Jake had a little less than one hundred dollars left. He picked up his bags and took a deep breath before entering the front yard. He exhaled loudly and long with his lips pursed. "The weird prodigal has returned," he thought. He grabbed the old, wrought iron gate's handle to lift the latch with his thumb. As he swung it open, the corroded hinges gave a familiar squeak. He shut it carefully to a crisp, metallic click. He headed toward the front door fifty feet ahead. He stopped for a few seconds at the concrete steps to take another deep breath. He blew hard to exhale. He examined the familiar entryway in an effort to make a few adjustments in his mind. The dark green storm door with an oval window was new. He was finally back home, but was this still his home?

Jake noticed that some lights were on downstairs and upstairs. He felt a mild evening breeze on the back of his neck. He heard the faint report of evening news coming from a television. The household appeared so peaceful. "Why disturb them?" he thought. Suddenly he felt foolish and even afraid. He felt like turning around. He considered what got him to this embarrassing moment as a thirty-year-old man. He thought about the Japanese maple and the bloody beating he got with the old

23

guru's keisaku and wondered how much he would tell them about all that. He felt ashamed, then in his mind he thought back to what led him to drop out of school ten years earlier.

2   Making Fate

An ancient pond
A frog jumps in
A splash of water
—Basho (1686)

Jake stepped out of the desert heat through double security doors into the cool corridor of the campus lecture hall. He walked by the unattended information desk to a bulletin board. "Room 108," he said to himself, as he turned toward the right, appearing lost. He nearly bumped into a young, thin woman with red-rimmed glasses. "Excuse me," he said as he maneuvered to avoid her.

"You're excused! Can I help you? You look lost," she said with a smile.

"Uh, yes; I'm here to attend a lecture in Room 108," he said, reading from the brochure. "It's *Buddhism in America: A survey of modern times.*"

"Oh, just follow me," she said. "That's where I'm going, but it was switched to 113."

"Thank you," Jake said. "Glad I bumped into you." He followed her without saying another word to her. They entered Room 113, a small lecture hall with cushioned seats that sloped down to a raised stage with a podium and drop down screen for video. Jake took an end seat midway down the aisle. No one sat next to him.

The guest speaker was a frumpy, unattractive woman who approached the microphone, tapping it first to see if it was on.

"Hi," she said with a reserved smile. "I am Professor Gertrude Pedersen, and I am here to talk to you about my research regarding Buddhism in America. I am working on a new book about the subject. I recently returned from a sabbatical during which I traveled around the United States and Canada to visit over twenty

Buddhist churches and organizations. I spent on average ten days at each venue as a participant-observer. I will be showing some pictures as we go along. Please reserve your questions until the end."

The professor paused to check her projecting equipment. The first image appeared on the screen blurred. As it came into focus, the audience saw an Asian family in casual clothing at home watching television. The father relaxed in an easy chair. The mother sat on a plush couch with two young daughters. A toddler stood inside a playpen next to a sleeping Golden Retriever.

"This family worships at a Buddhist church in Seattle. One of my goals has been to assess how much American culture changed this mostly Asiatic import. For the most part I selected innocuous Buddhist communities that were established several generations ago. But I also included six controversial movements founded by foreign as well as non-Asian, American Buddhists."

She spoke before a mixed group of fifty adults that included teachers, students and interested people from town. With the image of an average Buddhist-American family on the screen, Pedersen gave a brief history and description of Buddhism for fifteen minutes before launching into her project. "So, although it exists among the so-called world religions, Buddhism does not focus on an all-powerful deity. Buddhism is the most *humanist* of the world religions. Buddhism is an ethical philosophy more like Confucianism and not a theology like Islam, for example." To Jake, she seemed engaging and well-informed from the start.

It was the August after the end of his spring semester in 1997. School had not been going well for him. His grades suffered. He had become obsessed with philosophy and a deep urge to resolve early religious indoctrination. The existential crisis drove him to and beyond the fringes of accepted academic study. He sought direct experience. He tried meditating on his own. Buddhism captured his attention after he read *Siddhartha* by Hesse and the poetry of Matsuo Basho.

He remained in Arizona that summer to work at a Tucson golf course as groundskeeper while he contemplated dropping out. He expected in the very least that the air conditioned lecture room would be a welcome relief from working in the hundred degree heat outside. He did not expect the lecture to be a life turning event.

The lecturer was an unassuming, shabbily dressed woman in her mid-thirties with a page boy haircut and round, wire rimmed glasses with thick lenses. Clearly, she was not trying to sell anything in her purple T-shirt, long floral skirt with the unflattering elastic waistband, and small feet covered by white socks inside of violet Crocs. She complemented her talk with a slick Power Point display of images and outlines.

"When we consider this image inside a Japanese Buddhist church established in Seattle nearly a century ago, it looks at first glance like any established congregation of Christians with mostly older folks in pews, most of which are empty, as you can see," she said casually.

Many of the people in the audience laughed in response

"As with well-established Christian denominations, this Buddhist church meets every Sunday. It has a wide range of community activities including children's programs, a soup kitchen for the poor, mental health services, and sports with a basketball team, a baseball team, and, believe it or not, a Buddhist bowling club and bi-monthly Buddhist Bingo."

More laughter.

"Buddhists number less than one percent of the American population. For most of us, this remains an exotic religion with no direct experience. When we see Buddhists acting like average Americans, we are surprised; we laugh." She stopped to scan the audience. "We expect the colorful examples displayed in popular film. For example: *The Golden Child, Kundun, The Razor's Edge*, and, due to its location in Tibet, *Lost Horizon*." Poster images of each film appeared in succession on the screen.

Next, she summarily showed them portraits of Buddhists in traditional clothing in Nepal, Myanmar, Japan, Thailand, Mongolia, and Vietnam. She paused at a picture of the Dalai Lama wearing the traditional robes and headgear of his Yellow Hat sect.

"Almost everyone knows of the Dalai Lama and the plight of the Tibetan Buddhists. We see images on television of Tibetan monks in maroon robes and rural

Buddhists living simple lives as we imagine Native Americans did over a hundred years ago, as you can see here." She showed them several dramatic images culled from *Discovery* and *National Geographic* programs. "In the American mind, that creates a stereotype that hardly represents the variety of common Buddhist folks throughout the world and here in America."

She showed them images of ordinary American Buddhists of Asian descent who had adapted quite well to varieties of American life in attire, housing, and politics. The speaker ended her survey with examples of Buddhism as adopted by the Beat and Hippie generations. She mentioned *Dharma Bums* by Jack Kerouac in literature and the evolution of the liberal Naropa University in Colorado founded in 1974 by the Tibetan Buddhist exile, Chogyam Trungpa. Trungpa appeared large on the screen, both in traditional garb as well in a business suit and tie.

"Trungpa, of course, was highly controversial—all puns intended."

A few people in the room laughed. Jake raised his eyebrows and noted her remark in his journal. She smiled; then continued.

"Some considered him a brilliant teacher while others found him abusive. His dependence on alcohol and cocaine as well as his licentious sexual behavior diminishes his legend and legacy. He died young in his late forties in 1987. Nevertheless, the Naropa Institute continues in his name to sustain many hundreds of students with courses ranging from body-mind awareness to interdisciplinary studies in music, the arts, ecology, peacemaking and the politics of change. If you are deep into New Age ideas, this may be the place for you," she said with a flourish.

A portion of the audience laughed. The lecturer clicked her remote again. An image of a thin, bald Japanese man in black robes appeared. He posed with hands folded and with a pleasant smile.

"Oh. I almost forgot I put this in. Just last week I visited a small and entirely new Buddhist center in New Mexico. The gentleman you see here in black robes arrived from Japan a mere few months ago. He is called Roshi which means, literally, "old teacher" but perhaps more accurately, *elder master*. He seems to have made an immediate impact with a dozen or more students, nearly all of them Americans, whom have moved into what appears to be the beginnings of a new Buddhist monastery."

The next slide revealed several smiling students seated at a large table. They were eating.

"While I was there for two days, they fed me well with delicious vegetarian meals. I found the students to be open and full of hope. They seemed quite impressed with their new teacher. The one in the center is Marga."

Then a full screen image of Marga's serene, exotic face appeared. Jake felt an immediate attraction to her and what she represented. He wanted what Marga appeared to have found. He felt a certain resonance with, even a jealousy for the freedom of a purposeful life.

"This nice young lady spent many hours talking to me and showing me around. She is typical of most people I met there. They come from diverse backgrounds and have a common interest to pursue a simple, spiritual life. She grew up in Hawaii in a mostly secular household. She is a recent convert to Buddhism yet exhibited a remarkable grasp of the essential teachings already. She credits her teacher."

The final image was of an endearing black kitten seated on a large granite rock and gazing into the camera lens.

"This cute little creature has nothing to do with anything in my research. Some called her Margaret. The Japanese assistant called her Neko. I snapped this picture as I was saying goodbyes to Marga and the rest in New Mexico."

With that said, she ended the lecture portion of her delightful and educational presentation. Everyone including Jake applauded.

"Now I would like to open it up to your questions," she said with her arms extended.

Jake sat silently throughout the lively question and answer session. He noticed two main lines of questioning. Half concentrated on the meaning of Buddhist concepts like nirvana, sunyata, and the no-self. The other half featured curiosity about American policy toward Tibet. One person asked about actor Richard Gere's role in foreign policy.

"You will have to ask Richard," the speaker said in a serious tone but with a wink. People laughed.

A middle-aged man with long hair, wearing a frumpy sport coat and speckled tie, raised his hand. The professor pointed to him to ask his question.

"You showed us examples of a subculture of scientists and atheists who embrace Buddhism. I teach physics at a local college. I have to say that I am inclined to Buddhism myself if I were to choose a religion. I was surprised to hear that I have a community out there! Could you elaborate on this science-Buddhism connection?"

"Buddhism views the human person as not having a soul or self. We are, each of us, an aggregate of physical properties, mind stuff, emotions, senses, consciousness, etc. The Sanskrit term for this aggregate is *skandhas*: s-k-a-n-d-h-a." The speaker paused to print the word on a white board. "There are five skandhas. Some scientists find that consciousness is as elusive as I or ego. At death all these skandhas appear to dissolve or disintegrate just as they seem to come together after birth, thus offering strong evidence that the Buddhists are correct. Whatever holds this aggregate we call a self together is illusory. Buddhists might call it desire and desire is the root of all suffering or attachment to samsara, a term we defined earlier."

"So, Buddha was an atheist then?"

"Actually, he would not speculate about metaphysical domains or attributes. The gods or a God was irrelevant to living a right-minded life. He might answer your question by stating: *The question does not fit the case.* He tended toward a practical solution to the problem of suffering."

The professor's answer suddenly struck Jake as utterly meaningful. It was at this point that he stopped using *I* in his journals for the next ten years. He would refer to his self in the second person, as *you*, as if observing the ego and not identifying with it.

"One last question. Yes, you, back there," she said as she pointed to a woman in the back row.

"I am a born-again Christian and I think Buddhism is anti-Christian and it is a satanic religion," the small woman stated nervously.

The professor's eyes opened wider. She smiled at the small woman and nodded, taking a moment to reply carefully. "Well, you may have a point. The two religions are irreconcilable. Without an eternal soul or body, there can be no such event as a resurrection as proclaimed by an orthodox interpretation of the Gospel. But in my experience, Buddhists have no more history of evil behavior than Christians or members of any other religion."

The small woman did not reply. She grabbed her purse, stood up, left her seat and walked out the back door. Without further ado, the speaker thanked everyone for their kind attention.

People applauded. Most of them made their way to the exit. But a handful came forward to speak to the lecturer in private. Among them was Jake. He waited impatiently with his arms crossed until everyone else finished. When his turn finally came, he offered to help the speaker break down and pack her small display that included two statues of the Buddha, a tangka or scroll painting, and several reference books.

"Professor Pedersen, I was curious about that last group you showed us, the one in New Mexico," he said as he watched her carefully tie off the rolled up scroll.

"Ah yes. I think they're calling it Samuwabi, or something like that. What would you care to know?"

"Are they open to visitors?"

"Oh, yes. Very open. In fact, they give lectures weekly and offer workshops, including for martial arts."

"Did you interview the Roshi? I mean, what did you think of him?"

"His English is poor but he has a Japanese assistant who speaks well enough. He was pleasant with me. His achievement as a teacher in Kyoto is impressive but I could not confirm anything. Then again, I have not had time to try," she said with an apologetic smile and a shrug. "The students he has seemed quite happy with him though!"

"Did you meditate with them?" Jake asked as he lifted a cardboard box off the floor.

"You betcha. I'm a meditator."

"Are you Buddhist then?"

"No. Actually, I'm a Catholic nun," she said as she placed a statue of a Buddha in the box.

This revelation took Jake back a few steps in his mind. Pedersen could see his surprise. She chuckled as one might after delivering a punch line.

"I get that a lot. It's okay," she said. "When I'm doing research, especially with people in other religions, and considering the reputation of the Church today, I try to appear as neutral as possible. I consider feedback from this audience as research at this point."

With that said she pulled her silver necklace from under her T-shirt to reveal a simple but meticulously engraved silver cross. "This was gift from my family when I took my final vows as a Dominican nun." She released the cross to let it dangle visibly over her breast.

Jake still looked confused. "How did you reconcile doing it then, if the religions can't be reconciled, as you said?"

"At the risk of being simplistic, I'll say while a Buddhist struggles to achieve emptiness or no mind, I, as a Catholic, struggle to maintain communion. From the outside, it all looks the same. We all *just sit*, as they say in Zen, in a tranquil pose."

"Not sure if I see the benefit of one way over the other."

"No reason you have to, but I see it as a choice, an act of the will."

"An act of will?" he asked, "Like Nietzsche's notion of *will to power*?"

"Ah, you have encountered Nietzsche! No, I think he was onto something entirely different than Buddhists or Christians regarding will. Buddhists meditate to rid themselves of wrong relationships with this world, with gods or metaphysical powers, and with people. As a Christian, I seek to strengthen my relationship with God through Jesus and by serving my fellow humans. I seek to be in accord with Jesus as cosmic Lord." Jake looked puzzled, so Pedersen added, "I am not saying one way is better than the other."

"But, why bother studying Buddhism?"

"Good question. I had to apply for permission from the order—the Dominicans are a teaching order—based on a paper by my dissertation professor. He concluded that in the future, the global religious debate will not be dominated by atheism verses theism, or Islam verses Judaism, but Buddhist philosophy verses Christian Gospel."

Jake retreated from further probing, sensing that he was getting in over his head. Instead he stated the reason he waited to talk with her. "Do you have any contact information for that group?" Jake wondered.

"Which one?" she laughed.

"The last one, the one you visited in New Mexico."

"I have a brochure somewhere." She searched in her leather binder and found two brochures and a card. "Here, you can have one. The business card is from Marga who is an aide to the Roshi, but I need it for follow up with her."

"Thanks. The brochure will do," Jake said while perusing the map on the back flap.

"You seem quite interested in the place. If you go there any time soon, tell Marga I said hello."

"Sure."

Jake walked the nun to her 2002, red Corolla in the parking lot. Heat from the sun beat down on them as Pedersen thanked Jake with a slight bow of her head. She tossed her box into the back seat and got in the car. Jake closed her door for her. "Peace of Christ be with you," she said, as she rolled up her window.

"And with you," Jake responded. He waved as she drove away. And then he mumbled, "Like, whatever."

Two weeks later, Jake drove to the golf course to pick up his last paycheck. He stopped by a tree-lined water hazard, a quiet spot he favored for breaks when he was on the job. A warm desert breeze rippled the surface of the man-made pond that stretched ten yards from the trees to the edge of the 18th green. A few withered leaves swirled around Jake as he sat at the edge of the murky water under the shade of a large, aging cottonwood. He answered his mobile phone, a gray Nokia 2000 series model handed down to him by his older brother Harry. As expected, the call was from Sarah, his lovely, round-faced and slightly overweight, brown-eyed girl friend. Sarah was from Guadalajara and also a student at the university.

"Hi," he said as he fumbled to switch the Nokia to his right ear. The switch freed his left hand to hold a cheap, ball-point pen. He prepared to write down an address that she would give him. The pen would not work until he shook it and scribbled a few loops onto the bottom of the notebook page on his lap.

"Hey, it's me," she said.

"Hi, Sarah! Did you get my message? Where can we meet?" he asked with some urgency.

"Where? Where what?" she asked softly. Sarah paused to collect her thoughts using her phone to tap her ear as if to loose memory. "Oh yes! That's why I called. You left a message on my machine. I'm sorry. I don't want to meet for lunch," she said with conviction.

Jake shoved the pen into the back pocket of his khaki pants. He gripped the Nokia hard and grimaced at it before returning it to his ear.

"Can't we just do this face to face? I mean, like, we don't have to have lunch," he pleaded.

He stood up easily, leaving his backpack and note pad on the ground. He began to pace through the uncut grass by the water's edge.

"What's the point?" Sarah objected. "We've been through this twice already. Besides, I already started seeing Kai. I don't want to complicate this any more."

"You started seeing him? What does that mean?"

Jake stopped in his tracks with his left foot crushing a California poppy. He stood facing the water. His gut fear was not that she would start having sex with someone else; rather that she was abandoning every sense of intimate companionship they shared.

Sarah was his first real love after years of short-lived affairs of his adolescence. They were together for nearly a year, a year that seemed the most important of his life. He shared his deepest thoughts with her without hesitation. He was awakening to a new awareness of himself and his world. Until this conversation, Sarah seemed open to, often amused by, and even intrigued with his intensity.

"Why do you always want to know what everything means?" she challenged.

"You always say *everything*. That's not true," he said with a tone of condescension.

"Oh, you mean everything has *not* changed since Nietzsche declared that God was dead," she countered with equal sarcasm. "You said just last week that everything changed when he said that."

"I meant that the God we created is dead. He was talking about why the god of the Christians is no longer viable," he explained. "Nietzsche saw that we had to break out of old stuff; that's all."

"And is that why you stopped being a Catholic?"

"Who said anything about that?"

"You told me you stopped going to church after you read Nietzsche, just before we met."

"I wasn't going much anyway. He makes a lot of sense."

"What, by irritating Christians?" she quipped.

"What do you care about Christians? You don't believe in any of that."

"No, you are right. But you're dropping one thing and going into another. Can't you just take a break? We used to have fun until your latest kick."

"What do you mean, kick?"

"You're like a man on a mission to another planet. I feel like I'm holding you back. I want to stay here on Earth."

"Okay. Okay, let's drop it. I wanted to know what seeing him, the new guy means."

"What do you mean, what does that mean? I like him. He likes me. We're dating," Sarah replied with some irritation, referring to her new lover Kai.

"But I thought you hadn't made up your mind."

"Jake, honey, listen. We're like not on the same page; maybe even not on the same planet. I don't know what you want. One day you're dropping out of school, the next you say you will finish. Like I said, I feel like I'm holding you back."

"I was hoping you would, like, go to New Mexico with me," Jake blurted out.

"What?" Sarah was genuinely surprised. She laughed out loud. "You mean to that Buddhist thingy?"

"Uh-huh."

"Are you, like, crazy? You wanted to do that alone two weeks ago! You wanted a break from our relationship—remember? Anyway, I'm not interested in meditating with some strange Yoda from Japan."

Jake stopped pacing. He squatted on to his haunches by the pond's edge startling a minnow-sized goldfish that slipped out of sight into the deep.

"I guess I wanted you to be with me after all. But you're right. This is about me." Jake sighed quietly. He leaned back, plopping from his squat position onto his butt. The slight jar to his spine shifted his thinking. "It's about desire—I have a lot to learn yet."

"Huh?" Sarah asked. "You lost me there."

"Nothing. This isn't going to be so easy, is all," he said before clenching his jaw.

Whether or not she understood his intent, Sarah ignored his reference to Buddhist detachment. She turned in her seat to check the time on the clock on her desk. The motion tangled the phone cord under her armpit. She brushed back her abundant, dark frizzy hair to expose an ear to the phone again.

"Are you still there?" he said.

"Yes, but not for long."

"You going to see Kai?" Jake said instinctually.

"None of your business," she snapped coyly and with a giggle.

Jake hesitated before he asked, "What's he do, if you don't mind telling me?"

"Why?" she asked, dragging out the word.

"I want to know if you're going to be okay," he said with little affect.

"You're jealous," she said in a sing-song.

"Sure. I'm going to miss you, you know."

Jake's concern was genuine. Sarah relented. She briefed him on Kai.

"Okay. He's graduating with an MBA. His uncle in Finland offered him a position with a company he owns. Kind of an international rep position with an office in New York—they sell wood products. Anyway, he's kind of cute, blonder than you and taller but not by much. He's really good at tennis and he's going to teach me."

"Oh," Jake said flatly, hearing more than he wanted to know.

"Oh? What—not deep enough for you and Camus," she stated mockingly.

"No, I mean, he sounds good. I hope it all works out, I mean, I want you to be happy."

Jake could think of nothing more to say. It suddenly sunk in hard that their relationship was over. She seemed really taken with this new guy. No more tender touches from Sarah, he thought.

"I want you to be happy too, Jake. I really do."

She allowed a brief flash of images to surface. She recalled the handsome if geeky lover with the slim, sinewy body, and chiseled abs. She recalled his expert hands, his mop of sandy hair, and his ready smile with the one crooked tooth.

"Drop me a note when you get there," she said. Tears emerged from her closed eyes.

"Okay," he said as he stared at nothing in the pond.

"Good bye. Love you!"

"Bye, Sarah."

Jake stood up slowly. He felt off, even dizzy. His heart was pounding. He gulped air several times, and then held his breath trying to calm down. He leaned over bracing his upper body on his knees. Nausea nearly caused him to vomit, but he held it back. He took deep breaths and exhaled loudly several times. He stood straight up, then returned to the edge of the pond. He sat again; this time with his back against the large tree trunk. He dropped his phone into his worn *Jansen* backpack that he tossed to the side, only to retrieve it immediately to search for something. He instantly forgot what he was searching for. Irritated with himself he slammed the pack against the ground.

"Damn it!" he exclaimed as if shouting at the air.

Tears formed. A young man sobbed quietly by a Cottonwood tree. After collecting himself and staring at the sky for a minute, he reached into his pack and he took out his phone again. He called his mother in Pennsylvania.

Hello, this is Monica," she said speaking into her cordless phone.

"Hi mom, it's me."

"Jacob! Are you okay? You sound unhappy," she said as she stooped to slide a full wicker basket across the gray ceramic tiles of the laundry room with her free hand.

How does she always know, he thought? Then he answered, "I'm fine, mom, really. Do you have a minute? It's important."

"Yes. Let me take care of this laundry and I'll find a seat," she said as she shoved a damp load of white linens and sheets into the dryer and turned it on. She walked into the kitchen and sat down.

"Are you sure you are okay? You sound serious."

"It is serious, sort of. I'm following up on something we discussed last week."

"Are you still thinking of dropping out of school? Is that what this is about?"

Monica sat at her kitchen table. She set her elbow on the table and leaned her forehead into the palm of her hand.

"Yes, I'm going through with it. I'm going to see my advisor now, but I wanted to tell you first," Jake said in a soft voice.

"Jacob, you know we are disappointed in you," Monica said. "Neal and I discussed it. He feels frustrated. You know he feels responsible for your welfare too."

Monica was referring to Neal's ersatz role as step-father to her two adult sons. Their father passed away eight years earlier when Jake was twelve and Harry, fourteen.

"This is not about Neal being there for me or about dad, mom. It's something I feel I have to do."

"Please talk to Neal again. I'll get him," Monica said as she hurried to the stairway. She held the phone against her abdomen as she yelled for Neal to come down.

"Neal, Jacob is on the phone. He says he's dropping out. Please talk to him."

She could not hear Jake's muffled complaint.

"Mom, I don't want to talk to him now. Don't bother him."

He could tell she was not listening.

"Mom! Mom! Are you there?"

Monica handed the phone to her husband.

"Hey, Jake, it's me, Neal. What's going on?"

"Hi. Okay. Okay. Listen, I do not want to bother you with this."

"No bother. What's up?"

Neal raised his hand to shush Monica who was about to say something.

"You know—the school thing. I told mom I'm leaving here for New Mexico. I leave tomorrow."

"So, you decided to try Buddhism after all. Why can't you finish your degree and go next year? I still don't get it."

"We've been over this. I thought it over. Look, if this doesn't work out, I'll finish later."

"Later may never come, Jake," Neal said peevishly as he scowled at Monica. He was not happy that his wife thrust him in the middle again.

"Exactly, Neal, and that's why I want to follow up on this now."

Jake had what could be construed as a brief argument with Neal about the wisdom of dropping out and the risks of not returning to school. As before, they talked about the economy and how tough it was to find good jobs in the current downturn. The more practical Neal waxed, the more irritated Jake became.

"Damn it, Neal. I'm not going to go to some nine-to-five minimum wage job like you did when you left school. I'm not you."

Neal dropped his jaw, holding his defensive reaction at bay. He resorted to his group therapy skills. He took a breath. "All I'm suggesting is for you to think about this," he said in a calm, measured tone.

Jake's phone was nearly dead.

"Neal, I'm losing power. Tell mom I'm getting rid of the phone, so this might be the last call for a while. I'm cutting down on expenses."

Neal told Monica about the phone.

"Jake, she says she wants you to keep the phone. We'll pay for it."

"I've made up my mind. No phone. I do not want any more support from you guys. You've given me more than I deserve already. Listen, I'll keep in touch. There're pay phones around. I'll call collect if I have to, okay?" Jake knew how anxious his mother would be if he did not contact her with some regularity.

"Okay, okay," Neal replied in exasperation. "Well, I tried. Listen, I want to wish you well. And stay in touch. Visit us when you can, okay?"

"No worries. Bye. Tell mom I love her."

"Here, tell her yourself," Neal said as he handed the phone to Monica.

"Bye, Jacob. I'll be praying for you."

With that, Jake's phone went dead. The son did not hear the mother say she would pray for him and she did not hear him say good-bye. Jake took one last look at the Nokia. With a flick of his left wrist he tossed it into the middle of the pond. With a small splash, the mobile device sunk from view. He slung his pack over a shoulder. He turned away from the pond to walk to the maintenance shed where he left his car. He drove directly to the campus to meet with his advisor.

"Sanity?" asked Professor Gomez. "So, you are dropping out to get some sanity—can you elaborate, Jake, please?"

Gomez doubled as a student counselor and an archeology instructor. He was a husky fellow, graying and mostly bald with a thick beard. He wore a drab, linen jacket and a green tie loosely exposing an unbuttoned, white shirt collar. His brown rimmed reading glasses sat along the mid-bridge of his nose, allowing him to observe Jake above the lenses. Jake was taking one of his advanced classes in archeology at the time.

"Yes," his erstwhile student answered. "Maybe I'm nuts for doing this, but I need a break from school. Things are crazy for me. Things don't seem to make sense right now."

"And why must things make sense all of a sudden?"

"Huh?" Jake looked puzzled.

"Nada, nothing. Just making a bad joke," Gomez said with a drawn out, humorous emphasis. He collected his thoughts and cleared his throat. "Did something happen? Are you having a problem?"

"For one thing, I broke up with a girlfriend," Jake offered. "Well, to tell the truth, she like, ditched me," he said to be more exact.

"Ah." Gomez appeared sympathetic. "But you are a young, good looking fellow. I can't see where that will be a problem for you. Broken hearts can heal. What happened, if you don't mind my asking?"

"No. She met another guy, one who has a career, a future."

"Well, there's a lot to be said for security in a relationship. Money woes can tear people apart." Gomez nodded and paused a few seconds, as if to indicate he had been there. "Give it time. Maybe you need a little counseling, but you should be able to handle a few classes to finish your degree, no?"

"That's not bothering me so much anymore—I mean the girlfriend—I knew it was ending a week ago. The main thing is, I don't really know what I want to do with a degree," Jake said, shaking his head slowly as he stared out the window.

"What undergrad does know? At least half or more change their plans after graduation. It is the degree that matters, that gives one an edge."

"I'm not looking for a career—at least, not right away."

"What then?" Gomez raised his eyebrows in anticipation of what he might hear.

"I plan to stay at a new Buddhist center in New Mexico for a while. It's like a retreat where I can sort things out. I like the idea of pursuing *empty mind* right now," Jake said with no hint of irony.

The good professor raised his eyebrows even more, indicating his surprise. "But you are so close. One more semester should do it. Can't you empty your mind later?" Gomez asked with a tilt of his head and a simple but wry smile.

Jake took the question as a subtle insult. Gomez noticed immediately in Jake's blank expression that any intended humor was lost. The husky man leaned forward, making a crumpling sound in his worn leather chair. He removed his reading glasses and tucked them into the vest pocket of his tan linen suit jacket. He spread his thick-fingered palms flat on the desk, as he considered his pupil. His rugged hands revealed the effects of decades of field work. The Mayan cultures were his specialty.

Gomez considered the young man with the abundant, sandy-colored hair and clear hazel eyes sitting across from him. He thought of years past. "Sorry about that. I get it," he said pointedly. "I am not making fun of you. You know, Jake, many of you kids are looking to me more and more like retreads from the Sixties. And you—I see a dropout looking to tune in. But tune in to what?" Gomez leaned back into his chair again.

"Enlightenment," Jake replied without expression.

"Ah, yes," the professor said thoughtfully. "So, I was right." Then, in his best, guttural German accent, he remarked, "Was ist Äufklarung?"

"Vass ist—what was that?" Jake asked

"Immanuel Kant. I was quoting Kant who asked that very question in one of his works: *What is enlightenment?* But I have a feeling you are not going to look into Kant's conclusions."

"No, you're right. No, I don't want to merely read about it anymore," Jake said flatly.

"Well, I was not suggesting you actually read Kant. Heaven forbid! He can drown you in inexplicable questions and if he does not drown you, you might be swimming in his questions for the rest of your life!" Gomez spoke with a flourish, stirring the air with his hands.

His remark and gesture brought a smile to Jake's face. The professor actually did get it, even though Jake was clueless about what he meant about Kant's inexplicability.

"And, how do your parents feel about this?" Gomez had to ask because puzzled and angry parents had called him over the years when students failed or quit school.

"My dad died, you know. Mom was confused when I tried to explain it to her. She's worried now, especially after I got into an argument over this with Neal, her new husband."

"Your step-father?"

"Yeah. You can call him that. He and my mom married after I left for college. He actually knew my dad in a way. He works with vets, you know, as part of his work as a psychologist. My dad was a vet."

"And what did Neal say?" Gomez asked nonchalantly, while stroking his beard.

"He was actually pretty good about it until I said something about him being stuck in a lousy job. I may have hurt his feelings. Anyway, I reassured them that my plan was to, like, take a year, and then I would consider going back to finish a degree."

"A year can be a long time or no time at all," Gomez opined. "Do you think a year will be enough?"

"I can't say," was all Jake could think of as an answer.

"You are tempting fate, Jake. You are tempting fate," Gomez repeated half to himself. "The Fates are fickle." Gomez shook his head. He pulled a business card from the box on his desk and handed it to Jake. "Drop me a note when you feel so motivated. I would like to hear how this goes for you. Deal?"

"Deal," Jake said as he stood to shake hands. Jake never did get back to him, at least not for the next eleven years.

"You should sign some papers at the school office before you go," Gomez said as Jake approached the door.

"Already did that," Jake said with a certain cocky inflection. "Thanks again. Buenos dias, professor!"

"Vaja con Dios, son," Gomez replied half-heartedly. He shook Jake's hand with a firm grip. He slumped back into his chair as Jake turned to go. "Vaja con Dios," he repeated softly as his student exited the office. The professor sighed. He turned his chair to face the window that overlooked the students walking in the campus below.

3   Going Forth

After the storm, high up above the pond hangs the branch of a Ponderosa Pine.

You see a large seed cone wet with rain dangle from a branch.

A drop of clear water forms under the seed cone.

The drop flows along a long pine needle to its needle tip and it hangs there for a
*   second. A ray of sunlight breaks through the cloud illuminating the drop.*

The illuminated drop falls, yet every moment remains still as the world around it
*   moves and changes.*

Which is it, you ask?

All that moves moves from one perspective, and we measure it as time.

Gravity moves it to its grave as one drop loses itself in itself.

$H2O$ is $H2O$—Sept 1997

Jake paused, holding his pen a few inches above the page. He was in rapt attention pondering his last two lines. The sacred equation of life struck him instantly without words. Others may express it as earth to earth, ashes to ashes, dust to dust, he thought. Yet others from diverse religions might say, "I Am That I Am or That Thou Art."

    Then he wrote as if questioning his insight:

Are you the alpha and the omega?

Are you indestructible?

Energy can neither be created nor destroyed. What about life?

After the final splash there is no trace that anything happened save for a few minor,
*   unenduring ripples.*

Extinction.

Only stories of ripples remain to remind you of a drop.—Sept 1997

He contemplated extinction above a modest magma heated pool in the Lower Rockies. He tossed a rough stone into the clear water and watched as it sunk from view. He watched rain droplets form and launch from an overhanging Ponderosa pine branch. He contemplated his self-imposed sabbatical. He wrote in a common black and white marble, tape-bound, composition notebook. Someday he will fill a sizeable stack of the notebooks.

The thought about being open to possibilities lingered with him in 1997, as he lit the flame of his seldom-used, dual fuel Coleman stove. He poured water from a plastic bottle into a small pot that he set on the stove. He placed a *Stash Tea* teabag into a plane white mug and set that down on a flat, pinkish granite rock. He noted that it took a minute or two longer for water to boil at that altitude. His unremarkable campsite was at 7,000 feet, more or less. This was high desert territory in the Jemez range. He was above the village of Jemez Springs near Los Alamos, New Mexico.

The Jemez area, known for hot springs and pools of heated waters emerging from fissures in hot volcanic rock, attracted Jake for many reasons. He wanted to see and feel the geological world of the Rockies. He read that a series of ancient volcanoes formed Valles Grande, one of America's largest calderas. He drove past the caldera to get where he was. This was where the ancient Indians or Anasazi he read about in Gomez's class once thrived. But other, more current features in the area attracted him. He read about a non-descript Zen center and a quietly notorious Catholic retreat in the Jemez area. He visited both places briefly, earlier in the day, more out of tourist curiosity than serious interest.

The *Servants of the Paraclete* retreat center, established on 2,000 acres of forest in 1947, housed and treated alcoholic and sexually deviant Catholic clerics until 1994. The deviant priest controversies and how the Church hierarchy mishandled the cases over the decades were some reasons among many that caused Jake to veer away from his family faith. He rarely attended church since he left high school. He never went when he was away from home. But he was curious about this remote facility that was evidence for the Church's damaged image. For decades, deviant priests and clergy would be treated there then released to work at another school, parish or diocese as if they were cured through therapy, penance, prayer and forgiveness.

Jake parked his car down the road from the attractive white residence hall for clerical staff. As he sat in his car he was not sure why he even bothered to come there. Perhaps it was a subconscious anger that drove him to it. He took out his notebook.

Is God this simple-minded? How can liar priests remain in good standing? Satan lurks in the sacred halls seeking victims. Where are the guardian angels? Where is mighty Michael? Man's conscience cares not about angels and demons—why would a man fear the cartoon heroes he creates?—23 September 1997

He decided to walk off his irritation before leaving the place. He intended to walk over to a fast running stream nearby when he encountered a middle-aged fellow in a dark suit but with no tie and carrying a briefcase. The man introduced himself.

"Hi. My name is Leon," he said. "Do you have a minute? I'd like to ask a few questions."

"Hi. The name is Jake. What's up?" Jake shook his hand.

"I'm doing a follow-up on an earlier story about *Camp Ped*. Do you work here?"

"No, sir," Jake replied a little uneasily. "What's camp Ed?"

"Did you say Ed?" Leon asked with a puzzled look.

"Uh, yes," Jake answered.

"They wish it was called Ed!" Leon said with a chuckle. "It's ped: p-e-d. Ped is for pedophile. It's an old nickname people used for this place."

"Oh. That makes sense, I guess," Jake said with some hesitation.

Leon looked dismayed, sensing that he was not going get a story out of this guy.

"So, do you know anyone here?" Leon asked him indicating curiosity as to Jake's motives.

"Nope, I've never been here before." Jake began to wonder whether his presence there might arouse unwarranted suspicion. Maybe Leon thought he was a homosexual looking for a contact. Maybe Leon was a homosexual. With these unsettling thoughts in mind, he felt out of place. He decided to lie. "I was just checking out the stream that cuts through here. Thought about coming here to fish for trout later," he said with a smile.

"Oh. Sorry to bother you, sir. Enjoy the fishing!" With that said, Leon continued to his vehicle, a black Suburban with Massachusetts license plates. Jake surmised that Leon was a lawyer or a reporter. He decided not to even hypocritically go over to the stream. The place suddenly gave him the creeps, as if he inadvertently trespassed into a private club. He started his VW, backed it onto the roadway and drove in the opposite direction of the black Suburban.

Within a half hour after carefully following directions on his map, he parked his car at a simple yet attractive Zen center in the Jemez Springs area. Established in the 1970s, the facility exuded an exotic tranquility with its plain buildings and calm interiors. He could see that distraction was kept to a minimum, as he followed a gravel path and walked by a small sign that said *visitors* with an arrow pointing to a main building. On the way, Jake encountered a slim, Caucasian woman with short, graying hair. She appeared to be around forty, and she was wearing sandals, khaki pants and an untucked, blue cotton shirt. She was kneeling next to a flower patch and digging with a small shovel, when he approached. She stood to greet him after removing a soiled glove from her right hand. She made no effort to impress him, nor did she seem phased by his pompous bearing. Jake had already made up his mind not to stay, as if the place were not good enough.

"Hi. I'm Jake. Doing some gardening, huh?"

"Yes, if you want to call it that," the slim lady said with a smile.

"I read about this place. Can I ask you a few questions?"

"Sure. I'm Greta," she said. "People here call me Hiten," she said phonetically as HE-ten.

Jake did not ask her what it meant. He did not want to act too interested. Instead he casually glanced around the grounds, avoiding eye contact with Hiten as he spoke. "Nice place. I have some idea what goes on here basically. How come no one is around but you?" he asked.

"There are a few people staying here. Some are out running errands," she replied with her blue eyes intently following the movement of his. "Actually, we are between retreats."

"How do you support this place? I mean, there must be some charge for staying," he asked.

"There's an endowment, and we have set fees for small group retreats and lectures. We accept donations. You are welcome to look around."

"I might do that," he said with some hesitation.

"Someone is giving a workshop tonight on haiku. You are welcome. It's free."

"Uh, I may not have time for that. What do you do here?" he wondered, indicating he meant her with his eye contact.

"Besides gardening?" she remarked with a glowing smile. "I'm the acting director."

"Oh," he answered, as he glanced down at the ground to hide his discomfiture. Hiten's tranquil countenance and superior openness caused him to feel as if he had suddenly shrunk in stature in every way. He could not think of anything else to say. She noted his embarrassment.

"Well, nice that you stopped by. Stay as long as you wish. I'll be out here for another hour or so if you have any more questions," she said with her hand extended.

After a simple handshake, Jake nodded to her in silent appreciation, turned and walked away only semi-conscious of his rapid gait. He headed for his car. Hiten watched him for a few seconds, uttered a short Buddhist prayer for him, and returned to her gardening.

After this brief, unnerving interlude, Jake decided the place did lack the dynamic energy he sought. He was set on going to the newer, Chama commune anyway.

If Buddha was boring, there might be no Buddha—23 September 1997

After studying his road atlas further, he drove from the quiet Zen center to find a place to park and camp in the mountains for the night. A wind driven thundershower hampered his search. The VW got stuck along a sloping dirt road that had turned to mud. After setting a few stones strategically behind the vehicle's rear tires, Jake managed the gears skillfully enough to rock his small car out of the rut. He managed to wheel the car up a rising curve until he spotted a flat, grassy area off the road. He parked but remained in the vehicle to wait out the storm. With the seat tilted back, he dozed off under his green and white Philadelphia Eagles fleece blanket.

Sunshine struck his face through the fogged window. The bright light woke him. He stepped out into the open air, gazed up at the cobalt sky, and breathed deeply through his nostrils. The air felt fresh and crisp on his skin and in his lungs. Behind him he saw a portion of a double rainbow arched across the Sangre de Cristo Mountains to the east. He watched a thin slice of the magical arc through a stand of pine trees until it faded.

He was ready to create a temporary camp. Within fifteen minutes he was sitting under a lean-to shelter made by draping a green, waterproof tarp over a domed contraption patched together from fallen branches. He changed into dry clothes and settled into his rustic habitat. While enjoying the view, he played with a chunk of black obsidian with a sharp edge that he found while searching for branches. From its size and shape complete with thumb rest that fit well in his right hand, he surmised that it once served as a cutting tool for an Anasazi tribesman. He drew the serrated edge lightly over his exposed right arm, leaving a hairline cut.

"It still works," he said to himself with certain delight as he rubbed the scratch vigorously with his left hand. He tossed the primitive tool back where he found it. While his water heated, he pondered the water dripping from a large Ponderosa pine. He pulled his Nietzsche biography out of his pack, took one look at a bookmarked page, and set it aside. He opened his notebook to write.

You are a drop of universal stuff forged through evolution into awareness of being the stuff of universal stuff.

Is there anything more to life than to realize this and then to let the self absorb the self?

And what of Nietzsche now?

Jake recorded *Nietzsche* in his notebook as he would spell a mantra.

Nietzsche, Nietzsche, Nietzsche, Nietzsche you say until you tire of Nietzsche.

You have a hammer but you have no nails and no boards.

—22 September 1997

Mantra loosely defined means to cast a spell. Nietzsche's words cast a brief spell over Jake as Nietzsche might over any unsettled college age seeker. The spell of Nietzsche for Jake this time, however, actually meant to give the notorious Hammer of the gods a rest. One last time he browsed a few pages in the book. He scanned over a notable event toward the end of the philosopher's life.

In 1889 in Turin, Italy, and not far from the steps of his home, Nietzsche watched an irate carriage driver whipping a hapless if stubborn horse bloody. Nietzsche was moved to tears and intervened to stop the driver's cruelty. Sobbing, he ran over to hug the horse, trying to comfort the animal for a moment. As Nietzsche turned aside he collapsed in the street. Nietzsche was hospitalized after what can be construed as a nervous breakdown. He never recovered his sanity. He languished through his last ten years under the tender care of his mother and finally a sister who traveled all the way from her anti-Semitic commune in Argentina to be with him.

After reading this and setting the book aside, Jake built a small fire with sticks and debris left over from the lean-to dome. He tore pages from the Nietzsche biography, wrinkled them up and tucked them under the sticks. He struck a match.

The fire caught immediately. He continued feeding pages of the book into the flames until the book was gone.

No need of Nietzsche.'Go forth' and let the chips fly. You can gather them up later. Or not.

We imagine we are like gods and yet we are more like the animals than we like to admit. Dangle a carrot in front of a horse and it will move toward the carrot. Hit a horse with a whip and it will move away from the whip—if it can. We are more unlike the animals than we like to admit. Hug a horse and it will not hug you back like your mom or your lover do.—23 September 1997

Whipping a horse is not always equal to using a whip on a horse. Jake recalled reading of Secretariat winning the Belmont Stakes in 1973 by an unbelievable margin. On the same page, he wrote:

Secretariat had a heart twice as large as the average horse. Secretariat never hugged anyone but many hugged the horse that won for them. We love the winners.

Earlier, when he was scouring through pages of books, Jake pondered that Friedrich Nietzsche had, before his collapse, completed a ruthless attack on the message of the crucified Christ. He proclaimed that Christianity is a *hangman's metaphysics.*

Thus spoke Nietzsche: Dualism be damned! Man is the god that lost God to the dead. Enough. One literature professor told you the antidote to Nietzsche was Dostoyevsky.

You opened The Idiot and got to page 131.

Are you the idiot trying to find reality between a Nietzsche and Dostoyevsky?

—12 August 1997

During that summer, Jake also turned to extra-curricular authors generally ignored by college courses. He read *The Aquarian Conspiracy* about the new global consciousness and he read two of Carlos Castaneda's tales about the Indian sorcerer don Juan Matus. These old books were in his father's small library collection in a box in the family basement. Monica told him that his father briefly pursued a religious search after he returned from Vietnam. The books indicated direct experience under a teacher as the key to wisdom. He puzzled at why seekers sought the next step in evolution, the mystical transformation into Nietzsche's alpha mammal, the Übermensch. Was this possible? Were they on to something? Could he, Jake, move in that direction?

Could a superman occur through special effort?—12 August 1997

Jake read that Nietzsche would have tolerated the ancient Greek, Heraclites. Heraclites was a kind of radical loner who saw change everywhere and in everything. This idea of impermanence appealed to Jake. Heraclites spoke of a Logos before Socrates and John the Evangelist did. But Heraclites, according to his storytellers, ended badly, dying from dropsy at an advanced age a day after he attempted a self-cure by covering his body with cow manure and baking in the sun.

Jake wrote random notes about these philosophers, as any young man might without fully grasping context. Though he wrote this down, he may have missed something of Nietzsche's warning:

"Do you presume yourself to be free? If so, then I want you to tell me what is your ruling idea, and not that you have broken free of some fetter. Are you the kind of man who ought to be unfettered? For there are many who cast off their final value when they cast away their chains." (Thus Spoke Zarathustra)—2 February 1997

But this was eight months after he wrote that. Jake never reread his journal notes. The young man had no idea what a *final value* might mean anyway. This was September and the season was changing. A chill hung in the mountain air. Jake's water finally reached the boiling point. He dropped the tea bag into an empty white mug, draping the attached string over its edge. He heard a deep, melodic croaking from a bird. He looked around. He saw the raven perched atop a dead juniper cedar across the pond. He watched it take off to perform an extraordinarily playful stunt twice.

A raven watches water dripping from the pine tree into a pond.
A drop falls to itself, its fate, into its pond.
The black form leaps into the air where wings flap freely guided by the laser sharp site
    of its eye fixed on the drop.
The ragged black feathers, all of one purpose glide toward a simple target as the large
    black bird swoops down to snatch the drop just above the surface.
The bird returns to its cedar perch, on the ready to play again.
A new drop forms at the end of a pine needle. And again, it flies.
—23 September 1997

"No, not all drops fall cleanly into the pond," he thought without writing it down.

Death and life were on his mind as he sipped the hot tea. He was not concerned about how to die but how to live and live fully. Death was inevitable. Why worry. Living fully to him did not mean living financially fulfilled, but it did mean to feel and know that his life had immediate value. There had to be more to this life than what his college courses and his foundering faith had given him.

It was time for a break, a break from the cacophony of ideas in his head. He was near his goal outside of Chama when he wrote:

The first Buddha as prince left his wealth, wife, and child to join the mendicants. Seeing suffering started it all, so the prince sought to end suffering for all.—24 September 1997

Northern New Mexico had plenty of room for one more Buddha. One more moved to Northern New Mexico months before the dropout was to start his final semester to complete a degree. Jake was twenty years old; old enough to legally make his own decisions. And his decision was to seek ultimate freedom and to begin that process at a new community. Professor Pedersen said it was a choice. He was free to decide. And he liked the symmetry, the sense of newness and this community was indeed very new and perhaps the beginning of something important, something with Buddhism in it along the upper Rio Chama.

With Nietzsche bulldozing bothersome beliefs and childhood's church brainwashing out of the way, the Buddha's way seemed a good thing to try. Going forth, moment by moment toward nirvana while sharpening awareness, could be its own reward. Going forth meant commitment to undo all anxiety and burdens of memory. Going forth meant exercising compassion on all sentient beings. No complex metaphysics or epistemic pretzels to contend with. The Buddha of legend was a practical guru. The Buddha of Chama was his hope to find a practical guru. Professor Pedersen told him it was a simple sangha—it was a small community with an old, experienced teacher, and perhaps the best of both worlds, of ancient tradition living in the present, so why not check it out?

If certainty mattered little when he left the university, he was less certain that his old Volkswagen bug would make it. The Beetle, vintage early 1970s, once belonged to his father, a mechanic who kept it in good running shape. It kept running with a little help all the way to Arizona from Pennsylvania and now perhaps to Northern New Mexico. Jake tinkered with the bug's distribution system enriching the fuel as he gained altitude on the Colorado plateau in the lower Rockies. This may be a spiritual trip and the spirit or the Fates would guide him, but he still had to make his way there somehow.

Jake watched the road ahead and glanced in the mirrors at the road behind. Traffic was sparse on the open desert hiways. He traveled cheap and light. He stayed within the speed limits, so nearly every vehicle passed him for two days.

To save money he camped along the way in his lean-to tent and sleeping bag. He chewed granola and beef jerky. He drank gas station tap water out of a used plastic bottle. Since he had no cell phone, he figured most everyone else did and most people would offer the use of one to him in an emergency. There were no emergencies.

He crossed the Chama River and the village of Chama appeared ahead— population 1,100 the last time he checked. He passed through a part of the small town. He veered right from *Route 84/64* onto a rustic road that rose toward Rabbit Peak. When he saw the newly carved sign indicating *Samuwabi Center* with a red arrow hanging below and pointing right, he knew that he was nearly there—just one slight turn onto a bumpy, dirt path. He passed an official, green metal sign that said: *No Outlet: Elevation 7,550 feet.*

A new scene opened up to Jake. He imagined he was driving onto the set of a movie as it was being filmed. He heard the hallowed bong-bong of a hand-hammered Japanese gong that resonated throughout the rural compound. The dust cloud kicked up by his VW drifted past a few people marching out of step down a rugged trail. They were moving toward one of two main buildings. Jake pulled over to park next to a row of a dozen vehicles. He encountered a heavy set fellow exiting a van next to him.

"Excuse me! I am new here. Where can I get some information?"

"Hi," said the friendly fat man with his Aussie accent. He was holding two brown bags of groceries. "Follow me over there," he indicated with a nod of his head. "I'll show you."

Jake followed. He passed the dark metal gong that sat atop a rustic wooden pedestal. The gong was in the shape of a large bowl. A middle-aged American with a gray goatee and bald head struck the bowl again with a polished hardwood stick—a keisaku.

"The sensei must be calling us for a meeting," said the fat man.

Jake quickly learned from his guide that sensei is Japanese for elder person or teacher. The sensei's formal title was Roshi, that literally meant *old teacher* but had an honorific quality meant for the most exemplary teachers only. Jake later learned that many of the guys endearingly called him *the old man*, but not to his face. "The sensei lives with his Japanese assistant and with his oldest student. He's privileged. He's the main gong ringer. They live in the two-story, brown stucco home across the way," said the fat man. "There he is now," he said as he pointed to the house. Jake saw a thin, baldheaded man in a black robe emerge onto the front deck to greet students as they arrived for a midday meeting. Jake's heart rate increased. He felt as if he saw a legend come to life before his eyes.

The sensei's house was coated with tan stucco and topped by a pitched, red tin roof. The first floor with its large open area served as the hall for meditation and lectures. It could easily accommodate fifty. Only a kitchen and full service bathroom remained of the original first floor after workers remodeled it to suit the sensei's design. The residents and some guests stayed bunkhouse style in a nearby, newly constructed, two thousand square foot, adobe-style cabin with the same tan walls as the main house. Others stayed in personal tents and trailers. The bunkhouse contained two large sleeping rooms, large enough to accommodate up to fifty in over-under bunk beds. It had the feel of a European hostel. The lodging rooms were separated by a common kitchen and dining area with two, long, hand-hewn pine plank tables. Simple wooden benches surrounded the tables. Three highly efficient wood-burning stoves heated the entire cabin. At that altitude air conditioning was not necessary. High desert summer nights were almost always blanket cool. The cabin had three entrances: one central, one for men, and the other for women. Two blue portable toilets, tastefully camouflaged by several common piñon trees, stood well below the cabin. Jake followed the big Aussie into the dining area that doubled as a greeting place for newcomers.

"Looks like no one's here to register you now," the fat man noted.

"What do I do?" Jake asked. He looked confused.

"No worries mate. Go to the meeting and meditate there if you wish. Or just hang around. You will meet someone here in an hour or so."

"I was told to look for Marga. Is she here?"

"Ah sure, she's about somewhere. She'll find you. I'll give her a shout for you."

During his first days there, the college dropout shared a tent with a slim fellow from the nearby Jicarilla Apache reservation. They sat together by coincidence at Jake's first group meditation. The Apache offered to share his shelter. He spoke English with a unique northern New Mexican dialect influenced by old Spain and his Indian heritage, not by Mexican culture. They were the same age. So his first day, at the beginning of his new life, featured a long-haired Indian. "How cool is that," Jake thought.

Cool as the other side of the pillow if he had one. The two young men slept on pads while tucked in individual sleeping bags. A jacket piled over a smooth flat stone served as Jake's head rest. The Apache owned the relatively new, blue-green, supposedly four-man tent shaped like a dome. Two fit comfortably in it. As they settled down to sleep the first day, the Apache farted.

"Christ, Waylon! What the hell did you eat?"

"Sorry, bro. Grandma's rabbit stew."

Host farts are funny especially in tents when the guest has to step outside for relief. "Whew! You need to stay away from rabbit, bro," Jake suggested while waving a hand in front of his face.

"Can't."

"Can't what?"

"I am Rabbit."

"What are you talking about?"

"My grandma nicknamed me Rabbit when I was a little kid because of how I darted around all the time. But don't tell anybody, okay?"

"Okay, Rabbit. I won't." But Jake would continue to call him Rabbit privately, however, as an inside joke. The host and the guest quickly became friends thereafter. Both men slept soundly.

They woke up at the sound of the gong. The common meal for breakfast was simple: Cooked oatmeal with a selection of fresh fruits, teas, and honey. Guests and residents ate in near silence together—whispers only. The college dropout felt energized by the communal atmosphere. This was different than class. This felt spiritual and holy.

He was about to hear the old man talk for the first time. When it happened, what he heard was the assistant translating for the old man. Although it would improve over the years, the old man's English at the time in 1997 barely made sense. Happily however, the translation was in a Japanese accent, and that made everything spoken sound more authentic to the students. The talk was about the *Lotus Sutra*. The old man chose the Lotus Sutra because that was the teaching most emphasized in his sect in Japan. His sect founded by Nichiren was not a part of the Zen movements, yet the old man chose to integrate all he knew into his form of Zen.

Few if any of the students there knew if one sutra had more meaning or authenticity than another. Most, like our college dropout, read a few books about Buddhism—yes, he read *Siddhartha* by Hermann Hesse as did almost everyone else at that commune, but he looked into Edward Conze and other scholars on Buddhism too. Naturally, he knew that the deeper, cultural implications evaded his experience, but he was confident that he would absorb and adjust as he went along. As for original language, Sanskrit and Pali would remain as Greek to him as Japanese.

That early autumn day in New Mexico carried a chill despite the bright sun outside. Around thirty people sat inside a large living area, some on chairs in the back and others seated on the floor nearer the sensei. His bald head and gray wispy beard and mustache enhanced his image as a traditional and friendly sage in a Soto style, black robe.

After a student struck the gong, the sensei spoke and the young assistant from Japan translated.

"Sensei says that the Lotus Sutra teaches that between Buddha and human is a parent-child relationship. In fact, Buddha is like a father to all sentient beings. He loves and guides them to be what they are in essence. Buddha does not teach a religion. He teaches a way to enrich all beings because all beings have Buddha nature. Everyone here already has Buddha nature, but distractions and desires interfere with the way of realization. Some call this realization satori; others, kensho or enlightenment. Do not worry what to call it. There is no word for Buddha nature. It is as obvious as life yet like life it remains mysterious. Sentient life is special but how special depends on you, not me. What I am doing here is not special, as I have already said many times."

The sensei pointed to Jake and his Apache friend as he said, "We have two new guests today, so I will repeat things. Please excuse. But I also remind and will continue to remind. We tend to forget simple things that bring us peace and enlightenment every day. So my job is to always remind you, to bring you back to Buddha nature day by day. Someday you will get this, so you will need no more reminding."

The old man continued in a rambling fashion, telling many anecdotes about his life as a monk. He claimed that even before Sakyamuni the Buddha, there were teachers that taught of the Buddha nature.

"Many great sages taught the same thing before and after Buddha. Buddha nature has many disguises. Even Jesus taught that *I and my father are one*. This means the same thing as I and Buddha nature are one. These things are mysterious. But one can achieve Buddha awareness through meditation practice. Maybe there are other ways, but after searching I find this way of Zen most simple, most direct, and most effective. No craving for nirvana. No craving for this world pleasure. We sit. We learn to stay in right mind as we do anything. Sensei will guide you. The rest will take care of itself. As great Western sages say: *We will cut out all bull shit!*"

The old man paused for the laughter to subside.

"My teachers showed me much through skillful means. Sometimes I feel confused by my teachers' words and actions. At times I was angry at them for causing me to suffer. I thought this way was supposed to end suffering. I left the monastery of Kyoto for many years because I believed it caused suffering. But one day after I drank too much sake, I woke with very bad headache."

The old man paused again to hold his head in his hands while making a pained expression with his face. Jake noted that part of the old man's left pinky finger was missing. But it was another comical gesture. The old man had a sense of humor. He had good timing and an engaging smile. After everyone stopped laughing, he and his assistant continued.

"At that moment I had my first actual satori! I cause own suffering by my action and wrong mind. My teachers tried their best to get that through this thick head."

Here the old man stopped to pound his head with his fist. "Is anybody home? Ah, empty mind is good," he said with open palms aimed at his audience.

Again, they laughed.

"Of course, Buddha nature is always home. Buddha nature is always calling us. Perhaps for you it is time to finally answer the phone!"

The gong rang. Jake felt a cosmic hush as the sound emptied in to the students and into the atmosphere around them. He felt oddly, even magically drawn to the new environment. If this was Buddha nature, it felt like an overwhelming burden lifted from his back. He had climbed a mountain and now he could lay his pack down, enjoy the moment before the real work began. This place was with it and he was with it. He was not converting to anything but inside he felt old patterns poised to pass. The sensei may not be perfect but he was the key to a door that was yet to open. The old man rose from the floor, bowed to his group as they bowed back— Gassho. Sensei silently walked to his quarters followed by his assistant.

Jake felt an informal calm in that exotic setting for the first two days. No one pressured him to do anything. No one paid special attention to the newer members and visitors unless they asked. Jake picked up on what to do mostly by following the movements of the others and through casual conversation. He learned that new members would have to fill out a one-page form with identifying information and sign a brief statement releasing the Center and the old man from any liability.

A suggested minimum daily donation of twenty dollars covered two simple meals and incidentals that the Center provided for overnight guests. Guests made snacks and drinks for extra nourishment from community supplies in the dining area. A donation bowl on the counter sufficed as payment for extras. After a mid-morning talk by the old man, Jake and Waylon the Apache followed the assistant and an oriental-looking woman, who appeared to be the assistant's assistant, to the main cabin for further orientation.

"Good to meet you both," the male assistant said as he bowed. "Please, have a seat. This is Marga." The new visitors stood to greet the elegant and stunning young Asian woman who stood smiling before them. Jake immediately recognized her from Pedersen's presentation. He felt an immediate connection. She bowed slightly. Both men returned the gesture—Gassho.

The men sat at a long wooden table while Marga prepared tea for everyone. Jake noted her slim, willowy figure under the rather unflattering, long brown skirt and simple beige blouse. He described her as *skinny* in his notes. Her long dark hair fell to the middle of her back. Her smiling image, that impressed him when he first saw her on Pedersen's PowerPoint display, was even more striking in person. He felt awkward trying not to stare at her.

The young Apache appeared unassuming, quiet, and self-contained as he leaned back in his chair with his arms crossed. His black hair fell loosely along his cheeks and down to his collar bones. He stared ahead, seemingly without blinking.

The Japanese assistant placed a pair of simple brochures before both men. One was an introduction to the Center with an impressive if short biography and black and white picture of the old man seated as if in meditation. The other was a foldout with the projected plans for expansion of the Center. The assistant went over the plans briefly and then rose from his seat to leave Marga to answer any and all questions. The assistant bowed to the guests before exiting the cabin. Jake bowed awkwardly in reciprocation and the Indian merely nodded. Marga served the tea.

"Namaste," she said with her hands folded as she graciously bowed her head to the two new guests. She sat down lightly on the pinewood bench that served as seating at the apparently hand-hewn pine table. Jake ran his admiring fingers along the splendidly crafted surface. Marga noted his appreciation.

"A local woodworker made this table and benches for us," Marga said. She explained with pride, "Our sensei designed it."

She sat across from the men with her spine erect and shoulders relaxed. She made certain eye-contact with both men before speaking. She seemed self-assured and emotionally distant yet with an elegance and easy grace that made Jake feel positively curious. If she was selling, he was considering anything she had to offer.

"We hope you enjoy your stay here. I have been here for only two months and I can tell you it has been intense but fun at the same time. As you can see here on this sketch we plan to build a couple of new cabins soon. We also have designs for a large garden that not only reflects Zen ideas but will use all local materials. The idea is to create an atmosphere for meditation for anyone who wishes to pursue enlightenment, even if it is only for a day."

Marga's presentation was interrupted by a small black cat that jumped up on the table. It sauntered over to the brochure and sat on it while facing Jake. The creature let out a slight meow, and then began to purr. Jake reached over to scratch the cat's head.

Marga waited a few seconds before proceeding to snatch the cat by the collar. She held the kitten in front of her face.

"Bad neko," she said as she wagged a finger at the limp feline. "You know you're not allowed up here."

Marga took the young cat, sat it down gently outside on the portal, and closed the door.

"Sorry," she said. "She showed up last month and seems to have adopted us as her home. Roshi said a neko—that's *cat* in Japanese—wants to be a student too!" Marga giggled until she noticed that neither man sitting with her seemed to grasp the guru's humor. She cleared her throat and continued.

"Roshi has no desire to form anyone's future here, but he expects the environment to help support Buddha mind. Of course, he has the responsibility to teach but he says that Buddha nature will guide him and everyone who comes here."

"I'm not sure if I get this," Jake puzzled. "Do students sign on, like monks, and live here?"

"Funny—well, maybe not funny—I mean interesting that you would ask. Roshi gave us a teaching last week about just that. He will be accepting permanent students soon but he requires a one year probationary commitment before anyone can take the *three refuges.*"

"And what is that?" Jake wondered.

The Indian looked at Jake as if he took the words right out of his mind. He repeated, "Yes, what is that?"

"Early Buddhism required three things to support those who would commit to the path: The student took refuge in the Buddha or a guru, the student committed to the Dharma meaning the teaching, and the student joined the Sangha or community. So, in practical terms for our Zen center, that means to take refuge under Roshi, his teaching, and this community. It also means that one has to eventually renounce possessions and other attachments. He does not require it but he praises those who can do that, including detachment from family. Committed members who take refuge will attend mandatory sessions two or three times a month. It's called the Uposatha or Fortnight Assembly at every new moon and full moon. Some people from Hindu tradition call it an *Upanishad.*"

"What if someone misses an assembly?" Jake wondered with a hint of concern in his voice.

"Roshi said he would make that clear. Traditionally, monks confessed any wrongdoing at the assembly and punishment or a penance was meted out. Mostly, as I understand it, the confession was enough, but if the offense was grave, a monk could be suspended or punished in some other way. Roshi has the power to dismiss anyone from refuge. My hunch is that a member would be put on probation for a first major offense. If someone can't meet that level of commitment, to meet at the Fortnight Assembly, maybe they should drop their vows anyway. In the end, it is up to the student to decide what level to pursue and then commit to the rules."

The Apache made eye contact with Marga. He gazed into her eyes for long seconds before asking his question. "What convinced you to commit to this Roshi guy, this path here?"

The question indicated more than curiosity about her personal history, but Marga shared her story with them—the story of how she got there and why she stayed.

Marga was of mixed Asian-American stock. One of her grandmothers was Chinese and one of her grandfathers was Mongolian. Her mother was Hawaiian-Mongolian and her father was Chinese-Japanese. Marga's parents met in Hawaii where she was born and raised. She had good parents.

They owned a small, exotic fabrics and sewing supply store. Marga, the eldest child, helped to run the store from age fifteen. She had an instinct for organizing the business and developed a talent for it much to her parents' delight. Marga was very familiar with the Japanese culture in Hawaii. She spoke a little Japanese. This language trait endeared her to the old man immediately. As a child she attended Buddhist services with her mother but only a few times. She showed no interest in becoming Buddhist as a child. She was the old man's most valued though not most favored disciple—women had a lesser role to play in the old man's mind. But he needed someone to deal with the women in general.

The old man knew of Marga's past. She told Jake that she revealed everything to him early in her discipleship. She appeared at the commune shortly after her affair with a wealthy, but married, young Egyptian entrepreneur ended badly. Marga's family business was one of the Egyptian's clients in Hawaii. Her affair with the Egyptian endured for six stormy months. He was staying in Hawaii longer than usual in order to manage a new business project.

The story he told Marga, that he and his wife were about to divorce, was just a story. At least it was a believable story until Marga found a letter from the wife in his hotel bedroom. Marga confronted him with the evidence. They argued. He was drunk as was she. The lover beat her up badly and then left her crying alone in his hotel suite that night. In her depressed desperation Marga overdosed on pills from his supply of Valium. She took all twenty-two that remained in the bottle. Hours later, a housekeeper found Marga sprawled on the floor. The housekeeper called police to send help.

An ambulance rushed Marga to Straub Hospital, the nearest medical center. After a day or so of medical treatment, a doctor referred her to the behavioral health unit of the hospital where she stayed for several days. The therapy helped her see through the false relationship, but Marga's personal insight came not from her therapist. It came from another female patient she befriended. They happened to share a room for two of the three days.

The roommate, Amy, carried an admission diagnosis of bipolar disorder with mania. Amy was a patient there for a week and her symptoms subsided considerably by the time Marga met her. Amy was also a prime example of a religiously preoccupied personality disorder. She read and explored everything but without sustained discipline. Amy shared her volume of Hermann Hesse's *Siddhartha*, the modern novel about the Buddha's life, with Marga. It was the first spiritual book Marga ever read from beginning to end. Marga devoured it in two days taking its message to heart. She was ready for spiritual insight.

Life was about transcending suffering and realizing salvation for oneself and others. Attachment to money and pleasure with a man leads to suffering. It all sunk in and it all made sense. She vowed never to repeat that mistake again. She would find another way to happiness.

The hospital world of mentally ill people was disconcerting to Marga, for sure, but she found in Amy a valuable resource nevertheless. Amy helped Marga feel at ease in treatment. Marga liked her roommate in the same way someone might enjoy the experience of an engaging, dramatic stage performance. She learned that Amy lived off a family trust fund that enabled her quest for self-realization. She could afford to live in the alternate reality of the eternal quest for truth.

Amy represented a world of experience with spiritual people and places. Amy's gabby talk about that world intrigued Marga. It became more than a distraction from depression. There was hardly a topical guru that she could not name: Sri Chinmoy, Krishnamurti, Yogananda, Sai Baba, and Om Ram-something were among the few that Marga could recall

Amy told Marga about the *Lama Foundation* located north of Taos, New Mexico, the last place she stayed, for two days, she said. It was one of the Lama folks who drove her to a hospital. She was clearly in need of help, as she was not sleeping for days and babbling esoteric nonsense. Her father flew in from the islands to escort her back to Hawaii for further treatment.

Marga's roommate described Lama as a small but enduring intentional community. "It's quiet and in the high desert, away from everything. Some of the people there are Buddhist. It's been there since 1967," she said.

Amy told her that Lama was infamous among the early hippie communities. In 1968, the then young actor, Dennis Hopper, brought his crew to Lama to shoot the commune scenes for his new film, *Easy Rider*. Marga had no idea what film she was talking about but the combination of a quiet place and Buddhist meditation piqued her interest.

Marga contacted the Lama folks. She let her instincts guide her. Her father, satisfied that his daughter was stable again, gave her some vacation money. A few weeks after her hospitalization, she traveled to Lama for a month-long private retreat. It was there that she heard from someone passing through, a glowing report about the new Zen center outside of Chama. The new Zen center was one place Amy did not mention.

At the time of Marga's arrival, the Chama center was very new, perhaps three months in existence. She discovered that the founder used his inheritance from a wealthy brother who died in Japan to purchase close to ten rural acres. The property included an old but solid three-bedroom, two-story house with a functioning well and electrical power.

Soon after the sensei and his assistant arrived in New Mexico, they began to advertise his meditation classes. A regional religion writer with an interest in emerging spiritual groups interviewed the old man and his assistant. The feature article with photos appeared in Taos, Santa Fe, and Albuquerque news outlets. Word spread quickly among the regional seeker culture about the intriguing new Zen teacher. Marga felt encouraged by these early reports.

When Marga first met the old man, he had eight resident followers with maybe ten to fifteen visitors that arrived for open Saturday lectures. She heard him give a talk after she participated in an hour of group meditation. Despite his bad English and what may have been lost or gained in translation, the old man's proclaimed dedication to his followers and apparently keen grasp of Buddha's teaching impressed Marga immediately. She felt calm and *at home*.

"And that's my story," Marga said with some embarrassment. But Marga understood that the Indian wanted confirmation of the real power at the Center. She said, "Two days after I arrived here, which was a few months ago, I wanted to know the same thing, to find something that would convince me. My first day was good, I met good people, and I found the Roshi to be intriguing. I liked him. I slept well and got up with the others before sunrise for morning meditation. Ten minutes or so into the meditation I felt something shift inside. It was extraordinary like nothing I experienced before. It did not matter whether my eyes were closed or not. My ordinary sense of self dissolved. I saw things as they were in the moment, things from the stones on the ground in front of me to the entire cosmos all at once."

Marga paused to collect her thoughts. The men waited intently for her to continue.

"I was in a timeless space," she explained. "All fear left me as well as all desire to have to do anything. I felt like I was out of my body. I looked up to see Roshi standing near the gong around thirty feet away. He was smiling at me. I knew then that he knew. That sensation has not left me even though not much else changed. I still struggle with trivial things like what to wear or homesickness. But it passes and I return to what Roshi calls Buddha mind again and again at surprising moments. I found serenity, or maybe serenity found me."

"Ah," was all the Apache said as he nodded slowly.

Jake's mouth was agape. She spoke to his heart. This is what he wanted also; that simple awareness and tranquility that he did not yet have.

Marga spoke for a few more minutes, answered their questions—rather, she answered Jake's remaining questions until he was satisfied. The Apache merely thanked her when she was done. The two new friends walked out of the meeting silently with new brochures in hand.

Buddha nature very well may have guided everyone who eventually came there. "Buddha nature is mysterious—the sensei said it," she said. Jake felt at home; even energized. Anxiety drifted into his past. And he became intrigued with the whole package that included living in Northern New Mexico. He felt welcome to come and go as he pleased at the Center. He was in *The Land of Enchantment*, and like so many new residents in New Mexico, he became increasingly fascinated with the variety of native peoples and landscapes. New Mexico's northern districts had a unique history and culture informed by Native American nations and early Spanish settlers. But there was more, something he did not expect and that surprised him. Marga and other students he met reinforced it many times. "Sensei tells us that we must not trifle with Buddha nature once we are called. The chance comes only to a few who are at an advanced stage of awareness in their stream of consciousness in this incarnation. The teacher is all important," Marga said. "He is not the Buddha, but he is Buddha!"

Jake certainly felt like he had never felt before. His past seemed to melt away into the eternity of the present moment, especially when he meditated in the presence of the old man. He could not deny the feeling. He could not deny that the old man was a great teacher or Roshi, if personal experience was any guide. He could not deny that a weird set of coincidences led him to this community in Chama. A Catholic nun inadvertently initiated his fate as if his Catholic faith was a preparation for the next step to the Buddha and enlightenment. The synchronicity seemed uncanny. His life had been touched by a true transcendence. "So, it's true: When the student is ready, the teacher will appear," he said to Marga.

"When the student is ready, the teacher will appear," she repeated with a quiet emphasis. "Yes. But this realization comes with a price. Doubts will enter the mind. Old demons that we have not resolved will bite, scratch, seduce, and burn us to distract us from Buddha mind. Roshi compared this to the desert fathers in Christianity. Like Saint Anthony we may have to suffer through much from within to realize that we are worthy of enlightenment."

Jake took her words to heart. He would hear the old man say as much to reinforce this fact many times. "Not everyone is ready for this," he said. "As you see, many come and go after only a few weeks or months at Samuwabi. In Japan I had many students who lapsed, as you say in Christian culture. Some fell into a much worse state after rejecting the path than they were before it. Two committed suicide. Very sad for me because I believe they would be alive and happy if they stayed true to their calling."

Over the next five years, Jake used the Center as home base, sometimes working on jobs in the region for weeks or months at a time. He hardly noticed that his ambivalence toward a career or degree when he dropped out of school extended through the years. He enjoyed living in the moment, earning just enough to get by. It was as if he entered a timeless phase through a day to day existence. The Roshi seemed content to let Jake come and go as he always seemed to return with funds to share with the community. Whenever he had enough money, he stopped working to stay weeks at a time meditating and volunteering at the Center.

On one of his first jobs in New Mexico, Jake learned the essentials of local masonry from a stalwart Hispanic man who would hire him regularly. Jake appreciated and respected Mr. Anaya much as he might a father figure. Raymond Anaya told stories of how his father as a child traveled to the area in a covered wagon from Colorado in 1910. His family worked hard to establish a small sheep ranch but lost nearly everything during the Depression years. Ray owned what was left of it: Three and half acres, a small barn and a house. Ray specialized in smooth river-rock walls but he could do almost anything with stone, tile, and brick as well as plaster.

The smooth stones formed in arroyos where rushing waters ground rocks over each other in sand for hundreds and thousands of years. Each stone Jake held held a unique record of the passing of time for him.

The stones worn smooth by sand let me touch an era in an instant.
—November 3, 1997

Jake spent days of hard labor collecting the rocks and mixing mortar before Ray taught him how to set the stone. The experience gave Jake some idea of what the eleventh century Tibetan saint Milarepa must have experienced before Marpa the Translator, his guru, took him on as a student. Jake and many others at the Center read the biography of Milarepa. The old man encouraged it. The Center had a dozen copies in its library.

The story relates that Marpa commanded his student Milarepa to build, break down, move and rebuild a stone tower many times as a form of penance for practicing sorcery. Milarepa used black magic to take revenge on an uncle who stole property from Milarepa's mother. Milarepa conjured a hailstorm that destroyed much of the uncle's property and family. The remorseful Milarepa persevered through these excruciating tasks in frustration. Marpa's concerned wife intervened, asking Marpa to have pity on the young man. But Marpa did not relent until he was satisfied that Milarepa had paid off his karmic debt for a serious sin. Only then would Marpa teach his student the way to enlightenment. By comparison, Ray was an easy taskmaster and he was not a famous guru. The old man was another story altogether. His students saw a version of Marpa in the old man.

During those first few years in New Mexico, Jake read selectively while he practiced Zen at the Center. He volunteered often to expand the rock garden. He would resist taking refuge or permanent status as a student under the old man for five years. He was unconcerned about permanence. He had one girlfriend for a time in Taos, but she wanted nothing to do with the Center. She broke off the relationship. Jake learned his lesson. Buddha mind had tested him again, as if he had unfinished karma with his ex-girlfriend in Arizona. Through connections at the Center, he easily found places to stay or house-sit when he chose not to stay at the Center. To live there as a permanent resident, he would have to take refuge and commit to certain routines. He was not ready for that. He was not yet in strict orbit. But that would change.

After four years of following his unfettered fate, he felt anxious and maybe a bit homesick. He returned home to Pennsylvania for seven months to consider renewing his college career. For income he worked at his brother's auto repair shop. He enrolled part time at a community college. After finishing an unsatisfying course in journalism and another if only slightly more satisfying one in ancient culture, he decided to return to the Center in New Mexico again, much to his mother's chagrin. The yearning for Buddha nature drew him back and it was strong enough this time to overcome any remaining ambivalence.

So, he returned to New Mexico in 2002 in his VW with a renewed sense of purpose. Jake was happy to discover that Marga and his Apache friend were still there, but he noted something different about them as they welcomed him back. Both of them had sheared the hair off their heads indicating a new rule for permanent students.

"Yo, bro, what happened to your hair?" Jake asked Waylon.

"Nothing happened, bro," the Indian casually replied.

"There's nothing there."

"That's what I said."

"So there's nothing more to say?"

"Nothing's been said," the Indian answered with a smile.

"Are you sure?"

"No."

"If you are not sure, does it bother you?"

"Why bother, bro?" the Indian asked flatly.

"Oh, well," Jake shrugged. "It will grow back."

"To remind me that it grows."

"Does hair—can hair have intention? I mean, why remind?"

"Could be a new koan."

"Comes from nothing—"

"Nothing at all."

"This conversation is getting emptier," Jake said.

"Arigato," the Indian said, and in mock gratitude he bowed ceremoniously to his friend.

"Domo arigato," Jake replied returning the gesture with an effusive Gassho.

Marga used her training in martial arts to shove both of them hard. The two surprised clowns stumbled to the ground laughing.

After recovering his composure, Jake told Marga, "You look good in no hair." He was not kidding. Marga retained her stunning, exotic features. "So what else has changed around here?" he continued with his hand raised to stop the Indian from offering a nonsense answer.

"The Japanese assistant has gone away—he moved back to Japan. While you were gone we've increased to nearly thirty students that have taken refuge," Marga reported with a hint of glee. "Roshi has challenged many of us to increase our level of commitment to help his cause here."

Thus, after five years of struggle under the old man, the tiny community was thriving with committed converts. Jake felt the increased energy and he liked it. After five years of touch and go as a student, Jake was ready to commit, to forget the self and blend naturally with the group. He was ready for Zen dharma.

That next weekend, after his return, Jake stood before the old man in the lecture hall. He knelt down. He bowed his head until it touched the plush Oriental rug covering the pine plank floor. The old man took a pair of scissors, grabbed a lock of Jake's hair and snipped it off close to the scalp. Marga held open a small brown paper bag into which the old man dropped Jake's hair. Marga took the bag over to a woodburning stove. She tossed the bag into the flames and shut the door. After Jake stood up and exchanged bows with the old man, everyone in the room clapped and cheered.

And, thus, he began shaving his scalp and face regularly as a sign of his renunciation. He chose to give up attachment to possessions, sex, family, fame, and anything else that got in the way of the way to enlightenment. He had taken refuge. He was on the way, but to what?

4 Holy Madness

Margaret wandered into the dining area during the noon meal. Her sleek black form seemed to glide rather than step across the sealed concrete floor. Margaret was a hunter who often ate what she caught outdoors, but every other day or so she came inside to eat store bought kibble. Originally, the Center's residents called her Kitty or Gato. The old man called her a *neko*, which is Japanese for cat, but naming her Neko did not suit the old man. He said *neko* in another context could mean, "To be sick in bed or asleep." A young student, who was responsible for feeding the cat after it arrived, named her Margaret after her grandmother who had just died. It was a coincidence that Marga's birth name was Margaret. That name stuck to the cat for five years until one day, the day after Jake took refuge, the Apache addressed the cat in the dining hall just as it crossed Marga's path.

"Here Margaret! Here pussy, pussy."

Most of the men broke out in raucous laughter. Marga did not appreciate the lewd pun. She was already silently irritated with everyone calling the cat Margaret for the past five years, but Marga lived with the irritation as a test of her tranquility. The old man told her it was an opportunity to learn about the self, so Marga accepted the task as one might struggle with a koan. "An enlightened monk would not let such a petty thought linger in mind," Roshi said to her.

But this pussy thing put the old man's top female assistant over the edge. Marga gave in to a self-protective impulse gained from a searing personal experience she had with the married Egyptian man prior to coming to the Center. In any case, she knew abuse when it reared its ugly head even if it was meant in fun. Additionally, she wanted to reinforce respect for the celibate status of everyone who took refuge, especially for the women.

"Okay, that's it. Change the cat's name," she said with certain authority. "And I don't want to hear pussy jokes around here any more either—got it?"

There was dead silence in the room. The Indian apologized, sensing he had a hit a raw nerve. "Won't happen again, Marga," he promised.

The tension remained.

Rachel, a diplomatic, older woman broke the ice when she said, "How about we shout out a few new names and put it to a vote? I would call her Raven."

There was a collective groan with tentative laughter among perhaps half the students who recovered their giddiness.

"Too obvious," one male yelled out. "I think Blanche would be better."

An even louder groan with a few boos negated Blanche. More laughter ensued. It became apparent that this would be an election by acclamation.

After several more groans overwhelming minor cheers for Zenda, Inky, and Schwartz, the Indian called out to the cat that crouched nervously by the door.

"Come here Maggie. Here, Maggie," he said with his hand down by the floor.

The kitten perked up and responded immediately. She ran over to his hand.

"See, she knows her name."

"Hey, that's cheating, bro," Jake challenged. "She figured you had a treat."

"And it's a little close to calling her Margaret," grumbled Marga.

It did not matter. Everyone clapped at the cheap performance and accepted Maggie as the cat's new name. The Indian lifted the kitten high above his head.

"We christen thee Maggie, our Zen cat extraordinaire!" he shouted as he glanced sheepishly toward Marga. They made eye contact. Her exasperated smile let him know he was forgiven.

More cheers erupted and a number of students lifted their hands and clapped.

"Yo, Rabbit," Jake called out.

The Apache turned immediately, lowering the squirming cat to his chest. He made eye contact with Jake.

"That must be your name, eh?" Jake said half in jest.

Until then commune members called him by his birth name, Waylon. Only Jake called him Rabbit in private, recalling their first encounter marked by the stench of the rabbit stew fart.

"Must be my name," he said with a smile as he set the cat down on the floor. "Then, we christen thee Rabbit," Marga offered aloud so everyone could hear.

Cheers broke out again. The Indian accepted the change without resistance. Waylon carried many harsh memories. If this place was for deep change, then a name change made sense. He felt renewed as Rabbit, if only with community members.

When the old man got wind of the naming ritual, he approved of the spontaneity and fun. A few members had taken new names but there was no rule to do so. But this event inspired the old man to push the naming ritual a bit further, thus exercising a kind of guidance or control depending on your point of view. "You are Usagi," he announced during the next general meeting as he rested a hand on the Indian's shoulder. "Rabbit in Japanese is *Usagi*. Very good Zen," he said. "Right thing, right time, and right place." Everyone clapped.

As the months wore on at the Center, the original spontaneity of the naming ceremony waned. The old man saddled newer members taking refuge with Japanese names indicating virtues, flowers, animals, and the elements like earth, wind, and fire.

One time and one time only, the old man suggested to Marga that Jake be called Jun. It often was her responsibility to act as liaison between the old man and students. "It means *obedient*. What do you think?" Marga asked Jake.

"Sounds like a girl's name. Not sure I can deal with that. Tell him it doesn't feel right to me," Jake responded curtly. By refusing the suggestion, Jake unwittingly insulted the old man whose polite suggestions were understood as commands by students under his refuge. The old man took it a sign that Jake retained an independent streak despite his renunciation of all desire.

"This student might need a deeper lesson." Marga was not sure what her Roshi meant by this, but she felt he had Jake's best interest in mind.

Breakfast was over and it was time for two hours of chores. Everyone had an assignment indicated on a white board mounted on an easel next to the entrance door. There were five categories, each in a special color with student names printed in the appropriate color for that bracket. Students were permitted to swap chores. Two students were assigned to clean-up in the dining area and that included tending to the cat's litter box and taking out the trash to a dumpster a hundred yards down the road. Two others were assigned to the old man's house and lecture room to do whatever and that included cleaning, office work, and answering the phone.

A handful of students were assigned to Jake and Usagi, both of whom oversaw the grounds and gardens. Two students cleaned the pathways of debris that included dead leaves, fallen branches and paper scraps that were incinerated in a large barrel at one end of the property. The old man wanted a neat, natural feeling on the grounds. He always had gardening projects going which meant wrong rocks needed to be hauled to and from a nearby arroyo. Weeds had to be pulled and thrown into the compost. In the spring season new beds were dug for the ever expanding vegetable and herb garden. The old man often walked among the gardeners, even lending a hand when it suited him.

A small construction crew assembled from able students split up to get supplies from town and to continue with any building projects. Enough orders came in for harvest style tables with benches and coffee tables to keep a few students working daily. A rustic workshop complete with a table saw, a functional set of hand and power tools, a gas generator for heat and torches for welding enabled students to make elegant if rustic furniture year round.

Rather than outsource projects like this one, the old man saw an opportunity to bring in cash from the donated labor. Students, for the most part, were only too happy to comply. It was all part of the happy, *chop wood, carry water* atmosphere cultivated by the old man.

A start-up sewing industry developed among the women who made the traditional Buddhist robes worn by permanent members during formal gatherings. They also produced attractive variations of the robes creating tunics and loose pants that customers could wear as casual attire at the Center for any occasion.

The old man devised plans to establish a clothing brand once the designs were "right"—*Rightwear*. The project was overseen by Marga whose parents had a fabric business in Hawaii. She had some business experience from working in the family store from age twelve. Two or three women at a time worked at these sewing projects in the lecture hall whenever it was not in use for gatherings. Since sewing was labor intensive and slow going for small profit, the old man directed Marga to contract with a Chinese firm to produce their designs. They found several boutiques in New Mexico to sell them.

Overall, guests were impressed with the cheerful, productive atmosphere at the small commune and many volunteered to help as they could.

Soon after taking refuge, Jake approached Marga with something that had been bugging him for some time. Refuge included coming clean about everything and anything, to release oneself from desire. Life at this level was a tough psychological cleansing. "I need to tell you something," Jake said to her. "Can we take a walk?"

"Sure. What's up?" she asked as she set her clipboard with the daily schedule on it on her desk.

"Not sure how to say this," Jake said as they walked up the hill behind the Center, "but I've been attracted to you since I first saw your picture before I came here. After we met, I realized how committed you are to this, so I never said anything. I guess I want to know if there is any reason for me still feeling this way after five years."

"Do you want to know if I have been waiting for you to say something?"

"Wow. You get right to the point, don't you?" Jake was surprised by Marga's immediate grasp of his dilemma. "Yes."

Romantic territory had been a touchy area for permanent commune members. Attachment to things and people of this world was suspect. Commitment was to the community, to the Buddha in the guise of the old man, and to the Eightfold Path. However, the sensei also wanted to avoid trouble by not appearing too strict. Married couples were welcome, but only one couple ever took refuge, and then only for a few months. The brochures advertized an open policy. Anyone who had taken refuge could obviously just walk or sneak away, but nothing in print warned of psychological bonds. To walk away was never easy. No one would come that far to take refuge without a deep inner conversion. That conversion was often as strong as readiness to die for a cause.

Jake like Marga had taken vows to reject marriage or sexual partnerships as long as they were monks. If they broke this rule, they would be asked to leave. Jake was not so much tempted to break the rule as he was curious to reveal the reality of his desire for Marga. If she reciprocated, the challenge for both of them would be doubly heavy to resist. But he thought that they had to know. All desire had to be flushed out and confronted and then let go. Marga knew exactly why Jake brought this up, yet she was flattered. Her problem, however, would be attachment to flattery and not to Jake.

"You're not my type, if that's what you're after," she said with a sarcastic tone.

"You mean you really never wanted to date me or anything like that?" he asked with some apprehension.

"No, but I did recognize your affection at times."

"Like when I gave you a small fossil I found. Is that what you mean?"

"I still have the trilobite. It's cute!" she said.

"Whew," Jake remarked with a blow. "I figured that was it but this old desire kept coming up. Thanks."

"Thanks for what?"

"I feel like a load just lifted. I've had this, like, crush on you since I first saw your picture. Now I feel like my affection for you is like courtly love. You know, Platonic."

"You're such a romantic! Let's just say brother and sister. That's how I treat it. There's no need for you to fight a dragon!"

Jake felt childish all of a sudden. He blushed but Marga did not notice. She was negotiating a few steep steps to climb up onto a flat overhang. Jake followed her.

"We can sit here for a while to catch our breath before going back down," she offered. Jake sat next to her. There was nothing more to say. They were a brother and a sister at peace looking over and beyond the Center below.

Over time Usagi allowed Jake into his life as well, as a brother. Usagi said he was a *half-breed* who never knew his Anglo father. He heard that the man was good looking and charming and from the East coast.

"That dude that left my mother lied to her. She later found out that he spent four years in a Texas jail on drug running charges. He was a dark-haired Jew from Philadelphia who came to work for a season at the Jicarilla hunter's lodge. He was a chef. Mom fell for him and he moved in with her in her trailer. When he discovered that she was pregnant and not willing to abort, he left her. He just disappeared. Lodge managers suspected that he absconded with a missing ten thousand dollars."

Jake merely sat. His silence encouraged Usagi to continue.

"Later, when I was four or five, mom moved in with a local Indian guy who worked in construction. He treated us very well. Between what my step-father earned, mom's job as cashier at a grocery store, and the tribal royalties, we managed to get by."

"What royalties?" Jake wondered.

"My people sell natural gas and oil from their land."

"Are you getting any royalties?"

"Some. Everyone gets a check every year. I started saving mine. I may use it later to go to school."

"How did you discover this place?"

"A brochure in Dulce. It fell at my feet off the bulletin board at the co-op. I thought it was a sign."

"Cool."

"And you?"

"I read Nietzsche."

"Not cool. I mean, you lost me, bro."

"His philosophy convinced me that the God in my religion was over. So I looked into Buddhism. A Catholic nun told me about this place," Jake said with a smile.

"I like my story better," Usagi said.

"So do I."

A few enthusiastic commune members came from Europe. One young woman, Nancy, who had just graduated from an American college, donated half of her inheritance, giving the old man the equivalent of two hundred thousand Euros. Another woman, Taylor, was recently divorced and gave the commune forty thousand dollars after she liquidated her estate. She intended to seriously practice renunciation. These two women were particularly enthralled with the old man and his vision of an integrated Buddhism. He paid special attention to them privately. They wanted to support his potentially world-changing venture.

"To change world you must first change the inner world," uttered the old man.

Cliché or not, the adage made sense to the women and other commune members.

"You cannot teach calculus before you learn it, and it is better to learn from a professor unless you are a born genius," he said with a chuckle. "If you are a Buddha already, then why are you here?"

Another key, even self-sealing lesson for all that took refuge created a deep, psychological reality for new and old members. According to Jake the old man put it this way:

Old man said the most important step is taking refuge. This is a step into eternity and most serious as well as nothing to worry about. He indicated that to not follow through with total submission, you risk horrible hell-worlds that can take hundreds of rebirths to disentangle. He said, "This is like a man that leaps from a one-hundred foot cliff. He must be very disciplined on way down to enter water smoothly. If he doubts or loses control—loses his razor's edge—he will go SPLAT! Not good."

That is why you must remain as disciplined as possible.

The old man took several trips a year to Japan after the major donations came in. He said the trips were necessary to maintain connections with a Zen center in Kyoto that sponsored his effort. Only Tadao, whose American name was Jerry, his young

American house assistant, traveled with him. The young devotee understood barely a lick of Japanese at first. The old man apparently wanted it that way during his meetings with some strange characters who seemed to Tadao to have nothing to do with Buddhism. The older devotee, Jiro, who lived with the old man as his cook and house manager, administered the Center in his stead while Marga tended to women's programs and to all new recruits.

The core members lived and worked at the Center. Jake was among the core members now. He continued to take small jobs as a stone mason in the surrounding community. However, he rarely missed weekend workshops when he was expected to assist with guests.

Guests came and went for Zen meditation workshops, lectures, and martial arts classes. Jake and Usagi helped the old man to teach basic martial arts. If the old man really had a black belt or the equivalent, no one could prove it. He behaved as if he did, even if he said that belts do not matter in the end anyway. In any case, for his age, he retained fluid movements from years of practice. He was good enough to impress his best students.

Some guests stayed or returned later to attempt a kind of novitiate for six months. Most new members lasted less than a year. Marga, Usagi and Jake labored among the dedicated core of a dozen devotees that remained from the first years. They believed in the dream of living and spreading an ancient tradition to pursue enlightenment.

However, not everyone was a happy guest or student. Some defectors left in bitterness after hearing rumors of the old man's promiscuity or feeling his pressure to give more money. Others could not tolerate the disciplines. A few felt his brand of Buddhism was more made up than traditional. Some started calling the Center a cult. The devoted wrote this off as minor problems all new movements have. Christianity started off as a cult too, some of them would say.

After one midday meal the gong rang to gather residents for the monthly *Assembly*. Guests not in residence found things to do like reading, writing, hiking or whatever sustained a form of mindfulness. Some practiced martial arts and Tai Chi which were normally taught by the old man with his assistants, but all of the teachers were at Assembly. Everyone maintained silence within earshot of the gathering inside the lecture hall.

The private Assembly took place during every new moon day. It was perhaps the most important day for the Center because this was when the old man interacted personally with his core following. The Assembly at full moons was less intense, more festive and remained open to all at the Center. On days of new moon Assembly the students chanted Om Mani Padme Hums and meditated intermittently for several hours. After that prolonged period of preparation and introspection, the old man's disciples confessed wrongdoings and asked about things that bothered them. They discussed ways to improve the Center. The old man left many questions unanswered. Students interpreted his ignoring a question not as ignorance but as part of the empty-mind atmosphere cultivated by the old man to maximize self-awareness in the student. It was a signal to work it out for ones self, thus following the Buddha's dictum. The old man taught that inaction often spoke louder than action. He sometimes demonstrated this empty reality with his brush drawings of remembered landscapes from the old country.

A few of the newer members at this Assembly asked the old man to elaborate on emptiness. After one of his quiet moments of non-response, the old man laughed.

"You ask Roshi to teach what is not teachable. Ha!" he said while stroking his thin beard.

He stood up and asked Marga to bring him a bamboo paint brush. He took the brush and stroked the air around him with an invisible calligraphy to illustrate his short speech.

"The deeper meaning of oriental landscape not so much in visible brush marks as in empty space and dragon line. Every mark on the page is connected to other marks with a dragon line. Dragon lines are invisible. Invisible lines bring all together.

This is like empty space around a gong or bowl. Emptiness in air is essential for sound to have material substance. Emptiness is necessary for something to exist. All visible things come from nothing—this is taught in Western teaching also. God in the Jewish tradition created from nothing. Therefore, nothing is very important!"

The old man rolled his eyes and chuckled. Everyone laughed even though most of the students had heard him use this pun before. He returned the brush to Marga who replaced it to a brush rack.

"Any more questions?" the sensei asked as he sat down in his chair.

"Yes, I have one," Jake chimed.

Jake rarely asked questions, so the old man asked him to stand up. The old man bowed to him and Jake reciprocated, and he remained standing.

"Last year, I met a Christian teacher in Santa Fe. He was interested in your teachings—I gave him your book. We sat in a café there talking and comparing Buddhism with Christianity. There seems to be a different view toward suffering between the two religions. He thought Buddhism teaches to avoid suffering. I asked him why Christians seem to embrace suffering. Did I ask the right question? Are the two religions divided over concepts of suffering?"

The old man motioned for Jake to sit down. He stroked his beard slowly and looked around at his students who were all very attentive. He sensed a potential string of more questions if his answer was inadequate. He recalled discussions by his teachers about the inadequacy of Christianity which taught less reliance on self for salvation and near total reliance on the *other*—on Jesus. Buddha taught his disciples to work out their own salvations.

The old man was troubled by the Christian tradition with its concept of a permanent soul and a permanent hell for unbelievers. His teaching on this topic continued to evolve as he grew to better understand his Western students. He sensed in Jake the same conflict that he sensed in most of his American students. He felt that they unconsciously retained primitive ideas about suffering from the pervasive influence of the culture that raised them. He would teach this lesson about suffering another way.

"Good question, Mister Jake. Someday I will have the right answer, but not today."

The Assembly lasted for another hour. Two students confessed that they had extramarital sex after taking refuge for two months. They talked about how difficult it was to recover from bonds of attachment to one another and how they yet struggled to remain celibate.

The old man responded with a casual approach.

"Sex can be fun or it can be healing or it can be another path when a couple wants to raise children. What is the goal? Is the goal a worthy one? All sex acts have consequences—cause and effect—that make a path to enlightenment more difficult. Why do you want to create more suffering? When you take refuge, you must refrain from sex to keep the mind on main goal. Main goal is Buddhamind. That is all. Then there is no suffering and you are at peace. There is a possibility to remain free from effect of sex act, but this is not for student. Only very advanced monks with special training for years can avoid suffering from such activity. You are still in elementary school."

"What should we do, Sensei?" asked the young man.

"This is serious," he replied. "If you are serious about enlightenment, one of you must leave the Center. You cannot be together. If you cannot do this, then you both must leave. Many lifetimes will pass before this opportunity will come for you again. Maybe you are not ready in this lifetime. That is what I see."

The male student who confessed sat on the opposite side of the room from his girl friend. After her initial confession she remained silent with head bowed. Nearly everyone already knew about their affair as gossip spread around the commune the way it might in any tight grouping of people. The old man knew about her too. He pointed to her and called to her to stand.

"You, Miss Taylor," he said. "You meet with me after Assembly, okay?"

Taylor was her first name. She looked up somewhat surprised. The sensei had

86

paid little attention to her except to suggest she change her name, a change that she continued to resist. She was new there. She had not yet made up her mind about a new name, a change that generally meant acceptance of full time devotion or refuge. She came from a wealthy family. Her family was already unhappy with her move to a New Mexico commune and the thousands of dollars she donated. A name change could cause more problems.

Taylor nodded her assent to meet privately with the old man. She sat down.

Taylor's confused and heartbroken boyfriend left the commune the following month. It was clear who the the old man favored.

Routines at the Center were sometimes interrupted by guest speakers. Typically, the old man invited someone known in Zen circles as a teacher or published author of poetry or teachings. As the years passed, a disturbing side of the old man emerged. An example of this disturbing side occurred the day following the Assembly mentioned above.

Perhaps thirty members and visitors gathered in the lecture hall to hear an American monk who had studied in Japan for many years. The monk had published a small book of poetry. The monk had a following of his own in the Seattle area. He was on a promotional tour for his new book. A video of his work featured actors in natural settings, reading the poems to simple flute music. His given name was Ben Hermann. His Buddhist name Gonin stood for *strong and patient.*

Gonin was a middle-aged man with wire-rimmed glasses that complimented a shaved head and round face. He was of medium height and dressed casually in loose black pants, black sneakers and a loose, black, button-down collar shirt that hung tastefully over his distended gut. As a young man, Gonin attended an Ivy League school for several years before dropping out to pursue his spiritual path. He worked as a marketing writer for a small business in Indiana for ten years until he made his way to Seattle to study Buddhism under a Japanese teacher.

Gonin rose in stature under his teacher and ended up leading the small community when the teacher died. The old man at Samuwabi knew of the deceased teacher's work. The old man was curious to hear Gonin, but he arranged a harsh surprise for his guest.

Gonin appeared for an hour or so, read from his poetry, and entertained questions. The old man sat silently in the back. When Marga announced that there was time for one more question, Chizan, a large student who had taken refuge under the old man for five years, stood up and walked over to Gonin. Chizan said nothing until he was inches from Gonin looking down into his face. Chizan blurted out a string of insults about Gonin's poetry.

"You call this crap poetry? I heard better from my six year old niece. When you describe a mountain, you sound like you never climbed one. When you present a waterfall, it feels like you are pissing in a pot. Maybe you should submit to Hallmark Cards! This is what I think of your performance." With that said, Chizan spat on the floor at Gonin's feet hitting one of his canvas shoes. Then Chizan turned, made eye contact with the old man, and walked calmly to his seat. The students had seen Chizan rudely confront speakers before; even slapping a couple. Most students were hardly disturbed by his insensitivity. There was no predicting when or if he would behave this way. Only the old man and Chizan knew.

Gonin was understandibly startled, red-faced, and agitated. Sweat beaded on his scalp and trickled down along his brow. He took off his fogged glasses and nervously cleaned them with his shirt tail. He was speechless.

The old man stood up to acknowledge Gonin's performance by clapping for him. Everyone joined in the applause. He walked over to Gonin and shook his hand. They bowed to one another as a formality.

"Please forgive student Chizan. He is very sensitive about some things and still working on right mind!" The old man chuckled. A few students laughed. Gonin responded with an ambivalent half-smile. He gathered his things and walked out with his traveling companion without bothering to pitch his new book.

The old man instructed Chizan to offend certain guest speakers purportedly to test their tranquility, following the Buddhist dictum of cause and effect.

"Truly enlightened men will not react to insult or threat with confusion. An enlightened man will act precisely and calmly," he would say. The point was made: Gonin was not enlightened. Students should not be too impressed with his poetry.

Jake and Usagi left the hall with the others. They walked into a cool breeze from the west. The starry canopy glowed above them on this moonless night. They had seen Chizan perform the insult routine several times before and they knew the old man put him up to it.

"What did you think of his poetry, bro?" Usagi asked his friend.

"You heard the expert—greeting card stuff," Jake replied.

"No, seriously, man, I thought he was pretty good," Usagi insisted.

"He was. You know, I used to think insulting a guest to test for enlightenment was pretty cool. Like it was true Zen—what did the old man call it—crazy wisdom? Holy madness?"

"Yeah, like Chogyam Trungpa," Usagi offered.

"Yeah, like a Trungpa knockoff. Damn it. I can't believe I'm saying that now," he said recalling Professor Pederson's remarks about Trungpa immediately before she showed the images of the old man.

Usagi thought for a few moments before asking, "So, you think the old man was jealous?"

"Maybe."

"Gonin could have punched Chizan," Usagi offered. "More cause and effect. That would have been really crazy, bro!"

"Chizan would have wiped the floor with him," Jake retorted.

"Too much holy madness may be just madness," Usagi remarked matter-of-factly.

Jake did not reply. They continued in silence under the stars down the path to the bunkhouse.

5 Sword of Wisdom

You hope to know what might come next.
You did not see this coming.
Sometimes the sword of wisdom cuts.
It cuts deep into your sanity.—4 June 2004

Zen centers that mix martial arts training with meditation mimic a warrior-monk model rooted in ancient samurai tradition. It is Buddhism with bushido. By the time Jake met him, the sensei was an older man in his late sixties. The older man offered his version of Buddhism with bushido and Zen for eager seekers like Jake. In line with a bushido code of conduct, he stressed discipline, stoicism, and service for the warrior-monk candidates after they took refuge under him.

The old man hinted at his remarkable past to his new, mostly American students. They understood that he moved to America from Japan purposely without fanfare. Thus he cleverly cultivated an aura of mystery to add to his charisma. Students came to believe that he had attained supernormal powers in martial arts, but true to his humble stature, he would never display these skills unless absolutely necessary.

The old man moved with the grace and dignity of a lean and spry retired athlete. He retained indications of the old power he wielded once upon a time in his youth. He could still pack a punch. He moved gracefully through the fight routines or katas. He called his teaching Zen but indicated that he would give it something special. He taught that through him the *Buddha mind* would reach them in its essence. He would not impose the old forms on his students. Rather he would renew the old forms so that Buddha mind might thrive in new students as they were. In other words, he would not use old wineskins to store new wine.

"Buddha mind is not old and not new," the old man said. "It just is."

He taught the culture of the samurai (or what passed for that culture) to his male students. He taught the tea ceremony, monochrome ink painting, and rock garden design to all students. He composed haiku poetry. He gave delightful workshops in origami technique. He taught mantra chanting that filled the commune with haunting serenity twice a day. He conditioned his male students differently than female students, especially those females he favored in a special way. He inspired his male students to believe in the virtues of discipline even in the face of pain and suffering.

During meditation sessions known as *sesshin* or 'gathering the mind', the old man employed the traditional keisaku, a flat wooden stick or slat used to keep meditators focused and awake. Zen monks refer to the instrument as a *compassion stick*. The keisaku also stands in for the *sword of Majusuri*, the Bodhisattva of Wisdom. Traditionally, the meditator asks to be whacked but in some venues the master or sensei might decide the proper time. A whack across the back or shoulder brought a meditator back from drowsiness or disruptive daydreams.

The old man tailored his Zen custom just as he did his own keisaku. A Japanese woodworker crafted his keisaku from Japanese maple in Japan. It was one meter in length. Inscribed on the keisaku was the Japanese ideogram for *kensho* that means *seeing one's nature*, or, more commonly, *enlightenment*. The old man paced among the meditating men slowly with his stick in hand. His casual pace was a walking meditation considered an advanced form of mindfulness by his students.

Students trusted the sensei's compassionate Buddha nature. He would know or intuit when to tap or whack or peaceably pass by. In the beginning in 1997 he offered a firm tap or whack with the stick across a shoulder or the back. Sometimes the whack was more like a stinging slap. But as the years went by, as sensei advanced his male students, this ritual became less predictable and at times harsher and rarely requested. Some days no one was whacked. But during one significant week of the year his male students endured more than one or two slaps.

This was the week of the warrior in 2004 and the week of an answer to questions about suffering. The deeply committed students endured silently or tried to because they were warrior monks matured in consciousness and close to enlightenment— they knew that they were close to enlightenment because the old man told them so.

They were learning to endure discomfort and pain without breaking concentration. It was an honor to be trained by a master. It was honor to withstand harsh training. It was an honor to bow and thank the sensei after every sesshin no matter what or how he taught. Acknowledging the master with hands folded in front and a bow was Gassho!

By that time, that week, Jake's total commitment to finding enlightenment was more than two years running.

On that day the sensei appeared in his traditional black Zen robe. He wore black slippers. He embodied the image of a sage with his long, wispy gray goatee and bald head. He was not smiling. Sensei was especially sensitive that day but he seemed more irritated than aware. He did not like the way the students self-arranged in the meditation yard. He required at least half the men to move from their spots, to spread out. Eleven, maybe twelve men appeared for the morning sesshin on the east side of an elegant rock garden.

On this particular day, Jake was in his usual spot in the outdoor sitting area. The group meditated inside during harsh weather conditions that might include snow, rain, or dust storms. He was in high desert country in northern New Mexico where even in summer, mornings are cool. This particular sesshin was just after sunrise in early June. That day the sky was clear, the air was crisp at fifty degrees and calm. It was a good day to meditate outside. The rising sun illuminated the left half of each sitter as all faced south. The relatively flat ground under them was raked earth or sandy red clay with short tufts of buffalo grass here and there. The students sat on cheap, three-foot square, imitation Navaho rugs that the Center purchased through a Guatemalan firm. Most of the students including Jake removed their blankets or jackets for the sesshin. With right mindedness in meditation the cold should not bother them.

The small black female cat sat near Jake and his Indian friend as she was wont to do. The semi-feral communal pet bonded with Jake for some reason known only to the cat. The cat sat quietly among the men nearly every morning during meditation. If not there, she was most likely on a hunt. This day in accord with her habit, she sat facing Jake, at times purring, at times seemingly asleep, and at times with eyes wide open. Months before, Jake noted the cat's behavior in his notebook by quoting from T. S. Eliot's *Old Possum's Book of Practical Cats*:

> *"When you notice a cat in profound meditation…His mind is engaged in a rapt contemplation…Of the thought of his… deep and inscrutable singular Name."*

The cat's inscrutable demeanor suggested that enlightenment was just around the corner, one cosmic surprise or satori away.

You are an evolutionary leap beyond a cat, yet, and yet—.

All he need do is empty his mind of all expectation. The emptiness of an enlightened state reflected in the cat's face mirrored his task daily or at least it did whenever the cat showed up. The cat was not just being a cat. She was being the very cat that sat there in front of him. The humor of the situation was not lost on him. He knew that the cat was waiting to be fed and the cat knew that this human being sometimes fed her after the morning sit. It was not why she waited but how she waited that intrigued him. Only that cat could or would wait that way at that moment. That cat was being itself, no more and no less. If Maggie could do Zen so perfectly, why couldn't Jake?

An old koan from the old man: "Does a dog (or a cat) have Buddha nature?"

Cat hunger and cat Zen aside, the old man would remind the men that they may have a long way to go for true kensho but he could assist to shorten the journey with a special koan. Traditionally, the koans were statements or questions designed to shock the rational mind out of its common slumber. Koans were not meant to shock the body. Or were they?

Within minutes, most of the men settled into a relaxed yet alert state of mind familiar to anyone who meditates regularly. One doctor who studied the meditation phenomenon called it *the relaxation response*. Heart rates reduced and gentle breathing ensued.

Not everyone sat the same way. A few felt fine in the full lotus posture. The old man had no strict rules about how to sit. His only strong suggestion was to "just sit." The fat fellow with bad knees used a small yet sturdy canvas folding stool that kept him twelve inches above the ground.

The old man whacked the fat man hard across his upper back. The sudden sting surprised him. All students clearly heard the sharp slap, and then another slap. The fat man let out audible grunts that caused some of the students to chuckle quietly. Jake kept his mirth to himself. The black cat would have noticed a slight smile on Jake's face if she ever noticed such things. As Jake attended to the event with his eyes closed, his inner laughter subsided. As the outer and inner distractions passed, he settled back into the quiescence of the Buddha mind in his mind. The old man stepped around to face the fat man who acknowledged his master with hands folded and a bow of gratitude. The old man reciprocated with folded hands and a silent bow or *Gassho* to indicate that the lesson was given and received with mutual respect. Then the old man moved on slowly with stick in hand.

Sensei systematically whacked the next seven students even harder, each four or five times. All of them let out cries or grunts and one or two or more dropped tears reacting to the searing sting that remained. In each case the old man stood in front of the student until the student acknowledged him and bowed with hands folded. In each case the old man exchanged the Gassho before moving on. Usagi, the Apache Indian with his shaved head, was next. By this time no one was chuckling inside or out. Heavy apprehension hovered in the stillness disturbed only by the soft footsteps of the master.

No one knew how long this lesson would last or if the old man would return to strike again. Indeed, he passed by two of the men without striking. Usagi took the first hit without reaction—one might say even stoically. The second, a resounding strike, was not accurate or less flat forcing an edge to crush skin into bone causing blood lines to surface under the Indian's skin. This last strike caused the Indian to wince. Thrice more the keisaku struck the Indian's back seemingly harder each time. After the last strike the Indian arched his spine. This was no longer about warrior training. Something else was going on.

The stick smacked his back again. The Indian moaned.

"Enough," he thought, "the old man is out of control!"

Usagi opened his eyes and turned his head to catch an ugly scowl on the face of his master. The stick was poised to strike again. But this time, as if responding to a primal instinct for self-preservation, the Indian put up his right hand.

"No more," was the silent command in the Apache's gesture and the old man knew it was a command.

The old man let the stick sink slowly to his side. Long seconds passed between their eyes. In those few seconds the old man managed to regain composure and dominance. The practical tranquility of a master reappeared. Puzzled and impressed at the same time by the sensei's meek reaction, the Indian relaxed. He resumed the posture of a student. He folded his hands and bowed in recognition of another lesson to contemplate as his back stung mightily. The old man stepped directly in the front of the Apache to return the bow. The old man moved on in silent resolve.

Across the way, out of sight of the men, the female assistant walked with her stick among the meditating women. The tall, graceful Marga assumed her role that day, consistent with a tradition in Zen practice, to firmly tap any one that requested help to stay awake. To stay awake had a layered meaning. The obvious one was to help sleepy sitters from dozing off. Sleep is not meditation. To stay awake was to stay alert in a spiritual sense as Buddha mind. Buddha mind was what remained when the sitter emptied herself of all or entered no mind. Such seeming contradictions, such as Buddha mind is no mind and emptiness allows for the fullness of Buddha mind, sat at the core of each sitter's effort. Progress was individual. Insight was expected yet not overly desired. The old man taught them that enlightenment could come gradually or suddenly. He taught that Buddha mind was in the flame on the candle yet it was not the candle. The keisaku kept the flame burning brighter, enhancing a chance for enlightenment in this life for a rare few.

Marga carried the stick three days a week and she assigned others to wield it on the remaining days. None of the women engaged in warrior training because the old man taught the warrior way to men only.

A neatly raked rock garden separated the men from the women. A pea gravel and sand base with sparse but precise arrangements of native Buffalo grasses and a few small cacti accented the enclosure.

Out of sight and out of mind from the motley meditators, a brown and black Woolly Bear crawled intently toward a tuft of grass. The caterpillar moved methodically, urged on by its natural course to eat grasses and leaves. It would soon find a suitable twig habitat for the winter to prepare for its springtime transformation and rebirth as a Tiger Moth. The fuzzy worm remained within itself and its immediate experience. It took no notice of a motionless Praying Mantis perched ominously a few inches above on a rock. The two bugs were in tune with a natural right mind and right action. The mantis, the caterpillar, and the garden were one.

The old man taught with stories and metaphors from the Zen garden. He taught them about the mantis and the caterpillar. He said that in a proper Zen garden nothing is right or wrong, that is, as long as everything appears in natural order. It is either in harmony or disarray. Nevertheless, in whatever condition, the garden just is. A well-designed Zen garden was a metaphor for Buddha mind in its emptiness of disturbances. The Buddha mind remains still and eternal as all disturbance flows through and around it.

This rock garden maintained its serenity despite a microcosm of natural violence. Sometimes right action is not tranquil. The mantis easily grasped and held its wriggling prey. Mere minutes later the mantis sat satiated on the grass, again not moving for the moment.

"When mantis eat caterpillar, does Tiger Moth disappear?" asked the old man.

The old man caused Jake to wonder about such things. He actually observed the incident above one day while tending to the garden—a garden that he helped to build. In response he wrote:

You ask: Does Buddha mind exist in an insect that eats another insect?
What is suffering? Is it the hunger of the predator? Is it in the digested prey? Is it you
watching?
Food for thought.

Sensei stepped slowly toward the next sitter. From behind, he leaned over close to Jake's left ear blocking the sunshine on the student's face. Sensei spoke in a low, gravelly voice accented with a strong hint of stale alcohol from the remains of sake on his breath.

"So you wish to understand difference between Buddha and Christ? Today we explore question," he whispered gruffly.

The old man referred to the question that Jake proposed to him weeks before; the one the old man chose not to answer at the time. The lessons of empty space in a brush painting

Jake did his best to remain relaxed sensing what might be coming. This was a time for the brush marks on the page that will enhance the value of the empty space in the mind's landscape. This was a time for the stick to strike the gong. He felt he had better than average pain tolerance from years of contact sport in high school and construction work, not to mention the karate workouts that he sometimes led at the Center. This warrior stuff was one aspect of the experience he desired. He did not come there merely to create another sensitive guy. He had little interest in exploring the feminine in a man.

There is a time to watch and a time to engage
A time for peace and a time for pain.—4 June 2004

Sensei's first strike hit the middle of Jake's back. Like his Apache friend he took the first blow well with barely a noticeable flinch. The black cat slinked away behind a dull-green Chamisa shrub nearby. The cat crouched low to the ground with her eyes fixed on the old man and her ears pinned back. She assumed the pose of potential prey and not the predator that she was. The next three strikes by the old man were equally hard yet Jake remained in place trying to breathe normally. His back burned. With each successive whack he steeled himself to enter the pain, become one with it and let it go. The blows kept coming. Jake began to feel oddly excited until he felt the edge of the stick cut into his skin on the next strike. He arched his back in reaction but the edge hit again cutting skin and bruising bone. He grunted with eyes shut tight and teeth clenched.

A horned toad appeared a few feet from the cat. The cat showed no interest in the lizard. The lizard scurried into the brush a few feet away and disappeared. The cat watched a third and fourth and a fifth time as the edge of the whip-like kaisaku struck into Jake's flesh. Several stripes of blood oozed through his red ochre tunic that muted the evidence.

The bald-headed Apache turned to see what was happening to his bald-headed Polak friend. Jake was leaning forward with his mouth hung open in silence. He was drooling. Tears streaked his cheeks. Without a thought of how to act, Usagi sprung to his feet with hands ready to square off in front of the old man. Again the stick was up high ready to strike and again the grimace was on the sensei's face. Student and teacher held their snapshot poses briefly, locking eyes. In that brief moment, Usagi experienced enough rage to kill and enough devotion to submit at the same time, the latter conditioned by years of absorbing any number of reactions to unsavory behaviors in his teacher and letting them go in the name of enlightenment. Was he willing to sacrifice all that effort with one passionate act to choke the life out of his hated object? No, he was not. He merely froze in position with chest heaving from a burst of adrenaline. The old man lowered the stick slowly down to his side. Usagi relaxed and lowered his hands. The teacher was the victor. But this time there was no Gassho ritual. The old man simply turned and walked away grunting quietly, as if to no one, "Sesshin over."

Someone, perhaps the only male student not whacked by the old man that day, struck the gong indicating that indeed the morning meditation was over. The men slowly emerged from a seated position in differing states of pain. Many groaned and a few grumbled.

The entire, unpleasant and confusing incident lasted a little over an hour. It marked some of the men literally and all of them psychologically for some time to come. The old man had hit them hard before, marking backs and shoulders but never like this. The stories of this hour on that day would diverge into disparate versions but they would not disappear. The stories told at the time reflected the conditioning from a Buddhist scripture believed to be over two-thousand years old. This was a reason why the old man worked them hard at times or tested them so.

The old man made sure all his students read the 2000 year old *Fifty Stanzas of Guru Devotion* by Aryasura. The *Fifty Stanzas* with commentary carried much weight with the old man's students. Jake noted the following:

You read that gurus could beat disciples to teach them. We all read it because the old man mentioned the Fifty Stanzas. Part of Stanza 47 with commentary: "Powerful attainments follow from doing whatever your Guru approves."—10 June 2004

The old man pointed to the story of Milarepa too.

"Marpa scolded and even beat Jetzun Milarepa many times. Marpa did not personally dislike him, rather out of compassion he saw the need for skillful means to help his student grow. Thus if your Guru is wrathful with you try to see this as a method he is using to tame your mind and lead you to Enlightenment. As a Buddha, how could he possibly hate you?"—Geshe Ngawang Dhargey.

You are in the money now, Grasshopper. The old man knows what he is doing.
—10 June 2004

"Spare rod, spoil child, said Jesus. Jehovah did not spare whip on son Jesus," the old man told them. "And Greek gods did not spare Hercules the twelve terrible tasks."

100

The old man disappeared around a small bluff as he walked toward the main house. Two students dutifully followed the old man. One of them, Jiro and Jiro had some rank. He was not whacked that day. He was fifty-two years old and, as mentioned above, he was the old man's personal cook and primary administrative assistant. He had tried many paths including spending nearly nine years in Pune, India, at an ashram. Back there he was known as Ananda. Jake never learned of his actual birth name. Jiro said he no longer was that person. Jiro achieved a level of recognition at the Center he never had before in a career of spiritual pursuits. He cherished the chance to live and serve in the same house as a guru.

For the younger monk Tadao, which meant *satisfied* or *complacent* but whose Hippy parents named Sky, this was his first group experience. Besides traveling to Japan as the sensei's cabin boy, he was responsible for general chores like cleaning, answering the door and running errands. Why the old man chose this young student as a personal aide was not immediately apparent. Tadao received only two but unusually hard whacks that day. His back still stung. He carried the keisaku for the old man after the sesshin. Carrying the stick for the old man was an honorable task.

Tadao turned around to see how the others were faring, not sure at the moment if he felt sympathy, empathy, anger, or pride. He tried not to feel but to remain mindful. As with all of the men, save the old man, confused reactions arose in the young monk's mind. The extreme experience at this sesshin was too raw to evaluate properly. But was there anything to evaluate? Was the sound of one stick slapping students the same as the sound of one hand clapping? Was this another lesson too deep for the rational mind? Was this simply abuse?

The old man made no effort to explain the keisaku wisdom, no more than he would to explain a koan. Of course, he allowed questions and entertained commentary but his seemingly obtuse clarifications often left students more confused than enlightened. Was this crazy wisdom or holy madness? Would the question matter if the result was enlightenment? The old man seemed to goad students toward self-examination. Was he a brilliant teacher or was he faking it? Those who sought more reasonable teaching soon left the Center calling the old man thickheaded and annoying if not outright abusive. Those who sustained the ambivalence stayed on and called him brilliant.

The old man, the housemaster, and the servant left the men to sort out the events of the dawn sesshin. Two of the women joined the master who led his small entourage into the main house that served as the lecture hall and the old man's residence. The grumbling men commiserated in different states of pain and attire. Some wore black robes or red ochre Tibetan style garments while others were in jeans or khaki pants and drab-colored shirts and sweaters. They ambled and stumbled to the bunkhouse. They would change clothes and wash up before breakfast. Usagi and another fellow helped Jake to his feet. He appeared woozy. He was woozy. He grimaced from the pain but said nothing about it. For the next half-hour or so the men helped one another to treat wounds and ice bruises. The cat with her tail held high scampered after the men to the bunkhouse. She fully expected that one of them if not Jake would offer her milk and a scoop of kibble.

"That was crazy, bro," said the Apache.

"Ya think?" was all the Polak could think of saying as he steadied himself on the Apache's shoulder.

6   Benedictine Zen

When does a rabbit employ skillful means to attract a hawk to kill it?
—(an attempt at a koan by Jake, scribbled in a margin; not dated)

Weeks following the lavish beating from the old man's stick, Jake drove to Santa Fe to assess a promising lead for a stonework job. His back wounds had healed—he no longer smarted from leaning into a car seat. He would meet a woman in Santa Fe on Canyon Road. The lady, a journalist, needed repairs on a botched flagstone path and partially completed stone wall bordering her property. He intended to handle this job on his own, but upon inspection, he changed his mind. He would ask Usagi. The client was in no particular rush, as long as the job was done before cold weather hit the area. The Center expected Jake to be gone for several days at least, so he felt no pressure to return immediately. Besides, he was on a mission. He stayed overnight in Tesuque, a quaint village north of Santa Fe, with a couple that supported the Center. The old man called the wife a *danapati* or donor. He sent them a gift by way of Jake in appreciation for the last generous donation they sent the Center. The old man knew how to cultivate danapatis.

"Jake," Fowler said with a wide grin as he opened the door. "Was not expecting you until tomorrow! Come in. We have the back room set up for you." Rick Fowler was perhaps in his late 30s by Jake's estimation. He and his wife spent five days at the Center during a workshop the previous year. Jake noted that Fowler had put on weight, maybe fifteen pounds since they last met. Fowler lived in Tesuque with his wife and two daughters. He inherited his old, sprawling adobe house from an elderly aunt and her husband who once owned a copper mine in Mexico. The home retained some of the aunt's fine collection of regional furnishings and exotic décor that included several vintage statues of the Buddha.

"Nice place you have here, Fowler. And quite a collection of paintings!" Jake was looking at a particularly colorful landscape over a bench in the entry area.

"That one was done a hundred years ago. My aunt bought it during the 1960s from an eccentric neighbor who lived down the road. Her father, the neighbor's, painted it. William Penhallow Henderson. He designed and made the bench under the painting too. He was quite the Renaissance man—designed buildings, did some famous portraits including one of Tagore I am told, and murals. Henderson's wife Alice Corbin was a well-known writer in the area." Fowler paused, noting that Jake's attention had wandered into the living area.

"That's an incredible coffee table," Jake remarked. The massive, four-foot long table was crafted from a redwood burl with a fine polish that brought out the intriguing lacey grain on the table surface.

"Yes it is," Fowler affirmed with pride. "We bought it last year from a monk who used to build them at the monastery in Abiquiu. We commissioned it after he did such a good job restoring that bench by Henderson. Here, come in and have a seat." Fowler directed Jake to the plush leather couch by the burl table.

"Used to?" Jake asked as they sat down.

"You mean the monk? He sort of left the order after ten years. He lives up the road from us now, near *Shidoni*. He has his own shop." Fowler was referring to the famous foundry that had an impressive outdoor sculpture garden and to the order of Benedictine monks at *Monastery of Christ in the Desert* located along the Chama well off the highway above Abiquiu.

"Sort of left?" Jake looked puzzled as he slid his left hand across the table surface.

"I think he's on a sabbatical of sorts to decide whether he wants to continue being a monk."

"They let him do that?"

"I guess it is their protocol. If you met him though, you would not think that he's into it anymore. He dresses in layman's clothing and he lives with a guy—a male partner."

"Do they run the wood shop?"

"No. The partner is gay. He's a financial advisor."

"Oh. That explains it a little—I mean, why he left." Jake winced. He had a mild streak of homophobia, but he was thinking of the Roman Church's policy toward sexual activity.

"Have you ever been to the monastery?" Fowler asked him.

"Nope."

"You really should check it out. Anyone can visit whether you're Catholic or not."

Jake nodded silently. "Hey, where's your wife and kids?"

"They went to a mall to buy shoes. Karen will most likely stop at her mom's, so they won't be home until late. How about some left over lasagna? I can warm it up."

"Sounds good. I'll get my stuff from the car while you're doing that." Jake went out to his Volkswagen to grab some things and the gift box. He brought his notebook in also. He handed the box to Fowler who set it on the Henderson bench to open the lid. Inside was a set of six earth-gray mugs with the signature *kensho* motif of the Center.

"They're something for you from Sensei in appreciation of your generous gift." Jake was referring to a $5,000 check Karen had sent.

"Hey, very nice," Fowler said as he examined one cup under the glow of the ceramic sconce on the wall. "Karen's going to like these. I wonder what she *paid* for them?" he said with a chuckle. Karen had private savings accrued from significant investments.

Jake washed up in the rear bathroom that was richly tiled decades before. The lighting, sink, and commode were new, and the old claw-foot tub had been refurbished with retro plumbing and fixtures. A functional shower curtain surrounded the tub, to his relief. Jake was a shower person.

Fowler's home is impressive. Best of old and new. Santa Fe style all they way.
Hardly any sign they have kids. Housekeeper does a good job. The old man sure
knows how to work the donors.—(date omitted)

While they were eating, Fowler asked, "How's it going at the Center?"

"It's going. Been more intense lately."

"How so?"

"The sensei has upped his warrior-monk lessons. The sesshins have gotten tougher for some of us." Jake felt anxious after blurting that out. He was not about to reveal details. "No big deal. Can I have something to drink?"

Fowler went to the refrigerator. "Beer okay?" Fowler offered Jake a 7 oz Corona. Jake declined. "Oh, that's right. Foolish me: *No intoxicants once you take refuge.* How about iced tea? We have an *Arizona* somewhere in here," Fowler said as he searched for it. He found a can and handed it to Jake, then popped the beer cap for himself. "Glad you came by," he said as he took a sip of Corona.

"How's your business going?" Jake was referring to Fowler's apartment complex on the Ski Basin Road above Santa Fe.

"Still a line of people wanting to get in. We've been lucky, considering the economy."

"You keeping up with your practice?"

"Yes and no. I mean, I manage to get in a good sit once a week. I find it refreshing, even if I spend five or ten minutes in a quiet state. That was a good week we had at the Center with you guys last year. Marga is an impressive lady. My wife really liked her. We dragged out my aunt's Buddha statues after that and dusted them off." Fowler pointed to one large seated Buddha in the next room.

"Yes, Marga is great. Glad you got something out of it." Jake was about to tell Fowler about an upcoming workshop, but he emptied what was left of his cold tea instead. "How did you guys like the talk by the Sensei?"

"It was about nirvana, wasn't it?" Jake nodded, studying his host's expression as Fowler continued. "You know, we gained a new appreciation for the Buddha and his insight into life after that. Karen and I were not practicing any religion—we're not so sure about the God thing anymore—so, the idea that Buddha showed us how to stop time, to make nothing out of something, sounded brilliant. It's not easy to keep in mind, but I laugh sometimes when I find myself not taking life so seriously—applying the lessons. The river of suffering flows, yet we can always choose to be still.

106

I feel less pressure to have to fix everything right away. I think it was my Jewish guilt from my mom's side, not doing enough to make it. Somehow that week and the Sensei's lecture—that gave me permission to let go." Fowler paused. "Am I making any sense?"

Jake laughed. "Not much, but I get the drift!"

"What am I trying to say? How do you say that idea of river of life?"

"Samsara. You got the basic idea. Buddha taught us that the flow of creation never ends; no beginning, no end, which is very different from how we were brought up in Western tradition. The no self or Buddha mind is out of time and space, is how the old—er, Sensei puts it."

"Another way to get to eternity," Fowler remarked with some insight.

"You could say that, I guess, except without a god and without a self."

"I could say that, but coming from an ego like mine it sounds ludicrous, doesn't it?

"Yes." Both men laughed. Jake continued, "Hope you can come visit us again." Jake suddenly felt drained. He yawned. "Mind if I retire. I woke up early in Chama. Been a long day."

"No problem. The kids' rooms are at the other end of the house, so they won't bother you."

Jake rose early and packed to go. It was around 5 am. He mediated for a half hour. He read from *Yoga* by Mircea Eliade. The client he met in Santa Fe lent it to him. He had pulled it from her office bookshelf out of curiosity while waiting for her to prepare to show him the job site. He wrote notes for another hour before anyone else awoke. Karen, an elegant woman with straight blond hair tied back in a bun, sent him on his way with a toasted and buttered English muffin and black tea since Jake politely declined to stay for breakfast. He left Fowler's house before the daughters, who were twelve and ten, came to eat before leaving for school. He had the impression from Marga that they were quite spoiled. He was afraid he might say something wrong or look uncomfortable around them, thus leaving a bad impression on donors.

As Jake pulled into *Bode's* General Store for fuel on his way up Route 84, he thought about his role as a mule to cultivate donors. He was not happy about it. Before he filled his bug with gas, he went inside to prepay for it with cash and to buy coffee to go. He stood behind a bearded man in a blue denim frock with a hood. The man was picking up a package. Jake could see the address: *Monastery of Christ in the Desert*. The man took his package, and as he turned to go, he nodded to Jake who nodded back. As Jake was paying, he asked the teller where the turn-off was for the monastery. He saw the man in the denim tunic pull out of Bode's lot in a slightly battered, white SUV. It was out of sight by the time Jake pulled onto the highway.

A little way up the highway, Jake turned left onto a non-descript, rugged road that appeared to fit the description given by the teller. The white SUV was nowhere in sight. The bug rolled along rugged, unpaved surface at twenty miles an hour for the first third of the trip, passing fields of cholla cactus and sagebrush. A hilly section slowed the bug down to a down-shift crawl. The ruts from water and tire erosion had worn into the hardened clay and stone surface making it tough to negotiate without bottoming out. "Man, no one told me I would need a four-wheeler," he grumbled as the bug crept and swayed precariously. A half hour later, he arrived at a flat muddy spot, no doubt caused by a hidden spring, for it had not rained in weeks. Passing through the mud required more speed, so he gunned the engine to avoid being stuck, splattering mud over the rear end.

There were no signs. He had no idea how far he had to go. Jake began to feel lost. Was he on the right road? He pulled over against an embankment as well as he could in case someone came by, although no one did. The road was barely wide enough for one car. Jake climbed up the embankment to a ten-foot rise, but the view was no help. "More sage and hills," he said. "What the hell are you doing out here anyway, dumb ass," he mumbled into the air. He began to feel like he made a mistake. Was he betraying his Buddhist path by returning to something Christian, even if it was out of curiosity?

He was about to descend when he saw a blur moving from the right into his peripheral vision. He turned his head just in time to spot a large hawk pinning a small, struggling bunny into the dirt. In seconds the immature cottontail lay still, its carcass firmly in the grip of the magnificent bird. Jake's jaw had dropped. He stood there stone still, not breathing with his mouth open while watching the bird rearrange its kill before swooping away with it. Jake relaxed and began to breathe again, but his heart rate was up. He felt energized by the event as if Nature had presented him with a rare gift. "What could *this* mean," he thought aloud. He slid down the slope and returned to his car. "You should turn around," a voice in his head said. Then another voice asked, "Are you the rabbit, or are you the hawk?"

Jake leaned on the open door to his car with both hands as he stared into the ground. He felt slightly dizzy. Maybe it was the altitude. After a minute, he relaxed into the driver's seat, grabbed a plastic water bottle, and took a few large gulps. Maybe it was dehydration—he felt much better in a few minutes. He started the engine to proceed down the road toward what he hoped would be the monastery. The road swung close to the Chama River as he approached what appeared to be a red rock canyon ahead.

It was only thirteen miles but with more than an hour of driving when he finally saw the sign with an arrow that said, *Monastery*. From the top of the rise next to the sign, he could see a few adobe style buildings emerging naturally among the common pines and cedars. In the distance below a high red cliff was the adobe chapel with its signature cross crowning a steeple. The Chama flowed earnestly, fifty yards below the compound. He felt a pang of envy: This location was ideal for monks. He pulled along side three other vehicles into a parking area marked for guests. A small sign pointed to *registration*. Another sign cautioned guests to respect the silence and to restrict talk to designated areas.

The first person he met was the monk he encountered at Bode's.

"Hi. I'm Brother Andre. I had a feeling I would see you again." The monk greeted Jake with a knowing but, to Jake, irritating smile. Jake bowed slightly in acknowledgment. Jake revealed that he was from the Buddhist Center in Chama. "We've had many Buddhists here over the years," Andre said with no particular affect. The monk, who was shorter than Jake, said he had been with the monastery for fifteen years. The affable Andre, who doubled as the guest master and campus tour guide, led Jake to register in the gift shop area. He was welcome to stay the night. The monastery could accommodate fourteen guests. Only half the rooms were taken at the time. The recommended donation was easily affordable and it included two meals daily with the monks plus breakfast drinks and snacks in the common lounge area of the guest quarters. Andre led Jake to a small, single room among a row of guest quarters fronted by an extended portal. The quarters flanked a courtyard that featured a rough-hewn statue of St. Francis. Jake's room included a sleeping pad on a wooden platform, a small desk with a wind-up clock, a chair, and a wood stove. A burlap curtain covered a closet area. There was no electricity, but there was a kerosene lamp and plenty of matches. He would share a common shower room and toilet with ten other guests. He felt right at home in his cozy little room. He laid the *Yoga* book on the nightstand before venturing out to explore the grounds.

The chapel bell rang three times as he stepped out and faced the courtyard. He followed a flow of several silent guests toward the chapel. They were going to prayers before the midday meal with the monks. Jake followed them into the chapel.

The Benedictines established this monastery near Abiquiu around 1964 in a red-rock canyon along the Rio Chama. The chapel and main buildings incorporated the indigenous adobe architecture but with a twist that intrigued Jake. George Nakashima, the famous Japanese-American woodworker and architect, designed the elegant chapel with its simple and massive stone slab altar. Sparse and natural Zen style complimented the Gospel tradition nicely. Jake sat silently in the chapel, absorbing the atmosphere. Twelve monks in black robes and nine mostly middle-aged guests chanted psalms and said prayers. The monks removed their robes and hung them on hooks by the back entrance as they all left for the dining hall.

After a hearty but simple and silent lunch, Jake met a visitor from England who introduced himself. Brian was a gray-haired Anglican priest on sabbatical for the year. He wore layman's attire: standard jeans, sneakers, and a plane green, cotton T-shirt accented only by a small wooden cross hanging from a cord around his neck. He heard from Brother Andre that Jake was a practicing Buddhist. That first evening, after another relatively silent meal with the monks, Jake retired to the common guest area where he had tea with the priest and two women who were fascinated with Brian. The exchange rapidly escalated into deep conversation about religion and spirituality in that rarified yet casual spiritual atmosphere. Jake was surprised that the man knew so much about Buddhism. He was not surprised that the women excused themselves after two hours. Neither one was a Christian or a Buddhist in any formal sense. One was a practicing astrologer, and the other a self-proclaimed *life coach*. She came once a year to the monastery for personal reasons that had nothing to do with the Christian faith, and this time she brought her astrologer friend who was also a client. The astrologer offered to do Brian's horoscope for free.

"Good night, Harmony. And good night to you, Rozlynn. I will look forward to your reading in the mail," Brian said while hugging each lady in turn.

Jake could not avoid the hugs, but he also wished them well with a bow and folded hands, saying, "Namaste." He waited until they were well out of earshot before saying to Brian, "Are you really into astrology?"

"No, I place no stock in it. But she does, and I did not wish to offend her by refusing."

"I hate to say this, but I'm glad they left. They sure seemed to enjoy talking about themselves," Jake said wearily.

Brian had no comment about the women. He did crack a smile, however. Instead, he invited Jake to continue with an answer that Rozlynn interrupted an hour earlier.

As part of his sabbatical project, Brian was working on his long essay about Thomas Merton. Merton was a Trappist monk who once stayed at the Abiquiu monastery. Jake was familiar with Merton's autobiographical *Seven Story Mountain*. He knew less about Merton's serious inquiry into the relationship between Buddhism and Christianity, one that Merton came to accept as irreconcilable, just as Professor Pedersen, the nun, had told him years ago. The priest's project explained his keen interest in Jake who, in turn, took the opportunity to better grasp Pedersen's remarks. "You were talking about your teacher's claim to be a Bodhisattva," Brian reminded him.

"Oh, wow. I forgot where I left off. He never actually claims to be one."

"How does he put it then?"

"He lectured a few times about the Bodhisattva state and compared it to Jesus or Mary in heaven. They have yet to be absorbed into God fully because they choose to help mankind achieve salvation. Our sensei allows us to believe that he chooses to remain in embodiment as a Bodhisattva to help us achieve nirvana. How would you respond to that?"

"Well, I cannot comment on your teacher's motives or teaching style. That he *allows* you to believe that, speaks to his cleverness or application of skillful means. Interesting twist on ancient Mahayana doctrine," Brian said.

"Why Mahayana and not Zen?" Jake asked, as he wanted some elaboration.

"From what you told me, your teacher does not appear to teach classic Zen doctrine. But I think you know that—you said he adapts what he learned in Japan to a Western sensibility. We have a propensity to revere living saints, like Mother Teresa, or living heroes like a firefighter who saves a child, as role models who bring us closer to God or what God wants from us if we are to be saved. Your sensei may be using *upaya* or skillful means, which is a form of righteous trickery revered in the Mahayana. You know the Buddhist story of the burning house?" Jake nodded. "In other words, it matters not whether the teacher is actually a Bodhisattva, but as long as you believe in the principle of a Bodhisattva that he represents, you the student will strive toward the goal, which is to know that you are burning with desire that causes suffering. He may believe that he has a right—even a duty—to function as a Bodhisattva as long as disciples need him to be one."

"And that is supposed to be okay—to fake it or lie?"

"Plato called it a *pious fraud* or a necessary lie to guide less aware people to the truth that they cannot grasp—to save them from the burning house, sometimes you have to offer them a prize, even a fake prize, to get them out. Samsara, or the very fact of corporeal existence in the Mahayana, is in the end impermanent, therefore an illusion. There is some correlation here, and I emphasize *some*. The Buddhist acknowledges the effects that cause the living self, or that which the Dalai Lama once called *just me*, as real, but that me is empty, an illusion. It is the permanent emptiness or nirvana that remains the only reality. When Saint Paul said, 'I live now, not I, but Christ lives in me,' he indicates a similar human state, one of impermanence. The difference of course between Mahayana or Zen and Christianity, is in the person of the cosmic Christ and the impersonal state of Buddha. A devotional Hindu or Bhakti Yogi would say that the realized self as Atman in Krisna is ultimate, whereas a non-dualist would agree with a Buddhist and say it is impersonal, soulless or Annata."

Brian stopped to take a sip of tea. "This needs to be warmed up." He looked to the food counter. "Ah, forgot. No microwave here. I'll just make another. Care for one?"

"Sure," Jake replied, handing Brian his cup. It's getting chilly in here. I'll get the wood stove going while you're doing that." Brian fired up the propane burner, and set the kettle on the grate. He followed Jake out the door to help bring the wood supply. "The night sky out here is brilliant." Both men looked up into a vast vault of sparkling lights. It was a moonless night.

"Always takes my breath away," Brian whispered. Jake said nothing.

After the men settled back in the same seats but in a cozier room, Brian continued, "At the risk of sounding cynical, every mature Christian cleric, including the popes I would venture, has wondered if the entire Gospel and Church is but a skillful construct to not only attract us toward an ineffable truth, but also to keep us in line ethically and morally. Take the Eucharist. Catholics here at the monastery try their damndest to accept and believe that the blessed host and wine becomes the very body and blood of Christ. How skillful or merely deceitful that is, is another question. Yet every one, I guarantee you, struggles with what Jesus meant by, 'Do this in remembrance of Me.' Decades ago, a Penitenté sect in this region was known to yet carry out real crucifixions during Good Friday celebrations. They claimed to follow the literal command of their Lord. We cannot justify that, can we?"

Jake recognized the rhetorical question and said nothing. Brian continued.

"The question is: How far can one carry *skillful means* before it becomes sin, abuse, or a crime? Ethical teachers of the Mahayana tradition recognize the principle of *upaya* as a slippery slope. The Christian way of looking at this is that Jesus, after all, died to replace all animal and human sacrifice, especially that of the Temple in Jerusalem. Now, I can justify the common Eucharistic sacrament as a very real symbol of an eternal truth that just as corporeal life cannot exist without corporeal sacrifice, eternal life cannot exist without an eternal sacrifice. In other words, the Eucharist mystery is the Christian way to acknowledge and appreciate the essence of life itself in eternity. But we can overreach as teachers when we require human disciples to follow a path that is less than moral or ethical. We can't mock the cross by pretending to replace Jesus."

"I get what you are saying about upaya," Jake replied. "No teacher is perfect." He did not want to elaborate. "But, I was wondering whether you had any thoughts, after studying Merton, why Buddhism and Christianity are irreconcilable. I mean, I heard this from a Catholic nun I met as well. She was studying Buddhism too."

"Christianity, like Buddhism has had many aspects since its initial development. In its early Gnostic forms, it has some relation to Buddhist idealism that rejects this world as an illusion. In Gnosticism, only the pleroma or a heaven populated by Aeons or gods has any reality, and one must be somehow enlightened to achieve that permanent spiritual state. That state of being is nirvana to the Buddhist, or a state of emptiness without samsara, of all that is not permanent. In general, the Christian tends to be dualistic and relational, whereas Buddhism has a monistic feel to it because it is essentially a Hindu reform movement. And Hinduism in its most developed philosophy is monistic, or non-dualistic if you want to be more technical. Christianity reinterprets Judaism, which is highly dualistic—man cannot be God. Christianity adds a cosmic twist by offering us Jesus as both man and God. Thus through faith in Him, we become *one* with the Father, although that does not make a man God."

Jake stopped him. "You know, that is exactly where some New Age people I know say you are wrong. That does make us God if we are one with God, as you say."

"Ah, then your New Age people *know* better than I do. This is why critics of the New Age call much of it old Gnosticism warmed over. I can feel like I am one with my wife—that is if I was married—but she nevertheless remains distinct from me. This is more than a matter of semantics. Entire treatises have been produced to unpack this point."

"Okay. That aside, I become one with Buddha mind through devotion to the Buddha, his teaching, and his community. Isn't that similar to becoming one with God through the Son, his Gospel and his church on earth?"

"In Christianity, this is all accomplished through that most ephemeral aspect of God in the person of the Holy Spirit and the grace from that Spirit. In Buddhism's later development in Japan, there was the reformer, Honen, in the 11th Century and Shinran right after him, who taught something called *Pure Land*. Honen taught that due to a degenerate age or *mappo*, it was no longer possible to rely on one's own efforts to achieve salvation. Recall that the Buddha, in his last day, is said to have directed his disciples to 'work out your own salvation.' But Honen grasped an essential teaching from the Buddha that also includes the eternal Buddha's grace. So he taught us to rely on *the other* and not merely on the self, which, by the way, is empty of self anyway. There is no *you* in strict Buddhist ideology, as you know. This eternal *other* in Pure Land teaching is called Amitabha or Amida Buddha. It is in his *name*—I mean literally in his name—that we are saved. Pure Land devotees chant 'Namu Amida Butsu' just as Christian monks pray 'in the name of Jesus' to receive the grace that is freely offered. Grace is wholly free in Pure Land Buddhism also. But this is where the problem lies for the disciple: When you accept this grace you have to totally submit to it and the system or teacher that generates it. Saint Paul again: I live now, not I, but Christ lives in me. The Buddhist would void the self in similar fashion to achieve sunyata or emptiness so that the Buddha's grace can remain. In Christianity, Jesus emptied himself totally, thus was God."

Brian pointed to a Catholic crucifix with the dead Jesus on the wall. "In light of what we are saying, that gruesome figure is spot on as a symbol of a man dying or emptying one's self to let God flood him with grace. The fact that God is doing the sacrificial dying for us eternally is the mystery of the Christian faith. Buddha, on the other hand, sits in solemn meditation, emptied of all self, yet remains to guide us to that state of grace as well. One is the eternal guide to and state of nirvana; the other, the eternal act and gift of salvation. Having said this, I find the two religions very different due to the lack of an eternal self or soul in Buddhism—full stop."

Jake sat in silence as Brian studied his reaction. During their conversation, Brian sensed that Jake's teacher was abusing the practice of upaya. Jake got that point—there was something wrong with the old man's self-control—he knew that, even though he would offer no confession to Brian. He also found it uncanny that Brian mentioned Bhakti—he happened to be reading about Bhakti yoga the night before at Fowler's house. But Jake was contemplating more than that. He recalled the graphic image of the bunny attacked by the hawk, an image that was vividly etched in his memory. "The rabbit is the Christ," he said aloud.

"Come again," said Brian with a smile, noting that his companion was in a kind of trance. "What rabbit?"

Jake snapped out of his reverie. "Sorry. I watched a hawk kill a small rabbit on the way here. At the time, I wondered if nature was giving me some kind of omen— was I the hawk or was I the rabbit? Now I see it in a completely different light. It had nothing to do with me as victim or predator. The power of life was in the rabbit, not in the hawk."

Brian relaxed, neither affirming nor rejecting the younger man's insight. "Something for you the think about..." The 4 a.m. bell rang for vigils. The monks and a perhaps a few guests roused for prayer. Brian paused again before asking, "How would you like to go fishing, that is, after we've had some sleep? The game commission stocked the river with trout just last week."

The next afternoon, Brian took Jake fly-fishing along the Chama. He brought extra equipment, enough for a monk or two that cared to join him in his avocation. Before leaving for the seminary when he was a young man, Brian owned a small but successful bait and tackle shop in Lincolnshire, England. But we will leave this aspect of Jake's story alone. Suffice it to say, our protagonist had no immediate knack for the art of fly-fishing.

7 Dogging It

It is often safer to be in chains than to be free.—*Franz Kafka*

Jake was getting antsy as he finished washing the breakfast dishes. "Well, you want to come or no?" he shouted into the suds thinking Usagi was still in the room. He wanted to get an early start to get to Santa Fe before noon to set up the job. After carefully draping the T-towel to dry over the edge of the sink, he turned to discover that Usagi had disappeared. "Now, where is he?" he thought out loud.

A pretty, young female student, one that the old man named Mika and who recently took refuge at the commune, looked up at Jake from the table with her quiet smile. She was peeling potatoes for the next meal. Her short-cropped blond hair looked like baby bird down feathers. She indicated the rear entry path visible outside the screened door. "There," she said pointing with her eyes and a slight turn of her head.

There he was, canvas tool bag in hand, red bandana wrapped on his bald head, acting as if he were waiting.

"Hurry up," Usagi yelled. "We ain't got all day, you know!"

"Ain't got all day," Jake grumbled. "Mika, can you finish up here, wipe the counter and table?" All Mika heard was, "Wipe the table."

"And if I don't?"

"Then it don't get done, do it?"

"Do it?"

"It's a question, not a command."

"Sounded like a command," she said.

"Mika, I got to go. Thanks." Jake bowed to Mika with hands folded. She returned the expression with a smile. She was attracted to Jake but her wide-eyed projections put him off. He did not return the smile.

"See you guys when you get back. Be safe!" she said wistfully as Jake strode past

117

her. Mika picked up the remaining dishes. She worked slowly but steadily wiping down the entire dining area. Then she carefully and methodically swept the floor. She emptied the contents of the dust pan into a battered, gray metal trash can. She set the broom and dustpan in the corner next to the can where they belonged. That took all of ten minutes. She paused a few seconds to take in a moment of peace with her eyes closed. Her smile turned to a grimace as she hoisted the heavy plastic trash can liner with its messy contents onto the floor. She tied off the opening of the bag, picked it up with two hands and waddled with it toward the screen door. She turned around, snapped her butt into the door to swing it open before turning around to waddle with her load out to the large green dumpster at the edge of the entry road. She watched Jake's VW leave a trail of sun-lit dust rising above the scrub pines and junipers before dumping the trash bag.

The men were on their way off the grounds.

"Check out your mirror," Jake suggested.

"Looks okay, bro," Usagi said.

"No, I mean look at the golden light behind us."

"You mean the dust cloud? What about it?"

"The color is intense, man. I mean the color."

"It's just dust in sun. Keep your eye on the road, bro. There's a boulder," Usagi yelled.

Jake hit the brake and jerked the steering wheel to the left to avoid a sizable rock by the roadside. He downshifted to second to approach the highway at the end of the dirt path. After making the left turn onto the macadam, there was no more dust.

"Which way we going?" Usagi asked.

"The shortest way—down 84. Why?"

The Indian did not answer right away. He stared at the passing landscape through the side window. Jake found this irritating but said nothing. He never knew when or if Usagi would answer a question. Usagi seemed to lack any compulsion to follow conventional civility in conversation. If a response took longer to process, so be it. After a year or so of getting used to his friend, Jake realized that this behavior had nothing to with being rude or obnoxious. Maybe it was cultural, Jake surmised. Finally, Usagi spoke up.

"A girl I knew lived in El Rito."

"And?" Jake waited again as he had no idea what Usagi was alluding to. He slowed down to let a large truck pull ahead of him to avoid oncoming traffic in the passing lane.

"And we used to hang out together. I mean it was serious, you know," Usagi continued as he fumbled with the radio tuner. Nothing much was coming through on the two stations he found. The rest was static. He turned it off. "Crazy. I have not thought of her for over a year. I wonder what's going on?"

"Maybe we can cruise through on the way back," Jake suggested. "I thought of stopping at Ojo Caliente when we finish this job, relax for a couple of hours, and maybe get a massage, eh?" Jake was referring to the quaint but well-established spa that was built a hundred years ago at a natural hot springs used for centuries by Native Americans. Ojo Caliente was close to El Rito.

"She used to work there, bro. You know her?" Usagi asked.

"How would I know her? I went there once last year. I don't know who you're talking about anyway."

"Ah—don't mind me. I'm not making sense. I thought I told you about her. Maybe it was Marg—it was Marga I talked to."

"She, whoever she is, got into you. What happened?"

"Cassie. Cassandra."

"Okay, Cassandra. She dump you for someone else?"

"How'd you know?"

"Psychic, I guess."

"No, the guy was a con artist. He wasn't really a psychic."

"That's not—," Jake stopped himself. This was another Usagi non sequitur. "What kind of con?"

"He did something called *Rebirthing* in a hot tub. She said it helped her connect with her past lives. The last I heard, she went to Oregon with him."

"Hot tub, sharing skin, intimate talk—makes sense. Was he rich?"

"No. Actually, he blew town with her after claiming bankruptcy. You know, at the time I was angry, feeling rejected. Now it's more like I'm worried about her. Maybe that's why she popped back into my mind. I'd like to ask her mom. She works at the grocery store there. If we have time..." Usagi did not finish the sentence.

"We can make time," Jake inserted.

Usagi remained silent.

With that the men dropped the subject of Cassandra. They were more than halfway to Santa Fe when Jake pulled over at *Bode's General Store*.

"We may need an extra hose. They should have one here."

"I gotta piss anyway," Usagi said. "Want some coffee or anything? I'm going over to the café."

"Black, no sugar. Maybe a donut or muffin," Jake said as he pulled up.

Bode's was a landmark business first established in 1880 as a mercantile, stage coach stop, post-office, and jailhouse in a sparsely populated area. Over a century later, the area was still sparsely populated. The modern store no longer functioned with a jail but it did supply a range of goods and services for locals and tourists. Some tourists stopped there on there way to gawk at Georgia O'Keeffe's house across the highway. Others might be visiting the small, wild animal zoo nearby or going fishing or hiking along the Rio Chama.

Spiritual seekers on the way to and from retreat centers dropped in regularly. The Ghost Ranch Retreat was up the road as well as the exit for the Benedictine Monastery that Jake visited earlier. On the other side of the highway, the *Dar al Islam* mosque established in the 1980s served a local population of American Muslims who hosted regular group retreats. Despite the convergence of history, outdoor activity, and a spiritual atmosphere, most tourists and business folk tended to speed by unaware of anything but high desert scenery. But the sensei was aware of this religious convergence in the region. He had done his research. He chose Chama carefully.

Jake tossed fifty feet of new, flexible hose into the bug's back seat that served as a tool container. A green canvas tarp protected the actual seat from a stack of mason's gear, carpenter tools, a reddish steel mortar pan, two well-used hoes and a spade shovel.

"Here's your coffee, bro," Usagi said as he ducked back into his seat and slammed the door.

Jake set the cup into the makeshift cup holder that he screwed into the dash some years earlier. Usagi handed him a donut.

"So, tell me again," Usagi entreated, "what's this job about?"

"Old Ray referred this woman to me last month. She has several stonework jobs that were left unfinished by the last contractors."

"So, we have to fix what someone else fucked up? You sure you want to do this? Could be a nightmare."

"That's why I brought you along," Jake quipped as he drove the bug onto the highway. "I need to blame somebody if we can't make it work out."

"Hey, whatever; work is work. Did you bid on this or is she paying by the hour?"

"You kidding? By the hour plus costs. But we figured a week or more to get this done."

"Are we worried about the more?"

"Not to worry, partner. I was down here two weeks ago to look it over. Most of what they did is sound enough. There's a narrow flagstone path they set in sand. Now she wants it redone with the flags in cement. We can use the same pattern—flip them over and flip them back as we go. The wall on the ridge behind her house will be a bitch though."

"How so?" Usagi asked as he looked at his hands. "I'm going to need some calluses."

"We have gloves. The ridge is maybe ten to fifteen feet up a steep rise. We have a stretch of a river rock border wall to complete."

"Where we getting the rock?"

"Most of it, I hope, from a pile the other crew left behind."

Jake turned the radio back on and found an oldies rock station. Bob Dylan's *Rainy Day Women* crackled through the old speakers.

"Damn. Stones. Another coincidence," Jake remarked.

"What?" Usagi asked.

"Nothing," Jake said dismissively. He changed the station.

"We need a wheelbarrow or something to move that stuff, no?"

"No." Jake turned the volume up on the radio. A song that reminded him of his father was on. Along with Bruce Springsteeen, he sang, "Born in the USA..."

Usagi waited till the song was over. "Please don't do that again," he said with a pained inflection.

"Do what?"

"Sing. Hey, who're we working for anyway?"

"She's a widow, husband died last year—lives alone with her dog, Obi. Nice lady, maybe in her mid-forties? Name's Daisy Baker. Very wealthy, but the house is not that big."

"Wealthy folks like to live in Santa Fe," Usagi mused.

"Artsy ones too. She's got quite an art collection. I saw two Ansel Adams photos. She said they are originals."

"She let you in her home?"

"Sort of. I stood in the entry foyer. It's got a security system and her dog's a trained Pit Bull."

"Eeee! Don't trust those Pit dogs. Hope she keeps it locked up."

"He's big for a Pit. Maybe crossed with something—or maybe not."

The men cruised into Santa Fe and turned onto Paseo de Peralta. Jake slowed down after crossing Alameda.

"You see a sign for Canyon Road yet?"

"No, but I'll watch for it. Keep your eye on the road, man," he yelled. Usagi pointed to an old couple crossing the intersection ahead of them.

Jake resumed an earlier conversation. "He seemed okay with me—she wanted him to recognize me."

"Who are you talking about?"

"The dog—I was thinking of Obi again. He sniffed me, and then let me pet him. He hangs out in the yard where we'll be working as long as she's home. As far as a wheelbarrow, her husband left a shed full of tools we can use including a good barrow and a small tractor."

After the men cruised into town avoiding the busy central Plaza by using Paseo de Peralta, they turned left onto Canyon Road. They pulled over and parked along the narrow, winding, one way thoroughfare to eat lunch at a vegetarian bistro. They fit right in with tourists and locals despite their appearance in work clothes. Canyon Road with its many adobe-style galleries, quaint specialty shops, and eateries accommodated an eclectic clientele. Besides, our young men were still clean but that would soon change.

Daisy Baker greeted the men on her front portal. She allowed Obi free rein to sniff her guests. Obi was the basic Buster Brown dog with small white marks on three of his paws and one on his chest. He was clearly in good shape and well-muscled. Usagi noted a friendly wag of the six inch stub of what passed for Obi's tail. He felt relieved.

"Okay if I pet him, Ms. Baker?" Usagi asked.

"Please call me Daisy. Sure, but no sudden moves. Obi's okay with you guys now, Usagi," Daisy assured them. "Most of his tail is missing as you can see. He's a good dog but very protective. I rescued him from a shelter after he was abandoned by a convicted drug dealer in Albuquerque. He was injured in a fight with another dog at the dealer's house where he lost his tail. He should stay indoors if I'm gone and if you can't watch him."

"No problem," Jake answered.

"So, you guys ready to get this done? That last crew was certainly enthusiastic for the first two weeks. Then they left me with this mess. I am really glad you guys took the job. Ray vouched for you."

Daisy Baker described herself as a spiritual woman who found meaning in all the world religions. She enjoyed the spiritual climate and the variety of alternative groups in the area. Her positive reaction or "resonance with" as she put it to Jake was immediate when she learned of his commitment to the Zen center. She met the old man once during an open lecture at the Chama location and liked him. Later, in her search for a reliable mason, she called Ray but he was unable to fit her into his schedule. When Ray told her about Jake, she felt connected to him already. She saw and recalled Jake's fine work on the stone walls at Samuwabi.

The crew she hired first was from another local intentional community that believed in egalitarian principles—no one was better than anyone else. That meant everyone on the crew, male or female, shared all the duties and tasks of life equally, and that included construction trades. Every day on the job Daisy noted that the commune workers switched roles whether or not they were skilled at that function. Some days seemed to go backwards as workers had to undo what another one did the day before. No one seemed concerned as every one went about their work with a self-contained bliss. There was no recognizable leadership or boss from day to day—they all took turns supervising. Daisy's tolerance for their bizarre behavior and questionable progress finally wore thin after five weeks. She fired the lot of them.

"They follow the teachings of Gurdjieff," she told Jake as she rolled her eyes.

"Oh, yeah," Jake said. "Our teacher called him a Sufi rascal."

"That may be an understatement," Daisy retorted. She indicated that she had researched her subject. She stopped herself from saying more.

"Okay, you know what to do. I'll be in and out all week. Call me on my cell if you need anything. Use the phone in the guest house."

Neither Jake nor Usagi had cell phones. They shook hands with Daisy who promptly stepped into her silver, 1998 Mercedes SL500 and drove off to meet a friend for lunch. "I'll be downtown at *Pasqual's*," she shouted as she pulled out of her gravel driveway.

"She's pretty hot for an older broad, bro," Usagi remarked as he helped carry tools from Jake's car. Jake told him that Daisy Baker was indeed in good shape, no doubt assisted by a personal trainer at a local fitness club and a habit of never eating a large meal. She had a twenty-five year old somewhere, a son she had not seen since she gave him up for adoption as an infant, an indiscretion from a failed relationship with a Hollywood actor. She revealed all this to Jake upon their first meeting.

"Yep, she's still got it, whatever it is," he said at the end of his version of her story. "She said she imagined her son to be someone like me." Jake talked as he sorted through his tool bags.

"Daisy said that? She's living with a hole then," Usagi said as he pondered a bush hammer and a face hammer in his hands."

"You can put the bush hammer back," Jake told him. "We won't be doing any fine finish work here."

Usagi tossed the tool into the bag. He balanced the other with the handle end on the tip of an extended finger for a few seconds before flipping it over into a firm, right-handed grip. "I think this lady is lonely, bro. What does she do? Does she work?"

"Writes a column on women in religion. She's syndicated with some newspapers and magazines."

"That helps explain her interest in you. Man, everybody in this freakin' town has a story," Usagi noted while reaching down for a hose. "Is that where we get water?" Usagi said pointing to a backyard wall.

"Yep. I'm going to the shed to get a barrow for these tools."

Usagi walked over to an outdoor spigot with two coiled hoses dangling from his hands. "I bet she finds more work for you to do around here," he said as he attached a hose.

Jake ignored the implication by not responding. Clients often kept him on after a small job anyway. He depended on being dependable and doing good work, thus selling his talents. He found a wheelbarrow in the shed and immediately checked the tire. It was low in air pressure. He spotted a hand pump that he used to firm up the tire. The pressure held. "Good sign," he said out loud.

"What, that she thinks you're like her son?"

"What the hell are you talking about? I just pumped air in this tire. No leaks."

"Good sign," Usagi retorted.

The men got to work first on the smaller job of resetting the flag stone pathway in cement. They worked steadily without much talk. Zen concentration, with its economy of effort, brought them together in what appeared to be a choreographed rhythm within the hour. The pathway went so smoothly that they were nearly done with it by afternoon on the third day. Daisy had lunch ready for them this time on the third day so they would not have to drive into town. She brought avocado and cheese sandwiches along with homemade ice tea to an outdoor gazebo where they all ate comfortably with the dog Obi watching intently.

The bright sun forestalled a chilly afternoon breeze. It was late September in the high desert. Daisy was pleased with her new construction crew. She kept them there talking for over an hour until Jake indicated that they needed to size up how to approach the wall before it got too late. Usagi grabbed his cup and plate to take them inside.

"Leave it. I'll clean this up," Daisy told them as she threw a few scraps to the patient Obi. The dog ate hurriedly, and then caught up with his owner as she entered the back door. Obi followed her inside.

"You know, that is one great dog," Usagi remarked.

"Yeah, he's sweet," Jake answered. "I never thought I'd hear you say that about a Pit."

"Still don't trust the breed, bro."

"Is that a form of racism?"

"Breedism."

"That's not a word."

"It is now."

"Why—because you said it?"

"Why else?"

Jake chose not to answer him. Usagi knew it was a word.

During the next few days Jake and Usagi worked steadily ten hours a day with liberal snack breaks during which they took some minutes to meditate as well. Obi hung out with them watching their every move intently if he was not inside. Now and then Usagi would throw a tennis ball that Obi would fetch energetically and drop close to Usagi. The dog seemed very happy to have such entertaining guests.

Their focus on the job at hand increased day to day. The men achieved a rhythm after initial, clumsy efforts to adapt to the conditions. For example, when it came time to finish the ridge wall, they found that wheeling the rock and mortar mud up the slope was awkward and time-consuming. So they devised a way to toss and catch what they needed. The rocks averaged up to ten pounds each. Usagi wheeled a pile to a spot below Jake who stood most of the way up the slope. Usagi lifted a rock, swung it with two hands like an Olympic hammer thrower, spinning around and tossed it to Jake. Jake caught it with two hands, settled his stance, and then rolled the rock to the base of the wall until he had a large pile to set.

Next, Usagi mixed some mortar, or *mud* as they called it, in the barrow while Jake sorted through the rocks to choose which ones to set where. In similar fashion, when Jake was ready, Usagi swung a shovel full of mud and tossed it, shovel and all, up to Jake who deftly grasped the handle just behind the blade with its load. After dumping the mud into his bucket, Jake tossed the empty shovel down to Usagi. They mastered the technique after only several attempts.

After the wall was up and pointed, all they needed to finish was a crude but neat stone stairway that led up the slope. They set the stair stones on a bed of gravel that they reinforced with more gravel and wet clay. Usagi sprinkled grass seed over the disturbed soil around the stairway. Eventually, grass roots would reinforce the clay and sand to stave off erosion around the rocks. The stone wall would connect with a coyote fence made of six-foot rugged poles that was already in place on either side of the back yard of property. It was one thing that the previous crew had done right. To finish the job, Daisy directed them to fit a rustic wooden gate to the opening in the wall at the top of the stairs. The gate opened to what was state forest land set aside for public use as well as for free range cattle and horses. Daisy not only wanted to maintain a boundary to keep her dog in and the occasional range animal out, she also wanted to create an aesthetically pleasing visual boundary to her property. Fitting the gate would wait for the final day.

Daisy prepared dinner for them and a few of her friends at her home the evening before the men were to finish the job. She was pleased with everything they did for her and seemed to enjoy their company, being especially intrigued with their Zen practice.

Daisy invited Gerard who taught social psychology at a local college, Genevieve whose art studio was a few houses down the road, and Estelle and her father Diego who was basically non-communicative. He was eighty-one and suffered from dementia but pleasantly so. Diego and Estelle lived with their only servant in Diego's remodeled, two-hundred year old adobe style estate in Tesuque north of Santa Fe. Estelle, a divorcee who earned a living as a real estate broker, was a year younger than Daisy. She directed Diego to a couch.

"Siéntado aqui, papá."

She gave him a deck of cards and a glass of water. Diego smiled, mumbled with apparent delight, and stayed right there for the next two hours intently going through every card in the deck over and over. After Gerard and Genevieve greeted their old friend on the couch with a handshake and a kiss, both Jake and Usagi felt compelled to shake Diego's hand also. Diego smiled and nodded graciously to everyone, recognizing no one in particular. Although he had been bilingual, he spoke and seemingly understood only Spanish now.

Obi remained quietly observant by the couch.

Upon settling into the meal and after introduction-laden small talk, Daisy mentioned the Buddhist practice of her crew to her guests hoping to stimulate conversation.

"So, I noticed that you guys are up at dawn every morning to meditate. Please tell us about your Buddhist community, if you don't mind?"

"We just sit around mindlessly every day doing nothing in particular," Usagi offered in jest as Diego stared at a playing card on the couch. "Kind of like him," Usagi noted shifting his eyes to Diego. Usagi was only half kidding. He still did not feel entirely comfortable with meditative sitting after all these years.

Jake tapped Usagi with his boot under the table. His friend did not notice how his remark showed insensitivity for Diego, but the others did and Jake could see it in their subtle changes in expression.

"You flatter me, Usagi. I'm not that good at it. Maybe Diego knows something we don't." Jake winked at Usagi who suddenly realized his faux pas.

"Yo, I did not mean that to put him down. Sorry, Estelle. My mom raised me to be a better Indian than that!" Usagi said with downcast eyes.

Daisy smiled, holding back a giggle. She had become familiar with their banter. The other women at the table smiled too, sensing the intended humor but Gerard appeared less amused.

"I heard about your teacher, the Roshi, from a young student of mine who spent a weekend there. Your teacher has developed a reputation among local Buddhists. There's been some criticism. I don't mean to make you uncomfortable, and you don't have to answer this, but are you two familiar with the controversy? I'd like to know what you think of it—the sociologist in me!" Gerard smiled as he finished his question. The women looked apprehensive. Diego dropped his card on the tile floor.

"Here, let me get that for you, sir," Jake offered. As he stooped to pick up the *Jack of Diamonds*, he said, "We're aware of it, the accusations of sexual abuse and how he took money. The old man, the sensei, isn't perfect. We know that, but he's pushed us to appreciate being Buddhist. He's tough on us sometimes."

"How long have you been with him?" Estelle asked.

Jake looked at Usagi. "Has it been eight years, bro?"

Usagi nodded. "Since a few months after the sensei arrived in New Mexico," he said. "Jake and me got there around the same time."

Genevieve, a plump woman dressed in Santa Fe style with a fine, woven Mexican poncho, turquoise and silver jewelry, and her long, graying hair arranged in back in a single braid, spoke up jokingly, "Eight years is a long time to learn to meditate, is it not? I received a mantra from a Transcendental Meditation teacher twenty years ago who taught me to meditate in an hour. I still use the technique and find it helpful to relax me and clear my mind, although I must admit, not always."

"I think TM is basically a Hindu approach," Usagi responded. "This may be different. We value meditation as a tool also, but this is a way of life. We took refuge under the sensei, so we are more like monks at a monastery."

"Most of the money they make from working for me will go into supporting the community, as I understand it," Daisy offered with a sense of positive reinforcement for the altruism the young men practiced.

"I admire you guys. So young, yet wiser than most of the young people I meet. Sometimes I feel like I am on a meaningless treadmill, moving real estate for others," said Estelle.

"Well, I admire them too—eight years is quite an investment of time!" Gerard remarked. Then he turned to Jake. "You must have some reservations, though, as to the sensei's value as a teacher," Gerard stated almost as a question. "I mean, I heard that he uses a stick on his students quite liberally. Now, I understand that this is a tradition in Japanese Zen to help one stay alert. Someone I spoke with said he gets out of control."

Usagi glanced at Jake who was staring at his fork while fumbling with a chili relleno. Jake spoke up.

"Yes, the Keisaku thing does trouble some students. Some left because of it," Jake offered tentatively. "It's not for everyone. We think it strengthens our path."

"Which is what, if you don't mind? Again, you have to forgive me but I'm a curious bastard about social movements."

Daisy underscored Gerard's admission. "Yes, you are."

Jake believed there was more to his line of questioning, as if Gerard already knew the answers he was looking for. The recent complaints by former female students had spread to the Internet.

"The warrior monk tradition goes back a long way. We practice martial arts as well. Anyway, if I get your drift, the old man, the sensei, does overdo it sometimes. I guess it's a kind of test of endurance for some of us."

"Now, Gerard, just because you may not be capable of handling the sensei's training does not make it wrong!" Genevieve countered.

"Well perhaps," Gerard replied, "and many of my colleagues who study new religious movements would tend to agree with you. Such commitments are subjectively driven and merely another aspect of the flexible American religious experience, they say. People experience good and bad in major religions as well, and one cannot always go on what a former member describes."

Gerard paused to sip his red wine, a common French merlot. "Ah, that's a good wine, Daisy. Never had the pleasure before. I always enjoy your selections."

"Would you like some wine now?" Daisy asked Usagi and Jake whose glasses were yet empty. The men rarely drank in keeping with community policy, but under the circumstances and suspecting that Gerard already informed the others that the old man indulged in sake, they relented.

"Sure," Jake said with a cheerful, subtle hint to Usagi. "I'll have what he's having," he said indicating Gerard.

"Pour me the same," Usagi said as he held out his delicate stemware for Daisy to fill. Daisy poured a tasteful measure, filling their glasses to half.

"Now that we are all properly wined, I'd like to propose a toast," Genevieve insisted. She was working on her fourth serving. All at the table lifted their glasses. Diego, who happened to notice, raised his water glass along with them. "Good Diego,"Genevieve intoned in her sing-song way, "join us in complimenting these young men for a job well done and in good time. Your Zen training certainly proved itself superior to the approach from the last crew Daisy hired!"

"Here, here! So true," Gerard replied as he reached over to touch glasses with Jake, then Usagi and then with the women. He reached out to Diego also as the old man looked longingly at Gerard's wine.

"None for you! No vino papá!" Estelle insisted.

Diego looked down at his water. He set his glass back down. "Es mi viaje en breve?" he asked in a commanding voice.

"Todavía no. Más tarde, papá," Estelle replied gently. She turned to Usagi and Jake. "He constantly thinks someone is coming to take him somewhere. I have no idea who he thinks is coming for him." Then, as an aside in a low voice, Estelle said, "I think he grasps that he is dying."

"Ask not for whom the bell tolls, it tolls for thee," Genevieve spoke aloud. "We are not so different from Diego, are we?"

The evening wound down quickly after that remark. Estelle said she needed to take Diego home. He was getting restless, a sign that he would soon need his night meds that she did not bring with her. Gerard excused himself as well, claiming that he had several papers to grade. He thanked Jake and Usagi for putting up with him. They shook hands amicably. Genevieve stayed behind to help Daisy clean up. Daisy would walk her down to her home after they had tea. Usagi and Jake excused themselves.

"We want to get an early start, try to finish the gate by noon, and then clean up. Thanks for the great dinner," Jake said.

"Yes, excellent. Really appreciate it," Usagi said as he shook hands with Daisy and Genevieve.

The plump artist held on to Usagi's hand while saying, "So good to meet you both. I am happy for Daisy that she finally got this job done. It's hard to find honest, reliable men these days. In years past I would have made a pass at you, but alas the stars were not aligned," she said with eyes beaming.

"Oh, don't mind her. She's had too much to drink and she's always had a thing for Indians," Daisy said mirthfully.

Usagi waited until Genevieve relaxed her grip to move his hand. He bowed smiling to her with hands folded, then backed away silently to follow Jake out the back door. Obi followed the men outside, stopping to urinate by a Chamisa shrub. Daisy held the door open until Obi returned. Genevieve hummed something that sounded like the old Sixties song *My Guy* while tending to the cleanup chores.

The men sauntered to the guest cottage in the dim moonlight. They walked one behind the other down the winding flagstone path they installed four days earlier. They maintained silence half way to the entrance portal. Usagi spoke first.

"Don't say anything."

Jake burst out laughing quietly. "Do you want me to let her in if she knocks on the door?"

"I'll be out the window and over the wall before she gets inside."

"I know she's big, but what's the big deal? Think of it as a good deed."

"Will I get a merit badge, bro?"

"Scout's honor," Jake indicated with two fingers raised in a sign of peace.

"You know people burn in hell for making fun of fat people," Usagi cautioned.

"Then hell is full of comedians," Jake advised.

"I told you not to say anything," Usagi repeated. "Now we're going to hell."

Jake opened the heavy door decorated with Mexican motifs. He let Usagi pass and then followed him inside while running his fingers over the engraved panels. The tired men said nothing more to each other as they prepared to go to bed. Jake occupied the large Taos bed in the living area while Usagi took the sole bedroom. Jake was nearly asleep when a knock on the door startled him.

"Now what?" he whispered to himself.

He pulled on his khaki pants and fumbled with the zipper as he approached the door to open it. "What if it's her?" he thought. A slim figure in a hooded sweater stood in the dark. Jake flipped the switch to turn on the porch light.

"Oh hi, Daisy! What's up?" he whispered.

"Just wanted to let you guys know I'll be gone early, maybe before you get started. I have to be in Albuquerque to pick someone up at the airport. So, make yourself at home with the food. Oh, can you feed Obi lunch? We should be back by one or so."

"Sure. No problem. Good night."

"Thanks. See you tomorrow afternoon. We can settle then, okay? Good night," Daisy said with a lilt in her voice.

Jake closed the door. Then he heard a voice from the bedroom. "I was nearly out the window, bro. Good night."

"Night, bro," Jake said with a smile. He kept his pants on, curled up under the tan linen comforter, and fell asleep in minutes.

The morning sun rose behind an unusually thick haze above the mountains. There was a distinct chill in the air. The diffused light cast an eerie warm glow over the finished wall. Jake took photos with his cheap digital camera for his sample album. He surveyed the completed wall closely for the first time. At a glance one could hardly tell where the previous crew ended and Jake's work began. He and Usagi were able to scrub and re-point enough of the earlier effort to blend seamlessly with the new work. Next they sunk two posts to line the opening where they would hang an arched gate that Usagi built with rough planks the previous day. He worked in the shed with the table saw, a good set of chisels, and a hand-held sander.

The men meditated with their knit caps on, facing east, for fifteen or twenty minutes before work. After pounding two cedar posts deep into the pre-set vinyl sleeves, they drilled holes for screwing in hinges and a latch. Daisy provided decorative, heavy-duty, strap style wrought iron gate hangers she commissioned from a local blacksmith. The gate was ready to install by mid-morning. Both men had shed their sweatshirts as the day warmed up.

While Usagi went to retrieve the gate from the shed, Jake noticed a man on horseback coming through the trees along the trail that veered past Daisy's property. A mid-sized dog was running with him, a sturdy black and gray speckled Healer.

"Morning, friend," shouted the man as he tipped his western hat. He was perhaps fifty years old with a grizzled beard and longish hair that settled in a wave at his shoulders. "The name's Matthew. Wall looks great. You do this?"

"Yessir, my partner down there and me did. Hi. I'm Jake," he said as he stretched to shake Matthew's hand. The horse, a large roan Tennessee Walker, shook and lowered its head to munch on grass. Matthew leaned forward on the saddle horn to stretch his back. The dog sat dutifully next to the horse.

"Nice job. I passed by a few weeks ago when it was half done."

"A different crew started it. We just finished it for Ms. Baker," Jake said with some concern that the man not confuse them with the previous crew.

As they were chatting, the Healer walked over to sniff Jake. It then proceeded to mark the new post with its urine. "Joker, get away from there," Matthew ordered. "Sorry, he's got bad manners."

"I suppose he wants to stake his claim," Jake said with a chuckle as he knelt down to greet the dog. Joker cautiously sniffed Jake's hand.

Like a brown blur out of nowhere, Obi sprinted past a stunned Usagi. The Pit Bull bounded up the new stairs, growling. He slammed into the surprised Healer, knocking it back five feet or more. The Healer quickly righted itself on all fours, fangs bared, ready to do battle. A furious few seconds of gnashing teeth and posturing for a strike ended with Obi clamped on the smaller, squealing Healer's neck and shoulder. Obi lifted the smaller dog to shake it. Horse and rider spun around. Matthew steadied his skittish mount with one hand tight on the reins. In the other was a drawn Glock 9mm. Matthew fired two rounds that entered Obi's back and head. Obi yelped, went slack and fell to the side of the bloody Healer. Joker managed to pull away from the deadly jaws, but he fell immediately to the ground a few feet away. Matthew's quick reaction with a weapon came from decades of training. He was a retired Texas Ranger.

"Oh, shit!" yelled Jake, as it happened in a flash a few yards from his feet. "Oh, shit!"

Usagi saw the entire scene after Obi sped past him. He dropped the gate and ran up stairs to see what he could do, which was next to nothing.

"Oh, shit," he repeated as he approached the bleeding dogs. He knelt down to hold Obi's head. Obi gasped a few times, spasmodically kicked his hind legs, and then expired and went limp. He was dead.

Horse, rider, Jake, and Usagi froze in the moment.

"He's gone, man. He's gone," Usagi cried out. A tear formed in his eye.

Matthew quickly dismounted to examine his dog.

"Easy, buddy, easy," he said as he gently felt around the dog with one hand while gripping its collar with the other. "He's cut pretty deep in two places. You guys got a towel or something I can use on Joker here?"

Jake grabbed his gray sweatshirt off the wall and tossed it to Matthew. "Is this okay for now? We can look for something in the house."

"No. Thanks. This will do." Matthew tied the sweater around his dog to cover the bleeding wounds. "Is the owner of that dog around?" He motioned to Obi with his eyes.

"She won't be back till this afternoon," Usagi replied as he continued to rest on one knee next to Obi's carcass.

Matthew handed Joker to Jake to hold while he climbed back on his horse. "Can you hand him up to me. I've got to get him to a vet." Jake handed the whimpering dog up to Matthew who gently rested it across the saddle.

"You sure we can't help? We have a car."

"No thanks. He's breathing okay for now. Who knows? This horse belongs back at a ranch a few miles down the trail. I can't leave it here. I'll call ahead to locate a vet." Matthew sighed and shook his head in frustration. "Tell the lady I'll be back tomorrow to settle with her about her dog. I'll call this in to the local sherriff. I'm sure he'll be out here to talk with the lady. I know him. I'm real sorry. Last name's Young. I'm in the Santa Fe phone book."

"The owner is Daisy Baker," Usagi offered.

"I promise I'll get back to Daisy Baker." With that said, Matthew Young flipped open his cell phone. He used leg pressure to guide the responsive horse into a walk. In short order Matthew connected with the rancher who said he would follow up with his animal doctor immediately. Matthew slipped his phone back into his shirt pocket. He urged his mount into a loping canter. Jake watched the rider with his wounded dog disappear behind a clump of ragged cedars. He closed his eyes. He wished this whole thing would disappear like a bad dream.

"This is crazy, bro. What are we going to do with Obi now?" Usagi asked.

Jake opened his eyes. "What?" He looked at the dead dog. The weight of the situation sunk in. This was no dream. "Don't move him yet," he ordered. Jake fetched his camera from his tool bag. Instinct told him to snap a few pictures to show that Obi died outside of Daisy's property. Instinct dictated that this could be a legal matter. Dogs had value. "The Healer may be a valuable working dog at the ranch," he said.

Common sense told him that nothing much would come of it beyond a remorseful Matthew talking it over with a tearful Daisy. They would work out a deal without legal recourse if at all possible. This was New Mexico after all with its enduring Old West character, he thought. Then again—who knew?

Usagi lifted the limp, sixty-pound dog with some effort and held it up against his chest. He managed the steps without stumbling and carried the dog to the back of the main house. With Jake's help, he eased Obi's carcass onto the back patio in the shade. Jake found an old Army blanket in the shed. He draped it over the dog. The men lingered for half a minute in silence. "Let's get that gate hung," Jake suggested. They walked with a sense of purpose back up to the wall.

"A few more minutes, Obi would still be alive," Usagi surmised as he held the gate in place.

Jake did not answer him. He concentrated on the job. He eased the gate onto the hinge slots as Usagi held it in place. Next he tapped in the pins. They swung the gate shut a few times, making minor adjustments to the latch each time until it worked precisely.

"Yes, a few more minutes. Fate is funny—and if Matthew didn't have a gun, then what? Joker may have been killed," Jake said. "Daisy could be sued or fined."

"I didn't think of that. How did Obi get out?" Usagi wondered.

"Don't know, but we'd better get an idea before Ms. Baker comes back."

They finished the job and had cleaned the area around the wall before Daisy's car pulled up in front of the house.

Daisy slumped on the back patio bench next to her dog. She lifted the blanket to see his head. "Oh, Obi, sweet Obi," she sobbed.

Her lady friend visiting from California sat next to her, trying her best to comfort.

"Tell me again how this happened," Daisy asked. She blew her nose in a tissue.

"It seems he got out a side window, the best we could figure. It was open when we checked," Usagi said with some relief. The door was properly closed.

"I sometimes leave that window cracked to let in fresh air. He's never done that before, but I guess he nudged it open. He's strong. He's also sneaky," she said with a tearful smile. "Or at least he was—the horse and rider were too much for him I guess. He had to get out, to protect the house, you know?"

Jake sensed that Daisy would approach Matthew reasonably over this. "What do you want to do with Obi?" he asked her in a low, careful way.

Daisy's guest Carrie stroked Daisy's arm. Carrie was a tall, elegant woman who owned a new women's magazine. She wore fashionable jeans, high-heeled black boots and a black linen jacket. She travelled to New Mexico to arrange a contract with Daisy for a series of articles. Carrie spoke up.

"We can discuss this over coffee or tea. Just show me where and I'll make it." Her suggestion ruled the emotion of the moment. All three followed her into the kitchen.

The men dug a large round hole nearly four feet deep in Daisy's main garden. With little ceremony Jake and Usagi lowered Obi into the hole with the blanket. They gently rolled him into the raw earth. He settled in a curled position as if he were sleeping in an earthen bowl. Daisy said a few words, thanking him for the few years they had together and offering praise for the God that gives us all a life to share with one another. She tossed an old chew bone and Obi's favorite if worn out sleeping pad into the hole. She nodded to the men to bury him.

Carrie walked arm in arm with Daisy back into the house. Usagi padded the remaining dirt into a smooth mound above the grave. Then he raked the surface to blend with the surrounding garden mulch. Jake selected a finely worn, pinkish granite rock to set as a grave marker. The odd shaped stone weighed more than the dog. It was not a good fit for the wall but seemed appropriate for garden décor. The men wheeled it over to the garden grave with the barrow. It was 4 pm.

"Thank you so much. I like the stone," Daisy said, much more composed. "If you guys will clean up now, I want to treat you and Carrie to dinner down town. Carrie is staying at the La Fonda. We can all eat there before you leave. Please join us. We can leave in an hour."

"Sounds good, right Usagi?"

Usagi shrugged and smiled. "I'm hungry, bro. Let's do it."

"We'll follow you down there," Jake said to Daisy.

Usagi ordered the *Roasted Root Shepherd's Pie* at La Plazuela because it sounded good. La Plazuela was once an open air courtyard in the La Fonda. Rain would send guests scampering. Now it was protected by an elegant skylight canopy.

"I'll stick with the Rellenos," Jake answered when it was his turn to order. Daisy ordered her favorite Enchilada meal for herself and Carrie. Daisy requested a bottle of white wine for all to share. After ordering, the women excused themselves so Carrie could check on a conflict with her room at the desk.

"We haven't drunk this much in years," Usagi remarked.

"Much? Hell, we didn't even finish half a glass last night. I don't think I could keep up with that group at dinner."

"Daisy downs at least a couple of drinks every night, it seems, no?"

"I think she does. Must be part of life on the upside of society."

139

"Why, you think we're on the downside?"

"Man, look at us. T-shirts and work pants in a place like this."

"Man, look around," Usagi suggested. "There's a guy with his family over there in jeans and T-shirt."

"His jeans don't have old stains and holes like yours."

"Mine are distressed—that's in fashion these days, bro," Usagi smiled with a hint of pride.

"You think Ms. Baker's going to be okay about her dog?" Jake asked. "Hey, they're coming back now."

"We could check on her later. She will have a few hard nights, I think," Usagi said as he stood up to help the women into their chairs.

The women sat down, both smiling, clearly enjoying one another's company. During dessert Daisy handed the men each an envelope.

"Your checks are in there and a little extra. Do something for yourselves. You deserve it," she said.

Daisy tugged on Usagi's clean but faded and torn red T-shirt. The men got the hint.

"Yeah, Usagi. Distressed does not mean disgusting," Jake intoned.

"Next time we'll show them. We will appear here in our Zen robes," Usagi countered.

"Zen robes?" Carrie asked with raised eyebrows.

"You didn't know. Jake and Waylon—I mean Usagi—live on a new Buddhist commune near Chama. They study under a master teacher from Japan."

Daisy wrote the check out to Usagi's formal name.

"Ah, how interesting. Are there women among you as well?" asked the magazine producer.

"Yes, more than half are," Jake answered. "It's small, maybe twenty-five to thirty total on a good day."

"This could be another story for our magazine. We concentrate on women's issues. May I come for a visit sometime?"

"Sure, we're on the Internet. Email us. Ask for Marga."

"I have their info at home, Carrie. I'll show it to you later," said Daisy.

The men could not have known that Carrie's feminist nose for news would soon lead to two women telling their stories of sexual manipulation under the old man. The story in her magazine would have serious consequences for the Center.

With the meal at an end the men said their goodbyes, wishing Daisy well. Daisy took Carrie for a stroll around the Plaza. The young men walked over to the lounge where they took a seat to examine their envelopes.

"Wow. Two hundred fifty cash on top of our checks! Now that's the *finest* tip I ever got, bro," Usagi exclaimed.

"You've had other tips?"

"Hell yes. I made ten dollars extra once after cleaning a horse barn."

"You know, this is a cause for a little celebration. How about a beer?"

The men retired to the lounge of La Fonda. The beer stimulated conversation about the week's events, their futures at the Center, the meaning of right action in Buddhism, and a call for several more Heinekens. They were suitably drunk by nine o'clock when they left the bar. After ordering coffee to go from the bartender, they got into Jake's bug and drove into the night to get home.

There was no news from Daisy for two months until she contacted Marga for an interview with Carrie. Marga printed out the email partially addressed to the men:

"Please tell Waylon and Jake that Matthew Young did call and come by that evening after you both left. He brought flowers that we placed on Obi's grave. He was utterly gracious. We cried together. Sadly, his Joker died too that same day. He asked me out to dinner. Now we are dating regularly. Odd how things work out. Thanks again for a job well done. Stop by any time. Ciao, Daisy Baker."

"That's crazy news," Usagi said, shaking his head slowly. "I still miss old Obi."

8 A Last Supper

"Chama Guru Sued by Former Disciples"

The headline ran in the regional news as well as the *Santa Fe Examiner*, a monthly that published a longer feature. It was 2005 during a wet, early autumn when members of the Center met to discuss the bad publicity. There was a chill in the air that evening. Usagi helped to load and light the firebox in the dining hall with wood from the dry stack under the front portal. The burning piñon permeated the space with its distinctive aroma. It was incense for a non-sacred event. The old man did not attend the meeting. He remained in the main house with his younger male aide, Tadao.

Twenty-four students sat around the long harvest table on benches and folding chairs. Jiro, who was second in rank behind the old man—a distant second—brought the meeting to order. He appeared casually in a plane black cotton tunic over his faded jeans. He was clean shaven save a gray goatee, neatly trimmed. The old man had given him the name Jiro, which meant *second male*.

Jiro bowed before everyone to indicate he was ready to speak. This gesture signaled everyone to sit quietly. Jiro stood in the silence with his eyes closed for a full minute before saying, "Thank you for coming. Sensei asked me to fill you in on this ongoing attack on us by two disgruntled students. Some of you have read the article in *The Examiner* that came out today. Sensei is limited as to what he can reveal. His attorney will advise when he can speak more openly. I can tell you that since this broke in the news, more reporters are calling. Marga told me that even the Buddhist magazine *Tricycle* wants to know what we have to say. It is important to keep in mind that our sensei is innocent. We all know that sometimes he is exacting and challenges convention in his teaching methods but we have a choice to leave or stay. Sensei has compassion on the two women who are bringing legal action. He says that they may have been confused or misled by a few disgruntled students that left last year."

Jiro held up a packet of papers. "We have some suggestions on one page for everyone regarding how to answer questions regarding these accusations. Marga, will you please pass them out."

Jiro finished summarizing the feature in *The Examiner* leaving out the more lurid details. "We must keep in mind that the closer we are to enlightenment the more we will be tested. Sensei often used the examples of Jesus who sweat blood when feeling doubt before his crucifixion and of the Dalai Lama who withstood devastating criticism and persecution from the entire government of China. We will get through this; another lesson in samsara," he said.

Two of the newer female students stood up and walked out silently. Apparently, they had heard enough. They never returned.

Jiro remained calm through the commotion and murmur among some of the students. He waited for the noise to subside; then he announced an event for the old man.

"Sensei deserves our support. We plan to celebrate with a simple banquet in his honor this Sunday. It will be eight years since his arrival in America after he purchased this property. Samuwabi has been his dream to help sustain the tradition of the Buddha as we all know. Please plan to attend. He will address this problem then and answer all our questions." With that said, Jiro left the dining hall.

Jake and Usagi had not read the damaging articles. They did hear that Carrie's piece in her magazine was picked up by a paper in Santa Fe. They had just returned from a job that day. The two friends sat apart from the others as they talked.

"Yo, Usagi. You know something I don't know? Are these chicks for real?" Jake said as he took a sheet from Marga. She kept moving, not paying attention to them.

"You mean about boinkin' the old man?" Usagi asked.

"Yes, that and about the money thing?"

"Well, yeah. I think he did it."

"How do you know?"

"One of them, Taylor, came to me. Told me all about it, bro. She was, like, crying, you know."

"You never told anyone?"

144

"No, man. It was like a confession. She didn't want me to say anything. I think she was confused about it," Usagi said in a low voice.

"Confused, how?"

"You know his thing about advanced teaching for certain students. She said it was tantra—sacred sex. But she did not feel good about it, especially after she thought about the thirty thousand she handed over to him."

Jake looked puzzled. He had heard rumors all along of this side of the old man. He ignored it using the excuse that the old man used private methods for different students, knowing their individual needs for advancement. But now it was in the open. "How do you feel about all this?"

"Like shit, bro. It stinks," Usagi said as he folded up the paper Marga gave him and stuffed it into his back pocket. "Hope he's got a good explanation, like Jiro says."

"I guess I'll read the articles and then see what he has to say on Sunday." Jake left his instruction sheet on the table. "I'm going for a walk. See you later."

On the following day, Jake discovered that Carrie managed to find the two women who were suing the old man after she interviewed students at the Center. The complaints were clear enough. *The Examiner* article was the most damaging as the women spoke more openly than they had with Carrie. It appeared to Jake as part of a strategy to press for settlement to avoid a long, drawn out civil case.

The stories revealed that the old man could not control his bad habits. He drank sake and expensive cognacs, a daily indulgence known to his chief male assistants who covered for him whenever possible:

Sensei is not feeling well today. Marga, could you please lead the lecture? Sensei feels a burden to meditate and pray privately. He will not appear for class.

Whether it was his charisma or mere hero worship is hard to tell in these matters of the longing spirit. Certainly, the women had not expected their guru to publicly declare his affections, and he never did. This was a sacred trust to them.

The old man hinted to his mistresses about a secret tradition handed down by the Buddha. In ominous tones he said it was such a powerful teaching that only the highest initiates under the guidance of a qualified teacher should attempt the rituals. The rituals derived from tantra were dangerous in unenlightened hands.

The disgruntled women exposed some of the tactics he used to bed them. He invoked strange words including *maithuna* and *panchatattva* with elaborate descriptions. He convinced the women that through sexual encounter he could elevate awareness of occult forces that would bring blessings. He modestly mentioned how he had acquired extrasensory powers through ritual practices, powers he would never lower himself to demonstrate.

"I do not perform circus acts," he said in response to one disciple who asked about his hidden powers at a general meeting. The old man was good at side-stepping the matter of his chi power.

Incredibly, his inner circle of devotees assumed the stories of power were true more so because the old man refused to perform anything paranormal in public. One story retold by members alleged that sensei could suspend gravity, allowing him and certain named objects to levitate. The believers spoke of his humility and awkwardness as evidence of his honesty. Jake would write in his journal:

Old man say:
Karma not about good or bad or universal justice. Karma just action. Learn to watch ripple in pond. Do not become ripple. It just passes through. Western mind see too much in karma. Sin, reward and punishment for good act, bad act. I teach you to let go this wrong idea. You will have peace—let go and be.

Old man full of shit. The women could not let go when he inserted his desire in them. They tried and that was their mistake. They knew that no effort to resist him was the way.—29 September 2005

The women that the old man seduced gave themselves over to the sacred tantric concepts behind sex more than to him. He showed the women images of sensual figures sculpted onto temples. One was *Khajuraho* in India that harbors mysterious erotic forces. The mysterious forces remained mysterious. Apparently, the old man's performance of tantric ritual lacked the elegance of his description. As one woman facetiously stated, "He was so skilled that he could perform this elaborate ritual in a few minutes."

The women reported that he had bad teeth and his naked, sinewy body revealed pale, flabby skin on a thin frame. The women described fancy tattoos of a dragon, two chrysanthemums, and of carp on the old man's torso and shoulders—evidence of his old Yakuza ties and to organized crime. The article said that the women sexed him for personal enlightenment, not for pleasure. This was tantra, after all. One can only guess the old man's intent. But he was their teacher and the master who, at the time, knew better than they did, they said.

The proverbial cats fell out of the old man's bag when one of the women who believed that she alone was his sacred lover talked to another who believed the same thing. After commiserating about their mutually devastating revelations, the two women contacted a local lawyer who asked them for thousands of dollars in advance to run the case. They did not have the money. But in the process, they discovered stories of more forlorn lovers after connecting with more ex-members.

Carrie, the magazine publisher, appeared at just the right time for the two women who felt empowered by her to speak out publically. The subsequent article in Carrie's magazine attracted the attention of an Albuquerque law firm that offered to take the cases on contingency. As a result, one of the women sued the commune to get her inheritance back. The other sued the old man for monetary and psychological damages stemming from sexual assault and fraud. She was seeing a therapist. Several ex-commune members offered affidavits in support of the litigants.

That Saturday, the day before the banquet, Roshi, Jiro and Marga appeared in mediation with their attorney and the attorneys representing the alleged victims. They met in a nicely appointed conference room complete with tan leather chairs and full food service at the Eldorado Hotel in Santa Fe. The old man seemed small as he sat quietly in his black robe in a large, stuffed chair. He listened to offers and counter offers for over two hours. Marga acted primarily as secretary for the Center, taking notes. Jiro, dressed handsomely in black slacks, a crew-necked black shirt and gray sport jacket, helped with clarifying the policies at the Center. There was some discussion about the liability waivers that every student including the women signed.

"These releases are essentially worthless," asserted the attorney for the alleged victims. "We will prove that the teacher here broke the contract."

The Center's attorney took the old man and Jiro aside to discuss options. They found empty seats near a piano in the main lobby. Marga remained in the conference room. The attorney asked a waitress for three waters. As she walked away, he turned to Jiro and the sensei. "I'm sorry to tell you this, but you have a weak case. No matter what your stated motive, I highly doubt any American judge will buy what may be culturally appropriate for a teacher of your stature. The appearance of malfeasance and manipulation or undue influence is very strong here. All the witnesses are credible and they are all women," he said. "Also, I think by settling, we can avoid a potential criminal charge here."

"Criminal charge?" Jiro repeated with concern.

"Yes," the attorney said emphatically. "In the very least they could appeal to an attorney general for misdemeanors. That would go on the public record even if you beat it in court. This way, you could shut down the noise and get on with your good work. My sense is that they want this behind them too, that they want the money they donated, and they want to pay their attorneys."

"Sensei," Jiro said as he turned to face his teacher, "our entire bank account will be drained and we will have to sell some of the property to cover all this."

"Selling could take months," said the old man. "How can we manage that?"

"We can set up a bridge loan, I think," said the attorney. "Marga mentioned that a rancher on the adjoining property expressed interest once. I think it's doable." The old man asked to speak with Jiro alone for a few minutes. The attorney returned to the conference room. "This puritanical country is a lawyer's paradise," the guru said to Jiro with a laugh. "Like he said, I think it best to settle. We can handle this and the women will be happy." The old man paused, noting that Jiro seemed in accordance. "I learned my lesson. No more private lessons to teach the Tantra. Americans are not ready. But you must forgive me, Jiro. We have made things more difficult. That was not my intention."

"We all have something to learn from this, Sensei. I am humbled by your request. Of course, all is forgiven."

So it was agreed to settle with the standard rider that all parties agree to no longer discuss the case for publication or reveal details of the settlement. The old man decided that by not admitting to anything he could claim to be a victim of the American legal system—the price of doing business. The Center would sell some of its property as well as drain most of its monetary assets to pay damages and return donated monies to the women.

After the Sunday morning meditation, everyone seemed to be in better spirits anticipating the banquet. Banquets at the Center occurred several times a year to honor Buddhist holidays as well as the old man's birthday. These festive events always included a variety of delicious main courses and desserts. Center members looked forward to a break from the lean daily cuisine. They also were looking forward to the old man's talk about the recent debacle.

Jiro took Stanley, one of the newer students, with him to buy fresh ingredients for salad. Stanley had been there for a year. He was tall but rail thin with a nervous disposition. He suffered growing up in an abusive family in Kentucky and he spoke with a thick Kentucky accent. He often helped with the cooking. He found Jiro to be more approachable than the old man. Stanley was very sensitive, even effeminate in his bearing. He did not like the way sensei used the stick on him or anyone else during meditation, but he did rationalize the necessity of the ritual beatings.

"Stanley, we're going up to the hills ahead get mushrooms. I picked some last week. Looks like a good season for them," Jiro said as he pulled off the highway onto a rural road that wound up to one thousand feet above the highway. He parked the white van off the dirt road near a wire fence. The fence had an opening with a cattle guard. Within fifteen minutes they reached the beginning of the forest.

"There, over there in the meadow, I see some already," Jiro pointed out. Stanley stopped to catch his breath. He felt dizzy. Stanley had a difficult time adjusting to the high altitude even after a year. Jiro waited for him as he pulled several plastic shopping bags out of his jacket pocket. He handed a bag to Stanley. "Come with me. I'll show you what we are looking for."

Jiro bent down and picked a large white mushroom from the ground. He held it up for Stanley to see. "This is a Horse or common field mushroom. See if you can fill a bag with them but half a bag will do if that is all you can find. That should be enough. I'm going up ahead to find some boletes. My Italian grandmother called them *porcini*. They are excellent. I found some up there last year." Jiro pointed to a stand of large fir trees.

Stanley went about picking a number of field mushrooms until he filled his bag halfway. He strolled up the hill where he spotted a few more of the white balls popping out of the ground under a pine tree. He threw them in the bag. He sat down on a rock to wait for Jiro who returned with his prize finds a few minutes later.

"Look at these," Jiro said proudly as he opened a bag to display a number of large boletes, some with eight inch caps. "Sensei loves these sautéed in butter!"

The students gathered in the dining hall around two in the afternoon. The main courses consisted of mostly Indian haute cuisine prepared by Jiro, Stanley, and a few women at the Center. They first served a variety of delicious vegetarian dishes spiced with curry along with the sautéed boletes. Instrumental Japanese music featuring guitar and flute played through four speakers mounted high on walls creating an exotic Zen surround sound. Everyone seemed relaxed. Everyone was having a good time.

Salad was served after the main courses in keeping with a European preference introduced by Jiro. He convinced everyone that salad after a meal helped with digestion and that it was a great palate cleanser before dessert. Stanley was responsible for making the salads. He served three large wooden bowls. One contained tossed greens, raw veggies and chopped mushrooms. Another was similar but with no mushrooms. And the third was primarily spinach leaves with sesame seeds and feta cheese. Students lined up with bowls to serve themselves Marga served the old man.

Several trays of small dessert cakes and cookies appeared next. All of these were made by Marga and a few of the women. The old man smiled broadly upon seeing his favorite daifuku cakes with strawberry filling. Tea was served. He signaled a student to tap the gong. The room went silent save for a soft flute melody coming from the speakers. He stood to address his students.

"Before we eat dessert, I will say a few words. I will be brief. As you know by now, we decide to settle with the two ladies who complain. We agree to not discuss details of disagreement. In the end, such disturbing details are not important anyway. Let them pass."

Here he paused for a few seconds to allow his last statement to sink in. "I must say sorry for any suffering I have caused by my action. My teaching them was meant for advancement only, but I offended them. This is not good. Even a teacher can create karma, as you see. As long as we live, we remain in samsara. We must be careful. I must begin repair this damage. I will spend next seven days alone in meditation; no food. But today I eat and drink with you. Please enjoy dessert now."

Jiro stood and began clapping, thus encouraging everyone there to do the same. Jake found him self standing too, feeling as he clapped that the old man seemed genuinely heroic in his struggle to transcend human frailty day by day. Jake felt that same innocent transcendence as he did the first day there one more time. It was that feeling that kept him going in his quest for enlightenment and kept him there for two more years.

After dessert, students volunteered to clean up. It was done in less than an hour. During cleanup, Stanley volunteered to walk with the old man back to the main house to help him settle in for the night. Jiro was putting away the clean silverware when his cell phone rang. "Yes, Stanley, what is it?"

"I need your help. Sensei is complaining of severe pain in his stomach. He's throwing up."

Before Jiro could explain why he had to leave the kitchen, he was feeling nauseous as well. "Sensei is not feeling well. I'll be back," he said with a grimace. Usagi and Marga merely shrugged when he ran by them and the large table they were scrubbing. The screen door slammed behind Jiro. He was only halfway to the main house when he doubled over with painful stomach cramps. He began to sweat. Then he vomited next to the path.

Back in the dining hall Jake found Marga to tell her five of the students were feeling very sick with similar symptoms. "They're cramping up and some of them are vomiting."

"I'm calling for an ambulance now," she said as she picked up the wall phone and dialed. "Roshi is very sick too and so is Jiro. It might be food poisoning," she said.

"What the hell," Jake said. "Is it salmonella?"

"I'm not a doctor Jake," Marga said with some irritation and motioning for him to shut up. Marga reported the problem to a 911 operator who suggested everyone with symptoms get to an emergency room as quickly as possible. In any case, she would send an emergency medical service to examine and treat the sensei due to his age.

Jake and Usagi felt fine so far, so they volunteered to drive the van and a station wagon. Usagi took four of the stricken students with Marga and Stanley tending to them in the eight-seat van. Marga and Stanley felt okay as well. Jake drove Jiro and the remaining sick girl with help from the one the old man named Mika. Mika was only too happy to go along. They rushed to a clinic in Chama.

The doctor and the physician's assistant at the Chama clinic both agreed that some sort of food poisoning was responsible. Everyone but the old man was sent home after a few hours with medication and instructions on how to avoid dehydration until symptoms subsided. The clinic kept the old man on intravenous fluids overnight. Stanley remained at the clinic to tend to his guru who was discharged the following afternoon.

Two days later, none of the stricken students felt completely well and the old man was getting worse. The cramps were gone but pain increased throughout his body. Jiro was still in bed as well. Marga was worried. Instinct told her something was seriously wrong.

"Usagi, we need to take Roshi back to the clinic right away. Something's not right."

Back at the clinic they found another doctor, one who doubled as the medical examiner for the county. He reviewed the old man's condition and looked him over carefully. His patient's breathing was labored. His eyeballs were yellow. The doctor ordered an IV and a blood test. He said that he suspected liver failure. He interviewed Marga and Usagi at length about the banquet and what they ate. They recalled that Jiro and Stanley had picked fresh mushrooms and one salad had the white ones in it.

"Can you get Stanley on the phone?"

The doctor discovered that Stanley picked a smaller variety of white mushroom that he thought was an immature Horse mushroom. He cut several of them up for the salad and put the rest in the cooler. Stanley gave him a detailed description of a whole one that had begun to spread its cap.

"I think I know what happened. You better get the rest of your group that feel ill in here right away," the doctor urged.

"Amanitas, when young, can resemble Horse Mushrooms," the doctor told them. He showed Usagi and Marga pictures from a mushroom guide at the clinic. Though rare, this was not the first case of mushroom poisoning for the physician. *Amanita virosa* was the identified culprit. "It is commonly known as the *Destroying Angel*," he said.

Jake showed up with Jiro and the rest of the sick students within the hour. Mika and Stanley came with them. Stanley brought one of the smaller white mushrooms to show the doctor.

"That's it," the physician said. He pulled out the guide. They all could see that the picture and description was a perfect match.

The doctor put them all on intravenous penicillin G after determining that none had allergic reactions to that type of drug. None said they did.

Despite all efforts to save him, the old man died the following day, but the students responded well to the antibiotics and recovered their health in short order. The examiner explained that the toxin in the Destroying Angel mushroom continues to ravage the liver and kidneys after a victim recovers from the initial nausea and discomfort. Feeling better is an illusion. Certain death can come for the unwary within several days without proper treatment. At first the examiner surmised that the sensei ingested more of the deadly Amanita, therefore suffering major damage, or the students just got lucky when they vomited. Later, after an autopsy, he discovered that his patient's liver was severely weakened by cirrhosis. The years of alcoholism contributed to his death.

Jiro believed this way of dying revealed the old man's Buddha nature. One legend said that the Buddha died after eating a meal prepared by a disciple. The Buddha's last supper, according to that legend, inadvertently contained a deadly mushroom. The coincidence was auspicious for Jiro and a group of students that favored him as a teacher.

After all they had been through, Jake and others thought otherwise about the old man's Buddha status. He may have taught the basic principles well, but he was no Buddha. Most doubters at the Center sustained devotion to Buddhism and to the Center despite losing respect for the old man. Only a few defected outright when the old man died. The devoted monks around Jiro debated the cause. Was it murder, an accident, or sacred suicide? Everyone had an opinion but eventually the students divided into two groups.

154

Jiro felt it was a sacred suicide. "Sensei knew this would happen. Remember he said he would go into meditation for a week and eat no food? He said he would take on this karma to help us heal. He sacrificed his life for us. Jesus said it: Greater love hath no man than to lay his life down for his friends."

The local sheriff's department questioned all the students. The sheriff came to the conclusion that it was an accidental poisoning, basing his opinion primarily on the medical report. In any case, the old man's death revealed rather than created a schism among his students. Jake, Usagi, Mika and those who doubted the sensei's pure Buddha nature turned to Marga as their natural leader. She felt honored by their acclamation but took on the role reluctantly at first. "I believe in this place and why we are here. I want it to continue," she said. "I will do my best."

Jiro was not happy that he was outvoted two to one among the twenty four students present. On the following day he gathered with Stanley and six others to determine a new course. Jiro's group decided to move to the Seattle area where an elderly aunt of one of the students lived. She was willing to allow them unlimited use of her large, empty beach house on San Juan Island. The beach house needed a lot of work but it was down the road from a small town with quaint shops and cafes. After the student's uncle died in 2004, the aunt stopped using the place, choosing to remain in her comfortable condo. The housing market was so poor that selling the beach house for a good price was futile. Repairs were prohibitive on her fixed income. By pooling their resources, the group would repair and remodel the place in short order. Jiro determined he would continue where the old man left off in an attempt to sustain his legacy as a true Buddha.

Marga and Jiro met with a lawyer to sign an agreement regarding ownership of the old man's property. Jiro would retain a fifteen percent share of the corporation based on a vague will in which the old man indicated that Marga and Jiro were to run the place if he died. He wrote it in Kanji ideograms that a professional contact on the Internet translated for them for a small fee.

Marga arranged for cremation.

Stanley was beside himself with grief and guilt, or at least he appeared to be.

Marga and Usagi sat up with him all night after the examiner revealed the evidence. In hindsight the young monk knew exactly what happened. "The bad mushrooms were near the good ones," he said. As he talked to Marga, he repeatedly revisited the mushroom gathering event as if trying to undo the past. "If only I had asked Jiro. I had a feeling that those were different. I had no idea they were poisonous. I cut and mixed them in the salad. It killed him. Death is final," he sputtered.

Before the funeral, Marga phoned the old man's relatives in Japan to announce his passing. Purely out of respect, she invited them to come. As expected, all of them politely declined to participate in any way. "He dishonored the family," is all one cousin would offer as an excuse. Apparently, he left a bad reputation in Japan. Also, the family had less interest when they discovered that the Center was in debt after a lawsuit. The calls confirmed for Marga that no one in Japan sponsored him as a legitimate teacher. He had merely taken family funds to set up his eccentric enterprise. The cousin suggested hiring a Buddhist priest he knew in Japan to officiate at the funeral. Marga knew that the traditional Buddhist fee would be exorbitant not to mention expense of travel. The Center simply could not afford it.

After the funeral service, Marga and her staff interred the old man's ashes in a shrine at the edge of the rock garden. In preparation for the ceremony, two days before it occurred, Jake and another monk built the shrine by forming river rocks and mortar into the shape of a small, elegant stupa or chorten.

"It may be the only stupa in the world built of river rocks," Jake said to his helper as they stood back to admire the finished product.

The stupa included a three-layered, stepped square base with a barrel middle section and a slim conical peak. The stony structure finished at four feet tall. They cemented a round, black stone on top. Jake left an opening in the middle for the reliquary urn of ashes that was sealed inside later with a matching stone and mortar.

The funeral was a hodgepodge of traditional ceremony and improvisation; perhaps a harbinger of what was to come if the commune was to survive. Marga's instincts were good. She surmised that old religions like new cults must adapt and adjust to the surrounding culture to thrive. Out of necessity Marga did the best she could to create a pleasant and memorable event. She finished with a haiku by the old man. Even in translation, Jake thought it had a weird eloquence. It felt right. He wrote it down in his journal:

Autumn winds howl
A great tree bends
Seed cones hit the ground far away.

You liked this kanshi side of the old man. He could recite and write from memory many poems composed by the great ones in his tradition. Basho! Issa! His calligraphy was superb. You did learn to appreciate something to take with you.
—11 October 2005

Jake agreed at the time with Marga that what mattered were the Buddha's teachings or the Dharma and not the flawed man that taught it. The Center had to return to the essentials of the Middle Way.

As Marga put it, we must be:
A lamp for those in darkness
A mother for children
A ferry for those in need of a boat
A fire to warm those who are cold
A garment for the naked (Buddhist saying)—8 December 2005

Despite the sheriff's final report, speculation continued among the students about the nature of the old man's death. Was it fate? Was he betrayed? Why the coincidence with the way the Buddha died? If he had Buddha consciousness, did he know he was eating deadly poison? If the latter, then he was a hero, a Socrates calmly accepting what fate brought to him. If someone intentionally poisoned him, then he could be a martyr. If he died by accident, then no one was to blame.

"Maybe it just happened," said one monk with Zen dispassion. "Accept it as one would accept a thought or image passing through the mind."

The flame on the candle—extinguished! Maybe this was the last lesson from the old man, the lesson of impermanence of the body and the imagined self.

Marga believed that many lessons would appear in time. She sought the positive message without allowing for grandiose speculation. She only noted that in dying and after his death the old man was still provoking the most profound questions among those he taught. The good from the old man's spirit will continue to preside over the commune to guide and protect. The old man's good work must go on. Forgive the bad work. Forget the bad behavior. Keep the good work. Keep the Buddha mind.

You sat there at the gathering after the funeral feeling empty and not holy. The others found the holy pulse and measured it among themselves. Your holiness died before the old man died. Why did you stay for two more years then? What hope were you hoping to find? You lived for the others, for their hopes, their gospel.

 You measured and gathered the rocks for the shrine. You took pleasure in building and you were attached to the finished product. You want to say you did that. The stupa's purpose had no purpose for a dead man's ashes. Ashes feel nothing. The living needed the stupa to reflect their feeling. The living told you how beautiful, how simple, how the old man would praise the effort. The shrine is for the living. The shrine houses nothing. Sunyata.—20 September 2007

Marga told Jake that the hush money cost the commune half its land or ten acres of prime property.

Hush hell. Somehow, the entire mess leaked to a nosey reporter from The Journal. —20 September 2007

Through it all, Marga never wavered. Marga gave Jiro's group permission to visit the shrine at the Center as long as they maintained respect for the new rules she established. Marga answered every reporter with a direct answer to every question. As best she could, she always told the facts and no more. Soon the questions faded. The accusations of cult faded along with the critics as positive reports on the commune's status ended further public curiosity. Marga took over gracefully but her graces had little influence over Jake's fate.

9   Retreat from Emptiness

Sanity's angel struggles to find you again.
Why would a spirit seek one man lost in metaphysical space?
Where else would an angel look?

You sit Buddha-like like The Thinker who is not the Buddha.
The Thinker sits on bronze rock at the Rodin Museum, an authentic bronze faking
    a naked man sitting on a faked rock.
The statue contemplates Hell's Gate by Rodin
What hell?
Three Fates dangle: grace, meaning, and temptation, above the hero's head as he
    contemplates the people imbedded in bronze and frozen in some kind of
    purgatory below.
Neither here, nor there. Purgatorio!
Ah Dante, Dante, Dante.

Where is judgment and where is Rodin's muse Michelangelo? Women on tour come
    and go from the museum thinking not of gates, thinking not of Michelangelo. Do
    they know? Do they know of Michelangelo?
There they go! They come and go.

Thoughts wander toward dakinis holding human skullcaps filled with elixir in
    one hand and a curved, sharp-as-hell hunting knife in the other. Nearly naked
    and sinuous nymphs with long messy hair move catlike in the brilliant night.
    Two tantalize you with a dark dance slowly swaying and lightly leaping rising
    floating toward your face. The more they leer through seducing eyes, the more you
    fear. Will they cut you to pieces again?

You cannot run where there is no ground to grip. You want to breathe but no air
enters parted lips. You scream soundlessly into no atmosphere. Yet the dancers
smile, even laugh as if hearing you, the taunted man.

Why do they appear?

What do you know? The sky-dancers are simultaneously terrifying and soothing,
slithering round and round you, daring you to touch what is both declared taboo
and tasty delicious. As if you could touch a wraith with other than thought stuff
for fingertip and tongue.
Think. Think. Think.

You do not want to know these dancers, do you? Yet you have no control. Where do
they come from?

They have knives.

This is crazy. There are no directions here, no signs, no patterns, nada. Is this just
mind stuff? They are nothing, yet these no things would test you. What power
must you demonstrate before the succubae slink away? Before ordinary mind
conquers without effort? Try to stop trying.

Close enough now, you feel her warm breath on your face and her silky hair drag
across your naked neck. Moist scent of delicate musk on skin runs up your nose.
Your intoxicated brain entertains a rush of floral ecstasies. The dancing Sirens
sweat; sweet, salty and sexy. You want her. You want her. You want her. Ssssssss...

Merde! So this is what ten years of meditation and struggle with celibacy got you?
Another vision of holy sluts!

162

You think-chant, 'sunyata, sunyata, sunyata' softly as the dakinis retreat into darkness
one after one until they disappear.

Someone strikes the large gong. A deep metal chord-like note moves in all directions
through the high desert competing with the rush of air through the pines and
the cedars.
Sesshin session over

This is over. You are out of here! You are out of here tomorrow.
Shanti, shanti, shanti, you are off to the wasteland.......... It is way past April.
—*14 September 2007*

Jake wrote the above after reading *The Wasteland* and *The Love Song of J. Alfred Prufrock* by T. S. Eliot, after his last attempt at Zen tranquility after thousands of attempts, after years of meditative effort. It was early autumn in 2007. Some things had changed in the five years after Jake took refuge and some things had not. Jake looked back over his recorded history for the first time. As he flipped through the pages of notes, he mused how often he questioned the same things over and over without resolution, how often he punted the deep questions into a future time, and how most things at the Center went in circles with the seasons and the serious questions faded by the way.

Along the high mountain slopes near Taos the masses of quaking aspen created yellow swaths among dark evergreens. Dull green and silvery blue Chamisa shrubs that some locals called *rabbit brush* flowered bright yellow once again. Migrating Monarch butterflies from Colorado fluttered south over the Center on their magical way to the Transvolcanic Range in Mexico. Jake watched them fly high above flickering in the late afternoon sunlight.

The keisaku continued to assist the teacher at the Center but only in measured, traditional strokes. The new director Marga really did whack him that last day but only enough to spark attention. He had dozed off.

The notes above were part of what Jake wrote in his journal two weeks before he ended his decade with the Center. In further notes, Jake recalled how he helped to build the Zen garden. He raked the sand around the rocks regularly, ritualistically, as if in meditation. Some intentional communities called free labor *seva*, he wrote This one called it *samuwabi*. The old man named the commune *Samuwabi Center*—the Center, for short. The old man said samuwabi stood for "work-duty" and "refined poverty." Traditional interpretations of that translation were whatever the old man told them they were. Jake added a note about his garden work:

> *You comb sandy spaces between rocks unnaturally set to harmonize naturally with beauty in the old man's mind. You comb sand with a bamboo rake. One person could arrange our rocks thus. We depended on the old man. We knew nothing. We wanted to learn. The old man's mind is beauty here. We agree with the old man's mind and the rocks as they are without the old man's mind to mind them. How can we disagree with rocks? The rocks never disagree with us. Your mind is empty. Your mind cannot disagree. The old man told you when to move the rocks.*
>
> *Why did you move the rocks?—1 October 2007*

After the old man died, Marga's newly acquired charges at the Center were a ragtag group of more or less twenty white American and European converts and Usagi, the one half-breed Jicarilla Apache fellow.

During the two years under Marga's firm yet compassionate rule, Jake remained ambivalent and unresolved about everything. He had to leave. Things in his head were getting worse. The dakini with knives vision was a sign that things were getting to him. His feelings for Marga had changed. They were partners for so many years. Now there was this strange tension between authority and attraction. His primal feelings remained unrequited out of respect for her dedication. She was still as unapproachable as a goddess. He had to bow out to avoid an inevitable clash of

164

emotions, if not with hers, then those within.

"Marga, I need a real break. Not just a month or so. This could be it." Jake caught her steady gaze. She was on to him not being here nor there. "No, this *is* it," he added emphatically.

Marga looked at him quietly. At that moment she made an effort to read his mood and his intent. He seemed uncharacteristically vulnerable and truly serious. "I felt this coming. I saw you leaving a couple of years ago. I'm surprised you stayed so long but I am grateful you did. We're going to miss you."

She motioned for Jake to take a seat near her under the portal. She sat on the old, turquoise-colored rocker. He stopped at the top step, and then slid down onto the deck with his back resting against the sturdy log post. He flicked a large soldier ant off his boot. He checked around for more ants but found none.

"You? Miss me? Haven't you learned anything either? Desire and attachment lead to hell in this world. You know, lately I've been having visions of swimming naked with you?"

"You're a donkey's uncle. You know what I mean."

"Yes. I know. I know." Jake lowered his head. "Because of that I find it hard to leave. You, uh..." He hesitated to say more.

"Me, what? Say it," she insisted.

Jake looked away into the setting sun. Golden red streaks appeared in purple forms above deep blue hills. Another enchanting sunset in the Land of Enchantment, he thought. "I'm going to miss this place too. You have found a way to be here. The sun rises and sets with you here. It revolves around you. Every day the wind moves through the trees to greet you. You embody the Center. Without you the others would soon drift away."

"I can't tell any more when you're being sarcastic," Marga protested. "But somehow, this time, I think you want to mean it," she said clearly avoiding his romantic flattery.

"You know what I mean. We bought into the bigger thing. I know I wanted to. This was Buddhism and more. It was a way to the ultimate meaning. We felt it. You still do. Somehow you transcended all the old man's bullshit. Ah, bullshit." Jake laughed at his characterization. The old man liked to say *bullshit*.

"Now you're mocking me. C'mon, Jake, stop it."

"No, no, that's not it. I'm laughing at how much we projected onto so little—on him, I mean." Jake ceased his merriment and collected himself. He turned to face Marga. "You did it though," he continued. "You out-Buddha'd the old man. Somehow you were able to glean meaning from the flawed messenger. I think he saw that too. I'll have to give him credit for that much. Maybe you reminded him of what he lost a long time ago. He chose you."

"He chose Jiro as his second, not me."

"No. He chose Jiro just to save face because he was a fucking Japanese chauvinist pig. But privately, he held you in higher esteem."

"Watch your Japanese," Marga scolded.

"Gomenasai," Jake said apologetically.

Marga resisted the reality of him leaving. She felt a need to convince him to stay. "If you saw the bigger thing or bought into it, why the confusion? If this is real, it's real for good. You know the teaching. We're not perfect here but we're here to work toward right behavior, right speech, and compassion. You said it once. I really liked what you said: *Here, we can choose to be poets refining the language of our lives to help ease the suffering of others*," she said.

"Yeah, well, sometimes I'm full of shit too. I feel unsettled, even damaged by this. I don't know anymore." Jake picked up a stone and tossed hard it into a bush.

"The Buddha said we must doubt—continue to question everything," she argued.

"Sure. So did Socrates and Nietzsche. One ended up with a death sentence and the other went crazy. Listen, I don't want to argue with you. You win. You won. I lost. I'm lost. The old man stole my drive for this sort of questioning. I tried for over two years after he died to be where you are with this. I can't do it anymore."

Marga's sadness did not show on her face. Her eyes fixed on his for a gentle moment. "I often wondered why you did not leave earlier, even before the sex revelations and lawsuits," Marga said with a hint of shame.

Jake knew what she was referring to. Marga looked away from Jake. She was not aware until later how badly or often the old man beat a number of the men bloody with the stick. She did not know that Jake and maybe Usagi got the worst of it, not until much later, after the old man died. None of the men went to a clinic for treatment but they should have. Jake's back bore several scars from sessions of crazy wisdom sesshin with the old man. Usagi had one long, ragged mark across his back. Some wounds did not heal well.

Marga continued, "You said you accepted the beatings as an adjustment to your wrong thinking about suffering. Like the others, you said that the next day you bowed each time before Roshi in gratitude." Recalling an Assembly she missed, Marga asked, "What was it you asked Roshi again? You thought it set him off for some reason. We never really talked about it."

"During a new moon gathering, I asked him in front of the other guys if he noted any similarity between the teaching of Christ and the Buddha about suffering, or something to that effect. He said there were parallels but did not answer directly—in fact, I think he avoided the topic—but he did say he would show me someday. Now I think that was his way of showing us his frustration. At the time I wanted to think he wanted me to know, Zen style or without knowing, that Christ suffered and not to think about what for. The "what for" was not important for me in the end. No one can atone for someone else's wrongdoing in Zen practice. If Jesus was God, then God worked out his own salvation on the cross. Now, today, I think that was only in my head. I think the old goat just wanted to beat the crap out of us because he was drunk and having a bad day. He wanted us to stop asking such questions, questions he had no good answer for, questions that irritated him. He may have been frustrated with my lack of total surrender. I don't know. I do know that what he did was criminal; not compassionate."

Marga looked away into the sinking sun.

"That bothers me," she said. "Some were hurt more than others. And I do not mean just physically. But it was you who gave me hope when all that came down with the lawsuits and then his death. You said we can still make this work."

"That's the point, Marga. That's the point. I said it before. I might have gone soon after he died if not for you. You lived what I wanted. Lately even that's changed. I find myself wanting to take you away with me. I don't know if it is because I'm afraid to enter the abyss without someone or if I'm jealous of this place and all it means to you. It is your lover. Please don't take that wrong. I repeat, you are the one thing, the one person, I cannot reject about this. I can't tell if this is just my desire to rescue you from an empty road or my need to feel secure in my decision to leave. No matter what, there is a price to pay. You lose what I give to this place and I lose all my effort here. Once I leave here, here is no longer real."

Then, a bit theatrically, he pointed to her and said, "And you own my soul."

Jake was referring to his enduring, brotherly love for her, one they discussed and accepted early in their friendship.

"You've been reading about the troubadours again," Marga smirked recalling how Jake once compared his affection for her to Courtly love. "Shall your Lady give you her white scarf as you depart on your quest? Do not dare return without the Grail, Sir Jake! Are there any grails in Philly?" Marga looked at him mockingly with a scowl. Jake blushed as he recalled that embarrassing exchange between them nearly nine years before. "Well, I'm flattered," she continued, "but I can't be responsible for your bloody soul. We Buddhists don't claim to have souls."

Jake shook his head slowly, seeing he was caught in a language game again. "You got me!"

He would miss her. Marga was a special woman. He had grown to like her on every level that a man might like a woman yet his respect for her ruled every desire.

"Where do you think this is all going?" he asked her.

"You mean the Center?" Marga quizzed.

"Yeah—what else would I mean?"

"The criminal investigation into his death," she answered.

"No. Not that. I can't see any more coming of it. It's been two years. And the sheriff here could care less about our weird guru."

"I hope so." Marga stood up to stretch. After breathing in and out deeply, she gazed at the dark horizon. "I see the Center lasting as long as we can renew basic principles and live them here. We want it to be a safe and pleasant place for people to explore these Middle Path things with us; maybe not as ambitiously as Roshi. Maybe I'm naïve."

A coyote's sharp yipping pierced the air around the two friends. More coyotes answered creating an eerie choir of wild things celebrating in the distant hills. Nothing unusual for that part of the country but the noise stirred Jake to ask about a missing black cat. "Hey, where's old Maggie been lately?"

Marga shrugged as she looked in the direction of the coyote choir. "Not like her to be away for this long, is it?"

Marga wistfully recalled the little black cat that appeared at the Center soon after she arrived. She shook her head in sadness. "I'm afraid she's been killed."

Jake stood up with her and laid a hand on her shoulder, giving it a squeeze. They faced the emerging stars in the western sky and said nothing for a long few minutes. Silences like this were not awkward at the Center. Meditation was a way of life whenever and however one got into it. After the simple pause, Marga touched Jake's shoulder to indicate that she was going back to her cabin. Jake watched her disappear into the darkness.

Alone with his thoughts, he faced the steely, gray-purple sky for a few more minutes until all color drained from the horizon. With hands in his pockets and eyes looking down, Jake strolled over the rise along a dirt path that led to the men's side of the bunkhouse. As he stepped under the portal onto the wooden deck, he startled a gray wind scorpion. The hideous little critter scurried past his boot. Jake took notice of the arachnid that some locals called *Niña de la Tierra*. He knew the enduring myth that these misnamed *children of the earth* were venomous to humans and a bad omen.

Local legends not only confused them with scorpions but also with Mormon crickets that inspired the Cootie Bug toys. Despite their menacing appearance and aggressive movement (they never walk or move slowly but seem to glide on the ground like the wind) the opposite was true. Wind scorpions fed on spiders and other small creatures but were harmless to animals the size of cats much less humans. Jake watched wind scorpions stop dead in their tracks to square off with the cat. The standoff lasted a mere second. Maggie was never intimidated. She easily caught and ate those that ventured inside.

"Who knows if she caught any outdoors," he said to no one. "She was not around to get this one." Jake leaned into the snug front door to pop it open. Inside, he saw his good friend sitting at the dining table. "Yo, Usagi. Why up?"

"Marg told me you may be gone by tomorrow. You want to talk?" "Sure." Jake noticed the cat litter box in the corner. It was clean and empty. "Hey, have you seen Maggie around lately?"

"Not lately. Why?"

"I haven't seen her in ten days, maybe. Not like her. Just saw a wind scorpion, or whatever you call those ugly bugs, on the deck. Maggie snacks on them."

"Earlier in the week one of the girls thought she heard a cat scream out there. She said the coyotes got her. Sorry, bro. I didn't want to say anything."

That confirmed what Marga said. Jake closed his eyes, letting the idea of no more Maggie settle in. "Another attachment, eh?" he said half to himself. "What the hell. She's really gone. Damn it." He felt like crying.

Usagi offered to make tea. "Here, take a sip." Usagi noticed that his friend had teared up, but he knew it was not all about the cat. Everything was changing and something was lost.

"Ten years is a long time, homes," Usagi said with a rasp in his voice. After clearing his throat he said, "Love knows not its own depth until the hour of separation."

"Where'd you get that, bro?" Jake remarked with a laugh while wiping away the tears.

"Kahlil Gibran, man," Usagi said condescendingly as if Jake should have known.

Jake looked surprised but said nothing. Usagi never quoted anything to him before.

170

"Smells like some of your Mormon tea," Jake quipped as he sat down. He stared at his feet for a few seconds, and then he leaned forward to grab his left boot. He pulled it off and slid it across the floor past the doormat. It stopped next to the empty litter box.

"Hey," Usagi retorted, "this is *squaw* tea from the popotillo. Mormons ripped *us* off."

"Yeah, and you ripped it back off the Mormons. Isn't that from the stash that Cindy gathered months ago?"

Usagi did not answer. He concentrated on pouring the finished brew through a bamboo strainer into a gray mug with no handle. Then he poured some for himself in a similar plane mug. The mugs at the Center were custom made to reflect the Zen tradition. A thankful guest created and donated fifty of them from his pottery shop in Tesuque. The eight-ounce cups appeared as a set, yet each one was unique with slight, *natural* irregularities. The tea shrub was *Ephedra nevadensis* used as a tonic and tea throughout Mexico and the Southwest by Indians since ancient times. Marga asked Cindy to stock a variety of store-bought teas as well as locally gathered herbs. Cindy was the herbalist among them. Usagi was using store-bought tea. Jake saw the open box on the counter. Usagi knew he did. Their conversation about the tea was intentionally ludicrous and it eased the tensions of the moment.

The friends raised their mugs in appreciation of one another. Offering only brief, affirmative nods, they took short sips. After setting his cup carefully onto the table, Jake leaned over to tug on the remaining boot. He pulled it off and tossed it across the room next to the other one. As he straightened up, he noticed Usagi looking past him.

"What are you staring at?" Jake turned his head. He saw nothing odd about the counter and cabinets in Usagi's line of vision.

"I see you are not done with this place. You will carry it with you," Usagi said laconically.

"No, I'm done with it. Been thinking about doing this for two, three years. Gotta go, Usagi." Jake looked away then glanced over at his worn boots before whispering as if to himself, "Gotta go."

"You going grow back your hair, bro?" Usagi noted that Jake's head and face stubble was beyond almost bald looking.

Usagi, Jake and a few other men at the Center had a habit of shaving up once a week. The bald monk look was not a requirement but it caught on as a sign of commitment. The old man was delighted with those who shaved. He said it showed detachment—not to mention imitation of him. To compensate for missing hair most who took refuge wore colorful knit caps from Mexico when it was cold. When they worked in the hot sun, simple straw hats served them well. Usagi retained a scraggily mustache and goatee. He still looked more Indian than anything else despite his bald head. Jake on the other hand could grow a thick Polish beard but chose to remain clean shaven as a monk.

"I hadn't thought about it. I'm not sure what I'll do—we're not supposed to care, right? To shave or not to shave is not really a question for me any more."

Usagi wondered aloud, "What's right? It's all style. Right's what lacks suffering is what the old man said. And that's all in your head. *When you in right mind, then you enlightened, umm.*" Usagi grunted after his last remark, imitating the old man who often grunted after finishing a pithy comment. "You know, Jake, the old timer had something. He may have lost his way, but I think he had some of what Buddha meant. That's what I'm holding onto here—at least for now."

Jake leaned back into his chair. He rubbed the fuzz on his face with his left hand as he looked up at the ceiling. Then he leaned forward for a few seconds folding his hands on the table while tapping his thumbs together. He brought his left hand back under his chin and continued. "I don't know if he had anything. He was colorful; I'll give him that. The more I looked into Buddhism these past two years, the more I see how eccentric the old guy was. His teacher followed the teachings of a Japanese saint named Nichiren who lived over seven hundred years ago."

He paused to see if his friend was paying attention. "I think what happened here happened a lot worse in a lot of places. I was reading about the *San Francisco Zen Center* started by Suzuki in the Sixties, and later led by his successor Richard

Baker. Baker really screwed up a thriving movement with more of the same crap that the old man did here—abuse of sex and power. You know, the old man only started calling what he taught Zen after noting that Americans identified Buddhism with that term. Books about *the Zen* of anything sell here. He knew how to push our buttons even though he had no training in Zen proper. He was an opportunist. His fellow Nichiren followers reject Zen. I think his young assistant knew it and that's why he eventually moved back to Japan—among other reasons."

Usagi grasped what Jake was getting at—they had similar discussions before but he did not know how extensively his friend had studied it.

"We have essential Buddhist teachings right here in books," Usagi commented. "The old man never kept us from reading the stuff. I don't think he was hiding anything except, maybe, who he was shtuping at the time. How did you figure that he was teaching from a—what did you call him? Nicher something? Did you say Neechee?"

"No, not Nietzsche, dumb ass." Immediately after cursing at Usagi, Jake realized that his friend was playing on his earlier devotion to Nietzsche.

"Sorry. Nichiren found the essence of the Buddha's teaching in the Lotus Sutra. Then he devised a mantra that captured that essence, you know, the one the old man said we could use for meditation."

Usagi recalled, "Yeah. *Nam Myoho Renge Kyo*. I tried it for a while but I prefer to just sit. The old man said it was no big deal whether I use a mantra or not."

"Sure, I know. But that is what I mean by opportunist. He was re-inventing his teaching as he went along, as he noted our reactions. I also think he did not want to be identified as a cult like the Nichiren Society of America group was, so he avoided the connection. They push that mantra like it has magical power. I believe members of his family follow Nichiren teaching which is why they did not like what he was doing here."

"What was he doing here in their eyes?"

"Creating a kind of personality cult. I mean look what happened. We helped edit and publish his lectures in Buddhist and New Age magazines. He claimed that book would revolutionize modern Buddhism. We gave away more copies than we sold. Some revolution! And I even helped build a goddamned shrine to him."

"Marga doesn't dote over the shrine thing like Jiro does," Usagi argued. "It's practically a garden ornament now. We're open about the old man's indiscretions if anyone asks."

"Yeah, but who ever asks anymore? I can't figure Marga. She really wants this place to become something significant. I guess as long as people come here and have a good experience, she'll keep it going. For one thing, she's in line with Nichiren's radical teaching that women can be enlightened Buddhas too."

"That's awesome for an Asian guy way back then, no? I mean, to accept women as equals in the enlightenment game. You've done some serious booking, bro."

"Yes, well the Buddha played that game with women 2,500 years ago," Jake reminded him.

Usagi got up to fill his cup with more tea. He paused just before pouring. While staring into his empty mug he asked, "So what's authentic Buddhism then?"

Jake leaned back in his chair to ponder the question. Joints in his chest cracked as he stretched his torso with his hands clasped behind his head. He leaned forward again.

"I don't know. I was reading Takeuchi's *The Heart of Buddhism*. His view feels right. It has a wide range, kind of like non-sectarian Christianity. I don't know."

Usagi looked over at his good friend. He thought about Jake's intensity.

"What's to know, man? It's about getting by as well as we can but with more awareness. That's all I use this for."

"That's all? You know, I wonder lately what you as a Native American—well, the half that's native—finds here that you do not find in your culture. That one weekend we spent together a few years ago with your mom on the rez, you know, that was an eye-opener for me. Remember, you said you felt awkward, almost ashamed of what I might see. I thought it was great, even if your step-dad was half drunk at dinner. I was not expecting something out of a Hollywood movie, you know. That one fellow, your old uncle who is kind of like a shaman, he surprised me when he said he goes to

Catholic mass every Sunday. He seemed completely at peace with being Apache and Catholic. What do you think of that?"

Usagi returned to his seat. He stared into his teacup and swirled the liquid around a few times to cool it before answering. "I thought about it. Mom never talked religion, so I can't say I understand my uncle's take on it. He took me along with his son, an older cousin, to the Catholic Mission in Lumberton once but I didn't like it and never went again. He taught a religion class to kids once a week back then. My cousin followed the Church for a while but dropped it when he went off to college in Albuquerque. My family hardly participated in religion, not even in Apache rituals. But uncle, he's another story."

"Is there a strong following of the old ways there yet?" Jake asked. "I guess that's what I meant."

"Besides dances and powwows at times with other Indian nations, not much. Maybe it's enough. People on the rez still do the adolescent initiation. My uncle has a mountain spirit costume and mask for ritual dances and ceremonies. There's a core of people who do that, but my uncle says it's a struggle for him to keep it going. My sister and I went through the adolescent initiation." Usagi took a sip of his tea. "There's nothing like organized Buddhism or Christianity with Apache spirituality but my uncle thinks the same old spirit that Apache priests worship is active in the Catholic mass. He said his role model is Black Elk, you know, the famous Lakota seer. Black Elk, he said, went to mass every Sunday. My uncle met him once. You grew up Catholic, no?"

"Yep. Mom enrolled us in a Catholic grade school." Then Jake chose to change the topic. "How's that online course you're taking? What is it again, statistics?"

Usagi nodded slowly in affirmation as he sipped his tea again. He knew his friend was uneasy about the Church. Jake knew that Usagi was pursuing sociology or psychology or both with a plan get an advanced degree. His plan lately was to return to the reservation to help troubled Indian youth. Using grants and a tribal loan, Usagi took on this project some years after he joined the Center. He had Jake to thank for encouraging him.

When Usagi joined the Center he was running from his roots, or lack thereof, seeking a change. Growing up without his real father and with a chronically depressed mother left him feeling alienated. Living at the Zen center for Usagi was like being far away in a foreign land with new people and ideas. He used the opportunity to get a fresh look at himself.

"I plan to use some of the single-parent kids at the rez for subjects in a study. I plan to follow up with them every five years or so—see what happens to language, culture, and career. They live in two worlds, maybe three. Many are torn between what's left of Indian tradition and how it is being absorbed into secular America and the international scene. Since the Internet gadgets and the new globalism, we all live in a same world, Apache people included."

Jake thought about his father, born in Poland and arriving at age five with his family in America. His father could speak kitchen Polish but Jake and his brother knew only a few words. Apaches come in many forms, he thought. Just like Poles go from Polish to Polish-Americans to Americans. Yet, it was not the same thing.

"So, how do you see it, Usagi? Are you Apache, Apache-Jew, Apache-American or American?"

"My mother was going to name me after her great grandfather who was called Ahanday."

Usagi stopped to see if Jake had any boorish comments. Jake gave no indication of forming a wisecrack, so the Indian continued.

"It means *a long way* or *far off*. I think he was a wanderer, so he got that name. But she named me Waylon after Waylon Jennings because she liked his music when I was born."

"Your last name—Largo—it's not Apache, is it?"

"One great grandfather adopted it, probably from Spanish influence. Many Indians retain Spanish surnames. Santiago Largo was a famous Jicarilla who helped to secure our reservation. Maybe he was related to my ancestors, but I doubt it."

"I thought about this a lot last year—about our identities," Jake continued, feeling less constrained now to talk about his background. "Here we are trying to be

176

Buddhists yet what does that mean? Here we're taught to *empty* ourselves of our past. Is it, 'I'm Polish, but I am not?' Like you, I cannot speak my native language except for a few words, so what's left? My culture in Poland is tied in with the Catholic Church, but how? Most Poles today probably could not give a proper account of their religion. Last year on my way back from a job in Santa Fe, I was passing through Abiquiu. I followed a tip from Fowler to visit the *Christ in the Desert Monastery*, you know, the one across the way from Ghost Ranch. I never said anything to anyone at the Center about it. It took me an hour over bad roads to get there, but it was worth it. Around twelve monks were there with some guests at the time. Impressive place."

Jake explained how his interlude at the monastery helped eventually seal his decision to leave the Center.

"So you snuck in to the enemy camp, eh?" Waylon kidded.

"Worse. I was embarrassed because the enemy knew more about Zen Buddhism than I did. Talking with this guy all night, the four hours of fishing with this guy was almost surreal. Here we thought the old man was such a special, spiritual person when an average Protestant priest by comparison was far less egocentric and better equipped to teach Buddhism! I did more listening than anything. He did not condemn Buddhism or diminish it in any way. I asked him what made Christianity work for him. He laughed. He said he would get back to me on that."

"You mean he has doubts?"

"He struggles like most of us. That surprised me."

"How so?" Usagi perked up to listen.

"Well, for one thing he pondered if allowing young men and women into monasteries or a clerical life is wise. He talked about how in Hindu culture the choice to renounce is the last or fourth stage of life. One should approach that stage only after being a productive member of society. He said that made sense, that maybe he should have been more productive as a worker first, maybe raised a family. I argued that after all, Buddha made that mistake too—he left his wife and young child before fulfilling his duty. Brian said if it was a mistake, he's sure God has a sense of humor and will forgive him."

Usagi laughed and he continued to laugh aloud. "Oh, yes. God must have a sense of humor. Look at us—different kinds of fool. That's good, bro, that's good. I like this guy."

"Well, you might not want to like him too much. I mean, he admits he's a loner. It's one reason he's attracted to Catholic monasteries. He says the monks understand guys like him."

"Is he gay?" Usagi asked with a smirk.

"No, wise ass. He doesn't fit that stereotype."

"My uncle thought I was gay for joining this place. Then, how does the guy deal with sexual urges?"

"Many of the monks he's gotten to know found ways to elevate their sexual inclinations in a steady, sacred lifestyle that transcends sexual behavior."

"Sounds like yoga, bro."

"Maybe it is."

"The old man wanted us to achieve that same thing, no?"

"Yes, but he was hardly a role model."

"And we were hardly model students."

"Except Marga—maybe Cindy, and maybe the cook."

"Oh, yes, the cook," Usagi repeated with a serious inflection. "He baled on other gurus. This time, he was going to do it right!" Usagi took a deep breath and exhaled. "Sacred is as sacred does," he said. The Indian turned his head, took another deep breath, held one nostril shut and blew a load of snot into the sink. "But did you catch any fish?" He turned his head again to blow out the other nostril and then he turned on the faucet to flush it.

"What?" Jake asked with a hint of bewilderment.

"Fish. You were fishing."

"Oh, yeah, sure. We got a few, but I truly sucked at fly fishing. He snagged three good-sized ones for the monks," Jake affirmed proudly, recalling how grateful the monks were. He next fixed his eyes on his friend. "What do you make of this guy, I mean Brian?"

The Indian felt the seriousness of the question. "He had his vision and followed it. He's taking it to the limit. I admire him. Lucky man if he's happy."

"Yes, he's a lucky man if luck has anything to do with it. He would call it grace."

Jake rose from his chair and walked back to the bunkroom he had been sharing with Usagi for the past few months. He came back with a shoebox and a bag. He took the lid off the box to examine his new white sneakers that he bought from a Walmart. They were not laced. Jake removed them and began to lace them on the table.

"I'm done with those boots," he said as he raised his chin toward the door. "No snakes to worry me where I'm going."

Usagi quietly watched as Jake carefully laced the white laces. The clean scent of new sneaker rubber drifted around the table.

"I bought new pants and a jacket at Walmart too—both on sale. It all cost me only thirty-two bucks!"

Jake opened the bag and proudly revealed the khaki slacks and a turquoise and white windbreaker.

"That's you all right. You can put it back in the bag now."

"Hey, no one asked you for fashion advice."

"Maybe you need some queer eye, bro! You are going back East in seriously geek attire."

"Time for me to crash. We can say our good byes in the morning." Jake walked over to his boots, picked them up, and threw them in the trash can.

"When was the last time a snake attacked you out here?" Usagi asked sardonically.

Jake thought about it for a couple of seconds. "I surprised a rattler once along a trail near Heron Lake."

"So, what happened?"

"It was poised to strike, I froze, and it slowly backed away from me."

"I guess the boots could have saved you if it didn't, eh?"

"I was wearing shorts and sandals."

Usagi shook his head slightly. "See you in the morning, bro." He paused a moment before quipping, "Those sneakers don't go with the jacket." Jake went to bed without another word.

Before Jake awoke at sunrise, Usagi already sat in meditation in the common room in his old jeans and a red T-shirt. It was 6 a.m. He had slipped silently from the bunk room a half hour earlier to join a handful of others. Morning group meditation was no longer mandatory at the Center unless one was attending or leading a workshop. There was no workshop happening at the time that week. Some of the permanent residents were away. The common breakfast was scheduled for 7:30.

Jake ceased his meditation ritual weeks before but knew where Usagi was, so he waited for him in the dining area. No one else was there. When Usagi appeared, Jake had two black espressos ready. Usagi retained his meditative silence as he grabbed a chair to join Jake who was already seated. They sipped the coffees in unison.

The silence was soon broken by a familiar female voice coming from the side hallway.

"Where's mine?" Marga asked as she came in the through the back doorway.

Usagi immediately offered her his coffee as he rose from his seat. "Here, take it, I'll make another one."

"Looks like you already started on it. No thanks. Sit, sit—please. I prefer one with steamed milk anyway. I'll make it," she said as she stopped at the new *Jura* machine with all the gadgets on it.

The coffee maker was one of the few luxuries at the Center. Marga found that guests appreciated a few luxuries. After the old man died, they installed another, larger hot tub outdoors with a stylish, eight foot tall coyote fence surrounding it. The Center's residents were allowed some discretionary use of these features, but a few of the men took liberties when mama was not looking. She caught Usagi more than once lounging in the tub during guest hours. Punishment, if one could call it that, was extra stints at washing dishes and cleaning the commodes. For a Zen monk in right mind all was *chop wood, carry water* anyway, and that was Usagi's attitude, but mostly it was he and Marga playing cat and mouse.

With her small mug in hand, Marga joined the men at the table. Jake looked quizzically at a relaxed Usagi who seemed to know what this was about. Marga spoke up.

"I came by to give you something—well, two things—from all of us as a farewell tribute. There's some money in an envelope in your car. We can't afford much, but please take it as a token of appreciation."

Marga raised her hand to stop Jake from saying anything until she was done. Then she held up a white bag. "And here, ta da, is our new T-shirt advertising the Center!" Marga opened the white bag to unfurl a charcoal grey cotton garment decorated with a silk screened white Japanese symbols on front. The ideograms said *kensho* for enlightenment. On the left sleeve was a small logo with the Center's name and address.

"Nice. Thanks a lot, Marg, to you and everyone."

Over the years Jake worked hard to improve the place for practically nothing. He was not expecting anything, so his appreciation was genuine.

"What about a monogrammed mug and baseball cap?" he asked.

"We'll mail them to you when they get here," Usagi said without smiling.

"You serious? What's going on here? I never thought we'd bend to a becoming capitalist enterprise," Jake quipped. "Where's the purity?"

"Hey, bro," Usagi retorted, "soon we will go public. Wanna buy some stock before you go?"

Jake got up as if to walk out the door. "I think I left some money in an envelope in the car—be right back."

"Stop it," Marga interjected noting that the tiresome banter between these two would typically get more ridiculous. "The T-shirts happened because so many of our guests wanted to take something home with them. Forget that. I have more to say before everyone arrives for breakfast, and I know you want to get going. Please, sit down, Jake."

Jake dutifully sat. "Yes, mama, I'm listening."

"Is there anything you haven't told me? I do not want you to leave with any grudges or misunderstandings, if we can do anything about it."

Jake thought for a few seconds. He thought about asking her what happened to Sensei's cognac stash, but thought better of it. "Well, two things. When those two women sued the old man, why were we responsible for his misbehavior? I mean, we could have left him hang all by himself."

Marga was definite. "We could have but without him we could have lost everything. He still controlled the assets here. Maybe it was selfish of the board, but we were also exercising some compassion for him as well as the two women."

"Compassion?" Jake sighed. "That one, the one with the silly laugh—I mean Taylor—she seemed almost cynical about the whole thing. What was it with her? I never got to know her well in the short time she was here."

"She came to me crying one time after visiting with the old man," Usagi said. "We walked around a while talking. She told me what he was doing, that they were screwing around, and that he grabbed and shook her when she said she was feeling something was wrong with the sex thing. She stopped buying into his tantra bullshit by then, and wanted to stop seeing him. She thought he was going to kick her out."

"So, you talked her into staying—she did stay for another six months or so, at least until she found out Nancy was screwing him too all that time. What did you say to convince her?" Jake wondered.

"Not much," Usagi offered. Then he stopped talking but with a satisfied smile on his face as if he recalled something pleasant. He shook his head slowly from side to side.

Marga and Jake glanced at one another.

"You didn't," Marga chimed in. "You did her too?"

"Well, she was so unhappy at the time—hell, she came on to me," Usagi said sheepishly. "We were in the hot tub and, well, you know, she needed some comforting."

"Great," Jake retorted. "What else did I miss out on—and who else was playing house here while old Jake was playing monk?"

He raised his eyebrows as he looked at Marga. Her scowl was his answer.

"Sorry," he said. "I just feel more of a fool now—thanks, Usagi, you prick." Jake smiled, and then laughed quietly to himself. "Was she good?"

Marga quickly stopped Usagi from answering by saying, "Okay, okay, let's put this to rest. Maybe Taylor was a slut and just out to get revenge for something, but Nancy had a bona fide complaint. He manipulated a lot of money out of her with flattery and the special tantra sex in the bedroom. Roshi called her his *dakini*." Marga was referring to a Tibetan tradition of the holy consort that services a Lama's spiritual and perhaps in a degenerate form as a mistress, sexual needs. Dakini means *traveler in space* or *sky dancer*. "He told Nancy the same thing that she embodied a goddess or special sky dancer. I talked to Nancy at length about it after she spoke with Taylor. She was really upset then and for good reason. Nancy also came to me crying—we did not have sex!" Marga was looking right at Usagi when she said it.

"Marga, you can be so self-righteous at times," said Usagi, "but I know what you mean. I was wrong. I admit it. Can I go clean the toilets now?"

She ignored his wise crack. She raised her cup with both hands and took a sip. At that moment Marga's fine Asiatic face took on a maturity Jake had not noted before. She was a real leader, he thought, but she was not *the* leader as if no one else could take her place. The old man was different.

A handful of his devotees could not accept Marga's less charismatic yet assertive style. They said she was not a true Zen teacher. Five or six rebels eventually left, all within a few months after the old man died. Two traveled to India to check out a famous guru despite all the negative press about the miracle worker. The others, according to Jake:

A few felt fine inside the circle slightly open but when it opened wider some saw a broken circle. They saw the Buddha's wheel broken but it was not the Buddha's wheel.—2 May 2007

"Jake, talk to me more about those beatings that day from Roshi. I thought about it more after we talked last night. I thought about it again. One of the guys that left after that was bitter. I heard he's in with a Jewish cult-watch organization now that might publish his story. How bad was it, really?" Marga crossed her arms over her breasts as if feeling a chill.

"When it happened it seemed so correct. We were already conditioned to expect some hard whacks from the old man. That day I think he whacked the others five or six times each before he got to me. He hit me maybe ten, fifteen times. I nearly passed out. Usagi, what did you see? I know you got up to stop the old bastard."

Usagi scratched his head above his left ear. "Bro, he was in a rage, a silent rage. Something was pissing him off that day. That was beyond a lesson. He looked like he was taking batting practice on your back and hitting for the fences. I was about to grab him from behind, but he turned around. He and I just looked at each other—a face-off. You all were sitting. He turned and walked away in a huff. Man, was I sore. We all were. Some of the guys, like me, were a little bloody. But you, bro, parts of your back looked like raw meat once we got your robe off in the bunkhouse."

"I never did thank you for butting in. Odd how we all rationalized it, isn't it?"

"Rationalize? Usagi, can you elaborate?" Marga asked.

"Pretty simple really," Usagi offered. "Once we bought into the karma talk we understood the beating as a blessing. He was helping us to advance our spiritual warrior lives. We all figured that Jake had a bigger blessing coming to him," Usagi said facetiously. "Besides, Roshi was soused on sake at the time. As I look back on it now, he had a lot of hang-ups just like the rest of us."

"Yeah, we were soused too, on Buddha nature," Jake said under his breath but loud enough for his companions to hear. Then he spoke up. "Marga, you found out from his family in Japan that the old man was into the Yakuza when he was a young man. You said his tattoos and the missing part of his little finger had something to do with it. A couple of the men here, like his live-in cook, said he had to cut off his finger and give it to the mob boss to show his loyalty. I found out that it's just the opposite. Disgruntled Yakuza members agree to cut off a finger to get out of the gang. Maybe it's a sign they still own a piece of you even if you leave. The old man was a complex character. In some ways I wish we knew more about his real history."

"Yes, his past might explain a lot. Who knows what else he was hiding. His family remains reserved. Maybe they have something to hide too," Marga sighed. "Anyway, I don't want to hear from any more reporters but if I have to talk about his behavior, I want to get it as right as possible."

Jake looked at her. Her eyes saw in his that talk about the old man's past was done.

"So, Marga, I think you want to know if I have any hard feelings. Look, I am not blaming anyone here for anything. The old man is gone. I respect what you have done to change things."

"I know that you are not blaming us," she said. "But you've got to have some anger or deep feeling. Are you going to be okay? You said earlier there was something else that bothered you. What was it?"

"I can't remember. Listen, I'll be okay. Who knows? I may meet an angel down the road if I need help."

Usagi took a last sip of his coffee before turning his gray cup upside down. He tapped on it with a fingernail as if it were a drum.

Jake stood up to signal that he was ready to go. His two friends stood up with him. Jake slipped into his new turquoise jacket. He stuffed the kensho T-shirt into his backpack. Usagi poured another espresso for Jake into a carry-out cup. He set it on the table before embracing his friend. The two men stood eye to eye for a second after they hugged. Many good years settled between them in a flash. Whether they met again was not important to Buddha nature, but they hurt inside anyway. Jake then turned to Marga. She could not hold back a tear. He hugged her quickly and let go, hoisted his bag, grabbed the espresso and walked out the door.

Fifty yards down the path he encountered his old Beetle, tossed his back-pack onto the money envelope on the passenger seat and got in. He pushed down on the clutch, shifted into neutral, and turned the key. After a prolonged sputter and puff of smoke the motor fired and ran as smoothly as it ever had that year. Jake shifted into first and quickly into second, leaving it there to ease his way along the bumpy dirt path. Marga and Usagi watched in silence until the Beetle turned right and disappeared behind a stand of cedars.

Usagi gazed at the familiar sight of a lone raven at watch atop a telephone pole. The black bird croaked a few times, as if to announce that something had changed. Dawn had broken without solar fanfare. Low heavy clouds hid the sky. The scruffy raven watched a noisy, pale-blue Beetle shrink into the distance.

10 You Can Go Home Again

Black cat face fills the entire screen of vision as you stand firm.

Poised with pedipalps extended you look as fierce as possible.

You wish now you had more size like your cousin the camel spider in Arabia.

Two and a half inches of body mass may not cut it this time.

This creature this time is too fast.

You will not turn and run to expose your back side again.

Run and die or fight and maybe live.

Choice is easy.

Freedom is not.

Black cat face filled the entire screen of vision.

The audience is gone.

Black cat face turns and sees.

She sees two coyotes too close watching.

Freedom is two coyotes away—5 October 2007

Passages in Jake's notes before and after he departed the Center left no doubt that he distrusted everything that he learned from the old Roshi. The freedom he sought died. Nevertheless, he retained a sense of humor. He wrote about funny instances among the monks who took turns imitating the old man's horrible *engrish* and Jake was especially good at it. Perhaps that was good-natured fun by man-boys acting normally. Perhaps it was a sign of imperfection, or worse, rebellion, or still worse, stupidity.

Perhaps perfection's brilliance dimmed for Jake over time. *Today we look through a glass darkly* was a theme from a letter of St. Paul that Jake mulled over in his mind repeatedly during his final two years at the commune. Jake saw a darker image of himself now. For two years after the lawsuit, in a heroic if impossible attempt to vindicate his first eight years with the old man, Jake explored many religious traditions and ideas. He made several excursions to Santa Fe spending whole days reading books and searching the Web in the city and state libraries.

Jake decided that the old man's approach lacked sophistication and openness, as all he taught was self-centered. The old man told stories about himself constantly, repeating many over and over again to make a point. Buddhism was more than this—and less. During his first few years at the commune, Jake was impressed that he had such an important man for a teacher, perhaps a Bodhisattva. He felt like one of the first humble followers of a Christ or a Buddha. The old man's stories rang true when he first heard them like new wine from a pure mountain vineyard. Now all had turned sour. What Marga was doing was not enough either. It was not wine anymore. Was it ten years wasted?

The lapsed monk packed what little he had into his beater of a Beetle, an old model 1973. The years of Southwest road dust had not stopped the motor and the radio still worked. All the lights and moving parts functioned as expected. He replaced and maintained the transmission and gearbox. The faded blue bug was a tribute to Jake's persistence and skill if not his success. Jake's father left a tattered, annotated *Idiot's Guide* for fixing a Beetle in it. His father scrawled his own ideas into the guide. Jake treasured his father's notes. They were the only writing of any significance that his father left behind. One large gym bag and one small backpack held all Jake owned. Most tools, books, bedding, and the computer he used belonged to the commune. A small, black origami bird dangled from the bug's rearview mirror. Jake flicked it with his finger spinning it clockwise.

Rock and roll down the road. It was Ten Years After on the oldie station as you drove away from Roshiland in a cute old car. Cute.—5 October 2007

Jake changed the station in the middle of "Choo Choo Moma" by Ten Years After. If Lady Fate was toying with him now, he was not amused. He listened to the news about killings in Iraq and Kenya for a minute. He turned the black volume dial until it clicked off. That ended the music and the news. The news was painful to hear but not for reports of people dying. Jake's pain came from recognizing his long time disengagement from things that once mattered to him: family, a secure future, and a loving mate. He let Nietzsche trump a normal, sane life. He followed a certain instinct to seek enlightenment. But that was ten years ago and this was ten years after and he was no longer certain.

You could not leave it alone, could you? You just had to experience it for yourself. Reading about Buddhism was not enough, was it? What did you expect? Did you expect to join more than a cult without knowing the culture? The old man had you by your spiritual balls from the start. You thought he was so fine, so wise, so... Buddhist! Where in the sutras was it written that the disciple knows the Buddha when he meets him? Ah, yes, at the end of Buddhism for Idiots!

They shoot Buddhas, don't they?—8 October 2007

A mere five miles past the Colorado border, Jake already felt his past passing away. The gray sky above him was lead heavy. Winter was around the corner in the mountains. A cold rain sprinkled and then fell hard against the windshield. The worn wipers sloshed enough water aside for Jake to continue carefully. An hour into his journey, he began to think ahead as he strained to see a sign for Route 160 east. He vowed to find a real job and to go back to school, maybe to graduate school. Jake figured he was "twelve lousy credits" away from a degree when he dropped out.

Thoughts of what could have been drifted around the agitated space in his head as the blue bug struggled over Wolf Creek Pass. One cylinder misfired when Jake downshifted to second gear. The bug climbed the snaking highway slowly to the continental divide at 10,800 feet. The engine strained to remain air-cooled, but it kept working. The bug rolled onward as he shifted from third to second gear and back to third to negotiate around the tight, downhill curves. "Maybe it has a few thousand miles left in it," he hoped. "Just get me to Philly," he prayed as tense miles ticked by in the pouring rain. From a distance the old bug sounded like a vintage sewing machine stitching its way along 160 past Alamosa to Interstate 25.

Thoughts of what to do for money occupied Jake as the bug puttered north toward Pueblo and Colorado Springs. He thought about why he worked for little more than room and board in the old man's commune. Intermittent work from the outside kept him flush. Ten years of effort led to barely enough funds to get to Pennsylvania, let alone to start over. Money was one issue. Self-esteem was another. Jake would visit his family—his mother and stepfather—and his brother. He had not visited family for five years. Only his brother Harry passed through on his motorcycle for a brief, one-day visit a year before the old man died. Jake would ask them all for help. He tried not to think about what he would say.

Jake spotted the obscured exit sign ahead through the raindrops pelting his windshield. It was just ahead of the rig to his right as they rolled onward at fifty-five. Another rig was coming up behind him. He did not want to miss the exit because he was running low on fuel. Jake downshifted to third and gunned the engine to pass the rumbling, eighteen-wheeler. He managed to pull ahead and in one severe turning motion he swerved to the right in front of the truck.

The risky maneuver worked—he definitely if barely cleared the massive Mack—but during the process the bug's engine reported a loud bang. The acceleration through the curve caused the bug to skid sideways onto the slippery, paved roadway of the ramp. The deep howl of a passing air horn created an eerie back note to the bang-thud-thud of the motor and screech-squeal of wet tires and straining brake pads. One very perturbed truck driver wanted to royally acknowledge and clearly curse the simple-minded fool in the tiny car.

As the car slid onto the ramp, Jake instinctively pumped the brakes to regain control. He shifted down into a grinding second gear. Almost at a stop, he tried to accelerate again but the wounded, noisy engine had no power. And then it froze. He shifted into reverse before setting the emergency brake. Time stopped as he watched raindrops run down the windshield for nearly half a minute. He noticed his heart pumping hard and he was breathing deeply. After loosing his vise like grip on the steering wheel, his hands began to tremble.

"What the hell is wrong with you?" he said out loud. Then, echoing the truck driver, with his fists pounding his head in slow rhythm, he chanted, "That was fucking stupid."

He took time to breathe and to calm down with his head resting on the steering wheel. After he felt less stressed, he grabbed his colorful knit cap from his backpack, slipped it onto his head, and stepped out into the rainy night to inspect the engine damage. While holding the back hood open with one hand, Jake guided his keychain flashlight across the motor. Despite the smoke and steam it took him all of two seconds to grasp what happened. He scooted back to the open driver's side door, slid in and grabbed an old white towel from under the passenger seat. He rolled down the passenger side window, stuck most of the towel on the outside, and then rolled the window back up. He turned on his emergency flashers and waited.

Shit. Here you sit near Colorado Springs. Off Highway 25, on exit 135 with a blown engine in the cold rain. White rag of surrender tied to bent side mirror. Back bonnet propped open. The piston shot right through it! Who will stop to help? Who cares? Satori blown to hell again? Or maybe this is IT. You could be mangled by eighteen wheels or dead but you are not. Detach, brother. Let it be. Mother of God, you are one messed up dude.

Fifteen minutes later, after many cars passed him by, he wrote:

A half-ton dirty white Chevy pick-up is slowing down, pulling over. Bearded man with a beat-up Broncos cap. Looks like a construction guy.—5 October 2007

The bearded driver pulled his Chevy over in front of the bug. Tom was a rangy, thin fellow over six feet tall with an engaging smile. He swung the Chevy door open and stepped onto the rain soaked gravel. He popped the hood of his dirty yellow slicker over his cap as he approached. Jake noticed cement and mud spots on Tom's

Levis and plain tan western boots. Jake got out of the vehicle to greet him.

Tom glanced at Jake's cap, then into Jake's eyes to size him up before speaking. "I'd shake your hand friend but my paws are dirty as hell. What's up with the Beetle?"

"Blown engine. Thanks for stopping." Jake reached out with his right hand to greet Tom anyway. They shook hands. "You working with concrete today?"

"Shows, huh?" Tom said sullenly. He looked tired. "At least until it got too wet! So what's the deal?" he asked as the wind kicked up blowing rain into their faces. Tom glanced under the open bonnet at the engine. He wiped the steam and rain drops away from his eyes. "You need this towed or what?"

"Yeah, to Pennsylvania! I'm tempted to leave it right here but I might get fined for littering. I really need to get rid of it," Jake yelled to be heard above the din of strong blasts of wind.

"There's a salvage yard about ten miles from here but it's closed till morning. We could call a tow truck to haul it there," Tom shouted back.

"I don't know about that. Got no insurance. Guess I could spring for it and stay in the car till they opened up."

"Got another idea," Tom said.

He walked back to his truck. He backed his Chevy close to the Volkswagen's front, chrome-metal bumper. The two men quickly ran a chain under the car onto its axle and hooked it, and then they fastened the other end of the chain onto the truck's rear axle. The simple contraption worked well enough. Tom drove the pick-up slowly while Jake put slight pressure on his car's brake when necessary to maintain six feet of taught chain between the vehicles.

Along the way, Tom used a cell phone to call his mechanic friend. Tom carefully hauled his grateful follower for a few miles to the friend's auto body shop. They unchained the busted bug and stepped into the warm, dry office to negotiate a deal. Jake asked if there was an airport nearby. There was and Tom would drop him off the next morning. Jake stayed at Tom's house as a guest that night.

The next morning at the Municipal Airport at Colorado Springs, Jake wrote:

Simple beautiful average. Work hard all day. Stop on a road. Help a stranger. Drive home. Take a shower. Eat a good meal with the wife and first grader kid Joanie. Write some checks to pay some bills. Help Joanie with a school project. Kick back. Watch some tv. Ready for bed. Make love whenever. Up before five and ready to go again. Tom makes fifty grand a year clear. He's a year younger than you. Small business. Small house of his own. Never went to college. Seems happy. Wants his girl to go to a good college and be a famous anything. Tom is America's hero. He was yours too. You can cry now.

Jake sat alone in a small café. He was lost in a reverie about what might have been had he not gone monastic.

"Northwest Airlines 1234 will board in ten minutes," said the ticket counter attendant over the loudspeaker. That was Jake's flight. He wiped his eyes on his sleeve.

Flight onetwothreefour—go. New start, is it? Dawn of my life? What life? It is 6 a.m.—6 October 2007

Jake stuffed the notebook into his shoulder bag, stood up and carried his things toward the gate.

Tom had dropped him off at the airport on his way to work. As mentioned above, he spent the night at Tom's house sleeping on the large living room couch. Jake slept well. His five feet, eight inches stretched out easily on the soft leather cushions. He felt safe. He felt lucky.

Back at Tom's it was still dark outside when Tom's wife tapped Jake on the shoulder while calling his name. Jake was already awake but he kept the covers over his head to prolong the sense of peace he found in Tom's house. He fantasized that Tom would hire him and about how he might go to work with Tom. Jake took in the pleasant mix of aromas from the clean sheets and pillowcase he slept on, the leather

193

of the couch, the lighted, scented candles from the bathroom, and the hint of damp ash in the fireplace. Holly called out to rouse him. Jake enjoyed the scent and sound of bacon sizzling in the kitchen. Only then did he notice the tears streaming down his cheeks.

They ate breakfast with little conversation among the adults but little Joanie chattered away. She was curious about the strange visitor. She met him the night before and determined quickly that he was safe. She managed to show him her drawings and dolls and tell him all about them before her parents put her to bed. Jake fell under her spell easily and Joanie knew it. She had his attention despite the protestations of her mother who apologized to Jake for her pesky daughter. Joanie sat next to Jake at breakfast asking him one question after another.

"Do you have any kids? Why not? Do you know how to draw? You can have this one—here, take it." Joanie gave Jake one of her sketches of a flower in the grass.

Jake did his best to get through breakfast without feeling awkward. He felt like a stranger in a strange land, an alien who nevertheless liked what he felt. He answered the little girl's questions with brief responses. He asked her for a sheet of her drawing paper. She gave him a yellow one. Jake folded it artfully. Joanie watched intently and silently with her mouth slightly ajar. Like magic Jake made a bird appear out of the folds. He presented it to Joanie as a gift to her delight and the delight of her parents.

"Look mommy, look daddy! Look what the man made!"

"What do you say to Jake?" her mother asked.

"Thank you."

"You are very welcome. And thanks again for the drawing."

Jake wrote down their names and address. He intended to stay in touch. Holly gave Jake a hug and wished him well. She kissed her husband as she showed them out the door. The rain had stopped. The sun had not yet risen.

She is America's wife and mother. Clean house despite Joanie's small messes. Worked weekends as a nurse. Twelve-hour shifts. Two months pregnant—not showing yet. No make-up. Radiant with ash-blond hair tied back. No bleach. Plain radiance.

194

Either Tom or his sister cared for Joanie when Holly worked. Extended family beauty. They have family and good friends nearby. Not static harmony like rocks in perfectly groomed sand. They dance and find rhythms even when the music stops. They are not perfect emptiness. They dance on an ordinary stage. You told them you ran out of work and had a job back East. You did not mention the old man's cult. Fool. Liar.—6 October 2007

Jake sold the bug for $350 cash to Tom's friend after an anxious but brief search for the title that was buried in a small envelope of papers under the front seat. The crippled Beetle would provide a good project for the mechanic and his teenage son. A tag shop was still open just down the road where they exchanged the title. With that money and what was left from Marga's gift, he had just enough for a flight to Philly. He would have to pay full fare. He felt an inner and anxious urge to get there as soon as possible. His flight was ready for boarding and he was in line, that is, until the panic narrated in chapter one.

***

With the drama of flight over, the drama of reentry was about to begin. The cab pulled away and the unremarkable prodigal stood before his childhood home. A large moth fluttered around the porch light above his head as he pushed the glowing doorbell button. It had been five years. He was back in New Hope. He pushed the doorbell again. The moth alighted on his head for a moment just as Neal opened the door. Jake swatted limply at the moth.

"Hi, Neal. Remember me?"

Neal paused to assess the moth-distracted man who addressed him by name. Neal did not have his glasses on but the voice sounded familiar. A familiar, if fuzz-filled face emerged to complement the familiar voice.

"Hey, Jake! Jake! What's the occasion stranger? Let me call your mother." On impulse, Neal turned around to face the stairway. "Monica," Neal shouted. "Monica!

Guess who's here?" He turned back to face Jake. "Come in, come in!"

"Thanks Neal."

Jake took two steps inside so Neal could shut the door.

"Looks like you've redone the downstairs here. New hardwood floor?"

"Only the foyer, front room, and kitchen, Jake. Come in, come in," Neal repeated as he headed toward the kitchen to turn on lights and clean a few dishes from the table.

Jake set his bags down along the wall near the stairway. He heard his mother shout, "Just a minute, I'll be right down." He noted a new display of several framed pictures on the wall at the base of the stairs. In the center was a finely framed photograph of Jake's father in military uniform surrounded by smaller, complimentary photos. There was one of Ziggy with his two sons in front of the auto repair shop a year before he died. Jake grimaced at the image of his innocent, smiling self at age eleven.

His father was with the 101st Airborne Infantry. The photo was taken in 1973, the year after his second tour in Vietnam, the year he was discharged with a disability. Memories and stories flooded back into Jake's mind. As a soldier in the chaos of combat, his father had taken shrapnel from friendly fire. His left leg was never fully functional again, even after several surgeries. Nevertheless, Jake's father remained active as a mechanic with his own shop.

Both Jake and his older brother spent hours of free time helping their dad in the shop. Ziggy was a hands-on dad who made work interesting for his sons, assigning appropriate tasks they could both handle. All that ended one day when Jake's father died in the motorcycle accident. Jake was twelve then. Harry was fourteen. Entranced in his thoughts, Jake recalled the smells of engine oil, gasoline and grinding metal.

He recalled the rumors that Ziggy killed himself on purpose. He overheard some of Ziggy's fellow vets talking at the funeral. He recalled a news article with an image of his father's Harley mangled against a brick wall. The article was somewhere in mom's scrapbook: "Ziggy Grzyb succumbs to massive head trauma after motorcycle accident." Everyone called him Ziggy. No one called him Sigismund except the IRS and VA. Noble names in Eastern Europe sound funny to Americans.

Ziggy got drunk nearly every weekend as long as Jake could remember. He did not know that Ziggy had a stiff drink every night before going to bed. Whatever was bothering him, he kept from his boys. He rarely got angry with his sons, but when he did, he could be unyielding and harsh. Overall, he was a good father even if a part of him was missing from them.

Monica descended the stairway slowly until she caught sight of the visitor. Jake saw that his mother's hair was shorter and grayer now. She looked thinner despite a plush, white terrycloth robe. She looked good. He had seen recent photographs of her with Neal included in a Christmas card but seeing in person was different. The live version of mom forced an immediate emotional adjustment. It had been five years, after all. Of course presidents age considerably in that time, was the odd thought that entered Jake's head. He watched Monica's expression go from curiosity to wide-eyed surprise and finally into mild hysteria.

"Jacob! Jake! It's you! Why didn't you call? I can't believe it? Are you all right? How did you get here?"

Jake had to catch his mother as she lurched toward him from the bottom step with her arms open. Instinctively, he picked her up and spun her around with a warm embrace. When she relaxed her grip, Jake held his mother at arm's length by her shoulders. He looked at her sheepishly for a few seconds. He smiled and nodded slightly.

"Yes, mom, I'm okay. I'm okay. I'm okay. I flew in. I took a cab from Philly. Sorry for the surprise—for not calling ahead."

Monica stroked Jake's face with her right hand. "You growing your hair back?" she asked. "In the last picture you sent us you were bald."

After several minutes of happy small talk about family and the house, Neal suggested they go into the kitchen. Neal took Jake's turquoise jacket and hung it in a hall closet. Jake followed Neal to the table. Monica prepared to serve drinks and her homemade cookies.

Neal proposed to Monica five years after Ziggy died, about the time Jake was preparing to leave for college in Arizona. Neal was an Army vet also, but one that never saw combat. His only tour was in Korea. Neal's older brother served in Vietnam. Neal's brother saw action and died there in 1970. The military tried to keep brothers from serving together in active combat zones to not repeat World War 2's horrible legacy of two or more siblings dying in combat. Monica met Neal at a support group for those who lost someone to combat or grieved for someone missing in action. At the time, Neal was the leader of that support group. Nine clients was a larger number than Monica expected to meet. She discovered that many thousands of Vietnam vets had committed suicide by then. She was among those left behind that yearned to find comfort with people who sympathized and understood.

Monica and Neal married and moved in together the year Jake left for college. Unlike Ziggy, Neal was a steady man who used no drugs and drank only at social occasions. Ziggy was known to light up a joint and drank heavily now and then. Neal had a daughter from a previous marriage who no longer lived at home. He worked as a psychologist for a large high school.

Monica served a bowl full of cookies and another with sweets from a box of chocolates. Before she returned with the iced tea, Jake fell into a quiet space—a trance. He noted the fine oak wood cabinets and new gray granite countertop. The refurbished hardwood floor extended from the foyer into the kitchen. Monica and Neal kept the old claw foot oak table and four, spindle-back Windsor chairs. As Jake relaxed into the familiar kitchen chair, he felt the past seep into recognition—nothing specific, just a feeling with an awareness of many meals and hours of homework, card games, and conversations. Jake pulled his sweating glass of iced tea closer. He did not notice that Monica had placed it on the table. He wiped the moisture from his fingers onto his pants. Monica noticed him doing it. She offered him a cloth napkin. Neal grabbed a cookie.

"Good as usual, hon," said Neal complimenting Monica for her baking skill.

Monica was about to sit down when Jake suddenly pushed his chair away from the table and asked to be excused.

The room moved sideways. Jake felt nauseous and panicky again. He felt the onset of uncontrollable confusion and terror. He stood up uneasily and then wobbled toward the powder room below the staircase. After shutting the door, he knelt down before the white bowl and wrapped his arms around it. He heaved but nothing came up. He splashed cold toilet water on his face several times. He rolled over in the tight space on his back gripping his knees in a fetal position. Jake rocked back and forth for a minute or two until the anxiety subsided.

Back in the kitchen Monica looked to Neal for reassurance. Neal merely shrugged and gave her a quizzical glance. Monica began to rise from her chair, but Neal grabbed her arm. "Jake will let us know if he needs us," he said. He called to Jake within the next few seconds anyway. Jake did not hear him. Neal walked over to the powder room door.

"Jake, are you alright?"

"Yeah. Just need a minute. Okay, I'll be okay," he grunted.

During the few minutes that Jake remained in the bathroom, Neal and Monica speculated whether Jake left the cult for good. His last emails indicated changes and improvements had occurred since the Roshi died. So, why was he here now? They would have their answers soon enough.

Jake wandered back to the table looking disheveled and pale. Water spots stained his shirt. He took a sip of his iced tea, cleared his throat and then took another sip. He set the glass down between his hands. He raised an index finger to tap the condensation along the bottom edge. He rubbed the moisture on his fingertip with his thumb.

"I owe you an explanation. Please let me talk first. After, you can ask questions. Okay?"

Neal and Monica nodded silently as Jake quickly made eye contact with them. Jake cleared his throat again. Then he looked down at his hands and the table before him while telling his story. He tapped his fingers in rapid succession like a drum roll on the oak surface several times before he spoke again.

"Okay. Uh, I left the Center. I am not going back. Um, it took me two years to make up my mind, so don't think this is just another vacation like the one when I was last here—was it five years ago? Anyway, I feel embarrassed right now, so bear with me. Uh, all I have and own is with me here. I need a place to stay for a while till I get a job. I thought I could use one of the rooms upstairs or I could just crash anywhere, maybe on a couch. I know you both have a good life here together and the last thing you probably need is an intruder."

Jake took a sip of tea. He heard Neal say they had room for him. He breathed deeply once, and then continued. "I can help around here, mow the lawn, and tend to things in the yard while I'm here. Um, about that incident just now with me in the bathroom, well, that just started this morning. It happened at the airport in Colorado. I guess I'm having anxiety attacks. I nearly had a bad accident last night. It was raining hard in Colorado. Oh, I flew in from Colorado Springs. I feel bad about this, about Ziggy's Beetle. The engine blew outside of Colorado Springs. I wanted to bring it home—I sold it. I had to."

At this point Jake looked up at the ceiling, shut his eyes and tried to hold back tears. He did. He wondered if he was making any sense. It dawned on him just how far he had drifted from a relationship with his mother in the past many years. Monica lifted her hand as if to say something, but she did not. Jake took a deep breath. He continued again with his eyes fixed on the table.

"Now that I hear myself talk about it, it seems insignificant—the car, I mean. Yes, I know, mom, you told me to get rid of it a long time ago. Ziggy would not care. But it was something to bring back. Maybe it was a symbol of something, a connection. I don't know. I practiced not being attached to desires for all these years. Yet, there was the bug, dad's Beetle." Jake paused to grasp what he just said. "Neal, you ought to get a kick out of the symbolism. I lost the possession, but the desire remains. We use—I mean used the bug at the commune in the beginning, but for me it became more than that. It became something I kept for dad."

Jake paused, lowering his head to swallow saliva. He took a deep breath through his nostrils.

"Neal, you were right about some things as it turned out. You couldn't have known, but you were right. I had little idea of what I was getting into."

Jake paused to take another sip of his tea, but he only touched the glass.

"It wasn't such a bad cult, not as bad as some. But the old man, the Roshi, he betrayed us and I did not want to believe it at first. Not for years anyway. Some of the women complained about how he manipulated them into having sex, how he got them to give all their money. Two of them sued us, the old man, two years ago, just before he died. We chose to settle. We sold off some land to pay it off."

Jake looked at Monica and Neal, noting that they remained attentive. He felt as if he were babbling. He continued. "The old man died of food poisoning soon after the scandal broke. It was so weird. Anyway, in my research I found out that almost all the significant Eastern gurus that set up groups here since the sixties did the same stuff with abuse of sex, money, or drugs or all three. I did not see it coming. None of us at the commune did, or at least none who stayed around from the beginning. Some who left were not so naïve. Some of them noticed right away what you warned me about. The old man's claim to being a Roshi was bogus. I liked him at first. I trusted him." Jake paused again to collect his thoughts.

"Marga and Usagi, the two people I got closest to, are still making a go of it to run things. Well, I know Marga is. Usagi may be leaving. You'd like them. Good people. Some of the workshops and retreats Marga conducts are popular. They wanted me to stay to help with the grounds and classes. I couldn't anymore. I went there for Buddhism and it did not happen for me. Now the place is changing to accommodate anyone. Kind of like a mini New Age spa."

Jake stopped to sip tea.

"I'm thinking of going back to school as soon as I can get some money together. That's why I came here. I need a place to stay 'til I get a job. Maybe a couple of months—uh, I guess I already said that. Anyway, if it's a problem I can check with Harry, but I thought I'd try here first."

Jake looked up at Monica, then over at Neal. Monica was biting her lower lip. Neal sat back pensively with his chin on his left hand as his elbow rested on the arm of his chair. He was reticent to say anything, so he turned toward Monica. She spoke up.

"Well, Jacob, your brother's place will not do. I think you need some rest and time to get yourself in order. Since Harold got his divorce, his place is a mess. He has girlfriends and friends over at all hours. Your nieces are there every other weekend. There may not be room. We would like you to stay here. We have room."

"Harry got divorced? Whew. Man, have I been out of touch. Sorry to hear that. I'll call him tomorrow. Why didn't you let me know?"

Monica spoke up again. "He didn't want me to tell you about it. You rarely wrote or called him. He thought you didn't care. And you know how he is. He takes after his dad—keeps everything inside. Your brother puts on a good show."

Jake took a long shower in a semi-familiar bathroom with the gray tiles and black trim. The tiles were original but Monica had painted the bathroom and the hallway a quaint Colonial blue-gray. The hallway had been wallpapered in a muted, striped pattern. The entire upstairs was structurally unchanged. Jake took the bedroom he once shared with his brother. The room was much neater now with one full-sized, four-posted bed.

The old stacked bunks were gone, as were the garish, pale green walls covered with posters of exotic places, motorbikes, and sports heroes. Monica forbade the display of scantily clad women and swimsuit models. Jake laughed to himself as he thought of those days with Harry in the room. He remembered where Harry hid the girly magazines. Now the old room would suit a hotel brochure. Monica must have made the checkered blue curtains. They matched her peculiar taste for gingham trim throughout the old house. Jake liked the change. It felt fresh and new. He felt as if he were staying in a standard, quaint bed and breakfast. It made him feel like he was not just another failure as a son coming home again. He was a guest passing through, merely visiting, but the reality was he had nowhere else to go. He unpacked his few belongings placing most of them into the drawers of a large pinewood chest of drawers. He leaned little Joanie's drawing of a flower in the grass against the chest's mirror. As he lay in bed Jake left the small flat screen TV on low volume on a news channel. Candidates were campaigning in several states. He was not thinking of the news when he fell asleep. He was wondering why so few if any children appeared at the Center. He was thinking of why he had no children. The image of Joanie asking all her questions brought a smile to his face. He slept for nearly six hours until the stark and ominous figure in the dream woke him.

You saw a form of a man at first in silhouette, then in an odd light like overexposure. The man was also a woman or a feminine something smiling. The figure walked slowly past a small boy. You heard a voice say "Avalokitesvara" as the figure raised one palm up.

You watched the figure turn and beckon you with both hands. You hesitated to move.

Then the figure transformed into naked Kali wearing a necklace of skulls dangling. She, baring fangs.

You could not move.

Enough to wake you up. What was that about? We had a statue of Kannon at the Center. Kannon. Quan Yin. Guanyin. Why?

Why were you sweating?—October 2007

11 New Hope in Old Places

Jake knocked on the front door several times. "Harry! Harry, you in there?" Harry's house was nearly five miles from Monica's place. It was an older, single, one and half story, frame building in an old neighborhood. It had a pitched roof with brown asphalt shingles. The white wood slats needed paint. Jake noted a band of algae and wood rot to his right along the north corner. The downspout needed repair. The lower section was missing.

Jake raised his hand to cup the reflected sunlight from his eyes as he peeked in the front window. The curtain trim on each side of the window did not match. A television was on. Jake could see no one in the front room. He stepped back, turned, and then hoisted himself over the white wooden railing at the side of the front porch. He landed lightly on the sidewalk with his left hand yet on the railing.

Jake followed the concrete walkway to the back door. The wind whipped up fallen maple and ash leaves around his feet. These leaves still held their vivid yellows and mauve reds. The sidewalk tilted slightly away from the house. The back door was along the side of a rear, mud room entrance. The smallish back yard ended at a shed or garage with a back alley entrance. A metal swing set with a green plastic slide stood along the metal storm fencing that separated Harry's yard from a neighbor's.

No one was in the back yard. A pickup truck rambled through the back alley. Jake looked up at several gray clouds drifting toward the east. It might be raining again soon, he thought. He tested the screen door. It pulled open easily. The solid wood, walnut stained door was cracked open. Jake knocked twice with the brass knocker. No one answered. He pushed the door and stepped inside. "Harry! Yo, Harry! You here, bud? It's Jake!"

The back mud room smelled of engine oil, stale cigarette smoke, cat piss and beer. Empty bottles and cans piled high in the blue plastic recycle tub. Harry's work clothes hung from hooks along the wall. Two shiny motorcycle helmets sat on a shelf above the hooks. Grease-stained work boots sat below the shelf next to the blue tub.

Two tied-off white bags of garbage sat by the door. A cat box along the opposite wall needed attention. Jake looked down at the door mat. He wiped his feet to remove the wet leaves stuck to his shoes. Just then a female voice called out his name. As he raised his head he noted bare feet, then a pair of shapely, naked legs topped above the thighs by a dark green Philadelphia Eagles football jersey with a number 5. His eyes rested on a pretty face framed by a mop of disheveled, bleached blond hair. She stood in the doorway to the dining area.

"So you're Jake? Welcome! Harry's inside getting presentable." The young lady held out her hand. "Hi, I'm Lindy."

She looked directly into his eyes as if eager to have him return some recognition and acceptance. Jake gingerly clasped her right hand as she wrapped both her hands around his. Jake noticed her long pink fingernails. She had a strong grip. He felt himself blushing.

"Hi, Lindy. Good to meet you. I guess Harry told you I was coming over. I hope, er, hope I'm not here at an awk-kward time."

Jake felt awkward. Lindy was disarmingly attractive. The endearing young woman continued to hold his hand as she led him into the kitchen.

"Take a seat," she said. "I'll get some coffee going. Harry's anxious to see you."

Jake sat down. He pulled a crushed plastic shopping bag out of his jacket pocket and put it on the table. "Coffee would be good. Thanks."

Lindy lit a cigarette. She was about to rinse the coffee carafe, but she stopped suddenly. "Sorry. Mind if I smoke?"

Jake waived off her apology, shook his head and smiled. "But don't offer me any. I don't smoke."

"Cream and sugar?"

"No sugar. Just black, please."

Lindy dragged smoke from her cigarette and blew it toward an open window. As she did that Jake pulled a T-shirt from the bag and held it up.

"Do you think Harry will look good in this?" he asked wryly.

Lindy took another drag and blew smoke out the window again. She set the filtered Winston Lite on a clear glass ashtray on the windowsill. Then she cocked her head to the side as she tried to grasp what she saw on the gray garment.

"I don't get it," she said while staring at the oriental ideogram.

"Well, there's nothing to get—it's a Zen symbol. Means enlightenment."

"Oh," Lindy said. She took one more drag on her cigarette and put it out. "He'll like it," she said matter-of-factly. "It reminds me of the tattoos on his arms." Lindy connected the Japanese calligraphy to the Chinese symbols that Harry favored.

Lindy turned her head toward the open hallway. Someone was walking toward her from the side bedroom.

"Hey there, boss. Want some coffee?" she shouted.

Harry appeared in the kitchen as he fed a belt through his loose fitting jeans. His wet blond hair was slickly combed back. Jake noted that his brother had put on some weight. Harry was shirtless with a faded green sweatshirt draped over his shoulder. He smiled broadly as soon as he spotted Jake. He turned slightly to give Lindy a peck on the cheek before approaching the guest.

"Morning, babe," he said. "Jake! Looking good, young man! Good to see you."

"Here. Try this on, brother!"

Jake tossed the gift T-shirt to Harry across the table. Harry caught the shirt out of the air as he dropped his sweatshirt onto a chair. He held the new shirt out so he could peruse it before putting it on. Harry was slightly larger than Jake. Harry played guard both ways on their small, Catholic high school football team while, Jake, two years younger, played defensive back and back-up running back. Harry took after their father with his coarse, Polish looks, blue eyes and sturdy, six-foot body. Jake had some of his mother's features, more refined and he inherited her brownish eyes. Jake was considerably thinner yet fitter from all the outdoor masonry work he did over the years since Harry last saw him. The extra-large shirt from the Center hung very loose and long on Jake. It fit Harry much better.

Jake stood up as Harry approached. After exchanging kisses on both cheeks, the brothers embraced for a few seconds. Then Harry pushed his brother away by the shoulders, but held on. "Let me look at you. What's with the scruffiness? You're looking like Bret Favre! I figured you'd be bald."

Jake ran his hand over his head and beard. "I guess I haven't shaved in a few weeks. Didn't mom tell you I left the Center? Anyway, I did—so no reason to shave up."

"Wow, man. Big move. Big move, man," Harry remarked with a hint of pleasure. "Here, here, let's sit down. We have some catching up to do."

Lindy placed a cup of coffee with cream and sugar in front of Harry. "Thanks, babe," he said as he patted her on the backside. She brought another cup for Jake. Lindy sat down with them curious about what would transpire between Harry and his long lost, intriguing younger brother.

"Mom told me about the divorce. Sorry, man. You guys seemed so good together." Jake stopped himself, suddenly realizing his insensitivity as he glanced over at Lindy.

"Oh, don't mind me. I know all about it, believe me." Lindy emphasized the "all," indicating with her wide open eyes and slow nods that Harry vented his grief about the marriage on her.

"Yeah, she knows everything. Poor Lindy has put up with my belly-aching since last year."

Jake felt awkward again. He wanted to ask if they were living together, but did not. "So, what do you do, Lindy? I mean job wise?"

"What, besides being your brother's mistress?"

Lindy somehow picked up on Jake's unspoken question. She stuck her tongue out at Harry before going on. "I bartend and go to school part time. Harry used to come to the bar I was working at to have a beer or two when he and Julie were breaking up. That's how and where we met. He thought I was his shrink."

"I tipped you well, didn't I?" Harry reminded her.

"You bought me," she said with a wink.

"Yeah, well you did a hell of a sales job."

"So, how's it running so far, boss?"

"No complaints. No complaints," Harry said with finality. He sipped his coffee not wanting to turn this into a drawn out analysis in front of Jake.

Lindy turned to Jake. "I call him boss because I help with the books there too while I go to school."

"Going to school? For what?" Jake inquired.

"Don't laugh if I tell you."

Harry spoke up. "She thinks I need a manager at the shop. She's studying auto mechanics."

"And taking a business course," she added proudly. "Since Harry will take over the shop in a few months, we figure he will need help with accounting and management."

"Take over? What's happened to Harper then, dad's old partner?"

"He's had enough. Harp's in his late sixties, his wife inherited her family's estate in South Carolina and she wants to move down where it's warmer."

Jake wondered aloud, "Are you two serious then? Marriage in the works?" As the words came out of his mouth, he wished he had not said them.

"No, man, no plans for that," Harry insisted. "Lindy's been great, but I'm still licking wounds from the first one. You have no idea what I went through."

"Whatever. You can lick for as long as you want," Lindy offered with a lewd undertone.

Her pun was not lost on the men even though Jake showed no reaction. Harry shrugged showing some embarrassment.

"But, actually, Jake, I have ulterior motives too," Lindy said in a businesslike manner. "Bartending is getting old. I need a new challenge."

"See, Jake, women just use you as long as they get what they need," Harry said with emphasis on need. "There might be something to your celibacy thing at the commune after all." Harry paused to take a sip from his cup. "So, tell me what happened. Why'd you leave it?"

"Why did I leave it?" Jake repeated as if bored by the question. "I probably should have left it years ago. Things just began feeling wrong for me. I stayed on because of a few people there. We had gotten close as friends. That was the toughest part—to leave them."

Lindy asked with genuine curiosity, "You mean you couldn't have sex there?"

Jake looked up at her. He wondered if she would grasp why anyone might abstain from sex for spiritual reasons. "Well, we could but we were taught that it was better not to indulge in that. The idea was to detach from desire that causes suffering. It's a Buddhist thing, but other religions teach versions of abstinence too. Anyway, unless you're into the idea of a religious life, it all sounds pretty bizarre, doesn't it?"

"No, no. I didn't mean to imply that. Hey, I had a cousin who went to a seminary in Cincinnati for a while. He was going to be a priest. I get that," Lindy said.

Jake asked, "Had?" Jake wondered if he was yet alive.

"Her cousin is gay," Harry blurted out. "He met some guy there while they were in group therapy. They moved to Portland in Oregon." Then with unmasked sarcasm, he quickly added, "Not that there's anything wrong with that!"

"You're an ass, Harry," Lindy retorted. "My cousin's very happy now and that's all that matters." Lindy turned back to Jake. "Anyway, you must think I'm awful, greeting you half dressed and all."

She pulled on her shirt to cover more of her now crossed, shapely legs. Then she got up. "I'm going to shower and change into something decent. See you soon." She left holding her shirt down behind as she headed for the bedroom.

"She's really cute," Jake said after she disappeared. "You done good, Harry."

"Yeah. You should see her in heels and a dress," Harry said with a wink. "We get along well, so far. I wonder what she sees in me," he said in a self-deprecating manner. "But seriously, I hope we did not upset you. You must be going through a lot right now. The last thing you need is my screwed up love life in your face."

"It's okay, really, Harry. It's good for me to see how normal people live. This celibacy thing was overrated. I'm not stuck on it—at least not anymore."

Harry rubbed his chin as if feeling for missed whiskers after shaving. "Normal? Now that's a novel description of my life!"

"You know what I mean, compared to what I was doing."

"We can talk about that later—I mean why you left—if you want to. You're

210

really not going back then?"

"Nope," Jake said with certain finality.

"So what's the plan? What are you going to do?" Harry tugged on his new shirt that was slightly twisted around his waist. He pulled it away from his gut to admire the ideogram.

"Mom and Neal offered to let me stay with them till I find work and a place of my own. I'm thinking of going back to school."

"Did you see what mom did with our old room?" Harry rolled his eyes.

"Yes. I already moved in." Jake paused, and then said, "C'mon Harry. Mom did a really nice job."

"I almost moved back there too for a while but my ex finally decided to move in with her boyfriend."

"Who is he? Did I know him?" Jake asked.

"No. He's a business executive. Moved here from Rochester. Julie met him at her job at the health club. He's ripped and looks good in a suit. They moved into a McMansion near Valley Forge. They plan to be married soon. She must have been a hell of a personal trainer!"

"You're still bitter, then," Jake noted.

"Not as much as I was. Hey, enough of that. Listen, the kids are coming over next weekend. It will be my turn to keep them. They will want to see their Uncle Jake. They still talk about the neat Indian stuff you sent them last Christmas. Jenny wears her turquoise necklace and earrings a lot. Sam wore his sheepskin slippers all winter. He hung that shaman drum on his wall. That's really cool."

"Well, the turquoise jewelry was Indian made and maybe the drum; not the slippers. How old are they now?"

Harry pulled a recent, framed picture of his kids off a shelf to show Jake.

"Jenny here is thirteen now. Look, she has the necklace on, there. Scary how quick she's grown up. You might not recognize her in person—she's changed her hairstyle since this was taken six months ago. Sam there is eleven. I think he's turning into a nerd. He's a genius with math, not much interest so far in sports. He tried soccer last year but did not do well. Takes after his mom. But he's a great kid."

The brothers caught up on family matters until Lindy reappeared in the kitchen. She had slipped into her faded, tight jeans and put on a collarless blue blouse. With her hair combed and eyeliner applied she looked ready to go anywhere. Jake nodded his approval at Harry while Lindy had her head turned by the window to light another cigarette. Harry thanked Lindy for covering up. Lindy suggested they go out to eat breakfast. Harry called on his mobile into his auto shop to see if his two helpers could handle things for a while. They could.

They all got into Monica's 2004 Honda minivan that Jake had borrowed for the day. Lindy sat upfront with Jake to direct him. Harry sat behind them with his hand-held mobile device that did everything. He needed to check on business emails and customer schedules for the coming week. He was absorbed in that activity for the twenty minutes it took to get to New Hope. Lindy pointed to some new landmarks along the way. They drove along the Delaware River's old canal system toward town passing another stone colonial building being renovated into a bed and breakfast inn. It was late morning, close to 10 a.m. Parking could be a problem near the eateries but Jake managed to pull the minivan into a space just being vacated by a delivery truck. The sun slipped out between clouds as they stepped out of the van. They walked to Café Lulu's. Lindy led the brothers to an open outdoor table where they seated themselves.

Lindy and Jake both ordered the Feta and Sun-dried Tomato Omelet with Home Fries special on the menu. Harry asked for bacon and eggs over easy with no frills. Service was slow, very slow, but none of the three took notice as long as the coffee and tea kept coming. They were enjoying the morning respite. Harry mentioned that he sometimes ate with his biker friends there after a run. Indeed, there were a dozen Harleys and other large bikes parked along Main Street. As if on cue, a familiar voice came from the sidewalk.

"Yo, G'zhipp," a man called out saying Harry's last name, Grzyb with a hard G.

"Harry! How the hell are you? I was going to drop in at the shop. You closed today?"

The large, stocky fellow with sunglasses and thinning gray hair tied back in a pony tail maneuvered around the tables until he got to Harry's side. He slid his sunglasses up over his forehead. With him were two other rugged looking men wearing denim riding colors and carrying motorcycle helmets. Both wore dark blue bandanas. They stood back silently. The large man and Harry greeted by bumping fists. Jake recognized the man despite the many years that passed but he could not recall his name.

"Hey, old-timer, this is Lindy and you remember my brother, Jake, right? Lindy, this is our dad's good friend, Mr. Giles," Harry said. "They were in Nam together."

Lindy acknowledged Giles with a smile from across the table. Giles casually saluted her.

Harry turned back to Lindy. "You know, our dad used to come here to get together with vets."

Giles reached out to greet Jake with a thick handshake. "Jake, Jake, sure man. Good to see you again. I heard you were living out West."

"No. Just moved back. I plan to stay here for a while. In fact, I got back a couple days ago."

"Why, man?"

Giles expressed a common local reaction to anyone who broke free from the congested Northeast. He had been out to the Rockies around Denver several times.

"I'd move out there in a heartbeat but my old lady wants to be near her family," he said.

"Long story, Giles. Ten years was enough vacation! Time to get serious, you know?"

"Too bad. It's beautiful out there. Well, anyway, good luck Jake, with whatever you're doing. And welcome back."

"I'll be at the shop this afternoon, Giles," Harry noted. "So, you want to come by then?"

"I might. I need to borrow a truck first. My old bike needs engine work. It's running rough.

"Your old bike—you mean the '72 Harley?"

"Yes, that one," Giles confirmed. "First bike I bought after Nam."

"What are you riding now?"

"That 2001 Heritage over there," he said pointing over the fence. "So, what do you think?"

"This afternoon okay, say around four?"

"Yeah."

"You got a cell with you?"

"Yeah."

"Tell me your number."

Giles had to get his mobile out of his pocket to check it for his number. "I can never remember this. The old lady changed our provider again."

Harry entered Giles's information into his mobile. He immediately forwarded it to his shop computer. "It's all set. See you then."

Giles gestured for the two men with him to take seats at a nearby table as most places on the patio were taken already and guests were arriving in a steady flow.

"I'll be right with you guys. Order me some coffee—decaf."

Then he turned to Harry again. "Hey, if you're not doing anything tomorrow—today's Saturday, right—some of us from the club are riding to a harvest cook-out over near Phoenixville at Jim's. You know, at Jim McDade's, same as every year."

"Is that tomorrow? Damn, he did invite me again. Thanks for reminding me. I forgot."

Giles then addressed Jake. "He, Jim, knew your dad well. He'd be pleased to meet you." Giles paused a second or two before saying to Harry, "Bring Lindy and Jake and the kids if you want."

"The kids are with their mom this weekend."

"Too bad. Other kids their ages will be there. Come to think of it, why don't you guys ride with us? Jake, you can hop on with me if you don't have wheels. My old lady is driving over in the truck. What do you say?"

Harry looked to Jake and Lindy for a reaction. They both shrugged in affirmation. Jake smiled thinking to himself how lucky he was to have made new connections at his home base already. He was on his way to normal again.

"Okay, sounds good, man. Come by the house. We can leave from there," Harry said. Then Harry recalled that Jake was staying at Monica's. "You think mom can drop you off?"

"I promised her I'd go to church with her at, I think, the 10:30 mass. Maybe she can drop me off after that," Jake said.

Harry shook his head gently from side to side, and then said, "Mmm, mmm, she never gives up on God, does she? Talked you into it, did she? The only time I go any more with her is Christmas. Neal has an excuse—he's part Jewish!" Then Harry screwed up his face and asked, "Is that possible, to be part Jewish?"

No one answered him.

Giles waited till Harry was done talking. He said, "Then we can be at Jim's around two after a good ride. Glad you all are coming. There will be people of all ages there. Could be as many as sixty or seventy!"

"Can we bring anything," Lindy asked?

"Don't bother. As Harry can vouch, we always have plenty left over. But if you have a favorite wine or drink—bring that."

After breakfast, Lindy led the brothers to a shop nearby. She wanted to look for a special gift for her mother's birthday. The shop had unique hand-knitted sweaters that Lindy wanted to see. The men chose to wait outside for her. Harry lit a Winston. He coughed after taking a drag. He held the pack out—Jake declined.

"Still can't corrupt you, can I?" Harry blew smoke away from Jake. "How long you been a vegetarian?"

"I was strict about it for a few years but I started eating some meat again last year."

"You know, mom still prays for you. She thought you'd make a good priest since you're so interested in religion. She's been fairly upset since you joined those Buddhists." Harry spit on the ground, and then took another drag, this time without coughing.

"Yeah, well, I did what I did. Right now I'm not too happy about it either."

Lindy soon came out of the shop with a bag. Harry flicked his cigarette into a storm drain. "You found something, hon? Let's see it."

Lindy pulled out the top of a pinkish pullover to show them. Then she stuffed it back only to grab a smaller bag from inside. "Here, hold this." She handed the large bag with the pullover in it to Jake. "Go ahead, Harry, open it," she giggled as she handed the small bag to him.

Harry looked inside the bag carefully before taking it out.

"Well, what do you know; another damn mushroom!"

Harry pulled out the carved wooden figure of a simple red-capped toadstool to show Jake. "Ever since Lindy found out what our family name means she's been buying me these things. We must have a dozen or more around the place."

"Now I know what to get you for your birthday," Jake kidded. "You know, I rarely tell anyone what grzyb means. Hard enough getting them to spell it right!"

The next morning Jake drove his mother to church in her van.

A childhood pilgrimage repeats. Mother guides child to church again. You relate as a child almost helpless to protest any more not willing to hurt feelings. This is your mother and she mothers you always. But there is more. You seem curious. Has it been ten years? Has it been eleven years? Eleven years of mortal sins. Does anyone count sins in eternity? The eternal mass sacrifices only one, one that is eternal. How does that happen? You will see it happen again. You will see the blood separated from the body and offered to you and others unworthy. Lordy, lordy, you be not worthy that He should come into your heart, but only say the Word. You cannot say the word and you shall not be healed. The Lord says the word and you shall be healed.

Healed, forgiven, forgiven, healed. Take up your sick bed. You are forgiven. You can walk now. Get out of here. Go and try not to get crippled again. Next!—14 October 2007

Monica led Jake toward a pew near the front row where she was accustomed to sit. They passed the holy water fountain used for baptisms and for blessing. Monica dipped her fingers in it and blessed herself silently in the name of the Father and of the Son and of the Holy Ghost. Jake passed on the holy water despite a strong instinct to dip. He would watch only, he thought, as he entered a familiar yet strange world. He would watch himself watching the most powerful event in Catholic ritual; not as the ultimate participant-observer of the ultimate act, but curious nevertheless. He would watch a ritual he saw hundreds of times as a kid during which the God of all creation will be sacrificed on that altar, that very altar, and his body and blood will be fed to the people so that they might live eternally—God in them and they in God. He slid into his seat next to Monica who knelt to pray before sitting.

She believed in this but what did she believe, he wondered? He flipped through the missal looking for the appropriate readings. He looked at the people in the pews. The church was nearly half filled—or was it mostly empty? He did not recognize anyone. A nicely dressed Hispanic woman, most likely from the well-established Puerto Rican community nearby, and her two small children arranged themselves next to Jake in the pew. The young boy held a plastic figurine of Batman. When the boy glanced up with his big brown eyes to assess the man next to him, Jake smiled and nodded. The boy stared blankly at first, and then he smiled back. He stood Batman up on the bench next to Jake as if to say, "He's here too. Watch out!"

The church organist began to play and the small choir sang the hymn "Come Holy Spirit, Wind and Fire" by Saint Catherine. Everyone stood to greet the priest and his entourage of altar servers and a deacon. The deacon and the priest wore green vestments. The deacon held the Book of Gospels high above his head as the procession approached the altar area. The priest turned to the congregation and blessed them with the sign of the cross saying, In the name of the Father and of the Son and of the Holy Spirit. Along with everyone in the congregation Jake crossed himself from forehead to chest to left and right shoulder and responded with Amen.

After the introductory prayers everyone sat down. The little boy bounced Batman up and down from the pew to his lap. Monica took a missal from the rack in front of her. She opened it to the first reading from the Second Book of Kings. Jake did likewise. The lector read, "Naaman went down and plunged into the Jordan seven times at the word of Elisha, the man of God. His flesh became again like the flesh of a little child, and he was clean of his leprosy."

Monica was not an every Sunday Catholic before Ziggy got killed eighteen years before. To cope with that tragedy she converted her life to a steady cycle of church events. Ziggy rarely attended masses but he always encouraged the boys to go with their mother. Neal would accompany Monica twice a year for the Christmas and Easter celebrations. He said he enjoyed the cultural richness of the services. His Sunday ritual after marrying Monica was to drop her off at church, then drive to a local coffee shop to sit and read the newspaper until it was time to get Monica after mass to take her to breakfast.

The final reading was from one of the four Gospels. Everyone stood up to listen preparing themselves for "the word of the Lord" by making small crosses on forehead, lips and chest with the right thumb. The old, white-haired priest deferred to the deacon, a middle-aged, slightly balding man with an odd haircut—it was neatly combed back over his ears and it hung slightly over his collar.

Jake did not immediately read along from the open book in his hand. He was distracted by the boy who was making buzzing noises while moving Batman around. During one maneuver the boy dropped Batman under the pew in front. It was out of his reach. Jake knelt down to retrieve the toy for him. The mother quietly whispered, "Gracias, señor. Thank you." Then she whispered angrily to her son, "Hijo, quieto!" The boy sat obediently, Batman in hand. His sister stuck her tongue out at him. Jake stood up. He did not bother to look into the missal again. Jake drifted into a reverie of thoughts that he later wrote down.

Batman was next to you in church. Batman is a superhero without superpowers. He only seems superhuman. Batman is wholly if extraordinarily human. Superman is not of this Earth and only seems human in disguise as Clark Kent. Superman has superpowers.

Was Jesus Batman or Superman?

If Jesus were Superman his devotees would be similar to Monophysites and Cathars who saw Jesus as divine only. Clark Kent is the illusion who hides his superpowers. Superman as Clark Kent hides his divinity. But Clark Kent dies on the cross. Only Jesus resurrects.

If Jesus were Batman his devotees would be like Ebionites who saw Jesus as merely human. Bruce Wayne has no superpowers to hide. Bruce Wayne as Batman hides his humanity.

Batman is for the Atheists and skeptics.

Superman is for Gnostics and magicians.—14 October 2007

Jake snapped back from his daydream in time to hear the end of the Gospel reading. The lector read about Jesus admonishing his disciples to pay attention to what a dishonest judge says. The judge "neither feared God nor respected any human being." The judge nevertheless delivered a just decision to a widow who kept badgering him about her adversary. Jesus exhorts his followers to pay attention to this judge because he judges justly nevertheless, just as God will judge everyone. Then the deacon prepared to give the homily.

Monica leaned over to her son and whispered, "He's a new one, Jacob, and still learning. I wish you could have heard the pastor speak today instead. I like him."

Monica was very aware that her son fell away from the church because he felt little relevance in it to his life. The rituals were more like routines to him and they had grown stale. The last priest he talked with eleven years earlier at Monica's request could not convince him otherwise. And now the deacon spoke as if he were talking to a grade school class about how God will judge us in the end. The deacon's parental tone numbed Jake's concentration. He fell into a mild trance again as he recalled an encounter he had with a religious stranger in

Taos, an encounter he recorded on August 15, 2006:

Quietly meditating on a bench on the plaza waiting for Marga. She and a female Center member are posting flyers for our next workshop and Roshi's local lecture.

In the warm sunshine time, feels unmeasured with eyes shut.

You feel him sit at the other end of the bench. You open your eyes. A glance reveals that the casually dressed man in Wrangler jeans and a pale polo shirt holds a Bible. He catches your glance and immediately greets you.

Sir, do you know Jesus?

You tell the witness you were raised Catholic, but you mention nothing about the Center. He asks permission to share some verses from scripture.

You were polite and, maybe, you were curious. He was well-studied. Seamless scripture seemed to shore up simple truth. Pages and passages etched in neuropathways. Isaiah predicts the virgin born Messiah. Revelation exposes the Vatican as the home of the whore and the beast. The woman crowned with stars is not Mary. Darwin was wrong. The earth is around 10,000 years old. Dinosaurs walked with men. We have a picture of co-existing footprints in Texas. Once saved, always saved. King James rocks.

Admit sin, repent, and ask Jesus to come into your heart formula.

The poor guy threw his best curves and fast balls and you just sat there. The game was on but you never took a swing. Rome takes care of itself. Argue with Rome and not a fool on a bench.

Marga asked you who that man was. You said he was a good man fishing for souls and the bait was okay but the hook was inedible. You told Marga that the preacher left you feeling empty.

Marga smiled. She rarely missed a pun, even if you intended none.

—23 May 2006

Jake ended his Taos-bench reverie when the deacon stopped dictating. From his view on the pew Jake refocused his attention to present time. He watched the priest stand up to continue the liturgy. As if from hid subconscious mind an odd question surfaced: "What was the hook? To Catholics the hook is entirely edible," he thought. "The hook is the bait. It was time for the consecration of the host, the wafer of bread, soon to be the body of Christ, God-stuff used for the communal meal."

The priest continued with the liturgy of the Eucharist that leads to the Communion rite, the consummate people's ritual of Catholic faith. After the Lord's Prayer, or the "Our Father," the priest followed with the rite of peace. "Offer each other a sign of peace." Jake hugged his mother kissing her on the cheek as she hugged him back saying, "Peace be with you, son." Then Jake turned to the small boy who was occupied with a kiss of peace and a hug from his mother. The boy turned to Jake to shake his hand. They exchanged greetings of "Peace." The boy's mother also acknowledged Jake with a handshake. The boy's sister looked at Jake shyly. She kept her hands to herself. Batman lay at peace on the pew behind the boy.

When it came time to kneel for the communion rite, Jake felt queasy. The sensation came on suddenly. He felt a tingling in his fingers. The hallowed walls and pews began to spin slightly as if he had just stepped off a carousel. He touched his mother on the shoulder to get her attention.

"Mom, I'll meet you in back—need some air," he whispered. He excused himself as he clumsily slid past the boy and his family to get out of the pew. After locating the side exit he kept his eyes on the floor, walking with purpose, grabbing pew end after pew end to sustain a steady gate while trying to breathe slowly. Behind him the priest announced, "This is the Lamb of God who takes away the sins of the world. Happy are we who are called to his supper." Then all in the pews repeated, "Lord, I am not worthy to receive you, but only say the word and I shall be healed."

An usher and the preoccupied parishioners took little notice of him as he worked his way to the side door. He felt the blood draining from his head. He stepped outside. He paced anxiously but slowly along the sidewalk with his hands on his hips and his head hanging. He took slow, deep breaths. It was a brisk morning, so each breath of air soothed his lungs and his mind. He stood still, face to the sky with his eyes closed. Panic symptoms subsided. He leaned against the gray stone of the building to stay his equilibrium. The stone wall offered stability in the world that moved in and around him. He reached back with his hands to press the rough gray stone. Then he leaned forward resting his hands on his knees with his butt against the solid surface.

He noticed the cornerstone of the old building behind his feet. From his upside down view he saw *1892*, a simple cross, and *Our Lady of Mercy* etched into the smooth gray stone. Down by his foot he saw dozens of tiny ants piled on to a dead cricket. Busy workers dragged small bug pieces to a hole at the base of the cornerstone. Grains of sand tumbled down the hole behind a disappearing cricket leg. Jake moved his foot to avoid crushing more ants. He stood there until he heard the congregation singing the closing hymn.

After mass, Jake and Monica drove to the nearby cafe where Neal was enjoying his newspaper and coffee. They went inside to join him at his booth. Monica sat next to Neal while Jake sat across from them. Neal urged them to order something.

"Jake, can you eat with us before going the cookout? It could be four, five hours or more before you get to eat there."

"Sure, I guess. How's the service here?" Jake noted that nearly every table was occupied. He noted a wide range of people with some dressed better than others but most in casual daily attire. Single men sat at the counter stools. The better dressed people at the diner included an African American couple with three children and a gray-headed grandmother. They all sat at a round table near Neal's booth.

As if on cue, Neal introduced Jake to the family at the round table. After Jake exchanged greetings Neal explained, "We meet here nearly every Sunday at the same time." Neal had become acquainted with the family over the past year as they all tended to sit by habit at the same seats every Sunday. Then Neal addressed Jake's concern about time.

"I know this waitress. She can make it happen," Neal reassured him. "How was church?"

"Okay. Not much has changed."

Before Jake could go on the waitress appeared.

"Hi, I'm Kaylie and I will be your waitress. What would yous like to drink?"

It had been many years since Jake heard anyone use a plural form of *you* that way. He smiled at Kaylie, who was decidedly unattractive, plump and in her mid-twenties. She handed out menus. She returned his smile as she refilled Neal's cup. Neal asked her to wait to take their orders. They quickly looked at the menus. Monica and Jake ordered coffee and scones. Neal requested, "The usual scrapple and eggs over easy with wheat toast."

"Well, that was easy. I'll be right back with your orders." Kaylie took the menus and coffee pot to the next booth where two older men sat. Jake smiled again as he heard, "Hi, how are yous guys doin' this morning."

"What are you smiling about, Jacob?"

"Oh, nothing, mom—the people here are interesting. Feels good to be back"

Monica did not comment. She had another matter on her mind. "Neal, Jacob had another anxiety episode at the service. I'm a little worried. Will you talk with him about it?"

"Mom, it wasn't so bad this time. Stop getting all worked up. I'll be okay."

Neal raised his eyebrows, laid his newspaper down on the seat, and removed his reading glasses. He glanced at Jake who appeared fine to him.

"Monica, I'm sure Jake will know when to ask for help. By the way, Harry called me a bit ago. He and Lindy got up late, so we may have more time. He said he'd call when he's ready."

"Thanks, Neal, I mean, for asking Monica to ease up. But since she brought it up, what do you think causes my panic attacks? It's not clear to me what triggers it."

"Well, as I see it you're going through a big change, Jake. Some of this may be due to subconscious factors that may take some time to surface. This is not the place or time to explore this. Just keep an open mind about seeing a doc if this persists. Okay?"

"Yeah, sure. Can you pass the jelly, mom?"

"No, I'm serious, Jake," Neal went on. "You might have a temporary anxiety

223

disorder that is easily treatable in most cases, but something else might be going on."

"You mean I may be a head case? I already know that. I just wasted ten years of my life trying to meditate my mind away. Maybe there's brain damage. What do you think, mom?"

Jake made a crazy face with his tongue out to the side.

"Jacob, stop that," Monica chided. "I am not saying you are crazy. Do not even think that! Just that you seem out of sorts. Please see a doctor if this persists."

"Okay, okay mom. I should get a physical anyway. I'll look into it soon." Jake reached over to squeeze her hand to reassure her.

Monica looked at him for any indication of sarcasm. She felt he was sincere. Then she felt, for the first time, how desperate her son must have been to leave the Center. "Jake, do you really think you wasted ten years? You made some good friends. In your letters and when we talked you seemed to know so much about it. I thought you liked it there. Does any of that mean anything to you?"

"Mom, well sure, there are some good people there. Maybe I'll have a better answer for you later. Right now the best way to look at this is that I was part of a monastery that had an interesting but corrupt priest for a leader. As far as Buddhism as a way of life, I don't know. I can still see the logic in it. People who are skeptical of religion, especially about Western monotheism, find a lot attractive in Buddhism."

Neal asked, "Have you thought of exploring a more established form of Buddhism then?"

"I did. In fact I looked into it two years ago when I first thought of leaving the Center. I wrote to a monastery in Kyoto and had some exchanges with a monk there. He was pretty well educated in world religions. He even studied at Syracuse—his English was surprisingly good. He told me to read his professor's autobiography. The guy was an Austrian who became a Hindu monk."

"Did you say Hindu?"

"Yeah. He went by Swami Bharati. He taught religious studies at Syracuse when this monk in Japan studied there in the 1980s. Anyway, I read it, *The Ochre Robe*, and was quite impressed. It made me realize how backwards I approached all this. In his other writings Bharati recommended studying the language of the religion first and then its tradition before joining anything. So I looked into Buddhism with a broader view for a year. I even finally read Thomas Merton's autobiography, the one you recommended Neal, and some of the comments he made on Buddhism."

"*Seven Story Mountain*? Good book," Neal said. "I thought since you were into Buddhism coming from Catholicism, it might interest you. I can't recall any other motive for recommending it than hoping it would slow you down, make you think, you know. I'm surprised you remembered after all this time."

"I doubt it would have changed my mind then, even if I read it right away. I thought you and Monica were just trying to keep me in the Christian fold. But, yea, Merton looked into Buddhism, seriously. He died in India while meeting with Buddhists. Last month, I picked up a book that just came out called *Merton and Buddhism*. If anything, what I read only brought up more questions."

"Questions are good! You seem to be working this out fairly well."

Neal was about to say more, but Jake cut him off. "Neal, to tell you the truth I lost interest in that book halfway through it. I left it at the Center. Honestly, I wonder if there are a few loose screws in my head, or maybe I can't face reality." Jake stopped to take a sip of coffee. He was feeling both embarrassed and irritated. "Sorry. Didn't mean to cut you off."

"Er, nothing. Lost my train of thought," Neal said with some reserve.

After hearing Jake's admission to immaturity, Neal looked at him blankly. He realized that the young man was in the throes of a crisis, and this was no time to play therapist by acknowledging it. Monica on the other hand was at a loss for words. Unlike Neal, her grasp of Buddhism was not even rudimentary. She was afraid to say something wrong. She could read a son's mood as well as any loving mother. The ten years effort as a monk had not changed him that much. Jake did not like to be wrong.

"Can I get yous anything else?" asked the waitress who appeared at their booth suddenly, holding two coffee carafes—one decaf and one regular.

"No, just a check please, Kaylie." Neal pulled out his wallet.

"Thanks, Neal. One of these days, I'll repay all this," Jake said quietly.

"You're a cheap date, Jake. Forget it."

12   Riding for Normal

Giles pulled up from the alley behind Harry's house and stopped by the back shed. He dropped the kickstand on his black, 2001 Harley Heritage and cut the engine. Harry's shed served as storage for yard equipment and a garage for a silver-blue Super Glide Harley. The Glide was fitted with custom seat and sissy bar. Harry and most of his biker friends were part of the international Harley Owners Group or HOG. They met and rode at several events a year including for Rolling Thunder on Memorial Day when many hundreds of bikers rode into Washington, DC.

Giles pulled out his mobile to alert Harry that he would wait for them out back. He removed his aviator sunglasses and the black, German style half helmet that he set on the bike's seat. He lit a cigarette and took a drag as he leaned against the Harley's gas tank with his arms across his chest. The old, waist length leather jacket he wore did not rustle like a new one. It was rugged and rubbed raw around his shoulders, back and elbows. A few puffy clouds drifted overhead as a gentle breeze carried the exhaled smoke from his face. Giles squinted as he looked up to read the clouds. He figured the day would be without rain. Then he locked his eyes on a large dark dog in the neighbor's yard opposite Harry's. The dog's eyes were locked on Giles and it was slowly creeping in his direction.

The sturdy Giles slowly shuffled to the other side of his bike, never taking his eyes off the dog. As best he could tell, it was part Rottweiler—a big dark dog moving with purpose and not on a leash. Step by confident step it came forward. Giles flicked his cigarette away. The dog continued with ears now flat against its head. At a mere ten yards away it stopped as if to assess its prey. Ever so slowly Giles reached down to open the flap of his saddlebag where he kept his gun, a Glock 19. Just as his hand touched the gun's handle, a shout pierced the air behind him. He nearly jumped out of his skin.

"Metzger, c'mere boy!"

The dog bounded round the bike and Giles. It nearly bowled Harry over as it leapt up to greet him.

"Good boy, Metzger. Good boy."

Harry rubbed the dog's neck and back briskly. Then Harry turned to Giles who was looking none too amused.

"Scared the crap out of you, did he?" Harry said laughing. "Here, let him smell your hand first." Harry grabbed the dog's collar and guided it over to Giles.

"Damn, Harry. I was about to shoot the bastard if you hadn't come along when you did—shit, man."

Metzger sniffed Giles for a few seconds. Its clipped nub of a tail wagged rapidly. Lindy and Jake enjoyed the scene from the yard. As Giles tentatively held out his hand, he said, "He's one butt-ugly, nasty looking dog—what is he, Rottie?"

"Part, er, mostly," Harry said trying to recall what his neighbor told him. "I think Bart, his owner, told me one of his granddads was a Mastiff. I've known him since he was a pup two years ago. He used to be real cute then!"

Harry patted the slobbering animal on its head.

"He wasn't going after you, man," Harry explained. "He spotted me coming out the back door. I often give him a snack when he visits."

Harry glanced at his watch. "C'mon boy. Let's get you back in the house." Harry jogged ahead of the dog to lead him home. "Bart or Lil must have left the door unlocked," he shouted. "He's a real Houdini."

Jake thought of Obi.

"Metzger's a beast. Probably just busted down the damn door," Giles remarked mostly to himself with a hint of admiration. He lit another Marlboro and took a deep drag. He noticed that his hand was still shaking.

Giles insisted that Jake wear the half helmet. Jake did not argue. He eased himself onto the Harley's seat behind Giles. Harry lent his brother a pair of sunglasses to wear. In Pennsylvania at the time the biker had a choice to wear a helmet or not so it was legal for Giles to go without headgear. Instead, he wore his old black and orange

Giants baseball cap with its SF logo backwards, pulling it tight on his head.

Lindy wore a standard helmet that covered her ears. She felt quite relaxed behind Harry as he drove carefully down the gravel alleyway. They were a matched set with Harry's deep metallic blue helmet matching Lindy's that matched the Glide. The distinct rumble of the powerful V-twin engines emerged onto the paved street as Giles followed Harry to meet the others. Jake adjusted quickly to feeling comfortable as a motorbike passenger again even if it was over ten years since he sat on one of these. The older man's long gray ponytail flopped in the wind in front of Jake's face. His father wore his hair in a ponytail as well.

Ziggy took you and Harry one at a time on long rides on his Harley before the crash. At times Giles joined us and we both went. Ziggy always drove sensibly, never drank before, made you wear a helmet but he did not. Riding with Ziggy was a thrill as much for the ride as for where he would go. Once we visited an old farmer near Barto. He parked the Harley on the farmer's land at the edge of a wooded area with a steep slope. He led you through barely recognizable trails always pointing out the poison ivy. At one vantage point near a cluster of huge boulders he told you to look up. The boulder nearly eight feet high had the distinct profile of a man's head. He then led you to the top of the head. On top of the head boulder was a depression, like a large bowl. Behind the head cut from old gray rock were a number of seats. You sat in one of the seats. You envisioned a council of elders in feathers and buckskin. What went on there? Dad called it Indian Head Rock. He never tried to explain it but he said Indians made it.—9 November 2007

Their first stop was at a Wawa service center along a two lane highway. Three more bikers with two passengers were waiting for them, sipping on drinks and chatting as Harry and Giles pulled up. After brief greetings complete with fist pumps and hugs, the drivers of a Honda Goldwing, a Kawasaki Ninja ZX, and an elegant, rose-color Dyna Glide Trike joined the entourage. A woman Giles introduced to Jake as Gigi owned the trike. A GG logo stood out prominently on the front fender. Gayle Gordon looked sharp in her red Kevlar riding outfit with black trim and black helmet. Her passenger was a lean fellow whose name Jake did not get at first.

With Jake in tow Giles remained at the end of the pack as Harry led on the other end. The bikers paused twice to gather ten more motorcycles. Most were Harleys but the one that stood out for Jake's taste was a late model, black Ducati Superbike that looked more appropriate for a racetrack than a leisurely run. The oldest machine was a chopped Harley Hardtail with high handlebars and extended front end. It had a late sixties look with a deep purple base color accented with yellow, orange and pink flames. Jake heard the owner say that the original was a 1971 model. Jake recognized him as one of the men they met in New Hope the day before. The man on the Hardtail rode next to or in front of Giles the rest of the way. The twenty bikes, half with passengers, converged onto a highway on the way to Jim's cookout.

The way Harry led them wound through wooded areas, past dairy farms and over small streams. They rumbled through a classic covered wooden bridge creating a thunderous reverb inside that delighted Jake. Near Oley a couple of young boys on peddle bikes pulled up on a side road to watch the parade roll by. With smiles on their faces the boys pointed excitedly at the trike and the old chopper. Further along, as the road wound north past unharvested acres of tall corn, they passed a large, home-made sign stating: *Corn Maze ahead*. They passed stands of mailboxes of every description. Jake eventually relaxed behind Giles who was a smooth working part of his vehicle after decades of experience. This was fun for the sake of it; the feel of flying low to the ground through a picture-ready landscape.

On a straight rise ahead Jake noticed the bikes all slowing down to swerve, one after the other, to the middle of the road and then switch back to the proper lane. The man on the Hardtail ahead signaled to something on the ground to Giles who gave him a *thumbs-up*. As they approached the obstruction, Jake noted the dead deer with some of its gut freshly squeezed out on the tarmac. Giles pulled up behind the carcass and stopped. He parked the bike letting it run with the emergency flashers on. He waited for Jake to hop off before swinging his leg over to dismount. He was quite agile for a man with such a wide girth.

"Let's get this critter off the road. Grab the front feet and I'll get the back," Giles directed.

A pungent odor emanated from the carcass. The men slid the large, nearly 200-pound whitetail into the high grass and weeds along the road side. The deer, a large doe, left only a streak of body fluids and not enough guts on the road to impede traffic.

Jake rubbed his hands onto his khakis even though nothing moist touched them. He took one last look at the doe's head. Such an elegant animal, he thought. He took his jacket off, folded it and sat on it for the rest of the ride. It was a warm day. Further down the road they passed a dead skunk. Giles did not stop this time. Jake held his breath until they were well past the flattened roadkill. By that time they had caught up to the pack.

Giles yelled back to Jake, "Local roads are a slaughterhouse, man."

Following Harry's lead off and on Route 73, the lively group reversed course and turned south working their way along back roads through French Creek Park and into St. Peter's Village, then turning east onto 23. Finally, after the two hours jaunt they all pulled into Jim's small farm in Chester County.

Jim owned twelve acres of rolling, mostly wooded hills near a hamlet called Fox Run along Flowing Springs Road. The only farming he did was four acres set aside for Christmas trees or wood pulp. He kept two horses for pleasure riding but no other livestock besides a dog, a goat and a few cats. With the biker group's arrival the number of guests almost doubled. Activities and feasting were already underway. Kids and adults were playing badminton while others were throwing quoits.

The bikers tended to their machines, parking them all in a neat row on the lawn in front of the main house. Many of them removed riding clothes that included chaps, leathers, and helmets storing them in various carriers, saddlebags or inside the shed near the house.

Jake admired the old building, a restored colonial stone structure that had a stuccoed addition tastefully merged onto the back of the home. The plaintive sound of a Neil Young song, *Cowgirl in the Sand*, blared from several speakers hung on tree trunks. Jake took a deep breath through his nose. He took in the pastoral scene banked by hills flecked with early autumn colors from maple, oak, hickory, ash, beech, elm and other eastern trees inviting an impressionist's pallet. He saw children playing and adults talking. Some of them were cooking at a large smoky grill. This was America at ease. This was good. Then Jake sniffed the air a few more times. He turned around to examine a young, fifteen-foot tall tree.

Root beer was made from this tree Ziggy told us. We stopped once with Giles and Harry on one of our rides. Ziggy bent down after kicking away the dirt and cut some root bark slices with his penknife. We took the slices home, steeped some in boiling water and each of us took a sip. Sure smelled like root beer. Maybe we needed more bark. We did what the Indians and pioneers did. We made root beer tea.

 You saw a reference at the Center, a thick book with pictures and drawings of plants and herbs. The Food and Drug Administration banned sassafras bark in 1976 because of the carcinogenic properties of its constituent chemical, safrole. Safrole can damage the liver but it is a good insecticide.—9 November 2007

Gigi slammed shut the small trunk on her trike as Harry approached her. She was now in her black sleeveless top and short cut jeans that exposed a prominent tattoo of a thin snake wrapped around her left thigh. She was about to work on her short-cropped, dyed black hair after touching up her makeup with her eyeliner using the trike's mirror. Harry waited for her to finish, admiring her butt as she leaned over. The added mascara accented her bright green eyes. When she slipped into her sandals she stood tall for a girl, sturdy and slender at five feet six.

"Yo, Gigi, you're looking great girl. It's been a while," Harry intoned with a hint of irony. After his separation from his wife, Harry dated Gigi one time and once was enough for them to realize they were not suited for one another. They nevertheless remained friends. Gigi frowned at Harry as if to tell him to stop the B.S. She knew

Harry's compliments usually led to an agenda. She knew Harry's ex-wife Judy. The women spent some time together through the divorce proceedings so Gigi heard about Harry's many flaws. Still, after the divorce, she preferred to hang out with Harry and Lindy.

"Hey," he went on, "this is no big deal, but can we talk later? I'd like to run something by you about my brother."

Gigi's riding companion, a thin fellow, seemed uninterested in their conversation. He walked toward the main house to meet with Jim and his wife. Harry continued when the thin friend was out of earshot.

"My brother Jake just got back a few days ago. He was in some kind of religious cult in New Mexico. It was the reason we haven't seen much of him for years. I recall you were involved in something like that with a guru, right?"

"Yes, but that was eight or nine years ago, and I was out there for only a week or two. An old friend dragged me along."

"You sure talked a lot about it at the time with Judy, as I recall."

"It was an intense week, man! I got creeped out when I met the leader and when I heard about what it might cost me later, so I quit. In fact I quit looking into any of that spirituality stuff after that. Haven't thought about it much since. Was Jake really in a cult?"

"Shhhh," Harry whispered as he waved his hands in front of Gigi's face. He looked around to see if Jake or anyone else other than Lindy could hear them. He scanned the area and saw Jake at the other end of the row of bikes. He saw his brother holding a leaf in his hand.

"He doesn't like that word, but, yeah, kinda. He calls it a commune or the Center. Anyway, he may need someone to talk to about it, you know, in depth. Maybe you can use a feminine touch, eh? Get him to open up a bit." Harry cocked his head to the side as if to say, "Please, do me this favor."

Harry was not kidding when he noted how good she looked. Gigi was a full-time personal trainer at a gym, the same one where Harry's ex-wife worked. Gigi did not really have to work, she got by on an inheritance. She enjoyed the work.

Then Harry said with a more serious tone, "Listen, don't force anything. He's sensitive about it. It's just a thought. I'm worried about the guy."

"He seemed okay to me back at the Wawa. Could use a trim on that head and beard though. Where is he now?"

Harry motioned with his head. Gigi looked in Jake's direction.

"What the hell's he doing, Harry?"

Jake had torn the sassafras leaf and was sniffing the pieces in his cupped hands. From her vantage point it looked like some kind of odd prayer ritual. She watched him drop the pieces on the ground and wipe his hands on his pants. Then Jake inadvertently turned in their direction.

Harry waived at him as he shouted, "Did you enjoy the ride?"

"Totally."

"Come on. I want you to meet Jim and his wife," Harry shouted out. "What are you doing there?"

"Root beer!" Jake motioned to the tree behind him.

Now Gigi was clearly confused. Harry thought for a second and then yelled back, "Oh yeah, root beer." He recalled that day making tea with Ziggy. Gigi looked from one to the other brother quizzically. "Root beer," Harry repeated with a shrug. "He's having a flashback. Dad made us root beer from sassafras once. Good luck with him and thanks."

Harry did not explain further. He just walked away to find Lindy. Gigi waived to Jake, but he did not notice. He walked toward Harry while adjusting his sunglasses. Gigi shrugged, feeling no desire to pursue a meeting with him at that moment. She checked her hair and face one more time in the trike mirror.

Someone called out, "Food's on. Let's eat."

The Coldplay tune *Talk* followed Young's *Cowgirl*. The song opened with, "Oh brother, I want to talk, I can't get through," as a number of children and adults moved toward a newly mowed meadow. At its edge, a white tent canopy stretched over the food area. Jim and his help arranged several large picnic tables on the lawn. Each one had a red and white checkered table cloth draped over it. Hamburgers, hot dogs, chicken breasts and veggie burgers were ready to go with more on the way. Two large pots of corn-on-the-cob steamed away on serving tables next to the grills. Bowls of potato and pasta salads fitted with large stainless steel ladles sat in a row. Drinks inside ice-filled Styrofoam coolers included varieties of canned and bottled sodas and juices. There was a keg of beer and bottles of wines off to the side. Desserts that included ice cream, cake and cookies remained in the kitchen refrigerator for later. Jim directed the kids to go first in the food line. Harry came up to Jim to introduce Jake while they waited their turn for food.

"Jim, Jake here is my younger brother. I think I told you that he just moved back from out west. He's staying with mom for now."

Jim reached to shake hands with Jake who pushed his sun glasses up on his head before grabbing Jim's hand. "Welcome to the party, Jake. You plan on staying in the area?"

Before answering him Jake scratched his head, clumsily knocking his sunglasses off but he managed to deftly catch them behind his back. He folded and hooked them on the front pocket of his pants.

"Uh, if things work out I will. Depends on where I can find work," he said as he looked up at Jim.

"Harry mentioned you might be looking for a job. What are you looking to do?" Jim asked as he directed two small, unruly boys to get in the food line.

Again, Jake scratched his head. He also squinted and rubbed his beard stubble while answering hesitantly, "I do some masonry, set bricks and stone." He felt self-conscious as if he were not dressed properly for a job interview.

Jim noticed Jake's rugged hands that still showed the nicks and scars of a working man. "Talk to me before you go," Jim said. "I know a contractor in the area who has a big job coming up. He could use someone, someone he can trust to put in an honest day."

Harry accomplished his goal or at least one of them. He trusted that Jim would have the right connections for Jake. Jim was one of Ziggy's old customers from the shop. Jim wasn't a military vet, but he used to ride with them when he owned a Harley. Jim was a corporate lawyer who owned his own firm, something he built from scratch after years of hard work and setbacks. Since his earliest days as an attorney, he volunteered to help struggling vets to secure loans and medical assistance. This was the eighth annual harvest cookout. Almost everyone he invited was either family, an employee, or someone connected to his biker days.

Jim was a hefty, light-skinned black man standing six feet, three inches. He developed a weight problem after he injured his back from a spill on his bike. He stopped riding motorcycles after that. His wife made him promise. His youngest son, now twenty, still lived at home. Jim introduced his son to Jake.

"Yo, son. Come here and meet our new guest. And pull up your pants."

Dwight was standing nearby with two of his friends. He sported a righteous mop of dreadlocks. His jeans hung low, stylishly exposing checkered boxer shorts under his white T-shirt. Dwight was tall like his dad, but thin and darker-skinned like his mother. He greeted Jake with an engaging smile that revealed gleaming white teeth.

"Dwight's responsible for the music—my only request was no nasty gangsta rap—we got kids and sensitive old folks here, right son?"

Jim went on to brag about his son's ambition to form a band. "Music is his thing. Maybe we can convince him and his *posse* to play later."

Dwight sighed and rolled his eyes. "Sure, pops."

The young man pointed to his similarly clad, band mates standing nearby. They both waved. One was completely bald and muscled with an earring and a tattoo of a spider web that appeared partially above the left neckline of his brown T-shirt. The other, much shorter and perhaps Mexican, looked like Indians Jake met from south of the border in New Mexico. He reminded Jake of Usagi even if they looked very different. This fellow's black hair was very long, much longer than Usagi ever wore his. The trio made quite a visual impact.

"Good music," Jake remarked to Dwight. Playing at that moment was the old Beatles tune, *When I'm Sixty-Four*.

"Yeah. That one's for him," Dwight joked, pointing to his dad.

Jim protested, "I'm not there yet—don't push it."

"In a few months you will be." Dwight turned to Jake. "I downloaded a few hundred numbers on our MP3, set it on random and plugged it in! No biggee. Good to meet you, sir. See you later." Dwight revealed his shyness as he spoke while backing away to return to his friends.

Jake was surprised to hear anyone call him *sir*. He felt almost insignificant after years of cultivating a no-self. Sir sounded so official, as if he were somebody, as if had gravitas, as if he were older now. The impact of that *sir* surprised him as it unveiled the alien stage on what had been his role, his character in a play, for so many years. An eerie nostalgia hit him. Where was Usagi? Where was Marga? What were they doing at this moment? He half expected them to be here among the guests. Who here beyond Harry really knew him? Who would witness his transition from then to now? Jake felt quite alone at that moment in empty space between two worlds. Harry, Monica and the others here could only witness the now and knew little or nothing of the then.

You can't go home again, stranger in a strange land. Wolfe and Heinlein had it right but they were wrong, backwards, reversed. You must go home again. Strangers are not always strange in a strange land.—14 October 2007

Jake wrote that just before he left for mass that morning with Monica and Neal. It was one of the few entries he would write in his last notebook that ended in 2008.

As advertized, the food was plentiful and very good. Jake ate one flame-charred, turkey hot dog before settling for the pasta salad and a veggie burger. He still felt odd about eating beef. A Hare Krishna fellow he met told him, "If you eat a hamburger you risk reincarnating as many times as there are hairs on the cow from which the burger came." The point may have been metaphorical but it was literally real to the Krishna fellow. Hindu religion likes huge numbers to help the devotee grasp the infinite vastness of a universe and mysterious value of life. Jake understood that Vedic numbers were metaphors, yet the impact of the number of hairs on a cow stayed with him like a meme virus. "Why is that?" he thought as he passed over the hamburgers.

Beer was another matter. He and Usagi broke the Center's code more than once just as they drank beers in Santa Fe after the Obi debacle. Usagi was quite intoxicated and he got sick during the drive north. Apache liver could not tolerate booze like Polish liver. Marga scolded them later because they confessed. They had to confess. They were not right, and she saw that clearly the next day. And the old man drank.

Students generally excused the old man for his indulgence in sake and cognac. They were told sensei was so advanced that he could transmute the effects without attachment. Whenever the sensei lost his temper in a drunken stupor—when he beat the men on warrior training days—complaints wore thin when justification and rationalization were thick.

Jim manned the keg at the time and he skillfully filled a clear 12 oz plastic cup leaving a thin topping of foam for Jake. After taking a large gulp, Jake took his drink with his food over to a remote table under an enormous oak. He sat next to Giles who was sitting with a biker friend and Jim's wife. Giles introduced Sarah, a gracious woman with graying hair, natural and cropped short. She had a distinct southern accent. Jake learned that Jim met her in Atlanta where he attended law school. She graduated in law too, but she never formally practiced other than filling in as a paralegal whenever Jim needed her, which was often in the early years. She gave birth to their first two children soon after marriage.

She told Jake the whole story and said, "I wouldn't change a thing, child. We had some tough times early on, but things are good now."

Sarah extended her hands, palms up to indicate gratitude for her home. Jake smiled and nodded toward her in acknowledgment. Then he noticed that Giles was drinking an O'Douls.

Small talk dominated the first fifteen minutes at their table. Jake learned that Giles's friend at the table was Deuce, the one who owned the chopped Hardtail and the one who was with Giles at New Hope. This menacing man was actually a semi-retired engineer whose wife had passed away from cancer. His one daughter was grown and out of the house so he had time to tinker with several bikes he owned. When Jake first saw him at the café in New Hope, he thought, "Ex-convict." Deuce had a rugged face, mutton chop sideburns, and figurative tattoos up and down his arms. He wore a bandana. He was also drinking a non-alcoholic beer. Jake wondered why. Sarah, on the other hand, was sipping on red wine, so Jake did not feel odd with his real beer. Soon into the conversation, Jake realized that both Giles and Deuce came with their bikes, so that explained it.

Giles noticed Jake's question-mark expression aimed at his O'Douls.

"Don't get high anymore, Jake, but I like the taste of a brew. I quit right after your old man, my dear friend Ziggy, died. We used to drink together—on weekends."

Giles took a swallow and put his bottle down firmly. He stared at the label a bit before directing his eyes at Jake.

"I've been wanting to say something to you—about your dad. Now's a good a time as any, I guess."

Giles had a direct way about him, not unlike Ziggy did. He got right to the point.

"I'm glad you came back here. I watched you growing up and what you guys went through after Ziggy died. Your mom could always depend on me and my old lady to be there for her. But I guess you knew that."

"Yes. I sure do!"

Giles laughed out loud. "You haven't forgotten that day, have you?"

"Nope," Jake said with a broad smile on his face.

Giles as referring to an incident when Harry and Jake got caught as teenagers smashing mailboxes with baseball bats on a Mischief Night before Halloween. Giles stood in with them in juvenile court to help arrange restitution. Their criminal records were expunged after they restored or replaced every damaged mailbox under supervision by Giles. He also made them meet every mailbox owner and apologize personally.

"I told your brother this, but I wanted to tell you too, in person. About your dad, you know we were on tour together in Nam, right? Sure you do."

Sarah and Deuce both relaxed after they exchanged looks. Sarah crossed her sturdy brown arms and gripped her elbows as if she was holding something. She rocked back into her chair. They had heard this story before, but were willing to hear it again.

Giles breathed through his nose, collected his thoughts by looking first to the sky, and then ahead to his audience.

"As you know your dad was badly wounded in 1969, and after that his one leg was never the same. I know he never told you exactly how it happened, but I want you to know."

Giles looked past Jake into the distance. Then he leaned forward, pushed aside his empty plate and crossed his fingers on the red and white checkered table cloth.

"We were out one morning following a routine order to look for Charlie— you know—the gooks, the enemy. Our guys entered a village that we had walked through just the day before. There were two small families living in one building that we entered to search. The men were missing. We suspected the villagers were shielding soldiers and maybe a tunnel."

Giles squinted into the air as if he could see what he was describing.

"Suddenly, before we got within twenty yards of the place, air support started strafing the area behind the village. We never understood why. We all ran back for cover. The families, two moms and two kids as it turned out, did not know whether to come or go, so they stayed hidden inside. Me, your dad, and one of our best mates, Sergeant Eddie West, were together in the bushes nearby, hoping like hell the strafing would pass. It did. Then we saw a Vietcong emerge from the hootch."

"The what?" Jake asked.

"Hootch. Hut. Their home. Anyway, he was in black and armed. We leveled our M-16s at him as West yelled for him to drop his weapon. He did immediately, and he raised his hands, as if to surrender. West went first to take charge of him while we covered his back. Ziggy stood to West's side and a few yards back with his weapon raised and ready. Then, out of nowhere, an explosion went off just behind the hootch. Debris flew in my face. I fell backwards to avoid what I could.

"As soon as my vision cleared, I saw the Vietcong guy was blown out of the entrance. He was unconscious facedown. The blast knocked West and Ziggy to the ground too. The Vietcong must have shielded Sergeant West but West was bleeding from his face and shoulder, yet he got up somehow. He stumbled into the hootch. I don't know why. I heard more air strikes and explosions coming our way. Everything was dinky dau, crazy. I grabbed your dad by the arms and dragged him twenty yards or so back to a ditch where we covered our heads."

Giles stopped to take a deep breath before finishing his story.

"When we looked up, after the bombing stopped, your dad and me, we saw nothing by a mess of debris where the hootch or hut stood. Ziggy started yelling out for West, but I told him to shut up. We waited for a few minutes until everything got quiet again. I stood to see what happened. Ziggy got up to follow me. I heard him grunt in pain. He limped over to the smoldering mess with me to see what was left. We found body parts and"—Giles choked on his words—"two bloody children awkwardly wrapped in each other's arms. They were dead. West and the two moms were scattered, all gone to pieces. We found his dog tags later."

Giles skipped over some of the more gory details.

"We flew out of there in a chopper. West was a guy we liked. He did caricatures to pass the time. He did a good one of Ziggy—I saw him do it. I have it somewhere. I want to leave it to you and Harry someday. I kept it because it is West and Ziggy together in one image, if you know what I mean. That last incident for Ziggy, the one that led to his medical discharge, cut into his mind the deepest, seeing those little kids laying there mangled and dead and knowing West wanted to save them and their moms. He always had his leg wound to remind him. Ziggy flew out of Nam a couple of days later for extended treatment in Germany. My tour was over two months later."

Giles picked up his bottle and tapped it on the table. He wondered if Jake would grasp what he was trying to say. He wondered if he did justice to what he remembered.

"Jake, do you know why I brought this up? Maybe this wasn't the best place to tell it, but I thought I may not get another chance."

Jake allowed for a moment of silence before speaking up. He was not sure what to say. "Thanks for that. Harry and I knew that dad kept things about Nam hidden from us. It explains a lot about his drinking and maybe the accident."

"Yeah, the accident," Giles continued. "War can mess up a guy's head if nothing else. Some take it better then others. I came back lucky, in one piece, basically. The main reason I'm telling you this has to do with how some of us like your dad dealt with things. After Ziggy died, I went for help for the first time, because for the first time, I felt suicidal. We were wrong to try to drink it away the way we did as weekend warriors. I don't want to get into this too much, but I got to know a group of vets. We would hang out after NA meetings. That led me to group therapy for post war stress. That's how I met Neal, who also helped your mom later."

Giles paused again, blinked rapidly as he suppressed a frown or perhaps a tear.

"Monica spent many a night comforting your dad, Jake. Held him after his nightmares, you know, woke him up."

The Vietnam vet made eye contact with Jake before going on. He wanted to make sure the kid got the point that both his parents shared in the pain.

"If it weren't for the group sessions, I doubt I would be talking about this today to you. Right now, I might be stoned on my ass and sleeping here for the night—eh, Sarah?"

Sarah shoved Giles on the shoulder. "Danny Giles, now you know you don't have to be stoned to stay here. We have room, and we'd pleased to have you over anytime."

Jake and Deuce joined in the laughter. It relieved the tension.

"By the way, Jake, I wasn't telling you this to keep you from finishing your beer. Most folks that drink are not alcoholics. I don't really know if I am."

Giles looked at Sarah for approval, but all she did was shrug and smile.

"Here, here," he said with a flourish. "Let's toast old Ziggy."

242

Giles looked up as he raised his O'Douls to the sky.

"I know he's smiling down on us right now."

Jake lifted what was left of his beer. He drained it in a few gulps.

13   Almost Baseball

"Are you ready for some baseball?"

Jim's voice boomed over the music and the chatter as he waived and pointed to the direction of the newly cut meadow. There was a crude diamond already in place with base paths and canvas bags for bases. Jim's son and his friends carried the equipment. They had a few little league-sized aluminum bats, several soft balls and only one glove—a catcher's mitt. There was one catcher's mask as well. The field was hardly more than one hundred fifty feet square, but, with the small, light bats, the ball would not travel very far even if the larger men nailed one. Jim managed to round up thirteen willing players besides himself and Giles. Jim set the rules for Harvest Party softball:

"We play three innings. Everyone one on each team gets to bat once an inning. No one strikes out. You keep swinging till you hit it in play. Giles will do all the pitching, and I will catch and be umpire. Giles can help with the calls. Otherwise all normal rules apply for outs and base running. Deuce, you assign positions for the Bikers and Sarah will do the same for the Lawyers."

A flip of a coin determined that Bikers batted first. Sarah was in the outfield with Mohan, one of Jim's new attorneys, and Mohan's wife, Aisha, who stood in left field. Dwight played first base. Eleven-year-old Christine, the daughter of one of Jim's attorneys, played second and shortstop. Due to a shortage of one player on both sides, the second baseman switched positions from second to shortstop depending on who was at bat. Third was manned by Jim's long-time office manager, Doris, who was in fairly decent shape for a forty-five year old.

First batter up was ten-year-old Juanita, a small, slender urchin who appeared as if a stiff breeze could blow her over. She stood bravely at the plate with feet spread and bat cocked over her shoulder, eyes fixed on Giles. Giles moved closer to the plate to better throw a slow underhand pitch in an effort to give her a chance. His first pitch was too high and Juanita did not swing at it. Jim tossed it back to Giles without fanfare. Biker fans on the sideline cheered for their lead-off star.

"Go Juanita, hit it!"

Giles threw his next pitch carefully, again in a slow arch that, this time, dropped into the strike zone. Juanita stepped into it and took a rip with her bat. Crack! The softball flew directly at the pitcher's head. Giles was barely able to duck quickly enough as the ball swooshed by his right ear. He lost his balance and fell on his ass in the process.

"Go Juanita, go," shouted the merry audience, all the while laughing at Giles's expense, as their girl sprinted for first.

The ball made it into the outfield with the spunky Ozzie, Jim's gray and white Australian Shepherd giving chase. The bouncing ball got to Mohan, whose soccer skills were good, just before the bounding dog got to the ball. Mohan stopped the ball with his foot, flicked it up into his right hand and proceeded to throw it way above the head of Christine at second.

Ozzie kept his eye on the ball as he took off after it again.

Juanita ran the bases like a kid on a mission. She rounded second despite shouts telling her to stop. Big Jim called off his dog, as he collected the ball in the tall grass around twenty feet behind home plate. Ozzie dutifully sat in place, panting with his tongue hanging. Jim turned quickly only to fire a low throw to third. Poor Doris tried her best to catch the fast-arriving ball, but it stung so hard that she let it drop away between her legs.

Aisha came running to help while shouting, "I got it. I got it."

Jim scolded Ozzie. The dog stayed put this time. Juanita touched third and sped for home, easily touching the plate before Aisha's back-up throw dribbled past the pitcher's mound to the catcher.

"Bikers one, Lawyers zero!" Jim announced. "Second batter, up!" Before the next pitch, Doris asked to be excused. She wanted to ice her hand. It looked like she would not return, so Jim asked for another volunteer. After seeing what happened to Doris, no one seemed excited about the job. Jim petitioned Jake, "How about it?" Jake was sitting with the fans along the sidelines, satisfied to enjoy this spectacular parody of America's game and cheer. Since everyone else still seemed unwilling to play, he accepted. He was now a Lawyer, though he was, by inheritance, a Biker.

And so the game went. By the top of the third and last inning, Lawyers were behind 8 to 5. These annual events were relatively high scoring affairs save for one year, when they had to stop in the second inning due to a sudden and massive rainstorm. That year, the higher score was only 4. This year, in 2007, the Bikers were batting and were halfway through the last inning. Deuce was on third after popping up to Aisha, who muffed the catch and then under threw to second base—Christine had to run into the outfield to get the ball. The score was 8 to 6 after rangy Mark, the young guy who owned the Ducati, blasted a line drive that bounded to the edge of the woods into poison ivy. No one dared get the ball, and by that time Ozzie had lost interest in the game. Mark therefore hit a home run. Jim threw a new ball into play.

Earlier, little Juanita did not make it to base this inning either. Giles had moved back to the mound to pitch to her. He learned his lesson. She was thrown out at first her last two bats. Three more players were left to bat before the game was over, so conceivably the Bikers could win. However, according to Jim-ball, even if the batting team was winning everyone still had to bat through the lineup to end the final inning. Jim said it every year: "The harvest game is about playing and not about winning."

Batting left handed, Gigi stood at the plate ready to do battle with Giles. He threw a little harder underhand to her as he did to others who could play the game. She played softball in high school. She fouled the first pitch back over Jim's head. He ambled back to get it. Gigi slammed the next pitch over the shortstop's head. In this case it was over Jake who was doubling at third and shortstop. This was Gigi's first hit of the game so she took off excitedly letting out a loud warrior whoop. In fact, she ran out of her sandals before she reached first base.

The loud yell excited Ozzie who decided to pace the base-runner and not the ball this time. Mohan managed to grab the ball after one bounce deep in the meadow.

Gigi was headed to second in her bare feet. Mohan tossed the ball underhand to Christine who acted as a cut-off man in shallow left field. Christine was quite aware of Mohan's lack of throwing skills.

Meanwhile, Gigi with Ozzie in tow rounded second and headed right at Jake who stood a few feet in front of the bag at third waiting for the relay from Christine. Gigi put her head down meaning to run behind Jake to get to the bag but Ozzie, following instinct as an Aussie, nipped her left heel causing her to tumble. Gigi left her feet and converged with Jake just as he was catching the ball. Gigi shoved her hands into Jake's side as she turned and barreled into him, leading with her right knee and shoulder.

The collision threw Jake off-balance onto his left foot as he lost the ball. His right arm flew up, down and around to grab Gigi across her chest as much out of self-preservation as an old football tackling instinct. This was suddenly a contact sport. Holding onto her he fell backwards onto third base with her landing on top of him on her back. She still was not safe or out.

"Touch the bag, Gigi, touch the bag," someone yelled from the sidelines.

Christine, realizing the situation gathered the ball to try to tag Gigi. Meanwhile Jake held her tight with both arms not letting her roll one way or the other to touch the base. During her struggle Gigi let out a few curse words. Ozzie was yelping excitedly nipping at flying feet. Then the scene became more comical.

Christine tripped over the dog while attempting to apply the tag. This entire event took less than ten seconds but to Jake it came in slow motion. Observing the melee no one could tell for certain whether Gigi touched the bag or not. Neither could anyone tell if Christine had tagged Gigi before she touched the bag. As he held onto the wriggling, cursing she-devil, Jake broke out in laughter. He laughed like he had not laughed for many months if not years.

"I tagged her, I tagged her," yelled Christine who was now sprawled on the ground next to them while raising the ball high for all to see.

Gigi cursed Jake, saying, "I touched the bag, dumb ass. Let me go. Let me the fuck go. I'm safe!"

When Jake realized how incensed she was, he immediately relaxed and let her go. She rolled off her tormentor and pushed herself up to her knees. Then she realized how foul she sounded in front of all the kids.

"I'm sorry, guys. That was really bad. Sorry."

She covered her eyes as if to show embarrassment. Jake was yet laughing when their eyes met. When she saw Jake laying there with arms spread wide and Ozzie licking his face, she broke out into laughter too, joining in with everyone else on the meadow. Neither Giles nor Jim could tell if Gigi was out or safe, so they let her stay on third.

"Lawyers 8; Bikers 7," Jim announced as two last Bikers prepared to bat.

The next batter hit a single bringing Gigi home. The last batter grounded out.

"Tie game," shouted Jim. "Lawyers up!"

Giles pitched a little harder to the Lawyers to try to keep it even, even if three runners remained stranded. He had one last batter to face and it was Jake who had no hits thus far, having popped out twice. The sideline crowd was cheering for a grand finale grand slam or at least a walk off win. Giles fired a strike toward the catcher Jim. Jake swung and fouled it down the third base line, still not used to the undersized bat. Giles threw another one but slower. Jake missed it completely, swinging way early. On the third pitch, another fast ball, Jake connected and the ball soared high into left-center field. Deuce, now in center, moved toward the falling ball keeping his eyes on it all the way. The ball landed in his open hands and he managed to hold on. He and his teammates exchanged high fives as the crowd cheered his fine catch. The runner at third tagged anyway and ran home to win the game.

"Sacrifice fly, sacrifice fly," he kept repeating.

"Tie game. Last out. No sacrifice!"

Jim's word was final.

"Let's get dessert."

The festive afternoon merged into a mellow early evening. Out of the kitchen came the desserts carried by several women with trays. Many people took turns washing up inside before finding seats at the picnic tables. Typically, Jim's harvest cookouts began to break up at dusk and ended well before midnight. Jake limped a little on his way back to the tables. Gigi saw him massaging his right leg above the knee. She used the opportunity to engage him for Harry's sake. "You okay? I think I hit you pretty hard. Sorry."

"Just a bruise. Thanks for asking. I'll be okay." After they walked a few more steps, Jake collapsed onto the ground.

"Jeez, man, you're hurt. Let me take a look."

Gigi bent down, reacting instinctively as any personal trainer might with a fallen athlete. But before she could touch Jake, she noticed that his grimace became a broad smile. She realized she'd been had.

"Asshole," she countered. Then she covered her mouth again while saying, "Oops." She glanced around for the children. If anyone heard her, no one said anything. She was keenly aware that Jim had certain rules to keep the event civil. Some former guests were never invited again. It wasn't just about the game and a good time.

"Sorry, just fooling around," Jake said as he stood up. "I'm serious about the bruise though. It still hurts. You made a big impression on me."

Gigi gave him a slight shove. They both were laughing as Harry approached them.

"I was hoping you guys would run into each other!" Harry said as he winked at Gigi.

"Ha ha," she retorted. "That was really lame. It was purely coincidental, just part of the game."

Jake then said, "Yeah, we should stop meeting like that."

Gigi shoved him again.

"You both need new script writers," she said.

"I agree, girl," said another female walking towards them. Lindy caught up with them as they moved in unison toward the dessert trays.

On the way Jake stopped by the keg to draw another beer. He was feeling a thirst after the game but not from playing it. He felt a need to enter intoxication. Harry joined him but filled his cup only halfway. Jake suddenly felt better than he had in a long time save for his sore leg. He slugged down the beer and filled his cup again. After looking over tempting slices of pie and cake and varieties of ice cream Jake filled a paper plate with corn chips. He was looking for a place to sit not noticing that Gigi was waiting for him by a table. She yelled for him.

"Yo, Jake, over here!"

Gigi was with the thin man who came with her on the trike.

"Come and meet Don."

Jake hesitated for a reason he did not quite comprehend. Was it for fear of imposing on a couple's privacy, was it jealousy, or was he still the monk conflicted about seeking female companionship? He brushed the complex emotion aside and walked over to join Gigi and Don.

Gigi introduced them without explaining her relationship to Don. They sat down to share a table. Jake noted that Gigi was drinking bottled water. Donald had a can of white grape juice with his ice cream.

Jake figured to himself, "What the hell, you can drink a beer, but what is with the teetotalers here?"

Then he reminded himself that Gigi was driving too. He sat to join them.

"So, what's it you do, Don?"

Jake tried his best to feel neutral toward the man.

"Me? Not much lately, I'm afraid," Don said as he glanced over to Gigi for reassurance. He was unsure how much he wanted reveal to this relative stranger.

"Don used to exercise horses and look after them. That's how he met Jim years ago," Gigi offered. "He's also a farrier and a good one."

"I *was* a farrier," Don corrected her. "Actually, I work part time at a florist shop now."

Jake looked confused. Don did not strike him as strong enough to handle horses.

"I knew a guy in New Mexico who shoed horses. Tough work. I admire you."

"New Mexico? I've always wanted to go there. I hear Santa Fe is a great place.

How long were you there?"

Don seemed relieved to switch the subject to someone else.

"Around ten years."

"And?"

Don was genuinely curious.

"I worked in construction and landscaping but I spent most of my time with a Buddhist commune. It was in a remote area in Northern New Mexico."

Jake was surprised to hear himself mention the Center.

Don ignored the mention of Buddhism. His only comment was, "Like Georgia O'Keeffe!"

Don's superficial comparison threw Jake off. He did not immediately see the connection to O'Keeffe unless Don thought of the artist as a kind of recluse.

"I guess you could say her studio was a kind of monastery. No, we were a kind of cult, you might say, following a Buddhist teacher. He was from Japan. It didn't work out for me. It seems, like, longer now. I moved back East earlier this week."

Jake's tongue was loosened by the beer.

Gigi took it as a lead in when she heard Jake say *cult*.

"So, it didn't work out—why did you leave?"

She was not sure now if she asked this to please Harry or out of genuine curiosity. She felt a little dishonest.

"Oh, man, do we have to get into that? It's really not that interesting."

Jake inhibitions about revealing his past faded after another mouthful of beer.

"Anyway," he said as he swallowed, "if you really want to know, I found out, or maybe I finally admitted to myself, that the old guy who founded the group and who was supposed to be celibate was having sex with some of the women and misusing funds. It wasn't supposed to happen that way, I mean it was an ideal situation for me in the beginning, for what I was looking for. The old leader died a couple of years ago. The new leader, a great lady and a true friend, made some positive changes but I had had enough. Time for a change, I guess."

Jake took another gulp. He was not sure where his story was heading or if he wanted to go there. His thoughts began to swirl. He blushed as he changed the topic.

"So, Don, why'd you quit being a farrier?"

Don felt Jake's underlying anxiety in his careless attempt to tell his story. He could tell that Gigi's new friend was getting drunk. Don decided to get to the point.

"I have AIDs. These last two years have been rough. Meds aren't working so well. As you probably noticed, I look pretty wasted."

Don smiled as Jake sat at strict attention with his mouth slightly open.

"Jim and his wife helped me with my medical assistance and services. I had no insurance at the time and was avoiding treatment, maybe for too long. He's a great guy, Jim, you know."

After hearing Don's stark revelation, Jake looked at the man with a completely different emotion. He wanted to say something sympathetic but stopped himself.

"Yeah, Jim is great. Great bunch of guests too, present company included!"

Jake paused to look around. He noticed people moving toward the vehicles.

"Well, I hope the pie and cake was good. Are you two staying or going soon?".

"Going? The night is young! Not me. What about you?"

Gigi was trying to be upbeat noting that Jake still felt she and Don were hooked up. Jake's attraction to her was palpable but he had no clue that Gigi recognized his signals. Don noticed it however and he did not need to hear it from Gigi that she wanted to spend some time with Jake. He bowed out of the situation graciously.

"Well, I don't know about you two but I'm bushed. Doris is leaving soon and she offered me a ride. I think she's inside saying good-bye to Sarah. I'll excuse myself and go find her. Good to meet you Jake."

Don shook hands with Jake. He and Gigi embraced as she wished him good night.

"Thanks for the ride, girl. That was fun. I'm not sure I could handle going home in the open air though. It's getting cooler."

Don shuffled toward the house, now looking much older than his years to Jake.

"If you want, I can give you a ride home, whenever you're ready," Gigi offered. "It looks like Giles is settled into staying here for some time."

"Oh, I'm in no hurry, but thanks. I've never ridden on one of those, those trikes, I mean."

Jake finished his beer and set the cup down. He looked toward Don again as he disappeared into the house.

"He's in bad shape, then, isn't he? Have you two known each other long?"

"Don? We met two years ago here at Jim's annual. We're not an item if that's what you're wondering. He's gay. Since he got sick he's been coming to the club for physical therapy. I run a class for handicapped and elderly a few times a week. I got to know him better and we became friends. He's a sweet man. He thinks he has only a year to live."

"Real sorry to hear that. He seems like a nice guy. What club?"

"Oh, I thought you knew. I am a personal trainer at a gym north of Philly, but only part time."

"That explains third base. You really surprised me. I never expected you'd run that fast."

Jake tapped his empty cup.

"Hey, would you like to take a walk? I feel like I need to move. Maybe it's the beer getting to me."

Jake motioned toward the bikes. "I'd like to take a closer look at the trike if you don't mind."

"Okay."

Jake wobbled slightly both from pain and drunkenness after standing up. He collected himself quickly trying to not stumble or act foolishly. Nevertheless, Jake limped slightly to the row of remaining motorcycles.

Jake remarked, "Those wheels must have set you back some."

"Well it did set me back, kind of, but I used part of an inheritance for it. My grandmother left me a chunk a few years ago. I invested in a small home and bought this toy last year. It's something I did to reward myself."

"Reward?"

"Yeah. A gift and a reminder. The inheritance was supposed to go to me in full when I turned thirty if I cleaned up my act. My mother held the trust till then. You might as well know, if you haven't guessed already, I was a wild child in my early twenties. I dropped out of school after freshman year and just did what I felt like doing. You could say I was spoiled, an only child with well-off parents."

"And what school was that?" Jake asked as he climbed onto the seat of the trike.

"Antioch College in Ohio. Ever heard of it?"

"Nope."

"It has a history of activism. A year after I quit they wanted to invite a convicted felon on death row as a commencement speaker. Mumia Abu Jamal. Ever heard of him? It was all over the news then."

"Nope."

Jake was playing with the hand brakes in the trike.

"You were really out there then, I mean, out of touch?"

"Oh, yes, I was," Jake answered in measured words while squeezing the clutch. "So you're going to school again. What are you studying?"

"Just getting a BA for now. Majoring in psychology the same as everyone else who is trying to figure themselves out. I'm also getting certified in physical therapy. I have a year to go."

"Seems you started later than most to find a career, but I get that. I gather you had an interesting life so far!"

Gigi looked at him quizzically.

"I wouldn't call it that."

"Oh, I mean it in the Oriental sense. In some Asian cultures it's a curse to say *May your son have an interesting life*. There is a kind of cult of tranquility in the Far East," he said, but as the pithy words left his lips he felt like a pompous ass.

"Well, your life has been interesting then too. What's the name of that Eastern cult again?"

"What, tranquility? No, I didn't mean cult as in a bad group. There a devotion to harmony with nature. That may be a better way to say it. Umm, sorry. I'm babbling. I really don't know that much about Asian culture," he said as he took a deep breath to clear beer from his brain.

"Right. Why am I not believing you?"

Gigi laughed. She sensed that Jake's commune life was not as simple as he let on. This man with her had some depth to him. Though they were around the same age, they came from different life experiences, to be sure, but her drive to settle down seemed similar to his. There were some parallels. And she found him attractive.

"So, what happened after you dropped out of Antioch?" he asked.

"Actually, I got into a cult thing too, but unlike you I left it in less than two weeks."

"Oh?"

"Oh, is right. One big zero in my life."

Gigi checked her hair in the trike's mirror.

"Do you want to hear about this?"

"Sure."

"One of my best friends at school came from a really dysfunctional family. Her parents were divorced. Her mom left the family when my friend was fifteen to join a New Age school for enlightenment near Seattle. She and her mom didn't talk for three years. Then, out of the blue, her mom wanted her to take a workshop for a week there. Said she would pay for it. My friend, who thought this may be a way to reconnect with her crazy mom, thought she'd go but would only do it if I went with her. I saw it as an adventure. I had no idea. When we got there it was on this eccentric lady's property. She was the leader.

"We, maybe one thousand of us, crammed into what was once a large horse stable for the workshop. All I knew was that the leader, who was in her fifties, was the channel for a god they called Ram. Supposedly, he was the Hindu god Rama. Most of the people there were middle-aged women like my friend's mom, so it felt weird from the start. I don't know how much of this you want to hear."

Jake looked interested, so Gigi continued.

"People were cheering and hollering when the leader came out on stage, like they do when talk show hosts come out, and when she assumed the Ram personality, they went bonkers for it. I thought either I'm missing something or this is nuts, but I wanted to stick it out for my friend. Part of me found it challenging and exciting, I'll admit it. The crowd's energy was contagious, if you know what I mean. We listened to lectures, watched videos, learned a heavy breathing exercise, and did stuff outside mostly with blindfolds on."

"I heard something about this group. Some movie stars were into it, no?"

"Yes. Quite of few celebrities were into it from time to time."

"Why the blindfolds? Sounds like the old Rajneesh commune in Oregon. The old man who was our teacher used to make fun of him."

"It was different. They taught that with a kind of breathing-blowing technique we would be able to remote view things, you know, see without our eyes. By the fifth day I was crawling through underground tubes, blindfolded and bumping into sweaty bodies. Some people were freaking out, panicking. One older lady had to be removed from a tube because she had a breakdown and went catatonic. They took her to a hospital. I was with her when it happened. That night my friend and I decided to sneak away. Her mom never forgave her and wouldn't talk to her again for years again after that."

"You crawled around in underground tubes? What's that about?"

Jake leaned against the trike mostly keeping his arms folded across his chest when he was not massaging his thigh. He calmly watched Gigi's animated, roving eyes as she spoke. She could tell he was losing interest.

"Oh man, it's really complicated. If you found your way out, and some did, you experienced the *void*.

"Void?"

"Yes. It had something to do with going into the Void and not toward the Light when you die."

"Sunyata!"

"Sun what?"

"It means emptiness in Buddhism. Nirvana. Extinction. Voidness. The candle goes out—there is no light to speak of in the end."

"Maybe it was a Buddhist cult then? Never would have thunk it! Maybe we can talk about it some other time. Anyway, we took off for Fiji after that."

"And that's another story," Jake said as he hopped onto the seat of the trike.

Noting his interest, Gigi motioned for Jake to take hold of the handlebars.

"Would you like to take a spin on it? You can drive if you want."

"It's been a while. I'll need a lesson."

Jake watched intently as Gigi pointed out what did what. Old images of operating a motorcycle returned front and center. "You know, Harry had a Sportster that I learned on. I rode it for two years. Looks like the same works and I don't have to fear falling over! Let's do it."

After a little stop and go on the lawn, Jake had a feel for operating a bike again. The coordination of hand-clutch and shifting gears with his toe, feel for acceleration, and braking power came back easily. The only oddity on turns was his tendency to place his leg out or lean as on the two-wheelers.

"Just like riding a bike. You never really forget."

Gigi let the comment slide. Satisfied that her student knew what he was doing, she slipped on behind him and held onto his waist as he eased over the lawn onto the roadway. And off they went, slowly at first, on the narrow country road going south. Gigi guided Jake along a scenic route with elegant old homes tucked away far off the road. Dry set stone walls lined many of the properties.

They passed a couple of brown horses standing opposite in parallel to one another as if asleep behind a cedar fence just off the road. An old, white-headed gentleman working in his still lush garden greeted them with a wave of his green gloved hand. They waved back. Jake enjoyed the sense of taking control. He enjoyed the pressure of the female form against his back. The world was passing under them slowly at twenty-five to thirty miles per hour. It was fast enough. He reached back with his left hand, grabbed and firmly squeezed her calf.

"Thanks, Gigi. This is good."

She hugged him a little tighter.

After ten minutes more of casual riding Gigi directed Jake to slow down.

258

"Turn off to the left up ahead. I want you to pull up in the parking lot after the gas pump at the next intersection."

Jake drove about another half mile and parked behind an elegant old building. Gigi asked him to cut the engine. "I have friends who live upstairs. I told them I might be by this evening."

The building interested Jake immediately. "What is this place?" he wondered out loud. Gigi knew some of its history, so she led him to the front of the building at the intersection. An antique *Gulf* gas pump stood on the corner. An equally antique, painted wooden sign saying *General Store* hung over the portal. Jake noted the substructure was built using fieldstone. The framed part extended to a mansard roof complete with dormers.

"It looks easily over a hundred years old," he said.

Gigi corrected him.

"The original structure was here in the 1860s. The old post office still exists but the old general store is now this *precious* antique shop, as you can see."

Jake gazed inside through the window. A large wooden Indian gazed back at him.

She led him by the hand to the back where a wooden stairway led to an upper deck. They bounded, or rather she bounded up the steps with Jake hobbling along with an assist from the left rail for support.

Gigi found a note pinned inside the screen door. While she read it, Jake stood behind resting his vision on her distinct thigh tattoo below her cut-off jeans. He wondered briefly about the meaning of the snake until she spoke up.

"Looks like they're out until very late tonight but Trina says I can go in, make myself at home, if I want. They keep a key hidden under a potted plant back here."

14 Unoriginal Sin

Is it okay if I come in?" Jake wondered.

"No, you wait out here while I hang out inside," Gigi instructed with no hint of humor.

Jake was about to do as she said until she turned around with her fingers crossed in his face.

"You are a little weird, aren't you? You are my guest and any guest of mine is welcome here. Trina and I go back a long way. It's only her and her boyfriend living here now. But we can talk about that inside. I need to pee."

As Jake entered he noticed the large wooden dining table strewn with dishes and left-over food and a massive Maine Coon sprawled over the far end lazily staring his way. Clearly this cat was unfazed by a stranger. The place had a pleasant mix of odors that included something earthy, chocolate, and ginger with a hint of onions and incense of some kind. Jake suddenly felt hungry, sensing his mouth water.

"Make your self at home," Gigi said as she quickly grabbed up the plates and food off the table. "Trina has always been such a slob."

After scraping the food into the trash she placed the dirty dishes in the sink, and then wiped the table around the cat.

"Now I really gotta pee. The bathroom is in the back if you need it after me. Oh, and introduce yourself to Max."

Gigi skipped across the floor and disappeared through a door that led to a bedroom.

Jake pulled a high-back wooden chair with a wicker seat away from the table. He eased himself into it not far from the cat. Max blinked and raised his chin slightly. Jake reached over, trying to not startle the creature, to scratch its head. Max immediately began purring and rubbing his head into Jake's outstretched hand. The cat's calm reaction impressed Jake.

"Maggie was way less laid back than this guy," he thought.

He got up to look over the counter cabinets and how they were built. They appeared custom made out of old pine boards with a finely crafted finish that exposed the weathered grain. Custom wrought iron handles and hinges ornamented the entire unit effectively. The sturdy, contemporary counter was a slab of polished gray granite. It echoed the gray highlights in the cabinets.

He opened the large stainless steel refrigerator. Inside was a variety of drinks, imported beers, tequila, and all the basics needed for a kitchen: milk, eggs and butter, food in sealed storage containers, and a tray of brown cakes covered with clear wrap. To the left was a fully stocked freezer with ice dispenser. He grabbed a nearly full bottle of red wine.

"Pinot Noir," he said to himself. This was one wine he had never tried. "What do you think Max? This one okay?"

The cat had no reaction.

Jake noted the rustic autumn scene outside from the back window. The sun was going down but a wall of tall, leafy trees in the distance blocked any hint of sunset. The cork was tight into the neck of the wine bottle. Jake found a corkscrew dangling from a wrought iron rack above the counter that also held pots, potholders and padded patchwork mittens. He walked back to the refrigerator. After examining the contents he retrieved a large piece of cake from one of the trays. Then he settled back down into his chair with Max to his side. The great cat continued to purr.

"Here's to us, old buddy."

Jake nodded to the cat. He took a long, slow sip. He savored it as it flowed down his throat.

"Not bad at all, Max."

He teased Max by holding the glass under the cat's nose. This disturbed the cat enough to draw it to its feet. Max then sat down with his ears pinned back staring fully at Jake as if to dare him to make his next move. Jake got the message. He took another long sip before setting down his drink away from the cat. He then grabbed his chocolate cake and took a large bite. It was good in an interesting way.

"Not too sweet," he thought. He gradually ate it all, taking bites between sips of wine. He was chewing the last bite when Gigi reappeared.

"Ah," Gigi remarked after noting the crumbs on the table. "You found something to eat then? Good. And I can see Max is enthralled with you. He must like you. He can be a bit finicky though. Trina's last boyfriend tried to pick him up once and that was a mistake. Max left some deep gouges in the poor guy's stomach."

"Well, I was not about to pick *him* up if that's what you're getting at." Jake spread his arms to indicate the cat's size.

"Right. Don't try. Otherwise he's very nice. Hey, looks like you found the good wine too. You mind if I join you?"

"Sure. Isn't this a *mi casa es su casa* thing with Trina? Can I pour a glass for you?"

"Thanks, but I don't drink. Alcohol does not agree with me. She keeps a stash of pot somewhere in her bedroom."

Gigi left for a minute and returned with a small wooden box made in India with carved and inlaid decorations.

"I do weed on weekends when I'm in the mood."

Gigi found all she needed in the box: rolling paper, a self-striking match, and a plastic baggie half-full of marijuana. She proceeded to pour a small amount of the shredded weed onto a paper, licked the edge and deftly rolled a joint. She then flicked the match with her thumbnail. A flame appeared.

"I hope you're okay with this. Just a few hits. Do you want any?"

Jake waved it off as she presented it in front of his lips. Gigi nodded in understanding as she held her breath.

"I couldn't risk using any at Jim's," she said as she exhaled. "You know how he is about anything illegal. As for the booze, to his credit he never allows anyone to drive home drunk."

Jake was only mildly taken aback by Gigi's familiarity with marijuana. Marijuana use was ubiquitous among the construction crews he worked with in New Mexico. He rarely took a hit himself and he avoided the drug for the past five years altogether keeping his commitment to a pure as possible path to enlightenment. However, seeing Gigi toking up actually relaxed him.

"No, but go ahead. I was around it a lot in New Mexico," he said. With that admission he gulped down more wine. He finished half the bottle in the next fifteen minutes. He noted the lingering aroma of marijuana in the air. The atmosphere in the kitchen suddenly felt curiously cosmic.

After one more hit Gigi asked, "So, tell me more about New Mexico. I never really spent any time there. Passed through Albuquerque once, and saw a lot of empty road."

"It's different there, for sure. You know they call it The Land of Enchantment, don't you? It's a state slogan you see on all the license plates. The northern part where I was—nothing especially dramatic there like the Grand Canyon, but the combination of the high desert and mountains, the Indian cultures, the eccentric folk in out of the way places made it special. I spent most of my time around the Center."

Jake paused. He felt his beard as he considered the interesting people he left behind. He decided not to go into it.

"But I'm burnt out on all of that. All that effort and there is nothing much to show for it. I'm broke, no job, and essentially homeless if it were not for family. Right now I owe Monica and Neal." Jake smiled slightly. He drank the last sip of wine in his glass. He pushed the bottle away. "Whew," he sighed, "this is starting to hit me."

Gigi put out her half-finished fag and then flushed the evidence down the sink. She cleaned the table again, took Jake's empty glass and rinsed it. Then she washed and rinsed the remaining dishes. She looked into the CD player on the counter. Someone left a disc in the cassette.

"Do you want to hear the new Nine Inch Nails release? It's called *Year Zero*."

Jake shrugged in a playful, assenting gesture. He was not familiar with the music. He was entranced with the busy lady in the kitchen. She was his new found friend and yet she seemed to be a fascinating character in a scene in somebody's kitchen. He felt peacefully detached.

Gigi, who was familiar with NIN, put the music on low volume. The instrumental, "Another Version of the Truth," began with its chaotic introduction.

After wiping down the table one more time around the cat, Gigi sat down next to Jake.

Jake felt groggier. They sat there quietly for nearly a minute as if in a trance listening to the music until Max stretched out fully in between them. Max turned to Gigi. He rubbed her cheek with his forehead. He wanted to be petted or possibly fed. Gigi knew this cat. She checked Max's food bowl on the floor. It was empty. She got up to feed him. She filled his water bowl also. She found some cat treats in a cabinet knowing to not offer too many. The cat was on a strict diet since he gained so much weight the year before.

"Here, you feed him one." She forced a small cat treat into Jake's hand. "Go ahead." Then she giggled.

"What's he going to do?" Jake asked nervously in his stupor. He tossed the treat in front of Max. The cat not too casually flopped his butt onto the table, lowered his head and snapped it up. He looked to Gigi for more. She placed a few more bits in front him and then patted the cat on the head. She slid her chair closer to Jake. While she did this, Jake studied the tattoo on her leg again. He felt an odd attraction. He reached out to touch the serpentine form. When he did it seemed to come alive to the delicate stroke of his index finger.

"This is quite nicely done. I've been curious—why the snake? I notice it winds around three times."

Gigi gently grasped his hand and held it onto her thigh as she answered. Jake's hand stiffened.

"It doesn't bite!" she said while giggling. "It has three and a half coils, to be exact! I had it done in Indonesia." She held his hand in place until he relaxed.

"Indonesia is a big place." Jake said dreamily, waiting for further explanation.

"In Bali. It was one of those *had to* moments when chakras were the thing in my life. Do you want to hear about this?"

Jake merely nodded. He was enjoying an erotic rush. Gigi gave him a firm squeeze before retracting her hand. She continued.

"We, another friend and I, took yoga classes for a week with a Hindu teacher there. He explained the whole kundalini thing in such a beautiful way. So I wanted to do something with that after deciding to get tattooed. My tattoo artist did a great job, I think, but now it seems stupid because I no longer do yoga. I checked on getting it taken off last year, but that could cost a lot more than I want to spend."

Jake squeezed her thigh and then withdrew his hand.

"Well, it is truly a work of art. Nice snake, nice leg, and—and there is a beautiful woman connected to it," he said as he gingerly touched the tip of her nose.

"You think so? Maybe I'll keep it then. I can show you more tattoos."

Gigi giggled coyly this time, clearly flirting. She knew where this was leading and she was not going to stop it. Jake looked into her pale green eyes as he grasped her other hand. She looked back into his soft gaze and stroked his shoulder. Yes was the answer in the silence. They kissed softly at first. Jake stroked her neck.

She stood up over him, lifted his shirt up and over his head and tossed it to the side. He rose slowly while unbuttoning her black blouse. She helped him unsnap the black bra underneath before removing her blouse. The items dropped to the floor. They proceeded slowly. Clumsy and awkward touches nevertheless felt right in the warm glow of the moment with Nine Inch Nails finishing *Year Zero* softly in the background. Gigi took his hand again. She led him toward the bedroom.

After a mere two steps, Jake hesitated. He felt queasy. He felt his heart pound and his mind float. He felt both excitement and foreboding. Time took a chaotic trajectory through his brain. Seconds stretched like elastic warps. The white fluffy cloud in heaven just a moment before filled with gray swirls, storms, and graveyard visions. He took a deep breath.

Gigi sensed the tension through his hand. She reassured him. "Jake, honey, if you're worried about getting me pregnant, forget it. I'm protected. I doubt I will ever have kids anyway."

That was hardly on Jake's mind, but the revelation helped set aside one problem. He looked into her open, inviting eyes. He took a couple of deep, slow breaths. The anxiety subsided and excitement returned. He pulled her closer and then snatched her up off her feet like a child in his arms. He carried her to the bed as she giddily engaged him by caressing his neck. After he entered the bedroom with his prize, he shoved the door closed with his shoulder.

The cat blinked once in their direction from his post on the table whereupon he resumed licking and cleaning his paws.

Jake playfully dropped her onto the bed and then he rolled over her to her left side. The physical exertion helped him. He felt alert and excited. He noticed the hint of a perfume he could not identify. He stroked her leg with the tips of his fingers, slowly walking them to her breast. They embraced and began to kiss. He did not notice the pain above his knee.

Like Adam engaging Eve in the Garden, the two new friends melted into a primordial time when every touch of past and hint of future disappeared or at least seemed to. Their clothes were off. An ancient biological and teleological bargain coursed through veins and cells and brains and nerves into a one-pointed urge to mate, to enter into certain bliss, and to abandon all questions. Neither creature thought about cosmic meaning. Thoughtlessly they delighted in the flow of the moment. They thought not about forbidden fruit. The knowledge of good and evil had dissipated into anticipated and growing ecstasy.

Gigi enjoyed the affection, half expecting that this handsome, scruffy man could be a new boyfriend, half hoping that he felt satisfied with her. She could sense that he did. She urged him on into her most intimate pleasure.

Disturbed by the toxic fog in his mind, Jake nevertheless remained focused on one thing. He knew this was a merciful opportunity to break out of his pseudo-celibate attitude, an attitude that had bothered him for the past two years. She, this exquisite fallen angel, was more than just Gigi. She was both his savior from ambivalence and the priestess of a baptism that led to a new life. He would confess and he would sin again and his sin was his confession. She would take on his sin and would forgive him at the same time. She already forgave him. She was the source of the river to the new ocean. The insipid dam inside of him was ready to burst as the earth beneath it shook until the massive wall crumbled away. She was moist with passion, ready for him at any moment. All he had to do was—.

A nearly naked Gigi, wearing only Jake's T-shirt, fumbled for her mobile phone that she left in her shorts in the kitchen. She connected with Harry.

"Harry, Harry, get over here, please."

"What's up, babe? Where are you?"

"It's Jake. He's unconscious. I can't seem to wake him. I think he fainted or something. He fell out of a bed and cracked his head on the floor."

"What the hell? Where are you?"

"We rode over to Trina's, you know, above the antique store at Fox Run."

"How long has he been out?"

"A minute or so. I don't know."

"Call 911. I'll be right over."

"No, no, wait. Don't come on your motorcycle. Can you get a car or something? We have to get him out of here. We can't tell police to send anything here. Trina's got marijuana hid around the place and who knows what else. She doesn't know we're here. I can't risk getting her in trouble over this."

"Shit, girl!"

Harry spun around in his seat as he talked to her. He was now looking straight at Giles who understood something serious may have happened to Jake.

"Wait, wait. I'll borrow Jim's pick-up," he said into the phone as well as to Giles. "You sure he's breathing okay?"

"Yes, yes, it's like he's in a trance, but won't wake up. He moaned once when I shook him. But hurry."

Harry ran to Jim, told him that Jake was with Gigi somewhere nearby and hurt his head in a fall. He asked if he could borrow the pickup.

Jim said, "Sure man. Anything else the matter?"

Harry shrugged as if he had no idea. Jim told Harry the keys were on the seat.

"No, no, Jim," Harry said as he backed away. "I'm just irritated with them. I figured they'd be back by now. We were thinking of going soon. Thanks, man. I'll call you."

Harry motioned to Giles to come with him. Giles was ready. The men jumped into Jim's late-model, red Chevy with the king cab. Harry started the eight cylinder engine, put it in drive and then spun out on the gravel driveway. He immediately eased up on the accelerator to get better traction. Jim's Australian Shepherd gave chase to the end of the property. When the truck slowed down enough to make a sharp turn, Ozzie jumped up into the vehicle's bed. He enjoyed riding in the truck. The men did not notice the dog.

Giles spoke up first. "What's up, man?"

"I don't know but I'm afraid to think about it. Jake's been having panic attacks. Gigi said he's unconscious. Neal told him to see a doc a soon as possible. He hasn't yet. Damn it!"

"Why didn't she call for emergency services?"

"Longer story," Harry said as he sped down the winding, dark road to a destination that was a desperate two minutes away. "Gigi's worried that cops will come. Trina is known to have drugs in her apartment. She assured me Jake is breathing okay."

After a few minutes of harried driving they were there. Fox Run was only a few miles from the nearest medical center. The men spilled out of the truck, slammed the doors and jogged to the back entrance. Harry ran up the deck stairs with Giles puffing behind him. The dog watched for a few seconds as if studying the situation. Sensing there was a job to do, Ozzie jumped down to follow the pack.

Gigi was already waiting at the door to hold it open for Harry and Giles. She led them to the bedroom. They did not notice the gray, speckled dog that nudged the screen door open. The cat sat upright on his table to better observe the four-legged invader.

"Where is he?" Harry asked with an urgent tone.

As Gigi pointed to the other side of the bed, Harry looked at her and noticed her barely buttoned blouse. She had pulled on her panties and shorts and put on the blouse leaving Jake's shirt hung across a chair. Her bra was on the floor. Other items, including Jake's underpants, socks and sneakers were strewn around.

"What the hell, Gigi?"

He brushed by her as he strode to get to his brother. He found Jake sprawled out on the pinewood floor face down by the bed. Next to his mouth was a small stream of vomit. Harry knelt down next to him. Jake was breathing and his eyes were half open. Harry shook him once and then twice more. Jake's only response was let out a brief moan as his eyes rolled back. Harry felt a large goose-egg bump on his forehead.

"He may have a concussion. Okay, we should get him to an emergency room. We can call 911 along the way to Phoenix Medical."

Harry quickly examined his naked brother again and wondered out loud, "What's with the long scars on his back?"

Gigi looked closer over Harry's shoulder.

"Looks like old cuts or burns," she said with some concern in her voice. "He didn't talk about that."

"Looks like you did little talking anyway. I asked you to show him some feminine sympathy, not serve him the whole enchilada!"

Harry rolled Jake onto his back and tried to sit him up. Jake's body remained limp. Jake groaned, his eyes half-opened, but he did not seem to regain full consciousness.

"I'm sorry," Gigi said apologetically, but then retorted, "It wasn't like that, Harry. It wasn't."

"You've been sorry your whole damn life," Harry said angrily.

He grabbed and began to slip the pair of loose khaki pants onto Jake's limp legs with Giles attempting to assist.

"Here, make yourself useful," Harry barked at Gigi. "Help us lift him."

Giles knelt down heavily onto one knee. "Yo, Harry. Lighten up," he said. "It's not her fault."

The men struggled to find a proper grip. Harry began to laugh while struggling to keep Jake upright.

"What the hell you laughin' at?" Giles said with concern in his voice.

"You told me to lighten up. Princess Bride." Harry answered as he continued to chuckle.

"Princess bride? What's that about? Giles asked as he grunted.

"The movie, man. Jake and I watched *The Princess Bride* many times. We had the video. It's a spoof flick—there's a great sequence in it with this dude who remains totally limp after a goofy magician tries to fix him and his friends have to drag him around.

"Ha, ha," Gigi retorted with irritation as she struggled with Jake's legs. "So I'm a goofy magician now."

"It's okay, Gi. Sorry I snapped," Harry retorted trying unsuccessfully to hold back more laughter.

"I don't get what's so funny, man. Let's get him out of here," Giles ordered.

Giles grabbed a shoulder under the armpit as Harry grabbed the other arm. The men raised Jake's floppy torso as Gigi handled Jake's legs. They hoisted him readily.

The trio maneuvered around the bed and into the commotion in the kitchen between the dog and the cat. Snarling and hissing animals were not what they needed to deal with at the time. Gigi pulled Jake's legs over the table where they could rest Jake's butt. This freed her to deal with the furry melee. Max was on the counter hissing as the dog yelped loudly making sure the cat stayed there. Giles yelled over the barking dog,

"How the hell did he get here? Isn't that Jim's dog?"

"Obviously, he was in the truck, man," Harry said as he slapped Jake again to see if he would respond. Jake moaned.

"Harry, take it easy. He may have a head injury, dumb ass," Giles barked. "Come on, Gigi. Do something."

Gigi grabbed the dog by the collar not knowing what to do next. They had to get Jake out the door so she couldn't just put Ozzie out or he'd get right back in.

Giles noted her quandary and took charge. "Okay, Gordon, put the dog outside, shut the door. Next move the lion into the bedroom and shut him in. Then come back here to help us."

Gigi needed the simple directions that took her all of fifteen seconds to carry out despite one misstep. She was very upset and not thinking clearly, especially after the psychotropic enhancement from a cannabinoid. She let go of the dog and went to pick up the cat.

"No, dammit! Do the dog first—get him outside." Giles snapped as Harry continued to hold back laughter. Jake's head flopped to the side.

With the animal shuffle accomplished, out the door and down the steps they went as carefully as possible with the dog following quietly, his stubby tail wagging indicating its satisfaction with a job going well.

The men shoved Jake into the front of the cab. Giles slid in to hold him up. Harry gunned the engine, spun out backwards and pulled onto the country road.

Gigi went back to straighten up the place. She let Max out of the bedroom. He promptly jumped back to his throne on the table. He looked around warily before settling down again. In a dizzy rush Gigi gathered her bra, then Jake's T-shirt, his blue-checkered boxer shorts, white socks and sneakers. She locked the apartment, returned the key to its hiding spot and ran down the stairs to her trike. The dog was standing there waiting for her.

"Oh great, Ozzie. Now what?"

She grabbed her helmet from the trunk and shoved the clothes in. She hoped the dog would follow her back to Jim's.

"Come on boy, let's go," she urged as the dog easily kept pace at ten miles an hour. Jim's was only a mile away. When they arrived at Jim's driveway, Gigi stopped.

"Get home, boy. Go to Jim."

Ozzie dutifully returned back to the main house as Gigi drove her Harley down the winding road.

"Giles, dial EMS and tell them we are on the way. See if we can meet up with them somewhere."

"Hell, Harry, we can be there in ten minutes the way you're driving. Jake is breathing. Just go. I'll call the ER and let them know."

Emergency medical staff met them at the entrance. Within seconds Jake was on a gurney. The medical staff took vital signs and initiated a blood draw for labs. The emergency area was nearly on diversion due to a high volume of patients. One nurse could be heard saying "Must be a full moon!" Nevertheless, the staff attended to Jake quickly to rule out an imminent cardiac problem or serious head injury.

"The doctor is ordering tests and putting him on an IV for now," a nurse told Harry. "He's stable for now but not coherent. The doctor seems to think your brother may have taken something. Does he use drugs?"

"He was drinking beer the last I saw him," Harry said with a shrug and a look of exasperation.

Outside, Gigi arrived. She parked her trike and ran to the emergency department with her helmet on. She found Giles waiting in a chair. He was wiping his brow with a paper towel. Then he blew his nose in it. As he stood up to find a trash can, Gigi walked up to him. He tossed the paper towel away and then looked her over.

"You look weathered and worn, babe. The doc may want to talk with you. May I suggest you take your helmet off and maybe fix your blouse?"

"Thanks for the advice and compliment. You don't look so hot yourself. How is he?"

"I don't know. He was moaning on the way here. How much did he drink anyway?"

"Four or five beers, I think. He had some wine at Trina's."

Gigi removed her helmet and left it with Giles while she attended to herself in the rest room. She returned within a few minutes.

"Did he have anything else?"

Gigi was trying to piece together what happened.

"No. He refused a hit of weed."

Gigi paused with her mouth open.

"Oh, shit. He ate one of those large brownies!"

Gigi quickly pulled her mobile from her pocket and proceeded to connect with Trina. Trina picked up after a few seconds of a blues-riff ring tone.

"Yo, girl, it's me," Gigi started. "I was over your place earlier. Just left a bit ago. A friend of mine was with me… Right, right… Yeah, yeah, a new guy… Alright…Yes, he was nice… Yes, and good looking. Okay. Listen he helped himself to a brownie in the fridge. Was it loaded?"

Gigi listened to Trina explain the content of the baked goods.

"I don't know which tray he ate from… Yes, the remaining pieces in there are all smallish…What do you mean, 'Uh oh?'... Well, I'm here with him now in an emergency room. He passed out…Yes, he fell on the floor and hit his head. Well no, we did nothing like that…Hey, that's none of your business, sister… Stop laughing, this is serious… So you think he's just totally stoned?... A whitey?... What's that?"

Trina, an experienced pot smoker, now in her mid-forties, explained, "Some people are more sensitive to pot than others, girl. A *whitey* is when they turn a whiter shade of pale and faint after heavy use or doing too much, too fast. It won't kill him."

"Well, that's comforting," Gigi replied with sarcasm.

"You know, once one of our gerbils ate a chunk of hashish and it went into a comatose state for over two hours!"

"Yeah, yeah but he's not a gerbil."

Gigi looked up at Giles who heard her. He looked at her quizzically with his hands up as if to say *I don't want to know.*

"Shut up," she said to Giles.

"Well excuse me," Trina chimed in sounding offended.

"No, no, I wasn't talking to you, Trina. It's Giles and his smart ass remarks. Never mind. But listen, it's more complicated than the pot. He hit his head on your floor when he fell out of bed. He may have a concussion."

"That must have been some wild bumping, girl. Mmm, Mmm."

"It wasn't like that! This conversation is over. Okay? Gotta go and bye. And thanks."

Gigi turned to Giles. "Trina says that one of her old hippie friends brought hash loaded brownies to her party earlier. One large one may have been really loaded. The other one, she said, was cut into eights for people at the party. Jake ate the whole one. It was enough to get eight or ten people high. Oh, God, I'm so sorry."

"There you go again with the sorry business. I can't believe that ganja could do that to him," Giles remarked. He straightened his ponytail. "It must have been a helluva cake!"

"Well he started breathing funny, like he was gasping for air just when we were going to, you know, do it, then he hurled a little after falling and that was when he passed out. I wonder if anything else was in that thing or if he ate something else?"

"Maybe mixing it with beer and wine did not agree with him. Well, you better have a story ready. Here comes Harry with a doc and a nurse."

"Hi. Glad you got here," said Harry.

With her blouse properly buttoned and her spiky black hair neatly fluffed, she felt prepared to answer questions. She gave Harry a hug. He was no longer angry with her.

"Could you please talk with Doctor Blouse er, I mean, Doctor Blaise here?" Then Harry whispered," Sorry—slight slip."

Gigi glared at him. Then she turned to the doctor, facing him with a smile.

"Hello, doctor. My name is Gayle."

She spoke in her professional voice. She shook the doctor's hand firmly. She then wrapped her arms around her chest as if feeling a chill.

The doctor held the clipboard by his side.

"Hi, Gayle. Thanks for talking with us. We have Jake on fluids with an IV. We drew blood but the labs aren't back yet. We couldn't get urine yet. I have a few questions, if you don't mind. I understand you were with Jake when he fainted. We suspect he took something that may have triggered this episode. We're testing for a concussion. He's semi-conscious but not making much sense. His blood pressure is a bit low. What can you tell us?"

"Oh well, I may as well get this over with."

Gigi took a deep breath. She gestured nervously with her hands as she spoke.

"Only now, a few minutes ago, I found out from a friend that the cake he ate at her house was loaded with hashish, a lot of it. Jake did not know it was loaded. He had some wine there also. He was drinking beers earlier before we got there. We were on a bed when he started breathing funny—had trouble catching his breath. He fell like a stone head first onto a wooden floor. He threw up a little. I couldn't bring him to, so I called Harry, his brother."

"What about the grass stains on his pants? He also looks like he was outside rolling on the ground. And what can you tell me about the scars on his back?"

Jake was still shirtless and barefoot.

"Oh, the dirt? Well, we were at a friend's playing softball earlier. I don't know anything about the scars. We just met today."

Gigi noted that the doctor seemed perturbed. "What was he thinking?" she wondered.

"He has no identification on him," the doctor remarked. "Does anyone have his wallet or something?"

All three answered in the negative.

"He can't seem to concentrate clearly right now. We need some demographic information. Harry, could you help fill out some paper work?"

The doctor pointed to a young woman standing behind him. Harry followed her to a counter area where she could write. With Jake's name and birth date the social worker was able to confirm that Jake indeed seemed to have no insurance, just as Harry told her.

An hour passed. Jake became more alert but was hardly clearer in his thoughts. He was talking in disjointed phrases and intermittently passing out. The doctor thought he heard him mumble, "I want to die, just let me die." He took note of it.

In Jake's mind he was in a kind of dream. His past and his present seemed confused with musings and fears about the future. The doctor considered that psychotic breaks are not unusual in people under deep stress. Clinical depression

276

can cause a break with reality. Alcohol withdrawal can cause it but this patient would not yet be in withdrawal if he drank a mere hour ago, and he had no history of daily drinking. A high dose of THC from cannabis can do wonders to split the mind from functional reasoning. Patients with unknown histories exhibiting psychosis and saying they want to die deserve extra attention while under a doctor's care.

Dr Blaise decided to write an order for psychiatric evaluation. Jake appeared to be in no condition to refuse or consent at the moment so the doctor wrote a statement for an involuntary commitment. The doctor ordered the social worker to fax the statement to the new psychiatric emergency hospital in the county. An ambulance would be taking Jake there as soon as he was medically cleared to go.

Back in the waiting area Giles and Gigi showed signs of fatigue. They were unaware that Jake was going to see a shrink. Neither was Harry who came back inside after smoking a cigarette. He said, "I spoke with Lindy. She wants me to come and get her. Almost everyone has left the party. We have to get the Chevy back to Jim anyway. Gi, can you stay? Giles has to get his wheels too. I'll come back as soon as I can."

"You mean *we* will come back," Giles added insisting that he was in this for the duration.

"Sure, sure, I'm good. My bike is here," Gigi assured them. "I'll get some coffee and hang out."

She walked with them through the double set of automatic doors into the parking lot. She watched them drive away. She felt a chill in the air. With her arms crossed this time to keep in the heat, Gigi walked to her trike to get her riding clothes. She slipped them over her shorts and blouse. She locked her helmet in the trunk. She decided to keep Jake's clothes until she knew the outcome of his treatment. She felt properly dressed again and less vulnerable with her skin covered.

The Kevlar outfit was a high quality, pricey name brand and it fit her well.

Gigi made her way inside to a machine dispenser that brewed a variety of coffees. She fed a dollar bill into the slot, pushed H-3 and got a dark roast with chocolate. She did not recognize anyone in the lobby and she was glad for it. She sat away by herself in a single stuffed chair. Her coffee was too hot to sip so she set it down on an end table. It had been a long day for her.

She picked up her mobile to see how many messages she had been ignoring all day. Dozens of phone contacts and texts needed attention. She scanned the list quickly. She returned to a text she received early that morning from an old boyfriend who broke up with her when he left for Afghanistan. He was home again after a year of duty. When he left he said he loved her but did not want to hold her to a commitment, a commitment she wanted to promise. Perhaps he knew better. Now he wanted to get together with her again. She answered the text: "Call me tmrw nite."

Immediately after she pushed *send*, she saw herself as immature and unable to resist taking advantage of another opportunity to charm a man.

"What if he came back missing a limb or something?" she thought. "Yes, what if, Gigi girl?"

She put her mobile device away. She got lost in her mental world as she sunk down in her chair. Mellowing effects of the marijuana had not yet worn off and she was worn out from the long, eventful day. She went with the tired flow of feelings and thoughts in her head. Questions appeared.

"What kind of woman wants to do that? Is the game about control or is it about fear?"

Most men were especially easy prey for someone blessed with her rough elegance. She could turn on a *diamond in the rough* persona at will and just as easily turn it off. Despite the impression she portrayed in public, few men ever bedded her.

"So, why the tryst with Jake? Was I subconsciously offering a needy ex-cult member therapy? How utterly creepy and dishonest," she thought.

Her mind turned to another perspective. She glimpsed something else in herself. It was something more than she felt she could achieve in the past. With Jake she felt an urge to capture a relationship that could end this catty game. She liked his humor, she liked his mind, she liked his body and she liked his family.

"Might we be compatible? Maybe we could be an item for life."

278

The coffee was cooler. She took a sip.

"Ick," was her reaction.

She set the coffee down. A tear streaked down her cheek; then another.

Gigi went to a rest room to rinse her face with cold water. The cold water and a few deep breaths help her to regain composure. She looked at herself in the mirror. "You need to grow up," she sighed. She wiped off her face with a paper towel and returned to the stuffed chair where she left her coffee.

The social worker came to look for Harry. Gigi told her that Harry could come back if he was needed.

"What's the problem? Maybe I can help."

"The doctor wants Jake to get a psychiatric evaluation. He's talking to him about it now, but Jake seems reluctant. As soon as the behavioral health center accepts medical clearance, an ambulance will take him over there."

"Take him? You said he might not want to go."

"Well, the doctor wrote an involuntary request for evaluation. It's a legal document and it works like a warrant. He *has* to go. It will be up to the receiving psychiatrist to admit him or not."

After that sunk in, Gigi took out her mobile to call Harry. He didn't pick up. Then she punched Giles's number. He answered from Jim's place. She repeated what the social worker told her. While she was talking to Giles, Jake's doctor was on the phone with the psychiatrist at the *Community Institute for Behavioral Medicine* or CIBM but known locally as *Psych Hall.*

The psychiatrist, Dr. Patel, was new at the job. He had an inadequate command of American English. The doctors reviewed the labs results. Patel understood that Dr. Blaise decided that Jake was medically sound enough for discharge but not before a mental health assessment. He neglected to say that Jake was yet drowsy and loopy. He mentioned only that the patient was "rousable."

Dr. Blaise was most concerned to get Jake out of his busy department especially since he considered Jake to be more a head case than a medical problem. The concussion was not severe. He and the staff had had a bad night so far. He had no way of knowing it was about to get worse.

An ambulance crew consisting of two men in their late twenties was ready to transport Jake to Psych Hall. The larger man, Ben, approached Jake with the doctor's order. Ben was heavyset and wore wire rimmed glasses. Neither the doctor nor the social worker said anything about the transport to Jake to avoid a scene until it was necessary. Ben shook Jake.

"Hey, buddy. Can you please sit up? We are going to take you in the ambulance now."

Jake woke enough to hear "ambulance." He struggled to sit.

"What for? What's wrong, man? This has something to do with the old man. The old man," he mumbled. "What's—where am I? Are you taking me home?"

Jake had a foggy idea that he was yet in a hospital.

"We're taking you to a psych hospital for an evaluation. The doc says you may be suicidal. We need you to get on the stretcher." Ben pointed to the gurney behind him.

"Stretcher? I'm okay—can walk—I think."

Jake had no idea he was going to a clinic over ten miles away.

"It's the rules, Jake. We use a stretcher to transport patients."

Jake stared at Ben for a few seconds.

"Did you say psych hospital?" he asked slowly.

"Yes."

"I told the doc. No, not that. No. I'll, I'll be okay—just need some work."

"Well, you're not the doc, Jake. Nothing personal, but our job is to take you there."

"I'm not going. I need to find a ride back to, to Monica's."

Jake rubbed his head with both hands to try to erase the fog and the headache.

Ben signaled to his partner, Tracy, who overheard the exchange. Tracy reached behind for the handcuffs attached to his belt.

This team had done hundreds of involuntary transports to psychiatric hospitals so they knew the routine when someone resisted. Patient and staff safety were their major concerns.

Jake picked up on the change of attitude in their body language. Even in his drowsy mind, or because of it, he suspected force coming his way as Tracy calmly walked up to his side. Ben maintained eye contact with Jake. He continued to explain that they, as emergency techs, were just doing their jobs and that Jake had to go and it would help if he were cooperative. When Jake felt metal click around his left wrist he reacted instinctively, ripping the cuffs out of Tracy's hand. He was drunk and he was stoned but now he was scared and he was angry with adrenaline surging in his body. Zen warrior training instincts took over. Jake pushed off the bed. He landed unsteadily on his feet. He gained balance as man and beast merged into a fighting stance. He assumed the crane pose, then the tiger, freezing a startled Ben.

In the process, the loose half of the metal cuff ended up in the grasp of his left hand. With a snapping strike of his armed fist he nailed big Ben square between the eyes causing his glasses to fly across the room. Ben reeled backwards until he smashed against a metal counter with his arms flailing to gain balance. He knocked plastic bottles and boxes of stuff off the counter onto the white vinyl tile floor where he ended up among the debris.

The metal cuff had cut into Ben's skull between his eyebrows. Blood gushed immediately above Ben's nose creating a red mess on his face. More bodies appeared at the scene. Tracy and a security man nearby surrounded their dangerous patient. A lab tech came up from behind. A nurse witnessing the incident pushed an alarm button that set off a *code silver* throughout the floor indicating a combative person with a weapon.

Jake was on his feet whirling his arms with one wrist yet swinging the now dangling handcuff. More security and staff assigned to assist in codes came running from other parts of the facility but the added crowd was unnecessary.

Within seconds Ben rebounded from the shock of being punched. He was on his feet and loaded for bear! He squared off in front of Jake commanding his attention again. But the transport team had been through this act many times before. By the time several men arrived at the scene, Tracy had Jake in a full Nelson hold down on the floor with Ben piled on top essentially immobilizing both men with his wide girth. Ben took advantage of the situation by punching Jake hard in the ribs.

"Stop struggling, you son-of-a-bitch," Ben grunted.

The blow from his fist was hard enough to stun the function of Jake's lungs. Jake coughed and gasped for air as he felt a sharp pain. During the mayhem blood from Ben's forehead dripped onto and smeared on Jake's naked shoulder and upper back.

"Set up the restraints," Tracy yelled to security staff as he squirmed out from under Ben and the pile of men who had secured the limbs and head of the combative male. A staff member brought four leather cuffs and three webbed fabric restraint straps to the transport gurney.

The security men groaned trying to remain professional despite the insults and curses coming from Jake, whose anger was yet in full bloom. He continued to struggle ignoring the pain he felt in his side and thigh as men held his legs and arms. Tracy, now the team leader, maintained a sober bearing throughout the ordeal, taking control of the situation verbally.

"Okay, sit him up and hold his hands behind him."

The men forced the struggling patient up. Tracy finished the handcuffing he missed earlier.

"Now lift him on here—his head up this way," Tracy directed.

With Jake's arms secure, the men hoisted him up off the floor onto the lowered stretcher. Two men held his legs down as Ben quickly secured the restraint cuffs around his naked ankles. A female nurse fed the canvas foot strap through the cuffs and into the snap lock.

"Feet secure," she said.

The nearsighted Ben was practically blind without his glasses that lay bent on the floor. Blood continued to flow slowly down the bridge of his nose as he backed off Jake's legs. An aide stood ready to apply a damp towel to Ben's face and forehead. She helped to clean him up while a physician's assistant applied antibiotic creams and a butterfly bandage to the laceration. Jake continued to squirm, testing the foot restraint but to no avail.

"Jake, yo, buddy, listen to me," Tracy said calmly. "We're going to remove the handcuffs and then strap your arms down to the stretcher. This will go a lot easier on you if you relax."

Jake did not relax. He was still seething inside with legs straining on his cuffs as he continued to gasp for air. His side ached in this hunched over position. One man held his head forward to prevent potential spitting or biting while two others remained with their hands clamped over Jake's arms. With the handcuffs removed they eased him down on his back. Tracy continued to hold Jake's head down while others held his arms and applied the wrist cuffs. They strapped them tight to the sides of the gurney and secured three body straps across his chest, waist and knees. Jake screamed odd obscenities that caused Tracy to laugh because they made no sense.

"Don't fucking tell me to relax, you cop bastard. I was only playing baseball. Aaaaahhrr! Who the hell are you anyway?"

"The name is Tracy. I'll be your driver," he said as a matter of fact.

"Let me loose then, Teresa! Get me out of here."

"Well, sometimes I feel that way too," Tracy replied with a smile. Jake had no way of knowing it, but Tracy was bisexually inclined.

"Can't go. Can't do this. You guys aren't doing this right. Sunyata, no banana fish. I'm not, not. Call Marga. She knows. She'll tell you. Banana, bananas. Right, all right, then, just let me go. Aaach," he yelled.

Jake rambled from a dream world that made no sense to anyone in the room. They were unfazed by anything their patient said. They heard worse and crazier over years of dealing with out of control clients.

But how would they know that this patient referred to Seymour's suicide in J.D. Salinger's short story, *A Perfect Day for Bananafish*. Jake read it for a literature course in 1996. Images from that study surfaced after ten years in his addled brain, images of a sensitive young man who kills himself on his honeymoon.

"Sir, I think your mind is bananas," Tracy said in a low slow voice. "We're only trying to help. It's going to be alright. Take a few breaths," he said calmly. Then Tracy turned to the desk. "Did anyone order stat meds for this guy?"

Jake was shouting again hardly responding to Tracy as a person. The EMT was merely a voice connected to a character in a movie from another time—a time somewhere in Jake's head.

He continued to yell in agitated phrases. "I got to get back to where I was— where's Gigi? Eternity was so close. We fell. We fell. We fell. It was not hell, not hell."

Jake began to sob and gasp for air after making this statement. He was babbling as if he were talking in his sleep. He ended the rant with a long, loud, opened mouthed yell of exasperation. His head fell back and he lay still.

A nurse arrived by the side of the gurney with a loaded syringe. She had two male assistants with her. She checked the ID band on Jake's right wrist.

"Jake, my name is Kathleen. I'm a nurse here. The doctor ordered some medication to help you calm down. I'm going to give you an injection of two milligrams of Ativan, fifty of Benadryl, and five of Haldol."

Then she directed the assistants to roll Jake over enough to expose his buttocks. Tracy pulled down on the khakis to show enough fatty tissue for the injection. It was over in a few seconds before Jake had time to react. But as the nurse backed away, react he did. He began shaking the gurney from side to side until he nearly tipped it over. Tracy and Ben, who was bandaged by then between his eyes, steadied the unit while encouraging their patient to relax. They prepared to wait until the sedative kicked in before wheeling Jake out the door into their vehicle.

Just then Gigi walked into the emergency area to get an update. She heard a loud shout coming from Jake. She caught sight of Jake strapped on the stretcher. As she approached him he was mumbling mostly to himself but no longer yelling. She noticed the blood on his shoulder.

"What the hell happened here? Where're you taking him?" she demanded, looking first to Ben, then to Tracy.

"Who are you, ma'am?" Tracy asked.

"My name is Gayle. Jake knows me as Gigi. I've been waiting here all night to be with him. I spoke to the doc earlier. I know he's going to Psych Hall for an evaluation."

"Yep, that's where we're taking him. He struggled with us. He punched Ben in the face so we had to take control."

Gigi noted the tear streaks on Jake's face and the blood on his shoulder. She then looked at Ben. "Oh," is all she said.

"That's mine," Ben offered, referring to the blood on Jake. "We haven't had time to clean him up yet. We'll do that later at the Hall, maybe when he's calmed down after the meds take effect." Then Ben called to an aide to bring a blanket.

"What meds?" Gigi inquired.

"The meds of La Mancha," Jake blurted out lamely. Jake turned to Gigi. He stared at her as if she were a stranger. "I knew someone like you," he said.

Then Jake let out another long, red-faced shout, swelling the veins in his forehead and neck. He looked like a madman. Gigi felt horrible. She looked to Tracy for reassurance as he took the white blanket from the aide. Tracy went about his business, calmly covering his loud patient.

"Jake, it is me. It's," Gigi stopped talking when she noticed that Jake focused his eyes toward the ceiling. Suddenly he was breathing slowly and no longer tense. Either his attention had shifted or the medication began its work—or perhaps it was both. It dawned on her that maybe the doctor was right. Jake had snapped and there was nothing she could say at the time that would make sense to him. She turned to Ben.

"Can I follow you guys over there?"

Jake stopped responding. He continued to stare at the ceiling.

"You can," Tracy told her. "They may or may not let you stay. Privacy rules might apply unless this guy gives consent." Then he turned to Jake. "Is it okay for your friend here to stay with you while you get evaluated?"

"Her motorcycle won't fit through the door. It has three wheels, man. How's it going to fit through the door? Ha!"

Jake tugged at his wrist restraints again. His eyes rolled back as he arched his spine raising his torso with his neck muscles. He let out another moan when a sharp tinge of pain shot through his ribcage. He collapsed back onto the stretcher.

"What's wrong, Jake?" Tracy asked. Jake tried to indicate his ribs.

"My side, there," he said as he motioned with his chin. Tracy felt around the tender, now slightly bruised area. Jake winced. "You may have a cracked rib, buddy. Not much we can do about it, but I will note it in my report. They can give you something for the pain once Dr. Patel looks at it. Try not to breath too deep or make any sudden moves."

Tracy turned to Gigi.

"You can take your chances. Maybe the doc there will want to talk to someone who knows him. Do you really have a motorcycle?"

"Yeah. It's in the parking lot. He's referring to my Harley trike. We rode on it earlier."

"That's good to hear. At least he's in touch with some reality." Tracy chuckled and then turned to his partner.

"Do you have the paperwork?"

Ben pointed to the manila envelope resting over Jake's legs.

"Then let's get going."

They rolled Jake out the door while he mumbled something incoherent to his transport team. He seemed calmer. The sedative was taking effect. However, just as they were about to slide him into the back of the ambulance, Jake spoke up in clear, emphatic terms.

"I have to take a piss."

"Can't you hold it? We'll be at the Hall in twenty minutes," Ben said with irritation.

"Hold it. Oh, yeah. Hold, hold, hold on, whatever."

Jake was breathing deeper with a tense facial expression.

There was no way that the men were going to trust Jake to go to a bathroom out of restraints this soon.

"Let's get him into the ambulance first. I think there's a urine bottle in the box.

I'll help him piss in it on the way," Ben said. He would sit in the back with Jake.

The men shoved the collapsed gurney into the van. Ben settled into position in the back as Tracy pulled out slowly to give Ben time to help Jake to relieve himself. It was too late.

"Dammit. He pissed himself already," Ben shouted mostly to himself. "Go ahead, Trace, step on it."

With that Tracy engaged the flashing lights and siren as he sped toward CIBM.

Community Institute of Behavioral Medicine, known as *Psych Hall* to locals, was located on the edge of the large campus of old Pennhallow State School and Hospital. Pennhallow was established in 1908 to house and care for the *feeble minded and epileptic.* In its glory days it was a model program with the latest medical advances for treatment of a sorely neglected population of mentally and often physically handicapped children and adults, as many as two thousand.

The original campus contained a fully functional dairy farm, a large greenhouse for vegetables, and many productive features that supported a relatively self-sufficient facility. A series of ceramic tile-lined, underground tunnels connected main buildings so that staff and residents could easily walk from station to station in any kind of weather. The tunnel system also provided more control as residents were herded or wheeled from program to program. Higher functioning *retarded* residents manned the farm and provided most of the janitorial services. They worked for little or nothing other than the privileges of residency. One news reporter called it *slave labor.*

The Schuylkill waterway bordered one edge of the property that was located just outside of the small town of Spring City. Due to a series of media exposures about staff abusing residents and the poor, overcrowded living conditions, the large institution attracted lawsuits. A landmark decision came down to close the entire facility. New, humane laws required county-based services to provide local care for those with developmental disabilities. Over fifteen hundred remaining residents would eventually find their way into paid for private apartments, group homes and small, medically supervised treatment facilities. The last of the residents left the institution in the mid-1980s.

The large brick structures yet owned by the state were abandoned to natural forces. Thus began one human habitat's life without people. Within decades, due to lack of maintenance, severe weather, and creeping vegetation, the entire complex took on the appearance of a crumbling, haunted asylum. Indeed, it was haunted by unhappy memories that people would rather forget despite the original *state of the art* care the place offered a century earlier.

To fulfill a need for general psych services, a local council made a deal in 2003 with the state to rent a three-story, Pennhallow building that once housed the medical unit. The council then contracted with a private company to rescue the building from a quarter century of neglect. Happily the substructure and the general superstructure remained sound. It took almost two years to prepare it for both inpatient and outpatient behavioral health services. It wasn't perfect but it was clean, upgraded to code and functioning well as a fifty-bed clinic by 2006.

Ongoing repairs and remodeling continued as patient and administrative needs expanded. But compared to the large, empty buildings on the campus that stood vacant in various states of disrepair and decay, the new "Psych Hall" was a refurbished gem. Jake arrived there fast asleep, snoring, and in the dead of night.

Despite the late hour, the admission staff had been busy. The attending doctor was alone and had been working for nearly seven hours straight dealing with four admissions and several in-house incidents. It was four a.m. He was tired.

After wheeling their patient into a waiting area, Ben and Tracy gave the admitting psychiatrist a verbal report with the emergency department's paperwork. The doctor was both dismayed and relieved to see that Jake was out cold. The medications had done their job to chemically restrain the unruly patient but a proper psychiatric evaluation would have to wait until later in the day.

Psych Hall staff prepared Jake's intake contact information as well as they could without his cooperation. Dr. Patel could not arouse him for more than a few seconds at a time. He checked his vital signs again. Jake appeared stable enough medically, so the psychiatrist made his decision based primarily on what was written in the 302 statement and on the ED doc's report.

"Okay, we admit him. Please take off restraints now," he ordered Tracy.

"What diagnosis will you use?" a caseworker assigned to Jake asked.

"I think *Psychotic Disorder, NOS*. This look like drug-induced behavior. Too much drug and booze!" the doctor remarked lightheartedly. "We rule out depression for now."

In the meantime, Giles told Harry to stay with Lindy and to get some rest. He assured Harry that he and Gigi would ride over to Psych Hall to attend to Jake until his situation was resolved. Giles met Gigi at the Phoenix Hospital lot. The ambulance did not wait for her.

She followed Giles who knew which way to go. Giles led her by way of a shortcut that wound through the old state hospital grounds. He slowed down to a near crawl at ten miles per hour as they entered the unlit grounds. Pot holes and branches impeded their progress. They seemed to be obeying a defunct old metal sign at the entrance. It said *Slow* and it had a silhouetted figure of a walking man on it. Few men if any walked on that road for years and much less at night.

Gigi noted the eerie, empty brick buildings that rose out of the gloom as they eased by them, some three and four stories tall. Leafy vines clung to the red brick surfaces up to and over the rooftops and around and into broken windows. The vines inscribed the once stately facades with the organic designs of Mother Nature's relentless reclamation.

Most ground level windows and entrances were boarded up except where vandals had chopped through the thick plywood security panels. The rumbling motorcycles passed an area between two large brick buildings that had small signs and symbols attached to doorways and along sidewalks.

Giles pulled back until he was next to Gigi. She leaned over to hear him say, "The national guard uses these two buildings to practice urban maneuvers."

Gigi saluted him.

A sumac tree grew out of one window, then another. The trees and bushes appeared silvery gray reflecting the gentle light of a bright, three-quarter moon.

As they approached a turn, the real reason appeared for their slow going. Gigi nearly screamed when she saw the large animals emerge, but all that came out of her mouth was a little "Uh." Several deer glided ghostlike across the road ahead of them. She observed three skittish does and one majestic buck disappear into tangled brush that decades before may have been a well-groomed lawn.

The bikes cruised by the abandoned administration building that was the centerpiece of the architect's design for the complex. This once proud structure sustained a darker insult to its integrity. Thieves stripped the elegant cupola on top of all its copper, thus leaving a skewed skeleton made visible by moonlight reflecting from a cloud behind the building. The moonlight readily served to endorse the legends of a haunted asylum. Weeds and saplings covered the staircase below, deeply rooted below the cracks in the concrete. The bikes continued slowly around another curve where they could now see the glow of bright lights down the way.

As Gigi pulled up to Psych Hall she found a world apart from everything she experienced thus far on the grounds. The entrance was brightly lit by flood lamps that revealed tastefully arranged shrubs and trees below the rows of glass block security windows. The parking lot had new macadam with clear white lines and plenty of spaces for easy handicapped access. Nightshift employee vehicles lined the back end of the relatively empty lot. Colorful banners hung from the flagpoles inserted in the large pillars that framed the front portal. The clear message at this site on the decaying campus was that *we are alive and well and open for business.* The two bikers with helmets in hand arrived at the front desk shortly after Dr. Patel made his diagnosis and decision to admit Jake.

"We're here to see Jacob," Giles announced curtly to the pudgy male clerk.

"Jacob who?"

"G'zhib—g-r-z-y-b."

"Oh, that's how you say that! I thought it was misspelled. Is that Greek or what?"

"Polish," Giles said. He smiled at the middle-aged, balding man behind the desk. "We were with him all day and at the Phoenix ED."

"The doctor mentioned someone might be coming. Hi. My name is Thomas. How are you related?"

"I'm Giles. This is Gigi. Not related to each other or to him. We're his friends. I knew his father well. His brother will come over if necessary but I think we can explain as much as he can to the doc. In any case, Harry, his brother, will talk to you and the doc by phone anytime tonight."

After looking over their picture IDs the clerk said, "Okay. I can get you inside. You'll have to leave any matches, lighters, keys and metal objects here with me. You can take your cell phones in. I'll lock your stuff in here in the cabinet. I'll give you each a tag. You will have to pass through a metal detector back there before I open the elevators."

Thomas led the pair back through the simple but effective security system. He directed them to the elevator that led down to the rear intake area on the ground floor.

Gigi pushed the G button twice and giggled. She had been doing this on elevators since she was a kid. Giles frowned. The elevator came to a halt and the doors opened to reveal a pleasant but stark lobby. Giles stepped back to let Gigi out first. Upon exiting the lift Gigi spotted the ambulance crew behind a closed, clear sliding door. They were having a smoke. They had propped the outer security doors open.

"Hey guys," Gigi called out. "Tracy, where did you hide him?"

Tracy motioned to the end of the hall past the doctor's quarters. Then he put his finger to his lips before pointing to the frail female patient awaiting admission. She was asleep on a sofa.

"Oops. Sorry. Didn't mean to be so loud," Gigi whispered. Tracy gave her thumbs up as he blew smoke out the back door.

Giles and Gigi quietly walked past the sleeping patient. They encountered two bored police officers who sat on a bench across from a room where their shackled prisoner awaited admission in his orange uniform. The prisoner attempted to hang himself in the county prison early that day. At the end of the intake lobby outside the next waiting room they came to a young woman, a social worker, who was sitting by the open door in sight of Jake. She sat with a clipboard on her lap.

"Hi," she said quietly.

"Hi," Gigi replied. "Can we go in?"

"Sure."

They found Jake still on the gurney but now laying on his side in a quasi fetal position and out of restraints. The blanket was on the floor in a heap next to him. He was sound asleep under the influence of meds, a big hash brownie and fine red wine. And he was probably very tired.

"Christ, he's still a mess. Why is his crotch all wet?"

"He obviously pissed himself, babe," Giles remarked while sniffing the air. "Smells like piss to me."

Giles bent down to retrieve the blanket. He spread it back over Jake's body. Gigi leaned over to kiss Jake on the cheek. He did not react. "Let's go talk to the shrink," Giles suggested.

Dr Patel invited them into the office area that had several work stations. One caseworker, a young woman, was busy at a computer while talking to someone on the phone. She waved in greeting to Gigi who waved back. Giles followed the psychiatrist into a side office. Gigi was right behind them.

"Please, please, take a seat."

They sat on the tan leather sofa across from the doctor's desk.

"We can talk in here. I am Doctor Vidia Patel. So, let me tell you what is happening with your friend. We admit him here tonight. Someone will be down for him soon. I think this is a temporary reaction to stress and a drug but we want to be sure. In any case, we cannot send him home like this. There is a liability. He will be safer here."

"Where are you from?" Gigi countered in innocent curiosity. "You don't sound like you are from India?"

"Ah, you are hearing the Trinidad and Tobago accent! Very good. Most people assume I am from India. And you? What is your name?"

The doctor seemed delighted to talk with Gigi. He directed all of his questions about Jake to her. Giles sat quietly thinking to himself how easily Gigi attracted attention from men. He was tired and easily irritated. He picked up a brochure about the clinic's programs and looked it over while Gigi chatted with Patel.

After fifteen minutes Gigi opened her mobile to look up Harry's phone number for Dr. Patel. He took note of it as well as Gigi's. He passed both numbers to the social worker.

"Please inform the brother, Harry, after Jake is comfortably in a hospital bed and answer any questions he might have," he told her.

Finally, the psychiatrist reassured them that Jake would most likely be discharged within a few days but he could not promise anything. With that the two friends shook hands with the doctor, said goodbyes to the caseworker and the crew, and made their way back upstairs. Thomas returned their property. He walked with them to the door.

Jake remained out of it somewhere between here and there.

15   Angel of the Asylum

How many fragments of yourself will you see in a shattered mirror?
—4 November 2007

It was five a.m. Giles escorted Gigi to her house before riding his chopper back to his home. He rode home at a steady, slow speed so as not to make too much noise through the quiet neighborhoods. By the time Giles pulled into his garage, Jake had settled into his room in the men's wing of Psych Hall. Giles decided to soak in his outdoor hot tub under the disappearing stars before settling into bed. Soon the sun would rise again.

Songbirds chirped their signals to one another for reasons beyond his grasp but he did not care. Giles settled his bulk into the soothing heat in the tub. He closed his eyes and listened. He thanked the birds.

A half hour later, before going to bed, Giles left a message that he would be late for work at the office.

Gigi called in sick. She took a long shower scrubbing the day's dirt off her hair and skin. She felt awful. She wanted to feel ashamed but that emotion evaded her. She planned to see her therapist if she could get an appointment.

Harry planned to visit Jake that afternoon. On the way he would stop by Monica's to grab what clothes he could find for his brother. He would tell her then what happened. Harry left Lindy at her mother's house for the night. It was Lindy's turn among her two siblings to tend to her mother after her heart operation.

After parking his bike Harry locked the back shed and walked into his house alone. He spent a few minutes brushing his teeth and washing up at the sink. He collapsed into his bed for a few minutes but soon sat up to find the remote. He found an old war movie on a cable channel. Much like Gigi and Giles, Harry slept poorly.

Jake slept in the peace of oblivion.

Psych Hall stirred around seven a.m. as staff roused everyone—that is everyone who was not already pacing in the halls driven by racing or obsessive thoughts or hanging about anxiously anticipating the first smoke break of the day. Breakfast was at seven-thirty in the common cafeteria immediately after the smoke period.

Psych Hall was one of the few inpatient clinics in the area that accommodated smoking. For whatever reason, mental patients smoke tobacco in far higher rates than the general population. To eliminate another stressor, Psych Hall administrators accommodated the habit. Not all the fifty-two men and women in the clinic that day made it to breakfast.

Some patients refused, complaining that they wanted to sleep or be left alone. Some had no appetite due to the effects of detoxification. Floor techs took note of those who missed meals. Other acutely psychotic, severely suicidal, or dangerous patients who were under continuous observation remained in locked units. Staff delivered their meals.

As a precaution, Dr. Patel assigned Jake to the locked male section due to his violent behavior in the emergency department. He was not yet charged with a crime—he assaulted and battered Ben, an unarmed health care worker, an assault far more serious than hitting someone in a barroom brawl.

Jake shared a room with Paul, an older Caucasian man with schizophrenia. Paul was awake talking to himself when staff announced breakfast. Jake opened his eyes for a short few seconds. He glimpsed an old, scrawny, bearded fellow with long, stringy hair seated across the room upright in a fetal position, nervously tapping his fingers on his kneecaps. Jake rolled over to face the blank wall until he passed out again.

"Looks like Jake will skip breakfast. He checked in early this morning, Paul, but how about you? You want to come with us or stay here?"

Paul would not look at the tech at first. He pointed a gnarly finger at his guardian and kept tapping on a knee with the other hand as he said, "Do you have my pigeons? Why are you keeping me here? He did not bring the pigeons with him," Paul said swinging his accusatory finger and stabbing it three times toward Jake. "I have to wait here, here, here! The pigeons will need me when they arrive." Paul's rant trailed off into babble about electricity and a government document held in a secret place.

"Okay, Paul. You'll get a tray soon. Would you like some coffee?"

"Decaf shit. You can't fool me. You drink it. Fake coffee. You drink it. Bastards. You want my papers, don't you?" Paul hesitated, went into himself, and then said politely, "Cream and three sugars, please." He held up three fingers to emphasize his request.

"Sure, Paul. Cream and *three* sugars it is! Always three, right?"

The tech left to continue his rounds as he marked off his notations regarding Jake and Paul on the clipboard.

"Hey, buddy. He called you Jake. Is that your name? Are you the guardian? Do you know who I am? I'm Paul Traber. That's right, *the* Paul Traber. I know about Tesla's missing papers."

Paul glanced quickly over at Jake's back to make sure he was asleep. He continued talking while facing the door.

"Tesla gave us his secret papers. The feds keep trying to get them from us. They want to drive me crazy with radio waves using *elf*. You working for the government, Jake? You and the government. You and everyone. That's not your real name is it? I bet it ain't. The last time I was here they tried this. Can't fool me. Huh? Maybe you can't hear me. Huh? Maybe you're whacked. What's that?"

Paul stopped talking to listen to the radio signals in his head. He could hear the voice of an announcer calling a meeting into session. The meeting was about Nicolai Tesla and his death ray and about getting to Paul. Ten men in gray suits sat around a table. Paul called them, the *gray men,* who plan to control the world.

"Gray men plan relentlessly. They talk and talk and talk all at once so I can't make out what they say. Tesla wants me to keep his pigeons for him. They killed Tesla, Jake. Are you going to be my friend? Hey, can you hear me?"

Paul stretched, swung his feet to the floor and stood up by his bed. He stopped talking but was clearly thinking something as he gestured toward Jake. He walked over to the sleeping man. Paul stood a few feet from his roommate but would go no closer. He stood there in his striped hospital gown parted at the back exposing his white briefs. He hunched over slightly with his head cocked sideways like a bird as he watched Jake. He listened for a signal.

Paul arrived a day before Jake. Police in Philadelphia took him into custody at a center city café where he was preaching to the customers who were casually having lunch before he arrived. He was preaching to them about his relationship with Tesla and the government. Paul could get very loud when he was excited. The proprietor called police.

"Paul Traber is here again. Can you please pick him up?"

Paul was a public nuisance again as he had been many times in many places. Police invariably called his brother who would drive to the city, take custody of him and drive him to Psych Hall or any facility that would treat him. Paul knew the routine. He hated to stay in Philadelphia hospitals for irrational reasons connected to his mental illness. But he knew that police would commit him there if he did not go with his brother.

He believed that Tesla's free energy was stolen and misused in most Philadelphia buildings including the hospitals. After stabilization and release from treatment, Paul would eventually drift back to Philadelphia, to his ritual locations.

Not only was he treatment avoidant; he would also refuse housing that his casework team assigned him in his home county. Paul preferred the streets. He spent a portion of his monthly check on food for pigeons that he fed daily in the parks, especially the birds around Logan Circle. Without the free food at soup kitchens and at a local church, Paul could easily have starved. But he knew how to work the system. He had survived this way for over twenty years.

Paul had not shaved or bathed for several weeks, maybe months, when his brother brought him in. Staff at the hospital required every patient to take a shower before admission, or soon after. Despite his agitation and fear, Paul complied with the demand to suffer the invasion of soap and water on his skin. He was clean but still refusing medication when Jake arrived. Eventually he would get an injection.

Paul was once a promising engineer at age twenty-four until his brain disorder completely compromised his judgment and his career. He was now in his late forties but he looked much older. At five feet, seven inches, he was a bit shorter than Jake, but thinner. As seen on the streets he appeared in layers of clothing no matter what the weather, with stringy gray hair and beard.

He allowed staff to trim his beard whenever he was in treatment. Under proper medication, he enjoyed letting the staff tend to him because he imagined the attention to be a sign of his status as Tesla's protégé. His relationship with Tesla was a fixed delusion.

The staff at Psych Hall gave Jake a sponge bath as soon as he got onto the unit upstairs. They helped him put on a clean pair of jockey shorts, a white T-shirt and dark blue pajama pants. They placed a pair of black flip-flops next to his bed. Jake would not recall of any of this initial care. A tech checked his vital signs every hour for the first several hours. Jake seemed untroubled while he slept off the effects of the drugs in his system.

Hours later, perhaps an hour before noon, Jake felt consciousness return. He rolled over to see a small, thin man in his room staring at him.

"Hey, tell me about the pigeons, Jake. We need to feed them, you know," were the first words Jake heard that day and they were coming from this odd little man standing near his bed. Then Paul said, "We had seven, then three and three with one missing. That's why they put me in this room. They are hiding one in the middle. Do the math. Three there, three here, and one more, one more. Hear. Do you hear?"

Paul tapped nervously with his right fingers on his left hand knuckles.

"Tesla knew it," he said. "If you want to be a genius like Tesla you can't have sex. Do you hear me? No sex."

Paul signaled Jake with three fingers raised for no apparent reason.

Jake sat up slowly saying nothing but as soon as he moved Paul retreated to his side of the room, muttering incoherently.

Paul had been pacing back and forth, in and out of the room for hours monitoring his roommate. A tech sat outside Room 313 to monitor them. The doctor and nurse assigned to Jake wanted to meet with him soon after he awoke. The tech, or psychiatric technician, was one of many assigned to the acute section. He would alert Jake's treatment team that their patient was rousing. The doctor and a nurse would arrive shortly.

Jake took stock of his stark surroundings. He saw a single, five by four foot window made of glass block. There were air vents in the pale yellow walls up near the white ceiling. Two small but heavy white cabinets served as closets for clothes and other personal items. The floor was a red terra cotta tile.

He noted one flat light fixture on the ceiling with no switch inside the room. He saw no electrical outlets, no television, and no radio. One non-descript landscape print of a painting by proto-impressionist Corot under scarred Plexiglas in a heavy wood frame was bolted to a wall.

"Good morning, Jake. I'm Rasheed. If I can help you with anything, let me know."

Jake stared at Rasheed as if he were someone on television.

"Is this man actually talking to me?" he thought. He felt odd. Words would not come out of his mouth. He just stared ahead waiting for the man to speak again.

"I can show you where the bathroom is. Do you want to see?"

Jake nodded at the movie character. As he slipped into his flip-flops he winced from pain emanating from his side and thigh. He limped as he followed Rasheed to the common bathroom. The tech gave him a comb, a toothbrush with paste and a towel. Jake slowly washed up and even more slowly brushed his teeth, pausing often to stare at the face in the mirror.

He used the toilet down the hall but he felt constipated. A grouchy patient in walking restraints followed another tech past him to a sink. One friendly, younger patient waved and said "Hi" as he passed. Jake nodded once but said nothing.

"We will bring you something to eat soon if you want. I'll wait out here till you are done. The PA is coming to see you later," Rasheed advised him.

Jake merely nodded in response.

A female nurse and a physician's assistant pulled up a couple of chairs next to Jake who sat on the bed. It did not take long for the team to realize that Jake preferred to stay mute. The PA examined Jake's pulse and blood pressure. He checked his eyes with a small light. When he asked if Jake could hear and see him okay, Jake nodded slowly. He looked over the lab results and the intake notes.

"Jake, we're about to have lunch here. Would you like to go down to the cafeteria?"

Jake nodded.

"Rasheed! Could you please escort Jake to eat in a half hour or so? Thanks, man. Jake, I'm going to ask a psychiatrist to come see you after lunch, okay?"

Jake nodded again. It was not clear to anyone whether Jake completely absorbed what was spoken. It was not clear to Jake that there was anything to absorb. He was dissociated. His will to respond verbally had disappeared. He would try to keep these creatures happy. He would follow the others to the cafeteria.

A motley contingent of nine patients emerged from the elevators and merged with a stream of thirty or more men and women walking and shuffling toward a set of double doors that staff held open.

Jake passed by several large windows constructed with eight-inch glass blocks set and sealed in a kind of mortar. He ran his finger along the seam of cement on one window. "What is this stuff," he wondered. He could see that the sun shone on various shrubs and trees but images outside were blurred by the thick glass.

As he followed the group into the large eating area, a variety of food odors hit him. He felt slightly nauseous so he breathed more deeply until the sensation passed. Jake waited in line holding his tray behind an oddly bent creature with slurred speech and an unsteady gait. The patient appeared to nearly fall over as he swayed while sliding his feet in imitation of something that approached walking.

The twisted man who staff called Travis spoke loudly and brashly to insure that others might better hear him. Those who knew him understood him well enough. Travis had cerebral palsy as well as a nasty disposition. His group home supervisor committed him to Psych Hall this time after he assaulted a new, female nurse. Travis attacked her while she attempted to take his blood pressure.

During the routine procedure he asked her, "Do you want to fuck," but she did not understand him. Her response was, "Please stay still, sir." To make his point more clearly, Travis firmly grabbed her crotch. The next day, even after an hour of apologetic counseling by her supervisor, the nurse resigned.

The line moved along well. Jake took whatever foods appeared on the counter. He walked with deliberate steps, carefully holding his tray to a table near the far end of the room. He sat alone until three patients took seats next to and across from him. He did not acknowledge them nor did they address him in any way. Jake sipped his apple juice. He kept his eyes on his meal. He chewed slowly on a bite of what looked like Salisbury steak and spit it out. He ate every green bean one by one. He ate all the applesauce. He left the remaining meat and the overly baked potato untouched. His companions at the table continued to ignore him.

Simple body language and subtle psychological cues worked wonderfully to sustain boundaries among the patients at Psych Hall, most of the time. Nevertheless, Jake noted behaviors of his table neighbors out of the corners of his eyes and mind. He listened to their chatter. The two talkative women and the muscular man with slicked back hair were drug addicts admitted for treatment after claiming to be suicidal. One had made an attempt. Her left wrist was yet bandaged. All three had run out of drugs and money. The man had a swastika above a rose tattooed onto the inside of his left arm.

Jake noticed a date between the swastika and the rose: 20 April 1889. He did not recognize it as Hitler's birthday. The women were younger than the man. Jake heard the man tell a story about being in prison for a year before coming to Psych Hall. He was homeless. Jake heard them swap stories of where they could buy drugs in the area and of who to trust on the streets. They seemed happy to be with one another as they laughed and joked about their lives.

One of the young women mentioned that she might go to rehab after Psych Hall. The other said that the Seroquel was not working for her. She slept poorly and she wanted something stronger—she mentioned Xanax—but her doctor would not prescribe it for her. The swastika man said that Seroquel was worth good money on the streets.

Jake continued to observe everything as if he were watching a report on television. He felt tired again. He did not see Paul. Earlier he overheard Rasheed tell another tech that Paul was going to get injected that afternoon.

He wondered if Paul would be discharged after getting his injection. He wondered how many injections they would give Paul and him before they might be discharged. He wondered how long he would be stuck in this place and in this state of mind. Someone announced that lunch was over and that ended his wondering. Patients walked or shuffled through the main doors to go back to their rooms, to go to scheduled meetings or to get afternoon meds but not before fully half of them made their way to the smoke room. Jake followed Rasheed and the other men back to his unit. Paul was waiting in the room when Jake entered. He was waiting to tell Jake about the noise.

"The pigeons can hear it. Do you hear it? That's the nano radar. Nanotechnology can sort the air molecules all around us. It picks up the finer vibrations of thought. They know what we think but they have to tune in first. Tesla invented that. We could have free electricity now but they hid Tesla's papers. The coal companies work with the government to stop innovation. They made good into evil. They use his formula and changed it to tap our thoughts. The medications they give me do it. That's why they use them on me. They want my copy of the papers."

Paul avoided eye contact with Jake when he spoke. Paul paced about the room. He kept looking toward the door. Rasheed was not in his seat. He was standing and at guard to make sure Paul stayed in the room. When Rasheed stepped aside three male staff and a nurse with a syringe came into the room.

303

"Hi, Paul. It's Jamie. You remember me don't you?"

The nurse was an older woman with a sweet disposition. The nurse explained to Paul what the doctor ordered for him.

"Paul, I'd like you to please lay down on the bed on your stomach so we can help you get better. I have Prolixin and Ativan for you."

Paul shrunk back against the wall. He knew what was coming.

"Can I feed my pigeons? We have to go to them today. I have to feed them."

Then he tapped his fingers together nervously. His eyes were wide open but looking at nothing in the room.

"Maybe not today, Paul, but soon. Your pigeons will be okay. I'm sure others are feeding them. Come on, Paul, lay down here." She motioned to the bed with the syringe.

Paul was not moving. Jake lay on his side of the room watching the scene casually from his bed. The four men calmly walked up to Paul. Two of them grabbed the small man's thin arms. They deftly turned him face down onto the bed. The third man held Paul's legs. The nurse lifted his gown, lowered his briefs and smoothly injected him in the buttocks. She put a band aid on the tiny puncture after wiping the area with an alcohol swab.

"Thank you, Paul," Jamie said as she walked from the room with the staff.

Paul remained face down on the bed. Jake could not tell if his roommate was sobbing or merely talking to himself. Jake watched him intently. After fifteen minutes he stood up and limped over to Paul's bed. He touched him on the shoulder. Paul did not move. Jake leaned his head close to Paul's ear. He whispered in a flat delivery, "I will feed the pigeons as soon as I can."

"Thank you, man" Paul replied in an equally flat whisper.

Jake returned to his bed. He watched Paul roll over on his side and fall asleep. An hour later, Jake had visitors.

"Hello, Jake. My name is Doctor Joe Kelly. This young lady with me is a grad student, Ms. Alka Krol. May we visit with you?"

Jake glanced at the woman that Kelly called Alka. He nodded slightly in her direction.

"Good. I'm the psychiatrist who your doctor said would be meeting with you. Will you please follow us to the interview room down the hall?"

Jake followed them to a small room with a coffee table and four, green vinyl-covered chairs. The room was brightly lit and very clean. Dr. Kelly quickly surmised that Jake was not going to talk. This interview was supposed to take up to a half hour, but Kelly was done with his standard check list of questions in ten minutes. With Jake selectively nodding and refusing to write his answers, Kelly excused himself.

"See if you can get anything more out of him and report to me," he said to Alka. With that he left the room. Rasheed was on watch outside the door. Jake was yet listed as "unpredictable and violent."

"So, you're Jake Grzyb, the mushroom!"

Alka pronounced his name correctly with a smile. Jake stared at her blankly at first but flinched upon hearing his name.

"If you haven't guessed by my name, I know some Polish, so don't be surprised." She noticed that Jake squinted when she translated his last name.

"I can imagine that you put up with some odd responses with that name. At least you did not have to hear "Alka Seltzer" constantly! Once, a friend of mine introduced me to a man with the last name of Lloyd. Can you imagine?"

Jake wanted to smile but nothing more than a blank look appeared on his face.

"Anyway, as Dr. Kelly pointed out, I am a grad resident in a Ph.D. program in psychology. This is my last week working in this clinic. I'm not sure I want to do work like this for the rest of my life, but, hey, we don't know till we try it, right?"

Jake squinted again. He said nothing.

"Okay. You don't have to talk. I see here you have not said a word to staff since you arrived from the ER. From the notes, according to your brother Harry, you spent ten years or so out West in a religious commune until sometime last week. He said you practiced Zen. Now I have some idea what that is. Can you tell me about your experience there?"

Jake remained silent. He stared at her clipboard.

"Okay, plead the fifth if you wish. How about you nodding if I ask yes and no questions—can we do that?"

Jake nodded slowly.

Alka Krol's energy struck Jake as very different from the brash Kelly. She was much younger at twenty-seven to Kelly's sixty. Kelly was gruff, wore a crumpled tweed jacket with tan slacks, white shirt with no tie, and plain, brown leather walking shoes. His longish, wavy gray hair was unkempt. Alka Krol sat upright compared to Kelly's casual slouch. Her stylish eyeglasses with black frames accented her ash blond hair that she tied up in a loose bun. She was dressed in a dark mauve pants suit with a cream blouse. Her polished black shoes sported moderate heels. She was slim but did not appear underweight. Her large, unusually dark blue eyes had very little make-up.

In the next half hour she managed to find out that Jake dropped out of college, was not committed to a relationship with a person or to a group, did not take drugs for years before this incident, that he was unemployed, and that he wanted to leave the hospital. That was it. She changed focus onto herself, telling Jake bits about her background, her parents, and her youth.

"I want to explore why you spent time in New Mexico with a Buddhist group. Apparently you made a deep commitment, yes?"

No reaction.

Next, Alka took a stab at relating a personal story that might connect with her patient.

"My father was a member of a Middle-eastern Sufi sect for some time. He was very dedicated to a certain Sheik whom I will not name. He never talked about it to me or his other children but mom did. Our mother used to have fits over it because of the money he would send to this "fake-shake," as mom called him. To her, I seemed more bothered by it than my brother and sister were. She was right. To better understand my father I did some research on the sheik. That led to reading a few books and visiting a host of sites in the Internet. It seems to me there is a vast underworld of odd sects associated with all the great and small religions. If you want to talk about that, I think I can at least appreciate where you are coming from."

Jake placed his left hand up to his mouth. He tapped his lips a few times as he continued to stare at her clipboard. He dropped his hand back onto his lap without changing his expression. Alka got the impression that he might want talk but not at that moment.

"Would you like to talk about this some other time then?"

Jake squinted again. He felt an odd compulsion to say something but nothing in his thoughts made sense. He could not grasp how talking to this stranger would change the world he was in. Despite her seemingly failed effort to connect with Jake, Alka remained cheerful until Kelly returned.

"Well, how we doing here?" Kelly asked.

Alka shrugged her shoulders as she showed him her page full of notes.

"Still not talking, Jake? Look, son, we are trying to help you but we will not be able to discharge you until we are sure you are doing okay. The sooner you talk the better. In the meantime we will keep you on this unit for observation. I cannot tell if you are selectively mute or something really snapped in your mind."

Kelly thanked Jake for his effort to participate.

"Let's go Ms. Krol. We have three more patients to see before I go home."

Before she left the room, Alka stood over Jake for a few seconds. She leaned over with her hands on her knees and looked him in the eye.

"I believe someone very interesting is in there. I hope to see you well soon."

Jake heard her but did nothing to acknowledge it. He watched Alka exit his room. He liked her immediately but she seemed too remote for his feelings to matter. His thoughts were centered on what Kelly said. He might be in here a long, long time. He had a vision again of daily injections just as they had done to Paul. His worried reverie was broken when Rasheed announced that Jake had more visitors.

"Come with me, Jake. There are two people in the recreation area to see you— your brother and your mother, that is, if you want to see them."

Jake stood up in affirmation. Hospital policy was two guests at a time unless a treating doctor or the administrator made exceptions. The hospital did not have the staff to control a large influx of visitors. The acutely disturbed or disordered patients were unpredictable in their behavior so liabilities increased.

Jake walked over to a table to visit with Harry and Monica. He allowed them to hug him. They all sat down. Harry gave Jake some extra clothes that the staff had already inspected. He handed him a pair of basic blue jeans and a new pair of khakis, his white sneakers sans laces, two pairs of new socks and underwear, two plain black T-shirts and a new toothbrush.

Harry also brought a new novel by Dean Koontz. Harry had no idea what it was about. He thought the title, *The Good Guy*, would inspire his lost brother.

Dr. Kelly briefed Harry and Monica about Jake's behavior after interviewing them while Alka was with him. They knew not to pressure him or expect too much at this time. Jake's team wanted to wait a day or more before trying any more medications on him. After several minutes of one-way conversation, Harry turned to watch people visiting with another patient. Monica tried her best to dialog but to no avail. Jake fumbled with the clothes while Monica talked and cried. She feared that her son may not come back.

Jake did not make eye contact with her, but he did watch her fingers unconsciously pinching a holy medal of Our Lady of Guadalupe that hung from her gold chain necklace. The holy medal was a gift he sent her when he first arrived in New Mexico.

Jake waited until they left to shuffle back to 313. Once back in his room he methodically changed into his new clothes. He tried on the pre-washed jeans. They fit loosely but well enough to stay up without a belt, so he kept them on. He changed into the black T-shirt. He put on a new pair of socks and slipped into his laceless sneakers. Then he lay down in his bed elevating his head on a folded over pillow. He picked up the Koontz book.

"*The Good Guy*," he thought to himself. The subtitle said: *They want her dead. One thing stands in their way.* Next he turned to the introductory page with Koontz quoting Albert Camus:

I shall tell you a great secret, my friend.
Do not wait for the last judgment,
It takes place every day.

Jake tossed the book aside. He rubbed his face with his hands. His whiskers had grown into a near beard. He looked less like a monk due for a shave now, he thought. He looked like a mental patient due for a shave. He scratched at his cheek. The beard itched. Then he let out a loud scream.

"Camu—aaaaaahhhhh!"

Rasheed's shift replacement, Dennis, came running into the room. Paul sat up startled.

"He needs an injection. Hurry, get it," Paul said with a certain agitation.

Dennis observed Jake before making any rash decisions. He saw the book on the floor face down and open.

"Yo, cuz, you need anything? First peep I heard out of you."

Dennis picked up the book. He read the cover out loud to himself. He closed it and laid it on the small, plain nightstand by the bed.

"Must be something you read. Anything you want to tell me?"

Jake returned to his silent self as he stared at the ceiling, breathing slowly and deeply.

Satisfied that nothing more needed to be done, Dennis went back to his seat. In the progress notes he wrote, "Client let out a loud shout at 1635 hours after reading a book, then mute again. Resting in bed quietly."

At 1730 hours staff announced dinner. Both Jake and Paul followed the others down to eat. Paul was less agitated. His fingers tapped less. He thought to himself about Tesla, pigeons and his fixed delusions about the government, now and then saying a word or two to no one in particular. No one paid attention to him on the way to eat or in the cafeteria. The line of patients moved slowly to fill their food trays but efficiently nevertheless. Jake stood behind Paul.

For some reason Paul waited to see where Jake would sit. Jake passed him and went to the same seat he sat in earlier toward the back of the room. Paul sat next to him. He felt safe next to someone who had nothing to say. It allowed him to stay safe inside his own world. Paul sensed that Jake was in another world too and that was okay with him. Maybe Jake truly was one of the good guys and not a government plant after all. Maybe Jake would feed the pigeons too. Maybe the government was after Jake too. Paul continued to mutter about his precious pigeons while he ate. No one sat with them this time. They ate alone.

Behind them across the floor a maintenance man worked on an exit door. He propped the door open with a short ladder. The large man was rewiring something above the frame. It looked like a security device with an electric lock. The door was large, metal and painted gray. A sign on it said *emergency exit only*.

Jake ate little again. He felt nauseous and his body heat was rising. Sweat formed on his brow, his neck and in his armpits. He gazed disinterestedly at the maintenance man testing the wires. It appeared the job was finished. The man was putting away some tools.

Suddenly there was a commotion at the other end of the dining hall. Jake heard and saw nasty Travis cursing the drug addict with the swastika tattoo. Swastika man yelled back, "Get away from me, you fuckin' nut."

With that said, Travis leaned back, horked up a loogie and spit it full into the swastika man's face. The swastika man lunged at Travis, knocked him over, and proceeded to pummel him with a flurry of punches. The crooked man with cerebral palsy had no chance to win this fight, yet he attempted to bite and kick his opponent from below. Within seconds, blood streamed from Travis's nose and lip and blood was all over swastika man's knuckles. The altercation caught staff off guard. Initial intervention came from one male patient who managed to grab swastika man's arm. Someone eventually pushed the alarm.

The maintenance man was used to helping out in these situations. He instinctively ran over to help break it up. He was the second one on the scene to subdue the brawl. Jake saw him run by. He turned in his seat. He casually rose from his seat while everyone was distracted. Paul was unfazed by the commotion while staring at his dinner. Paul did not notice that Jake left his seat.

Jake deftly slipped passed by the maintenance man's ladder and through the security door. With his hand on a rail, he limped quickly down two flights of stairs and through a door into a dimly lit tunnel.

With the patients under control and swastika man restrained by three staff, a medic attended to bloody Travis. The medic called for a stretcher.

"Travis started it. He started it," yelled a couple of patients.

The techs knew that this was probably true. Travis was nasty. Nobody liked Travis. Nevertheless, swastika man would most likely face charges after an investigation. He used more force than necessary. He could have and may have seriously harmed the handicapped Travis. He should have asked for staff to intervene first. He would go back to jail.

The maintenance man returned to the exit door, packed his things onto a rolling cart, checked the door one more time and reset it on *lock* after shutting it. Evening staff and a janitor remained behind to clean up as everyone else filed back to their rooms or to the recreation areas. As they were leaving the cafeteria Dennis asked Paul if he knew where Jake was.

"313. He's up in 313. 313," is all Paul would say.

Dennis called out for Jake and checked the dining area one more time. "He must have gone up already," he thought.

As they were walking to the elevators, a charge nurse asked Dennis if he would accompany the ambulance that was taking Travis to an emergency room. They needed a staff person to sit with Travis until he was discharged or admitted elsewhere. The charge nurse said, "I checked with the other techs. They can cover for you on the men's acute unit. Things will be quieter up there now since Travis is gone."

Jake wandered into the dim light. He overheard patients say that the campus was once an asylum for thousands of *retards*. He did not hear anyone use the politically correct label, "developmentally disabled". What unfortunate souls had walked these halls and for how long? The question was barely an afterthought in his mind. He walked toward a red glow from a source high along the wall to his left. Within twenty yards he came upon a metal door, similar to the exit door to the cafeteria, with a lit sign above that said *Emergency Exit*.

He could hear rumbling noises outside and what sounded like rain against the door. Then a clap of thunder confirmed his suspicion that a severe storm had broken out. He pushed the handle but the emergency door would not budge. Perhaps it was connected to the system. Maybe the repair man had not finished the job after all? If this door opened, it might set off an alarm.

"Maybe you should not try it again," he thought. "No sense wandering around in a rain storm."

Jake backed away from the exit door with his hands raised as if the door were dangerous. He turned slowly to face the darkness further down. He wiped the sweat off his brow on his shirt sleeve. The motion of his head caused him to nearly lose his balance. He took a deep breath, then, step by step, he maneuvered with his fingers touching a wall for forty yards in near complete darkness until he touched the back end of the tunnel.

He backed away shocked that the wall seemed alive with a glowing atmosphere, as if it opened up in front of him into a mist. He shook his head, blinked a few times, and the mirage faded.

He stumbled on something, lost his balance, and veered a step or two to the side until his left hand rested on a wall. The tiled wall was cool and felt damp. He felt warm and sweaty. He groped along the end wall to his right until he felt the frame of another large, metal door. He turned the knob and leaned into it with his shoulder. Loose dirt fell from above the frame onto his head and shoulders. He spit to remove particles of dirt from his lips. He wiped his mouth on a sleeve.

A sharp pain shot through his side. He backed away from the door while hugging his ribcage. He brushed the debris off his head and chest as he continued to spit. He felt the door again and noticed that it had budged slightly. He raised his good leg and with a quick kick slammed his foot flat against the metal surface next to the knob. He jumped lightly up and down while muffling a cry as he tried to absorb the pains in his injured thigh and side. After settling down he saw that the door budged a bit more.

He saw a dim light through the crack. A bright slit of light from lightning flashed indicating a window or opening of some kind on the other side of the door.

One more time he braced himself to kick the door. He kicked it harder this time. It burst open attended by the sound of metal falling on tile. The force broke a rusted bolt lock latch that was probably installed decades before to keep anyone and anything from coming in or out that way. Jake stepped through the doorway. He then shoved the door shut behind him. Next he gave it a sharp kick to jamb it back into the frame. He turned around to assess his unwieldy situation. He was now in the old, decayed asylum proper.

He felt the cool, damp wall with his hand. A faint hint of urine and a musky odor emanated from the damp floor. Earth yellow ceramic tiles lined the walls. Long pipes with hanging rags of insulation ran along the ceiling as far as he could see. He could see no further than twenty yards or so which was where a small, dirty skylight let in the glow from a single security light attached to a nearby wall outside.

As Jake stepped forward, he felt something crunch under his laceless sneaker. A flash of lightning revealed lumps of dirt and scum emerging from several puddles in his view. He moved back a step to take a look. His eyes adjusted enough to see the skeleton of a small animal—maybe the remains of a small cat or a large rat. He saw and heard something run past his feet. It scurried up the tunnel out of sight.

The probable rat did not startle him. He was not interested in finding out what it was. His mind was reeling from physical discomfort and fever and who knew what else. The air felt thick. He took it in with short gasps. He stepped cautiously until he arrived at the light source. The skylight was fixed eight or nine feet above his head up the wall. He could figure no way to get up and through it unless he found a ladder.

After assessing whether or not to turn around, he continued walking cautiously with his hand feeling gently along the wall. He stopped when a spray of water from a crack in the wall hit his arm. He wiped it off on his shirt. After a few more steps he could see a glow low to the floor as it poured from under a door to the right. Sweat blurred his vision. He wiped the sweat from his eyes on his shirt sleeves again.

Jake knocked. No sound came from inside. He listened for a few seconds. Lightning flashed through the skylight temporarily blinding Jake. Thunder simultaneously cracked creating a very loud vibration down the length of the tunnel. Jake instinctively covered his ears. The door seemed to change color, to a pale orange. His heart rate rose dramatically. After collecting himself, Jake gripped what looked like a strangely ornamented, brass doorknob. It turned easily. He let it go when he felt a slight nausea and dizziness. He backed away from the door and leaned over, bracing himself on his knees until the fainting sensation passed. He felt a refreshing breeze from further up the tunnel. He decided to leave the door for the moment and explore some more.

He entered the darkness steadying his way with his hand against the tiles along the wall. He walked this way, step by careful step, at times crunching small objects or an empty can under foot. The dampness increased. An indistinct musky odor came with the breeze. After perhaps a hundred short paces he arrived at a barrier, a wooden wall that he felt with his hands.

He determined that the wall was made of large plywood panels that sealed off the area from the rest of the tunnel system. He could find no handle or door. This was a security installation for a condemned structure—perhaps it was a fire wall. The draft of cooler air whistled through the half-inch cracks along the sides. He tested the thick plywood panels with a hard kick but nothing budged. The large bolts with rounded heads that he felt with his fingertips were fastened or bolted from the other side. Jake decided to turn back to try the last door he found.

This time, while gripping and turning the curious doorknob, he leaned into the door with his right shoulder applying steady pressure to shove his way inside. The door gave in easily. Light entered from basement windows below the ceiling in the apparently large room. He spotted an old baseball bat near his feet on the gray cement floor. He thought it might come in handy. As he bent down to pick it up another thunderclap shook through the dank air and a bright light flooded the large space blinding him for a second.

When he opened his eyes, the room remained brightly lit. The door slammed shut behind him as if drawn by a stiff blast of air. Stunned by the light and the sound, Jake stood unsteadily. As his vision cleared, he stooped over to grab the wooden baseball bat. Before his hand reached the handle, he was taken aback by a sudden change in the room's atmosphere. He stood erect to determine what happened.

The contrast between what was inside the room and out in the tunnel was utterly amazing. The room glowed with continuous light from an unseen source. At a glance it appeared to be an exotically appointed living area. A large, stuffed red chair sat at one end on a slightly elevated stage. It looked to Jake like a throne that sat on a reddish Oriental rug with a rosette motif and white fringes. The walls were basically white with a pale pattern of some kind of exotic calligraphy from floor to ceiling. A huge, plush Persian rug, maybe twenty by twenty five feet, covered most of the rest of the light gray floor. The twelve-foot ceiling was bordered by white plaster crown moldings of a continuous, embossed fleur-de-lis pattern. Another stuffed red chair, similar to the one at the far end but smaller, sat in front of Jake.

Small, finely crafted wooden end tables flanked the right side of each chair. An empty, eight-ounce glass goblet and a glass pitcher of a clear liquid that looked like ice water sat on the tables. Two great urns decorated with warriors and horses sat along the walls on each side of the throne. They reminded Jake of colorful Ming ware. The entire effect was one of stark richness. The atmosphere was charged with something like electricity but pleasantly so. As soon as Jake wondered who used the room, a voice rang out.

Back in the hospital patients and staff settled into routines for the evening. Many patients piled into the main recreation room where a friendly tech shared his new

Pirates of the Caribbean DVD for all to view. Others sat around chatting in the hallways. A few went to bed early. One thin lady with manic symptoms continued to pace the halls talking to herself. Everyone avoided talking to her. In general things were running smoothly throughout the clinic. A rounds person with a clipboard went from room to room and person to person not in assigned rooms to check on every patient's status. Rounds checks continued three times an hour. After a quick head-count in the recreation room, the rounds person stood there for a minute or two, entranced by the movie. Then she called up to the third floor to report that she would be there next to finish up. The tech she spoke with said not to worry. Everyone seemed okay. No one in particular missed Jake for the moment. Paul was used to his roommates coming and going without notice. In any case, Paul was asleep.

"Master Jake, welcome!"

The voice startled Jake so much so that he looked to the floor to find the bat. He picked it up and turned, stepping quickly to the door. Jake pulled hard on the brass doorknob with his left hand but the door would not budge. He felt the pain shoot through his side, a pain that weakened his effort to pull. He was concerned about this stern voice that knew him and that he may be caught or trapped by hospital staff. In his mind's eye he saw another horrible emergency department scene repeat itself complete with restraints and injections.

"Fear not, Master Jake."

This time the voice sounded less ominous. Jake turned back to see a man standing next to the red throne chair. The man watched him calmly. He had his arms crossed inside large sleeves. He wore something like a loose Oriental tunic and baggy pants made of black silk with no identifying design. He wore black silk slippers with leather soles. Jake saw no jewelry on the man.

The man's dark, theatrical eyes appeared as if enhanced with eyeliner. His head and face were clean shaven. He seemed almost Asian but not quite.

At first Jake thought of the old man resurrected, but this fellow looked younger and sturdier and he did not look Japanese. His skin had an olive cast to it. The man appeared oddly handsome with his broad solid skull and chiseled face set on a burly neck and broad shoulders. He may have been Slavic or Tibetan. The man appeared larger than Jake on his stage. Jake could not really tell what height the man was from his vantage point. Was he the guest or the captive? The man spoke again.

"Please, Master Jake, sit down. Yes, you are the guest. Welcome to our discussion. This is a quantum event between you and me. I have been waiting for you patiently. And, I am slightly shorter than you."

"What?" Jake thought to himself. To Jake the strange man sounded like an American stage actor from the 1940s with a quasi-British accent. Jake knew enough about quantum physics to imagine what this man might have meant. The quantum world can seem to appear and disappear according to the observer's volition or ability to perceive—or so went the popular science. Whatever the cause, Jake's instincts told him this dream figment would fade soon. He was not about to take this dream seriously. Before Jake could complete another thought, the man spoke in a booming voice.

"That passive aggression will not do here, Master Jake. This is not some form of dream for entertainment. This is the place for discussion. Remember, you came to me. Now, either you decide to communicate or you will pay the consequences of your desire to die."

Jake felt a powerful energy surge around him. It infused the room with an aroma of clean cut steel and burning sandalwood. An eerie tinkling like distant waves of clangs from many bells penetrated the walls. Jake still wanted to believe that this was some kind of cosmic joke or maybe that it was a dream, but he feared he had actually gone psycho in a hallucination. Yet he could not ignore the experience itself. It engaged him and it was happening.

Less afraid now, Jake wondered why the man dressed that way in this age in this place. He still felt an urge to leave but he had no idea from what he was running or if he could.

Before finishing this last thought sequence, Jake began to choke. He could draw no air from the room. Jake leaned over trying again to breathe with no success. He felt the floor slipping away from under his feet. His body remained suspended as if in a rare atmosphere far above the earth. The wooden bat fell from his grip and rolled behind the chair next to him.

He felt a panic greater than any he had experienced or could have imagined. He was not ready to die. He looked up at the man in black whose unemotional gaze offered no sympathy. The man seemed to be breathing normally. Then the man raised his right hand, palm up, as if to ask what Jake wanted to do.

"Okay, I'll talk, I'll talk," is all Jake could muster in a hoarse voice.

With that spoken his feet returned to the floor and fresh air rushed into his lungs. After a few coughs and hesitant gasps, he forced himself to engage the man in black, whatever engaging him meant. As he thought about it the air around him began to disappear again. He remembered to speak his thoughts.

"Okay, I will play this game, sir. Let's get this over with," he sputtered. "Tell, tell me what you want."

"That's much better, Master Jake. But I will alert you now that this is no game."

"Then what is this? Who are you anyway?"

Now Jake was breathing easier, even as the pain subsided from his ribcage.

"First question, first. In one sense this is a review of anything you seem to want to resolve in your life, especially your spiritual existence. In another sense it is an examination."

The mysterious man moved to the front of his throne chair as if to sit, but he remained standing with his arms crossed. He had tucked his hands back into his sleeves.

"Your second question is both simple and complex to answer. You may call me Master G."

The man continued as if reading Jake's thoughts.

"No, G does not stand for God," he said sarcastically. "And, no, I am not those other Gs popping around in your agitated skull like G. I. Gurdjieff or Magister Ludi of Das Glasperlenspil. Your grasp of the esoteric teachings and spiritual novels

318

you came across years ago serve only to confuse here. And Gabriel, the great Angel? I hope I am not that terrifying! But I warn you again, speak your thoughts," he commanded.

Jake was surprised that this G fellow anticipated his immediate suspicions that Master G might be an angel or Gurdjieff or, vaguely, that this mystical rendevous might be a version of Hermann Hesse's *The Glass Bead Game* which Jake had read ten years before. This time Jake spoke directly.

"You seem to read my thoughts and tap my memory. Is that true? You can read my thoughts."

"You would be able to read my thoughts too if I did not speak them, if you cared to listen, as with any spoken conversation. I do and will continue to communicate my thoughts out loud. The intent here is twofold: That what you speak is what you think and that you grasp the intent of what you say."

G sat down on his throne chair. He extended his right hand while resting the left on the armrest. "Please sit," he requested as he gestured with his right hand.

"May I look around first?"

"By all means, do, if you wish. Time is not a problem, so take all you want. Again, I remind you: Speak your thoughts after formulating them. No secret self-talk. And do not bother trying to escape."

Jake took a few tentative steps to the left wall. As he walked he asked, "What gave you the idea that I had a desire to die?"

"Your mental status report stated you are suicidal. That is why you are in treatment, no?"

"I never said I would kill myself."

"You were delirious, my young man. Do you recall what you said?"

"You have a point. But I do not want to die."

Jake kept walking toward a huge urn along the wall to his left. Master G watched with an amused expression.

"And the past ten years, Master Jake—what of that ingenious effort? What else is the effort for the extinction of self but a form of suicide?"

"Now you're getting heavy with me. I suspect you know that nirvana is not a form of suicide."

"What I know is insignificant compared to what you do not know about nirvana."

"Now we are getting nowhere," was all Jake could think of saying.

And *now* you are *here*?" G said with glee with emphasis on "here," as if asking a question.

Jake approached an urn making inane, descriptive comments about it as he moved.

"Nice jug, bro. I like the smooth lines, all curves, nothing straight except the flat base."

He peeked into it just long enough to note that it contained a clear liquid.

G remarked, "All the vases are full of the same liquid—water."

He pronounced vase as one would say *chase* or *trace*.

"Water, Master Jake, merely water. No cause for suspicion."

From his position along the side wall, Jake could see another *vase* directly behind G's throne along the back wall. It sported similar ornamentation, a Chinese warrior on a horse. Jake walked clockwise behind G and all the way around the room. Indeed, all the vases were full of clear liquid. Jake dipped his finger in the third one. He sampled it and it tasted like water. G sat comfortably upright with his arms resting on the armrests.

Jake asked about the pale gold writing that filled the white walls from floor to ceiling. G identified the language as an ancient form of Sanskrit. He explained that the purpose was merely for a decorative effect but could serve as a symbolic stimulant for discussion if one wished.

"The wall pattern or calligraphy text comes from the Rig Veda of the Sanatanadharma," Master G reported in an off-handed way. "We can speculate why our room has these furnishings and that décor. I have no explanation."

Jake acknowledged that he had read the Rig Veda once but only in English translation. After completing a round of the room, Jake noticed that he felt no more pain in his leg or side. He sat down to face G and he sat slightly slouched with his arms resting on the arms of his chair.

"So, how did you get in here? I do not see another door," Jake asked him.

"I arrived the same way you did, through that door behind you. I was here when you arrived."

Jake shuffled his feet slightly, quickly forming a question on instinct about the obvious.

"Do you have power over me?"

"No. This place does however. We are, as you might say, *one* with this space. We are of the same stuff, if you will."

"Ah, I see," said Jake, knowing full well he saw nothing that made sense. "This then is a quantum world—a parallel universe—where matter matters but has no substance," he blurted out. "You and I exist in a paradox. Is that it?"

"Something to that. Language has its limits, Master Jake, but we will make do with what we have in our head."

"Am I crazy, dreaming or dead?"

"I am not your psychiatrist, nor am I your coroner. You are very much alive as we speak and you are as sane as you speak."

"Are you some kind of angel or demon?"

"Angel or demon—either way, something spiritual but matter-bound nevertheless. You will have to choose how you see me when you are ready."

"Ready, meaning what?"

Master G smiled at the question. He shook his head from side to side as if to indicate his pity for Jake. "Let us consider that you are not ready because you have not yet chosen. You will suffer from ambivalence in the meantime."

"Could this be purgatory?"

G laughed at the analogy and he clapped his hands.

"I applaud you. Your Catholic roots are showing, Master Jake! A good and bad question. Good because you touched a base in your heart. Bad because we have no idea what you mean by that. Let me ask you some questions then. The Buddha avoided metaphysical speculation. So, might we avoid it too? Once you achieve Buddha nature all questions about purgatory should vanish. Why worry?"

"Apparently my questions have not vanished. Purgatory still exists in my world."

"Good answer. But this leads me to the questions of faith verses knowledge. If you know, you do not have to believe because you know. If you believe without knowing, you could be wrong. So why trust faith at all? Odd conundrum, that."

Jake squinted to better concentrate on a response. "So, this seems to me to be one question. I recall the saying: *If you experience it as true, then it is true because it is true for you.* I cannot accept that any longer because it seems childish. Even the old man at…"

Master G impatiently cut him off again.

"The old man. The old man. When do you get over the old man? You have internalized him. Is it you or the old man that does the thinking?"

"What? What do you mean?"

"Simply put, I mean what you mean. You cannot live without communicating with me. I am the way, the truth and the life. Without me you have no idea what remains. Nothing, perhaps, if you can begin to imagine that, remains."

"I can't understand you now. What are you getting at?"

Master G merely shrugged with his hands open at his side. He continued as if Jake's question was meaningless.

"But is all this not overwhelming? In the quest for absolute justice mankind in every culture continually creates relative results. You related to the old man so long that now he lives within you, whether you like him any longer or not. And you continue to be related to him. He remains one of your most intimate relations."

"So is that it," Jake retorted, "you are a manifestation of the old man?"

"Your question is too simple, my dear young spiritual athlete. There is more."

When G said *more*, Jake wondered how much more. He wondered too long. When no air entered his lungs, he sputtered, "More, meaning what?" Then he took a deep breath. Jake had a sudden urge to run at or to attack G.

"Ah, the martial artist emerges! How will you fight without oxygen?"

"I could scream through it all!"

"You could try. Screaming however does not qualify as discussion, does it?"

"You got me," is all Jake could muster as he held back his frustration.

After that remark or insight, G stood. He bowed slightly with his hand held up to stop Jake from speaking, at the same time alerting him that not speaking is okay for now. Jake understood. He watched his host curiously while continuing to breathe easily. G walked over to the wall to Jake's right. He pointed to a passage of script at the end of the wall. Strangely, the exotic markings seemed to emerge as if brighter or lit up.

"Master Jake. Here we have the very beginning of one of the most ancient praises to a god known to man. Permit me to loosely translate the Sanskrit for you:

Praise Agni, praise the sacred fire, the chosen Priest, God and minister of sacrifice,
The one worthy of praise, lavishes plenty.
Worthy is Agni to be praised by living as by ancient seers.
He brings to us the Gods.
Through Agni man obtains wealth and plenty more day by day.
Most rich in heroes, glorious is
Agni, the perfect sacrifice which you encompass
Indeed, it all goes to the Gods.
May Agni, wise-minded Priest, truthful, most gloriously great,
The God, come hither with the Gods.
Whatever blessing, Agni will grant to the worshipper,
That, dear soul, is indeed your truth.
To you, dispeller of the night, O Agni, day by day with praise
Bringing you reverence, we come, Ruler of sacrifices, guardian of Law eternal,
O radiant one,
Increase in your dwelling place.
May you be approachable, even as a father is to his son:
Agni, be with us for our well being always.

"You see, we are surrounded by the earliest intelligent echoes of a human being's relationship with eternity. We in this room are as a microcosm of the entire universe just as quantum theory and holographic theory predict or imply. Only it is more alive here because you are dead to your normal self. But, Master Jake, I ask you: Who is your father? Have you rejected him when you rejected the Buddha in New Mexico?"

Jake winced. He still felt unsure of his decision to leave the Center.

Master G took no note of his reaction. He merely walked on to another section of the wall. He ran his hand over the script. He read a passage about praising the god Soma, known to ancients in the Asian subcontinent as a sacred juice crushed from a plant. He was about to go on when Jake stopped him, using the opportunity to keep himself from thinking about the center in Chama.

"I know about Soma. The ancient shamans used Soma as a means of transcendence. It occurs to me that this is some kind of shamanic experience. If it is, what is to become of me? I must rid myself of this room but how? Must I continue in this conversation with you endlessly in order that I might continue to breathe and live?"

"As you seem to know, the true shaman must die to be born again, Master Jake. He might be torn apart like Osiris in the spirit worlds, but will he have an Isis to find and repair him? There is no guarantee that he will survive the spirit journey mentally intact or alive. How many men and women have touched the limits of consciousness and not come back whole? How many have claimed to steal fire from the gods like Prometheus and come back producing only noxious smoke? Real Buddhas are rare."

Jake felt cold inside.

"Yes, I would say you are cold, meaning far from your original goal. What is enlightenment, indeed?"

"I feel stuck. This is not living. Is this what all those years of meditation led to? Am I stuck with a teacher in a room always?"

"That depends on what *you* do next," Master G answered as he pointed to his student.

324

A blinding light flashed surrounded Jake followed by a tremor that rattled the room. Everything including Master G faded into a kind of darkness like a moonless night in a forest. Sight gave way to sound. The tingling peals from the sounds of distant bells remained. An ominous sound of grinding emerged as if from a giant mill near rushing waters.

Jake's breathing began to slow down considerably. His mouth hung open in apprehension that something in the room was changing.

At first it was a speck of light, but as it drew nearer, he saw a glowing white mushroom emerge from the deep space. There was something odd about it as it came into focus. It was a patch sewn onto the front of a dusty black baseball cap. Jake heard, or thought he heard, the sonorous voice of his father call him as if from a loud speaker.

"Son, keep your eye on the ball."

Ziggy emerged and he was wearing the cap.

Master G sensed the change in his charge, his guest. The guest collected his wits as the volume of distant bells with rushing waters increased again. The scent of grinding steel and burning sandalwood flooded the room. G and the room reappeared to Jake. G returned to his red throne but did not sit. He stood patiently watching.

Jake stood up in front of his chair. He walked to the side of his chair. Underneath it he saw the handle of the old baseball bat—a *Louisville Slugger*. Jake leaned over and he picked it up. With a firm grip on the handle he took a couple of practice swings.

"You know," he said more to himself than to G, "my dad and I used to enjoy baseball. I recall him telling me, a year or so before he died in the motorcycle crash, *Son, keep your eye on the ball no matter what you do in life*. He would stand there on the mound saying things like that while we practiced hitting and pitching."

Jake ended his few seconds of recall with a last, firm look at Master G, who remained standing. In an effort to refocus and let go at the same time, Jake closed his eyes, took a deep breath, and opened them again to concentrate on a new vision that seemed to appear of its own volition. As he took another cut with the bat, Ziggy settled on the mound of a baseball field. He wore a traditional gray visiting team's uniform.

Jake smiled at the glowing white mushroom on the cap. Ziggy tipped his cap to his son before setting up to pitch. Jake stood ready at home plate with the bat cocked over his shoulder.

The scene was superimposed on the room in a subtle surreal sense, not as a double exposure, but as a parallel world. The vases in the room seemed to align with the bases on a diamond-shaped field. Jake was at home plate with the bat. He stood in front of his chair and table that had become a catcher and an umpire. The other players appearing on the field seemed insignificant, yet they were there. The battle, the game was primarily between batter and pitcher, always the key dynamic in baseball. The batter was prepared to swing. Throngs of vibrant voices cheered and jeered as if from a cosmic grandstand of anonymous fans mixed with versions of Master G who had by then shattered into a myriad of selves.

Ziggy went into his motion as a pitcher. He kicked high and he moved smoothly to deliver his pitch. The sound of bells mixed with noisy clangs increased in a cacophony of metal striking metal. Sandalwood incense aroma and smoke continued to fill the room. Jake could not breathe. The vision held as he held the bat and his breath. Ziggy uncoiled from his wind-up to hurl the ball toward the plate. With a split-finger grip, he sent the baseball into a wicked sliding motion. A tough pitch to hit but this son knew his father as the father knew his son. Jake remained in strict concentration, watching the pitcher's motion despite the increasingly louder knelling of bells, the pungent smoke, and a welter of distracting catcalls coming from a million Master G's in the stands.

"Master Jake. You will no longer exist if you disengage from this discussion. Nothing is resolved. Do you know what you are doing?"

Jake kept his eye on the ball.

"Master, Jake," the million Gs continued, "if you continue you will die and all will be over. You cannot do it this way. It is infinitely impossible for you to live this way."

The dancing Tibetan dakinis from his last meditation at the Center reappeared in a flash with their skullcap cups and knives. The dream wraiths whispered sensual invocations while kissing and delicately licking his ears from either side. Unable to distract their quarry, the feminine forms faded into a mist of memory as the ball streaked toward the plate.

Jake stepped into his stride with his right foot. He uncoiled with a tight grip on the old wooden bat. With his eyes fixed on the oncoming ball, his sinewy arms and strong wrists snapped the bat, whipping it smoothly. The bat struck true sending the ball high over the heads of the million Gs.

In the reenergized room, Jake stood small like a man, just a man, a tiny speck, a spark of life glowing dimly. The baseball streaked past eons of time erupting beyond the speed of light. A new vitality in the room expanded and then collapsed back into a kind of parody of its former self.

Still now and standing singularly at the front of the room, Master G folded his hands in a gesture of prayer. His fate was sealed with the room.

Jake lowered the bat and held it in his left hand. His shoulders sagged and his knees began to buckle under him. His strength and consciousness waned rapidly. Jake set the bat down like a cane for support and he leaned on it for balance. His mind slowly dissolved into a dark fog. He felt his delirium, pain and sweat return.

In the few seconds he had left, he watched the room decay around him. The red throne became an old, chipped wooden chair with a broken lower support rail. Storm light flashing through windows revealed that the chair sat across from him on a cracked concrete floor littered with paint chips, old papers, broken fluorescent bulbs, and ceiling dust.

Another flicker of lightning revealed more. A few gray metal laundry buckets lay around the room. One end of the room, Master G's stage, was slightly elevated above a large drain on the floor. Damaged metal pipes led to hanging faucet heads along one wall. Graffiti on the walls, most of it faded and illegible, spelled out names and dates and messages from the late 1980s.

Jake's body sagged into the dusty and wobbly wooden chair next to him. He managed to sit in it for a few seconds, long enough to spot a stark apparition opposite him. She was a poorly dressed mongoloid girl with Down syndrome and she was smiling. She smiled at him. She wore a knee length, ill-fitted, faded floral dress and scuffed up brown shoes with ill-matched white socks. Her brown hair was clasped with one cheap pink plastic barrette to keep her hair from her eyes. Her hair was cropped as if someone held a bowl on her head to trim it. She raised her hands folded in front of her face for an instant before she stumbled forward toward him, running duck-like, running happily with her awkward open-mouth smile.

As she approached Jake he heard her exclaim, "I safe!"

She jumped on what looked like home plate as she brushed past Jake leaving in her wake the strong scent of rose perfume. Jake turned slightly but just enough to see the tiny figure fade away into the same emptiness that now filled his mind. The turning motion caused Jake to tumble head first onto the dirty concrete floor with an unremarkable, unwitnessed thud.

16   Eye on the Ball

Hospital techs and security staff assigned to find Jake were frantic but organized. Jake had been unaccounted for a half hour. Within minutes of the alert, staff correctly figured out that he got past the cafeteria's open emergency exit door during the fracas. They surmised that he may have slipped out the tunnel exit door somehow without setting off an alarm. But no one could find any indication that he was outside. The outdoor security camera rewind revealed nothing. The stormy weather held a cloak of uncertainty over every searcher's hopes. Perhaps the camera missed something.

Inside, two men walked to the dead end of the tunnel with flashlights. They quickly checked the one side door at the end but it was jammed shut. Local police had been put on alert. The crisis staff called Harry and Monica. Harry readied his pick-up truck to search while phoning Giles, Gigi and others in case Jake showed up somewhere or tried to contact them.

Ben, who was on duty again that evening, asked the janitor and a charge nurse to walk him through where they thought Jake went in the tunnel. Ben examined the tunnel exit door again scanning the frame with his flashlight. Then he walked to the end to check the locked doorway that led to the campus underground system. He noticed that dirt was loosened above it. He saw two fresh sneaker prints on the door. With his ample bulk he managed to shoulder it open a tiny crack. Taking a hint from the sneaker prints, Ben stepped back to give it a hard kick. The door flew open on first impact.

The janitor, a small Mexican fellow, followed Ben down the unkempt section of the tunnel. They stepped gingerly over the cracked cat skeleton. Using their flashlights to scan the way they soon arrived at the skylight. The much taller Ben stopped to inspect the overhead windows for any breaks or potential openings. One window pane was broken but it was an old break with a hole too small to allow more than a small animal to enter.

Satisfied that Jake did not somehow climb up and out, Ben and his companion trudged on slowly. After taking many careful steps over the debris and muck, they stopped to examine a door to one of the old units. Another flash of lightning with a powerful snap of thunder felt like a blast of a bomb and stunned the men.

"Whoa, that was a close one," thought Ben. "What's up, Lopez," Ben shouted out. "Do you hear anything?"

Lopez pounded on the door.

"Jake, you in there? Anybody in there?"

The janitor looked at the door again as Ben approached.

"Ben, this door was recently opened and closed. Look at the broken spider web up there and the dirt down here."

Lopez stood back allowing Ben to shove the door with both hands. It swung open. Lopez scanned the room with his light.

"He aqui a Jake! Aqui! I think it is him in here. He's there on the floor!" yelled the janitor.

Ben's flashlight quickly found Jake as well. He seemed to be out cold face down. Jake's right hand rested on the end of the baseball bat.

"Here, hold mine on him too for me," Ben said as he handed his light to the janitor.

Ben crouched down uneasily into a squat to examine his patient. Jake's black shirt was damp. He felt warm. He was breathing steadily.

"Jake, buddy, can you hear me?"

There was no response.

Next Ben reached to check for a pulse on Jake's neck. No sooner had Ben touched him than Jake rolled and sprung to his feet like a startled cat. He snatched the bat near his feet with his right hand. Wide eyed with mouth hung open he held the bat high, ready to strike. With his left he tried to block the bright torch lights aimed at his face. Ben, who had fallen backwards on his butt, was struggling to get to his feet.

The janitor let out a short, "What the hell."

Jake retreated a few steps backward toward the center of the room.

Ben sputtered half in fear and half in anger as he rolled over onto his knees to get up, "Jake, what the hell are you going to do with that?"

He kept his eye on the bat in Jake's hand.

More light flashed through the high casement windows and another thunder clap rumbled through the room creating dramatic graphic images in the minds of the unlikely adversaries.

Jake suddenly realized who was talking to him. He immediately relaxed and said, "I already did it. I'm done."

Jake let the bat drop. It bounced on the concrete floor, then rolled briefly, and came to a stop near the drain.

"Is that you, Ben?"

"Yea, it's me. You scared the shit out of me."

"Sorry, man. You scared me too," he said as he shielded the janitor's light from his eyes.

Jake offered his hand to help raise Ben up off his knees. Ben accepted his assistance.

"You're talking again," Ben said as he brushed the dust off his pants.

The answer that Jake *already did it* confused Ben yet it significantly diminished his apprehensions. Then Ben returned to his role as an emergency medical technician.

"Are you okay, man? Let me check you."

The janitor stood by with the lights on Jake. Ben looked him over. He felt his forehead. He looked at his eyes.

"Fever—you're a little warm. Damn, you were soaking wet. Is it from sweat?"

"Maybe. I don't know."

"Here, use this chair."

Ben motioned for Jake to sit and he did. Ben felt for Jake's pulse on the left wrist.

"Your heart rate is fine. Strange."

Then Ben examined a small fresh abrasion on Jake's forehead. The new bump close to the older one he sustained with Gigi was most likely caused by his head striking the concrete. The blood specks in the bruise were fresh. Ben found dirt particles imbedded in the skin.

"You weren't out cold for very long, is my guess. Maybe a few minutes—how're you feeling now?" Ben asked.

"Fine—a lot better than I did a while ago. It seems that my mind has cleared up."

Jake was surprised at how alert and alive he felt. "I think I fainted after I got in here. I feel like I was wandering a long time."

"You've been missing from the unit for less than an hour, maybe forty-five minutes. You could not have been in here that long," Ben reiterated.

Ben flipped open his cell phone to call the front desk.

"Hi, it's Ben from ambulance. Listen, we found him, you know, Jake the missing patient. We're here with him where the tunnel enters L Building's basement. It's the old utility room where they washed kitchen equipment. Call off the search. I'm sending for a stretcher. The patient's okay—calm and cooperative. Tell the doc to call me."

Ben sent the janitor up to help his partner Tracy to bring a stretcher.

Jake spoke up insisting, "I can walk back. No need to go through all this trouble."

Ben laughed in Jake's face.

"Are you insane? After what you made everyone go through to find you? We're going to go by the book to make sure you are well. By the way, how's your side?"

Jake instinctively rested his right hand on his ribs as if to check.

"Still sore. Hard to breath at times. Don't make me laugh."

"I thought so," Ben remarked. "Tracy told me a rib may be cracked. Sorry, man. I laid my fist into you during that struggle in the ER. I want to apologize to you now that you're talking again. You have a right to press charges, you know. I had no right."

"Hell, man, I'm surprised you didn't do more damage to me. I must have been acting completely crazy. I really nailed you. How's your head?"

Jake examined the small bandage between Ben's eyes, one of which had turned black.

"I'll survive. So, are we even then?" Ben asked.

He was concerned more about what he did to Jake than what Jake did to him.

"Even? I need to thank you for doing your job. I haven't been in my right mind lately, that is, if I have a right mind," Jake replied with no hint of irony.

Ben missed the subtle Buddhist pun and he accepted the pardon. Then he realized that the recently mute and dangerous patient Jake was not just talking but talking quite normally and with a sense of humor.

"Tell me something. You seem completely different. I know the alcohol had something to do with your behavior at the ER, but why did you run? What were you thinking? You would have been out of here in a couple days, I figure."

"Yesterday, I imagined I might be locked in here getting injections every day like my roommate. I don't know what I was thinking. I panicked, guess. Everything was so distorted—I don't know."

"And how are you feeling now?"

"Besides crazy you mean? I'm not sure. I feel more at peace, like I'm back again. Clear headed. By the way, do you smell roses in here?"

Ben looked at him sideways after sniffing the air. "Nnn—no. Why? Do you?"

"I thought I smelled perfume when you woke me a bit ago."

The pleasant aroma waned as quickly as it came. And within seconds, it came again. The fragrance hurtled his mind back to the events of his vision in its entirety like seeing a large mural. He took a deep breath, knowing he would say nothing more about it. After exhaling, he sniffed Ben's shoulder.

"Fer sure it is not coming from you."

Ben ignored the insult. He called again to check with Tracy.

The gurney arrived within the next few minutes. Jake relaxed onto the wheeled cot as the men strapped him in. Ben and Tracy raised him up so they could comfortably roll him back to the ambulance waiting outside the emergency exit.

Jake spent most of the next four to five hours in an emergency room getting a medical evaluation to clear him for return to Psych Hall. The doctor gave him an antibiotic for a minor infection that may have caused his fever. Tests indicated a probable simple fracture in one rib. The doctor noted deep bruising in his thigh that may or may not have contributed to the raised white blood count. The intensity of the drugs and alcohol in his system had worn off. He felt no anxiety. His vital signs remained stable and normal after an hour of observation. The doctor noted that his patient's conversation was rational, his mood and affect appropriate. Jake rested calmly for one hour or so after the exam before they returned him to Psych Hall.

Gigi arrived at Psych Hall earlier than the others. She was alone with Jake for ten minutes before Monica, Lindy and Harry arrived. Gigi fumbled for words of apology. She was relieved that her strange new friend appeared okay.

"Well, are you still glad we met?" she kidded.

"Meeting you turned out to be one of the most fortunate events in my life. I can't explain how that is. It showed me something. About myself, I mean."

"What was that?"

"Oh, man, where do I start?" Jake gritted his teeth. "I wasn't ready for what hit me. No pun intended, but I had little control around you. All that supposed Zen training and self-awareness went up in smoke in one day. Maybe it was the beer acting or some primal instinct to hold onto you."

Jake laughed when recalling the image of the collision with Gigi squirming at third base.

"Sorry, but that was fun."

"Yea, fun for you! How's your leg?"

"Still bruised."

"Good."

"Good?"

"Yea, good. You were in my way. You weren't playing fair."

"Fair had nothing to do with it. I was trying to catch a ball. You ran into me—you could have gone around, you know."

"Yes, I could have, but the damn dog tripped me," Gigi said with some consternation. "Listen, I have a confession to make. Harry asked me to try to meet with you. You know, about the cult thing. I was not sure how to connect with you. So—"

"So the baseball genie intervened."

"It was meant to be."

"Everything was meant to be, on hindsight," Jake said with a resigned tone in his voice.

"That's romantic of you," Gigi replied with a hint of hurt in her voice.

"You really think what happened was romantic?"

"Well, it could have been," Gigi indicated with a little girl inflection.

Jake looked at Gigi for a sign whether she was being serious or not. Was she toying with him again? What for? He could not see that she read his confusion in a split second.

"You have a lot to learn about women, don't you?" she said.

"Huh?"

She leaned over and kissed him on the forehead.

"Do I have to hit you on the head with a hammer? Men are hungry fish and women are delicious bait. Sometimes there's a hook. Hooking up can be dangerous if you are not aware of who controls the line."

"So, you're saying that you were trying to reel me in."

"No, silly. Well maybe—a little. No, I'm saying I made a mistake. I didn't stick to the script. Harry asked for a favor and that was to talk with you. He thought some feminine charm would grab your attention. When it came down to it, I mean afterwards, I felt like a creep, dragging you into a conversation with, you know, physical affection. At the time it felt right, and I thought, Why not? We could talk about your commune experience later. The bottom line is we hardly know each other. Sex, well, it's never that causal, is it? Frankly, I'm ashamed of what I let happen."

"Well, I feel like I used you, you know, as a chance to break a sex-fast I no longer believed in. I'm not very proud of that either."

"I made it easy for you. It's not like I haven't done *that* before. Stupid love, stupid love," Gigi said grimly.

"Then we are forgiven. I'll let it go if you will."

Jake offered her his hand to shake. Gigi took his hand.

"Deal," she said. With her left hand she rubbed the left thigh of her jeans. Jake noticed her doing it.

"Are you going to keep the snake?"

"I don't know. On second thought, maybe not."

Then Gigi heard Harry's voice outside the door. She stood up to greet him. "Hey, look who's here! Hi, Monica—Harry"

After a few minutes of catching up with personal news, Gigi excused herself.

"I need to get to the club to prepare for clients. See you guys later. Bye, Jake. So glad you're feeling better. And thanks."

"Thanks? What'd you give her?" Harry asked.

"Hi mom, Harry. Thanks for coming." Then Jake turned to Harry. "I didn't give her anything. I thanked her for that extraordinary date we had. Thanks for setting us up, dear brother."

"Jacob," Monica chimed in, "that's no way treat your brother. He was only trying to help," Monica said with a bit of sarcasm at Harry's expense. "I heard what happened from Harry on the way here. He told us the whole sordid story. I'm not sure how much of it to believe. By the way, Neal sends his best wishes. He's at work."

"I think I'll see him soon enough. Anyway, I do feel a whole lot better. My head is clearer now. I'm glad Harry filled you in about my escapade. It was accidental—nobody's fault, really."

"So, when do you think you can check out?" Harry asked.

"I have to see my treatment team. I think it's basically Dr. Kelly's call. Because of the legal issue they say I have to appear in court tomorrow before I can be discharged. Dr. Blaise should be there to defend his statement. Whatever happens, I'm prepared to ride it out. I can't tell you how good it feels to see things more clearly, to breathe."

Visiting lasted for only two hours that Tuesday. Monica and Harry left in time to allow Giles and Jim in for a brief chat with Jake. The visitors all met in the lobby to determine who would go in and when. Jake was happy to see Giles again but he was surprised that Jim came along.

Jim was concerned about the legal matter—Jake's involuntary status meant he would appear in a mental health court to determine next level of care—as well as talking to Jake about work. One of the caseworkers explained the routine court procedure to Jim who called in earlier. He relaxed his concern that Jake needed an outside attorney. The county would provide a competent public defender who knew mental health law.

"It will be no big deal," someone who knew of the case told him.

Jim told Jake that as soon as he felt well enough, he could start on a new job in the area. A wealthy friend of Jim's was adding a back section to his colonial era stone home. He also needed major renovations to a barn to be converted to an office space. The crew chief would make room for Jake, starting him off as a common laborer. For the first time in five years, and maybe ten, Jake would be working to invest in his own future.

After his visitors departed, Jake asked Rasheed for a razor and cream so he could shave. Rasheed gave him a disposable blue razor and a can of shaving cream. He would return the razor as required to Rasheed after his shower.

Jake stood in the warm soothing spray of a shower to make it easier on his face. He shaved carefully and slowly, feeling his cheeks, chin, and neck with his fingertips as he scraped through the whiskers. He thought about the last time he shaved his head a little over two weeks before. It seemed an age away. After exiting the shower, he touched up his face at the sink, squaring off his sideburns just above his earlobes. Small nicks on his chin stopped bleeding after some pressure from a paper towel. He slipped into the new khaki pants and a clean, black polo shirt that Harry brought for him.

"You look much better, man," Rasheed noted as he collected the razor and cream from Jake.

"Thanks."

Later in the afternoon, Dr. Kelly came by again accompanied by his assistant Alka. Jake was no longer under continual observation so there was no guard at his door. When Kelly came into Room 313 he found Jake making an origami bird for Paul. Jake was seated on the floor near Paul's bed. Paul seemed almost disinterested in what Jake was doing. He sat knees up on his bed, back against a wall, and muttering. But Paul did acknowledge Kelly as he entered.

"You here for me?"

Paul glanced up at Kelly who smiled back as he pointed to Jake.

"He's making a bird out of paper. He's a good guy—not from Washington."

Kelly noticed the Koontz book and its title next to Jake's bed. Kelly surmised that Paul was making loose associations again but he knew that was base-line behavior for Paul.

"No, Paul. We're here for Jake. Jake, please come with us to the interview room. This shouldn't take too long."

Jake finished folding the bird, stood up and held the white paper creature out to Paul. Paul made no move to accept it so Jake simply placed it near Paul's bare feet on the bed. Then he turned to acknowledge Kelly with a nod. When Alka appeared at the door he said, "Good to see you again. You look nice today."

Alka glanced at Kelly who raised his eyebrows. He was pleasantly surprised with Jake's apparent turn-around. He was talking and appropriately! Jake followed them to the interview room. As they exited 313 Paul quickly stuffed the paper bird into his shirt pocket.

Kelly began, "So, Jake, I see we are talking again. Good, good. We read the report about the incident last night and how you got into the tunnel system. What the hell was that all about?"

Jake was prepared for this line of questioning. He was not about to tell Kelly

338

about the Master G encounter. But he did not want to lie.

"I talked this over with Dr. Blaise last night at the ER. To me everything that's happened since this all started seems like a dream, no doubt helped along by beer and hashish and a blow to my skull. Blaise seems to think I also developed a case of delirium from a fever."

"What else can you tell us?"

"Well, like I said, everything seemed like a dream. I think I was afraid I might be stuck in here or some place like this forever if anyone knew what I was thinking so I would not talk. I think when I saw a way to get out I did it spontaneously. I had no plan to escape prior to that."

"Can you tell us more about the content of your thought?"

"You mean, what I'm thinking now?"

"No. I mean from last night, in the tunnels, and before?"

"I felt panicky. This place felt like it was closing in on me. I imagined being stuck here in need of meds all my life like my roommate. The last thing I recall, in the tunnels, is seeing something like a mirage. I must have passed out right after I saw it because I recall falling from a chair where I sat. I saw a young girl in a plain dress. She looked retarded, you know. I heard her say "stay" or "safe" or something to that effect. Then she faded away. Next thing I knew Ben and the janitor guy, Lopez, were there shining flashlights in my face."

"Ah, a Pennhallow ghost! Interesting. You are not the first to see one, believe me. This place has given people the creeps for decades. The brain can produce strange things under suggestion and stress, eh Miss Krol?" Kelly rolled his eyes to signal his skepticism as Alka looked his way. "You could have made an unconscious connection with this place. It almost makes sense that you would see someone like that. At least you didn't have devils chasing you around, eh?"

Jake chuckled along with Kelly. Alka Krol remained reserved. Kelly continued.

"See or hear anything else?"

Jake shook his head thinking all the while that he did smell roses. Kelly did not ask about smelling anything.

"One more question," Kelly wanted to ask. "Are you suicidal or feeling like you might hurt yourself in any way? The initial report from the ER doc that committed you was that you said—let's see here," Kelly said as he sorted through the medical chart. "Ah, yes, and I quote: '*I want to die. Leave me alone.*'"

"I don't recall saying that. I do recall feeling like I was dying at one stage—the pain in my gut, and I had trouble breathing—and my mind slipping away. But no, not suicidal, especially not now. I want to get out of here and get to work."

Kelly finished his notes; then, he stood up to leave. "I think this is all drug related. You seem quite sober to me now. Ms. Krol, if you can give me your mental status and summary report later, I'd appreciate it. Jake, Ms. Krol will finish up with you." Jake stood up, shook Dr. Kelly's hand and thanked him.

With that appropriate gesture noted, Kelly left the room. He was satisfied that this was primarily a drug-induced episode and little more. Jake had no prior history of mental health dysfunction. He was inclined to discharge the patient as soon as possible.

Alka Krol was dressed more casually this time in fashionable blue jeans and a forest green shirt under a smart dark blue jacket. Her hair was up in a loose bun again, and she wore her glasses. Plain, silver hoop earrings accented her appearance. Alka went through a routine check-list of questions with Jake that took her fifteen minutes. Then she set her clipboard down on the table. She removed her glasses, crossed her legs and sat back in her chair leaning on her left elbow. She propped her chin onto her left thumb with her index finger along her cheekbone. She stared directly into Jake's eyes looking for any sign of anything.

He sat there with his hands on his lap staring back, waiting for her next question. At this meeting he found her not only stunning in appearance, but intimidating in personality. He could not be sure if it was her beauty or her demeanor that he was reacting to. He wanted to touch the skin on her cheek or neck, to feel that she was real. Alka let her hand drop from her chin. She sat up.

"You know, you look much better with that beard off your face. You have good features." She put her glasses back on. "You speak well. I was expecting something gruff, like Rocky Balboa."

This comment took Jake by surprise. He began to laugh then caught himself with an, "Unh." He held his side as he muffled his mirth. After gasping stiffly twice, he said, "You mean just because I'm from the Philly area, you expected a palooka? I wasn't expecting someone like you to come up with a crude stereotype," he snickered.

"Someone like me?"

"You know, you're educated and in psychology no less." Jake continued to muffle a laugh.

"Sorry. I forgot about your sore ribs. I had no idea I was such a comedian," Alka said with a hint of sarcasm. She methodically cleared her throat before continuing. "What I meant was your presentation the first time we met. You seemed very intense, afraid to express yourself. In a word, you were guarded. And you looked rather rudimentary."

"Yeah, like I might say, *Yo, Alka, wanna see my pet turtle?*" Jake barely held his emotion in check after his Rocky imitation. "Sorry, Ms. Krol, but for some reason it strikes me really funny."

Alka cleared her throat. "Okay, you made your point. Bad reference on my part. Let me try this again. I think there's a lot more you can talk about. You were in deep trouble when we last met, psychologically I mean. Now, after one day, you have a full range of expression and good control of mood with normal affect, not to mention your, ah, sense of humor. I understand that the drugs wore off. You seem to have come to your senses. But there's still the dramatic reaction you had, almost like a burst of a dam. I'm curious to know how much your experience at a Zen center for the past five or ten years added to your distress. Also, I think there's a lot more to your escape attempt last night than you're letting out here."

Jake leaned back into his chair. All the mirth left him like air let out of a balloon. Alka was a keen observer. He wanted to level with her in some way without spilling out details of an experience that he had no time to properly digest. He was suddenly afraid of saying too much again, enough to encourage the doctors to keep him in custody. If he told her the truth, she might think that he is really crazy. His instincts led him to talk about his cult experience.

"Well, you're right. There's a lot more but it's primarily a spiritual thing, how I view the world and questions about—what can I say about this—personal philosophy. To tell you the truth, I'm about fed up with myself for all the time I seem to have wasted in pursuit of this stuff. I want to get to work, save some money, get a normal life. I'll sort out the big mysteries later when I'm retired—or not."

Jake was a little surprised at his direct answer. He said it like he meant it.

Alka leaned back into her chair as well. She could see that Jake needed space, not pressure. He was definitely goal-directed and all immediate signs indicated that he was not at all depressed, let alone suicidal. Any signs of psychosis were gone. More time in a place like Psych Hall would do nothing for this man. She would recommend to Kelly that Jake be discharged to outside services after his mental health hearing the next morning.

"Before I leave I want to run something by you. Dr. Kelly mentioned that I'm a doctoral candidate in psychology. The reason I've taken an interest in your past, if you haven't noticed, is that my dissertation is about the psychology of spirituality—more specifically, brain function in the neo-cortex and how religious identification affects personality—what makes it beneficial as opposed to harmful. I'm researching a small aspect of this that I won't go into now."

Jake sighed in relief. His curiosity in Alka's work was peaked, however. "Were you ever in a cult? I recall you mentioned something about a Sufi thing." Jake asked.

"Oh, that was about my father. So you were paying some attention! Of course, my father's spiritual quirks stimulated some of my curiosity, but I was more affected by 9/11. I was only a junior in college then. I kept wondering what the brain of a religious terrorist looks like. Later, after I got my master's, I decided to switch, to concentrate on what sane religion looks like in the human brain. I am curious how irrational belief meets with healthy social behavior. Dr. Kelly thinks I'm nuts and that my hypothesis is too unwieldy, or in lala land, but at least he appreciates how I approach the science."

"So what can I do for you? You want to hook my brain to electrodes?"

"Hmmm, that's an idea. Just kidding—for now. Really, what I'd like to do is stay in touch with you. When you're ready, I'll send you a questionnaire and do an interview. Then the electrodes!"

Jake noted that she was serious.

Alka reached into her jacket pocket. She pulled out a business card and handed it to him.

Jake looked at it carefully. He noticed that Alka was with the University of Pennsylvania and that she lived close to campus. He looked up at her with an increased interest because of her research. He also felt conflicted because of it. Here stood a woman he would like to know better—someone to ask to lunch, perhaps. But, he could choose to become one of her lab rats. He felt oddly dejected.

On the other hand, he needed to slow down. His urge to find acceptance and romance needed moderation. He felt shamed by his attraction to her. What would someone with her accomplishment want with a college dropout, and worse, a man with little more than ten years of cult experience in his resume? He had no money, no place of his own, and no history of stability. Here he is in a mental hospital daring to think that a sophisticated, accomplished woman would care to see him as anything more than a patient.

"One pitch at a time, Jake," he thought to himself. "Keep your eye on the ball."

He snapped out of his brief reverie, catching himself staring at her card. He looked up into her curious, unflinching eyes. He felt a mysterious, calm connection to her in that instant

"Sorry, I was daydreaming," he said to her. And then in a flat tone, "Sure, I'll call or email you as soon as I can get it together."

Alka noticed the tone of disappointment in Jake's voice. She did not have to ask what was on his mind. She found him attractive too. However, she knew too well how easily transference issues complicate client-clinician relationships. She did not want to lead him on, but she was interested in his life at the academic level. For the coming year academia would dominate her life as she strove to finish her dissertation, submit it, and pass the orals.

"This is my last week at this hospital," she told him. After this, I'm not sure where I'll be assigned if anywhere. I have classes to teach. Anyway, when you're ready, maybe we can have coffee and talk more about where to go with this."

"Coffee? Sure, sure. I'd like that. Thanks."

Time was up for the session. Alka reached out to shake Jake's hand. He reciprocated. It was an awkward handshake as she gave him a firm squeeze whereas he did not want to seem too eager to touch her. Alka felt the calluses and workingman roughness in his hand. She felt his quiet, considerable strength, not that of a mug in a boxing ring but that of a cautious man intent on moving on, going forth. Jake felt that he touched a special woman, a special being and a perfect stranger. Jake's heart picked up a few beats per minute. He felt both energized and terrified. As they parted, he could not sustain more than a glance into her eyes, those deep blue eyes. He pulled his hand away in an effort not to contaminate her.

"Good. Don't lose my card!" she said.

"I'll keep my eye on it." Jake raised it in the air and held it there until she disappeared from the room. He felt like crying but he did not.

Jake followed Paul back to 313 from the cafeteria after dinner. They passed the recreation area where some patients settled in to watch a movie. In another area a young man played a Bach sonata on the piano. Jake overheard two patients arguing over which film to watch.

"We saw *Spiderman* last week."

"I wasn't here last week."

Paul seemed unusually agitated by the conversations around him. He avoided the recreation room preferring to stay in 313. The entertainment in his head was sufficient if one could call it that. Words, symbols and images became signs that fed into his world but hardly related to the actual environment. The recreation area provided too much stimulation for him to process. Sometimes the television talked to him as if it was observing him. This bothered him. He was very careful around television programs. Back in the room Jake gently confronted Paul.

"Hey, buddy. Something's bugging you. Can you tell me what it is?"

"I showed Maria the bird. I put it on the table at dinner in front of her. Someone took it. Maybe Maria thought I gave it to her. I didn't."

Paul reverted to his rapid self-talk that was hard to understand. Jake made out that he was angry with Maria, the government and someone trying to interfere with alternating current.

"I'll be right back, Paul. Wait here."

Paul was not going anywhere and Jake knew it. Paul was like a man on a chair lost in an extended daydream. When he was not agitated, hungry or harassed by hostile voices, Paul could sit quietly for hours entertained by his inner world. Jake returned in a few minutes with several sheets of construction paper: blue, pink and yellow.

"Look here, Paul. Watch this."

Jake sat on the floor near Paul. He went to work as his attentive roommate gazed at magical folds transforming flat paper into a bird.

Years before, in one the more pleasant days at the Center, the old man taught a workshop on origami technique. Jake learned to make a bird, a praying mantis and an ox. It was one of those memorable days when Center residents and clients laughed spontaneously at their clumsy efforts and when the old man's stick was nowhere in sight. The old man delighted in the chance to show off a skill he had as a child, a skill he learned from his mother and not from a Zen master.

Jake wondered what happened to the black origami bird that he left hanging in the Beetle back in Colorado. He talked to Paul as he worked his magic folds.

"Here you go, one done and two more to go, Paul. Maybe Maria is enjoying the other one. If she didn't take it you might not have three more. Think of that! But be careful with these if you want to keep them, okay? How about we put them in your property? Staff will give them back to you when you check out."

Within fifteen minutes Jake finished the birds for Paul. This time Paul reached out to take them one by one.

"This one we can name Tesla, this one Einstein, and this one—what should we name it?" Jake asked.

"Jake!" Paul smiled and then broke into laughter. This was the first time Jake noticed that Paul had a sense of humor.

"Einstein Bird—that's funny," Paul said. "Tesla knew more than him on a bad day."

"Paul, where did you last see your pigeons?"

Paul looked cautiously at Jake as if Jake was trying to get a secret from him. He decided that Jake was trustworthy. "Don't tell anyone. Logan Circle."

"You mean at the fountain on the Parkway?"

"Yes. Don't tell anyone."

"How about if I visit them when I get out of here? What do you feed them?"

"Hartz bird seed. Cockatiel food. It's what they like."

"Isn't that kind of expensive?"

"It's what they like."

Jake nodded. "It's what they like."

A makeshift court took place several times a week on the first floor of Psych Hall in a conference room next to the director's office. A long, boat-shaped, cherry wood table that could seat sixteen served as the bench. At nine-o'clock a social worker came to get Jake for court. His case was next on the docket. Jake got his shoe laces back. He wore a clean white T-shirt and his baggy khaki pants. While he was waiting in the lobby outside the courtroom a clerk came out to announce that Dr. Blaise did not show up and was unavailable as the petitioner for Jake's involuntary commitment. Therefore, Jake was free to go without a hearing since there was no new behavior that concerned the CIBM treatment team. The court referred Jake to a local outpatient clinic as a matter of protocol. Whether he showed up or not for follow-up therapy was nobody's business but his own. Monica and Neal waited for him in the front lobby. Jake returned to 313 to get the few personal items. Paul was out somewhere, perhaps at a group meeting or with his treating doctor, so Jake did not get a chance to say goodbye to him.

Dr. Kelly met with Jake one last time for ten minutes before his mental health hearing in court. Kelly told Jake he had a "substance induced psychotic reaction" as a diagnosis. He would consider or *rule out* an anxiety disorder. Kelly rehearsed what Jake already discussed with him earlier.

"Let's go over this again. Cannabis intoxication rarely causes a psychotic reaction but in your case you may have been hypersensitive to it due to prior lifestyle of an inordinate amount of meditation, strict diet, and perhaps stress from a radical change in your social environment and too much alcohol. That crack on your skull from the fall did not help," Kelly said as he leaned over to examine the remains of the lump on Jake's forehead. "I know I do not have to tell you this, but you need to be more careful when you go out partying."

Kelly also considered Jake's recent history of panic attacks. Kelly told him that with Ms. Krol's help, they ruled out a seizure disorder after examining several EEGs.

"Ms. Krol mentioned to me that you might follow up with her. She has a keen interest in talking to you about your brain and spiritual preoccupation. You are on your own with that one, son. If you have any further questions about the results, contact her."

Kelly was concerned that Jake's blood pressure tended to be low, but tests showed no irregular cardiac indications. The psychiatrist urged Jake to follow-up with a full physical within a month especially if panic attacks recurred. He said he may need a mild anti-anxiety medication.

Jake said, "Thank you. This has been quite an experience. I've learned a lot from you."

Jake went home with Monica and Neal. Neal was surprised how well-spoken and optimistic Jake was in light of everything that happened. Jake told them that the weekend in treatment was a wake-up call. He would "get real" with his life now, meaning immediately. Neal suggested that Jake take some time to relax.

"A week of rest might do you some good. Give yourself time to regroup."

However, within an hour of settling back into his old home, Jake made several phone calls to check on the potential job that Jim had arranged. The owner of Colonial Stone, Inc. asked him to come in at the end of the week with the understanding that Jake needed a few weeks of light work. Jake would be on probation.

Jake spent those first weeks at work observing, learning, running errands and picking up supplies for the two crews. He spent most of the following year working steadily for others. He eventually went into business for himself after hiring a two-man crew. He spent little money except for one short trip back to New Mexico. During that year he managed to pay off the hospital bills after Jim helped him negotiate a much lower rate for services. Jake offered to trade labor for the legal services but Jim would have none of it.

"Let's say this one's for Ziggy, son."

17 Ziggy Candle

Feed the city pigeons
Light the church candle
Then jump the broomstick—8 October 2008

Nearly a year of hard labor from job site to job site passed. Jake parked his 2001 white Jeep Wrangler behind Philadelphia's 30th Street Station. He hurried through the back entrance into the great foyer of the train station hoping he would not be late. He was on time with ten minutes to spare. As planned he waited near the giant art deco angel that dominated the east end and main entrance of 30th Street Station. It had been two months since he last saw her but this time would be different. Their communication had increased in the past four weeks. The masks had fallen away. She no longer required him for her research. He shed his mental patient skin among the walls of rock and stone he built. She completed her dissertation and anxiously passed her oral exams. He took control of his financial and social life again. She was now officially a doctor as Alka Krol, Ph.D. He had emptied himself of the ten year desire to empty himself. Her first job as a research psychologist landed her in the nation's capitol that month with a private clinic. She felt like it was time for a holiday. He felt like a kid on his first date.

Two months earlier, they converged in New Mexico to visit the Center. Alka met Jake at the Albuquerque airport where they rented a car. She flew out of Washington; he, out of Philadelphia. After four hours of driving and a short break for lunch, they arrived in Chama with a new appreciation for one another. There was nothing special going on at the Center beyond routines—there were no workshops or extra guests—so it was a good time for a short visit. They planned to stay for three or four days. Marga agreed to the arrangement to help with Alka's research. Jake convinced

349

Usagi to come back to the Center for a reunion and to give Alka an interview. Usagi quit the Center earlier that year to concentrate on a degree in social work. The Center's world was behind him.

Alka stayed with Marga at the main house, while Jake and Waylon or Usagi (Marga continued to call him that whenever he visited) found cots with comfortable foam pads in the newly expanded guest house. The old friends carried on as if they had never parted. Usagi's dark hair was long and shaggy again, much longer than Jake's who kept it shorter for work. They were both clean shaven. Although the trip was business for Alka, or field work, her experience at the modest Center was a revelation for personal reasons as well as research. She saw some of Jake's past fleshed out, so to speak, and found a model of what she was looking for in Marga.

The Center's director, as Marga came to call herself, exhibited the qualities of *sanity* that Alka expected to find in a stable religious leader: Marga presented as not only open minded within her adopted tradition but also firmly realistic in her priorities and goals. She helped establish a democratic form of governance whereby the Center's core members would vote annually for a director. Marga could be replaced any year. Jake suggested this model a year before he left based on his visit to the Benedictine Monastery that had the same democratic policy regarding its head abbot.

Marga greeted them in the dining area. Jake felt the friendship he had with Marga flood back into the moment. A year was not a long time. He was an age away, yet nothing much had changed. "Good to see you again," he said as he greeted Marga with a handshake and a kiss on her cheek. "This is Alka Krol."

"Hi, Jake. You haven't changed a bit." Marga was clearly joking and it was apparent to all in the room. She was aware of most of the changes he went through. She was aware of his hospitalization that they discussed at length during one phone call a few weeks after Jake's experience. They compared notes about psych hospital treatment and managed to find humor in it. They discussed the transformative aspect of a psychiatric crisis. Jake did not say anything to Marga about the visionary encounter he had. He hadn't told anyone, at least not yet.

"So, you are Alka. It is a pleasure to meet you in person." Marga hugged her. Jake watched as the women made eye contact. Alka was slightly taller. Alka was in jeans and sneakers and Marga wore a casual, long skirt and sandals with warm socks. It was a cool evening. To Jake's delight they seemed surprisingly comfortable with one another. Why he expected some tension was probably due to his mixed affections for them. He breathed a sigh of relief in any case. This was not so hard. He could relax and enjoy the long weekend. Dinner conversation that night went very well. The days went by much quicker than Jake expected. And on the last day or fifth day, Alka finished her interviews with Marga. They sat in the dining hall after dinner. Jake and Waylon, who had reclaimed his given name, were nearby cleaning up.

"It seems, Marga, you've never wavered from this commitment. What do you think makes it work for you?" Alka asked her.

"*Never* may be too strong a word. I think about what may have been at times but it passes because every day I have new challenges and good people to work with. I'm still growing and so is this place. I was asked to speak at a conference on American Buddhism recently, so someone has noticed us here!" Marga laughed indicating how tiny her enterprise was compared to other movements. "What makes it work? Ultimately, the answer to that remains a mystery to me. I think I am not as bound by the tradition as the Roshi taught it, so I tweak things as I go. It is Buddhist tradition that guides me."

"How so?"

"For example, two years ago some of us—I mean my current assistant Felicia, Jake, Usagi and me—noticed that some people reacted poorly to strict meditation techniques. They were getting more anxious, losing sleep, and two even started having involuntary hallucinations. They started hearing voices of ancestors or demons—the old man called them kami spirits—and having spontaneous visions. Nothing chronic but disturbing nevertheless. We talked to a psychologist at the University of New Mexico who pointed us to the work of Doctor Herb Benson and someone else—Newberg was his name, I think."

"Andrew Newberg?"

"Yes."

"Some scientists have criticized Newberg's ideas," Alka added.

"I heard—I mean we heard from that guy at the university that there are too many forms of meditation to lump them into a simple brain function or two. People's brains are not all wired the same. Also, prospective residents come from differing backgrounds; they may have suffered trauma, and any number of factors that could change the value of any one type of meditation. So, we still do traditional Zen sitting but I try to monitor reactions through observation and interviews. We now offer walking meditation, work meditation, and any number of options. Sitting is an option, not a requirement. The goal remains the same as self-observation and emptying the mind for a period of time. People seem happier with the experience here as a result."

Marga stopped for a few seconds.

"Oh, yes, we also stopped that detachment from family rule for full-time folks. It made no sense. It caused more suffering. We learn as we go and I have a lot to learn. Cause and effect is what Buddha taught."

"Now I can understand why Jake thought I should meet you. You are already involved in what I am studying! This is great. But tell me, why is it that you continue here? What is your motive?"

"Hmm, I thought about that many times. In the beginning it was more of a selfish goal—I wanted peace of mind and a sense of connection to life. Escape from pain was on my mind. I found that peace here because of and despite the sensei's personality. Enough of the tradition passed through him to make it work for me. But now it might have something to do with service to others and that I choose to stay here day to day. We try to cultivate what some people may only want to touch or experience once in a while but they always know they can come here to find it again." Marga shrugged her shoulders to indicate that it was a poor answer but it was all she could come up with.

"Chop wood, carry water?" Alka offered.

"Chop wood, carry water!" Marga laughed at the use of this old Zen adage. "I never chopped real wood."

"I see you doing more than that here, though," Alka said. "I see you applying what some psychologists call *positive psychology* to your experience. I mean, you could have let this thing collapse when the old man died but you made changes that appear to have helped this place flourish."

"I learned from watching his mistakes," Marga said. "Until he died I had no power to change anything. He got very strict at the end, you know."

"Looks like fate had something to do with your success here."

"Yes, and it still does." Marga answered without elaborating but she clearly had thoughts about it.

"You don't have to answer this," Alka said apologetically, "but are you interested in marriage or having children."

Jake was washing dishes within hearing distance in the dining area when Alka asked the question. He stopped doing what he was doing—making noise while stacking pots and pans—to unobtrusively take in Marga's response. He often wondered how she seemed to handle the celibate life so well. He often wondered if her female instincts to mate with a man had completely waned. He listened with keen curiosity.

"Oh, yes I am interested in marriage. We have married couples come here now and then. It intrigues me how that factors into a Buddhist path of detachment. But I imagine you mean, will I ever get married?"

"Have you ruled it out?"

"No," Marga said. She appeared to blush at this admission. "There's a guy, a fellow who stayed here a few months ago for two weeks. He owns a small chain of bookstores and has plans to sell off much of his investment. He wants to retire young, so to speak. He intends to try living here for six months. We talked a lot while he was here. We saw a movie in Taos. And Usagi—I mean, Waylon—no, we did not have sex! But I like him."

Marga smiled quietly reserving further comment. She let this revelation sink in to her two quirky male friends. Usagi looked stunned. All he said was, "Ah, someone is very lucky."

Jake felt a peculiar delight as he returned to what he was doing, scrubbing more pots in the stainless steel sink. He imagined that Marga healed a deep wound. He felt a happy tear drop from his right eye into the soapy water below.

"Well," Alka remarked with a matter of fact tone, "thanks for that. You answered my question."

Next, Alka turned to a page in her notes where she wrote about Marga's EEG results from the day before. Alka traveled with a portable device. She fitted her subject's skulls with a thing that looked like a swimming cap full of holes. She plugged sensors into the holes and applied a gel-like substance to points of skull contact to augment the current. The nearly one hundred sensors could capture brain wave activity at 2000 times a second. During the exams Alka asked Marga to merely remain quiet for five minutes, then meditate for eight or nine and finally to respond to various instructions including to carry on normal conversation about anything at all to end it. She watched for results on her laptop screen. Alka videotaped the session as well.

"Although I need to correct for artifacts caused by blinking and other factors, preliminary indications of the EEGs are that your brain is quite normal!" Alka announced.

Marga was not exactly pleased with this pronouncement at first. "I'm not sure if that is a compliment or an indication of my failure! I was secretly hoping for something extraordinary. Of course, normal may be extraordinary," she said with her finger pointing up. "What's a normal Buddhist brain supposed to look like anyway?" Marga felt her head with both hands as she said this.

"I don't know," Alka answered while scanning her notes as if the question did not require an answer. "I'm merely collecting data for now. Back at the university I have access to the fMRI and SPECT or neuroimaging technology. What I'm doing here is limited. But if I find out, I'll text you right away!"

She did not tell Marga that her thesis was about *sanity* in extraordinary religious behavior. Alka's working idea was that all religious activity is based on belief in something irrational, but a healthy spiritual path is sustained by sane behavior despite the irrational devotion. A healthy brain should reflect and complement sane behavior. She wanted to find out what a sane, religiously preoccupied brain looks like and how it performs. "The technology is actually secondary to what we observe through direct experience with our subjects," she insisted.

Waylon went through the EEGs and interviews with Alka as well, but she had a few problems with him. Waylon could not resist joking around with Jake thus skewing the results.

"Did she find my God spot yet?" Waylon wondered.

"Yes, she found it. Look here. It's connected to your gluteus muscles."

"Did you just call God an asshole? Is that a sane thing to say, Alka?" Waylon asked sarcastically.

"Sorry. I was looking at the readout upside down," Jake obliged.

"You can go rake the garden now, Jake," Alka firmly suggested.

Jake, who was assisting her, did leave the room at Alka's insistence. After Jake removed himself, Alka said, "Waylon, there is no *God spot*, for your information. That's a myth."

"That explains why I could never find it here. The old man was right after all. No God—only Buddhamind." Waylon sighed to emphasize his ironic intent. It mattered not to him whether there was a God spot or not. That was the way he was. In his conversations with Jake, he revealed that almost nothing had changed in his spiritual philosophy after the ten years he spent at the old man's Center. He still felt the Apache blood in his veins and the Apache connection to an animating spirit and the creator God or *Ussen*. Waylon held his spirituality in private. His people no longer had a main medicine man or priest-shaman as they did in the old days. The old ways were eroding. Many smaller tribal groups were going through cultural pollution or cross fertilization depending on how one saw it. Clearly, the dominant Anglo culture continued to creep into native life and Waylon was a product of that change.

"Do you ever think of the guy who fathered you?" Jake once asked him.

"What's to think about? He's no more real to me than a dog I never had."

Waylon said without passion or inflection. His missing father was a flat reality with all the implications of an empty relationship. In contrast, Jake missed his father. Ironically, the old man filled a psychic father hole in both their lives despite the contrast. The old man's charisma allowed for any number of projections.

"Maybe we were asking too much of the old man. He was ill-equipped to act as a father to us or anyone."

"I wonder what his father was like. Maybe he was a drunk too. Maybe he beat him. Maybe the old man *went forth* to renew himself in America just as we did."

"If he did, his limitations caught up with him."

"His caught up with us too, homes."

During their reunion at the Center, Jake and Waylon hiked up onto a high rise behind the buildings. They found a familiar rock ledge where many visitors and residents sat for private meditation throughout the years. The setting was ideal for that sort of thing. The grey granite ledge jutted out slightly or just enough for one sitting there to feel as if the rock hovered over the landscape. The evening sun shone brightly through a cloudless sky. As the men sat casually, an attentive jackrabbit appeared to them twenty yards below. Its large ears flicked and turned to note signals in the environment. The two men talking did not seem to be a problem. The rabbit resumed munching on the grasses.

"Man, in some ways I feel I never left this place, yet I am light years away. This view, this ledge, and that jack rabbit—it's all the same," Jake remarked. "Well, maybe it's a different rabbit, Rabbit."

Waylon grinned. No one called him Rabbit or Usagi since Jake left. "Those rabbits are all alike, homes."

"What kind of Indian are you? Rabbits don't all look alike."

"They all taste the same."

The rabbit scooted away.

"Now look what you've done. He was eating there peacefully, until you said that."

"I must be getting hungry. I flashed on rabbit stew when I saw it. Grandma sure makes great stews, you know. So, what's different with you besides the lovely lady you brought here to shrink what's in our heads?"

"Hey, don't get the wrong idea. I like her, but we're not an item," Jake protested. Before Waylon could make another comment Jake turned the conversation. "I was locked in a mental hospital for a few days last year right after I left here. That's where I met her."

"That's crazy, homes. For real?"

"For real, for real, *homes*. When did you start using *homes*, anyway?

"Some young dudes I work with still use it—lingua franca, man. When in Rome, you know—don't change the topic."

"I had a sequence of wild events after getting stoned back East. I spent time in a loony bin until they determined I was okay."

"Okay," Waylon said carefully. He leaned back with his hands set behind to brace himself. "What happened? I want to hear this."

Jake reiterated details of the outdoor party at Jim's, meeting Gigi, playing baseball, and how he ended up in the hospitals.

"And here's what I want to run by you. I have not told anyone about this weird vision, not even Marga, if that's what it was."

After taking a deep breath, Jake described his escape into the tunnels and the meeting with Master G. The narration took him nearly ten minutes. In conclusion he said, "That was almost ten months ago. I thought about it a few times but then let it go after writing it down. Nothing remotely like it happened since. What do you make of it?'

"That's esoteric stuff, Jake." Whenever Waylon addressed his friend by name, it meant he was mostly serious. Waylon continued with a story of his own. "Years ago when I was around fourteen my uncle, the one I told you about, the religious one, invited a friend of his over, someone he met at a conference. The friend, who was kind of an old Indian hippie, called himself John Redman but I think he had a different name when he was younger. Redman wrote a book about his spiritual experiences—I forget the title. It was something like *The Way of Sacred Pipe*. They were talking about vision quests at our kitchen table and wanted me and my friend Jay to listen in.

"Before Redman became a Christian like my uncle, he was into the Red Power thing in the late sixties. He said he felt like a fake because he had no idea what it meant to be Indian at age twenty. He was a quarter Lakota and something else— anyway, half white. He looked more like a Frenchman with his blue eyes but his hair was long and black. Anyway, he went to his Lakota grandmother on the reservation to ask her about how one goes about finding himself as an Indian. She told him about the vision quest of her ancestors. He decided to try it out. He fasted and he hiked into a sacred area in the foothills of the Badlands. He found a flat area below a cliff. He drew a circle around himself and stayed there for three days with only a blanket and some water. He tried to stay awake. He said by the second night he was having visions. He saw *Buffalo Cow Woman*, he had visits from real animals that seemed to talk, he felt that he left his body at one stage and traveled to strange lands. He said real feathers fell all around him from above.

"Redman went on and on telling us about all these miraculous events. He said after three days he went back to his grandmother's house to tell her what happened. He said she listened quietly while washing dishes as he proudly recited all the exciting things that happened. After he was done, he said she turned around, and then looked at him for a few seconds. She looked at him straight in the eyes. She told him, 'A man who has many visions has a weak spirit.' Redman said he was completely deflated. He said the lesson was that after a vision quest a man should be focused on who he is and what his mission in life is. Crazy people have many visions."

"But I was not on a vision quest. I was in a nuthouse and coming off of a drug high," Jake said.

"You've been on a quest for ten years, homes. Think about it. Something deep inside you spit that out. You better pay attention. What did Alka think about it?"

"I have not told her. Like I said, you're the first person I said anything to about this."

"You were serious then. You haven't been doing her." Waylon said this with genuine surprise.

Jake ignored the comment. "So you think the Master G connection means something?"

"No, I think the way it ended with you willing to die to play ball with your father meant something. Your father was real to you. Reconnection is real. Don't over analyze this. Let it be. It is what it is."

Waylon revisited his surprise that Alka was not Jake's girl friend. "That's some hot woman. And she's smart too! Please don't take this wrong, bro, but you're pathetic. You mean you haven't asked her out yet?"

"No. It's not like that. I'm only helping her reflect on her research now and then. We exchange emails mostly. Hell, look where I was when we met—it's embarrassing."

Jake was not very convincing. Waylon looked at him as if to say, tell me more. Jake said, "Look, man, I'm still living with my folks with little extra money to speak of. I'm in no position to get serious about pursuing anyone, let alone her."

"Who said anything about you *getting* serious?" Waylon countered. I've been talking to her the past few days. I think she already has you in her crosshairs. From what I can see, you're a dead man!"

"I'm not sure if I can believe you, but I hope you're right."

Waylon stood up, dusted off his jeans and he waited for Jake to do likewise. He grabbed his friend by the shoulders. "Look at me, Jake. You—you—don't have to do anything more for her. You are good enough."

"Thanks, Rabbit. I needed that."

The train arrived on Track Seven a few minutes late. Jake felt anxious. He thought about his panic attacks. He thought that he had not had any since his stint in Psych Hall. "Not now, not now," he quietly exclaimed. He took a deep breath and exhaled. He subtly shuffled from one leg to the other as he stood in one place. A crowd of passengers came up the stairs from Track Seven. He spotted Alka among them. Her hair was down, she wore a hip-length brown leather jacket, a white button-down blouse and tight jeans. Plain brown Converse sneakers completed the look. She looked plainly radiant to Jake. After she located Jake, she removed her glasses. All apprehension poured out of Jake that instant. The simple removal of her glasses signaled an open trust between them that had been building all year. He was cured for the moment of whatever excuses of inadequacy that he had. When she walked up to him he gave her a warm hug for the first time ever. Their meetings up until this one were friendly but with a professional comportment.

Alka hugged him back as they stood together under the great bronze *Angel of Resurrection*. The forty foot art deco angel holds a nearly naked, dead, railroad worker. It is a memorial for all the railroad workers that died in the World War II effort. The corpse dangles from the stern angel's arms. If either Alka or Jake noted any symbolism at the statue, they said nothing about it. To them it was merely a landmark where they could meet. They held hands as they talked happily on their way to his parked vehicle. Jake felt even with her for the first time. They had the day to hang out with no particular plans.

"So, doctor, how's the job going so far?"

"Good. I can't tell you much yet. I found out we have a major government contract."

"You mean if you tell me you will have to kill me?"

"No, but the man in the plain blue suit behind us will."

"I thought you weren't dating anyone."

"He comes free. We have nothing more than a professional relationship."

"Still, you're attached. Maybe we should call this off. You're scaring me."

Alka did not like where the joke was leading but she rebounded. "If you shoot him first, we'll have to hide forever," she suggested as she nudged his shoulder with hers. Jake turned around, faced the imaginary man in blue with a pointed finger and shot, "Bang, bang! There. Let's go." He grabbed her hand and led her at a slow jog to the parking garage. As they approached the vehicle Jake said, "But really, I want to hear about your work. I want to know how the government is going to tamper with our brains."

They settled into his job-scarred white Jeep and drove off. Jake pulled onto the Market Street Bridge over the Schuylkill to head into the city. Alka talked about her little corner of the lab and some of her projects.

"Our company has some support from private foundations, so it's not just government, thank you. There are also grants from several university departments interested in brain function and belief. Some of the money comes from drug companies but that's no surprise. I'm working on an aspect of the effects of psychotropic hallucinogens on a specific native healing cult in Central America. My supervisor is also looking into the devotion to the Lady of Guadalupe. I had no idea how extensive it was! There are so many implications beyond the religious. She uncovered interesting political and criminal affiliations within the devotional milieu, among the drug cartels, for example. Many Latino and Indian prisoners have Guadalupe tattoos. Her team collected loads of data. I do not qualify to do field work yet but I hope that happens soon."

Alka knew that she would be going to Central America for an extended time. Deep inside, she fancied that Jake might go with her.

Jake responded with a flippant interest in her venture as he negotiated through the stop and go traffic.

"I knew it! There *is* an Indiana Jones side to you. You have quite a future ahead of you," he said indicating he might not be in that future.

Part of him felt anxious about a future he hoped he might share with this disarming woman. At first he thought he might have to move to Washington. Now, Mexico? What about his plan to finish school? What about his inadequate academic status?

The sun suddenly broke through a cloud flooding their faces with bright light. Alka sensed his discomfort. She was silent as she fumbled with her purse to get her sunglasses. Jake noticed the reason for her silence. He spoke spontaneously from his heart.

"If I'm going to keep up with you," he blurted out as he squinted at a traffic light, "you'll have to tell me what to read. I find it all fascinating to a point. I finished the last book you sent, the one called *Brainwashing*."

"You mean the one by Dr. Taylor. Her research in brain science and her earlier papers helped inspire me to go for this field. I heard her speak in Edinburgh around three years ago. Did you like the book?"

"Yes. A lot there for me to chew on. I liked what she said about skeptics who often reduce religious belief to a psychosis. She said it takes as much use of reason to apply religious ideas to society as it does to apply science. It's in the application that we can tell if something is healthy or not. From her view the healthy brain function reflects the healthy behavior. Did I get that right?" He chuckled.

"I'm impressed. I was not sure how you might react."

Jake held his response until he negotiated a turn onto 16th Street. "Anyway, it's a good book. I might read it again. Made me stop and think about what I've been through."

"So, where, what are we doing? Are you hungry?" Alka asked.

"No not yet. And you?"

"I can wait."

"Let's walk around Center City then—maybe go to the museum area. I want to take care of something," he said. "We could walk down the Parkway and find a café later."

She said, "Whatever." She was familiar with the Parkway and its attractions.

He found an empty space to park the Jeep on Callowhill Street not far from the Rodin Museum. They walked in that direction.

"Well, which is it? Do you want to see the *Rocky* or *The Thinker*?" Jake taunted her in jest. "Yo, Alka. Wanna see my pet turtle now?"

Alka punched him in the side recognizing full well he was referring to the Rocky Balboa statue at the Philadelphia Museum up the way. Jake danced away from her with his fists ready for boxing.

"Rodin," she commanded in a haughty French inflection.

"Rodin it is, then," he said as he took her hand.

They walked a few blocks to the small but elegant gray stone building that held the best of Rodin. They stayed outside, walking past the large bronze *Thinker* to the bronze *Gates of Hell* mounted on the wall.

"I used to identify with that guy up there," Jake said indicating the contemplative, seated bronze nude with its elbow on a knee propping up its head above the gates, "but I can't now."

"So what's changed? You mean you no longer *think* about the ultimate meaning of life?"

"Not like that. I no longer bend myself into a pretzel over it. I have no desire or need to meditate formally any more. I mean, look at him. He looks tense, awkward, and taunted by the three fates above his head."

Alka paused a few seconds as she considered the statue. Indeed, Rodin's naked man looked more pained than contemplative. He was deep in thought as the uncertain poet, the unfulfilled philosopher, the agonized artist or the hero before battle. He contemplated the last judgment of souls in psychological ferment

"No happy Buddha there! I wonder what his brain looks like?" she said half alluding to her work and half countering Jake's darker reaction.

Meanwhile Jake extended his hands as if framing a picture.

"I think Rodin gave us an image of his mind—the sculpture is a brain scan," Jake said jokingly.

"Hmm," Alka replied with some surprise at his insight. Then she asked, "Was Buddha ever happy? Somehow the images of a happy Buddha, Jesus or Socrates do not compute with me."

Jake did not respond. He did not want to linger over his past in front of the *Gates of Hell*.

"Can we walk?" he indicated.

Jake's attention had wandered more to watching her talk and not listening to what she said. He turned her shoulders toward the City Hall. They passed flags of the nations hanging like banners from poles that lined the boulevard. A slight chill fell when gusts of wind whipped around them. Leaves blew by their feet. But when the wind settled the sun warmed them again. As they approached Logan Circle Jake said he wanted to tell her something that could take some time. They found a bench.

"There are some things I haven't told you about happened to me at Psych Hall and what led up to it. Since we went to New Mexico, I put some of the pieces together. I want to be honest with you."

"Jake, I have a confession to make…"

He stopped her.

"No, let me finish."

Jake was afraid she would say something that would stop him from telling about the Master G encounter. He gave her more detail than he had to Dr. Kelly about the hash brownie incident, his violent reaction to mental health commitment, and why he slipped into the tunnels. He no longer felt that Alka was his clinician. He was talking to her as a friend and perhaps more. He was burning inside to know her better. The fire he felt was a passion to mate with this woman. He wanted it to be right as it could be. If he was some kind of nut, she should know now. He relayed in vivid detail every part of the encounter with Master G in his memory. He conveyed the struggle with ideas and with choking and facing a kind of death to hold the vision of his father Ziggy as a baseball pitcher. He did the best he could to convey the cosmic character of layers of the vision and the transcendent grace he felt. He spoke of the lightning that illuminated the utility room at L Hall revealing it as it actually was to the normal senses. He spoke about the mongoloid girl who brought him such profound peace in an instant before everything faded into black.

"She did not say *stay* referring to *stay at Psych Hall* as I wanted Kelly and you to believe. She said, I think, in her garbled way, *I am safe*. Then I blacked out. And just as I blacked out she ran by me surrounding me with a powerful fragrance of roses. When I came to, the rose scent lingered for some time after Ben, the ambulance guy startled me."

Jake told her he had no more panic attacks after that, that he slept well, and that every day, except when he had a minor cold, was good health wise for the past year.

He felt connected to life and the environment.

"It's not as if I'm without flaws or some stress but something is very different at my core. I feel I recovered some lost years. I'm more secure than I was a year ago."

Alka looked at him with a quiet tenderness. She was forming a response.

Her pause caused Jake to say, "Do you want to put those electrodes on my head now? Or do you think I need more medication?"

She ignored the implication that he thought she thought he might be crazy.

"*I am safe.* How did you interpret that?" she asked.

Jake did not hesitate.

"*I am saved.* She made it home or to heaven without Zen, without theology, and without a guru. Her handicap would preclude her from a sophisticated grasp of any religion. A sacrifice saved her. Someone else had to bring her home as she patiently waited believing it would happen. She had already done all she could. She was a good kid."

"So, we cannot save ourselves? Is that the lesson?"

"Nope. Not without a sacrifice by someone else. We are not stranded in this universe alone."

"But you saved her then. Are you saying you stood in the place of Christ, the savior?"

"In a way but I did not do it alone. My father in heaven trusted me to hit his best pitch. I had faith that he prepared me well enough to pull it off."

"So there was a chance that you could have failed."

"Yes. And I would not be alive now."

"Okay. I hope you mean that metaphorically," she said with some alarm.

"I can't answer that. All I know is that I felt renewed."

Jake was curiously pleased that Alka actually paid attention to that detail of his story.

"She, the girl, affirmed I would be okay just before I passed out. Was she a Pennhallow ghost, a figment of a collective unconscious archetype, or a hopeful hallucination caused by brain dysfunction—how would I know? I do know that this specific girl appeared to me at a crucial moment and that she sent me a message that brought me to utter peace, like falling asleep in a bed of warm rose petals. I call her an angel."

"Your angel."

"Okay. My angel! We have no objective way to prove she's independent of me—at least not yet! That's going to be your job as scientist to figure it out."

Jake grinned at Alka.

"I can't see that happening any time soon," Alka said, "so what till then? I mean, how do you make sense of what offers no proof of existence?"

"It exists now in my memory, my imagination and in my stories," said Jake.

"As myth," Alka countered.

"Ghost story, myth, revelation—I guess it depends on how serious it appears to be."

"It cannot be both myth and reality, can it?" Alka offered.

"Well, we will either have to live in the great divide or take a side. Pure science either denies or compliments pure mysticism. Since both sides slide away into infinity we are condemned to live and die somewhere in the great dichotomy with our little certainties—or go insane."

"Does sanity require certainty then?" she said to push him to go on. He was on a roll.

"Sanity requires sane behavior at least, no? What goes on inside one's head may not be as sane as one behaves. But feeling certain of something reduces anxiety. My angel is my little certainty. She's totally retarded and a woefully unscientific proposition as far as evidence. But I admit that, so I am being rational. Yet in my vision if that is all that it was, she lives and God saves her. I also learned from her that God does not save only individuals in elite groups with refined ideologies. If God saves, God saves persons one by one according to individual potential and value."

Alka stopped him with a touch of her finger on his lips. "You talk of God as if God is a fact or a reality for you. How does that figure in your life now?"

Jake scratched his head. "I said God, didn't I?"

366

"Yes, why God?" Alka asked. "Why not the universe or the non-dual Brahman or Buddha's emptiness? Can't we have existence or good without God?"

"No. Without God, nothing exists, not even God. Call it a tautology or a conundrum or whatever. I have to warn you, I did a lot of contemplating with the bricks and stones and mortar this past year." Jake stopped to look at the pigeon droppings on the concrete pavement under his feet.

"Go on. I'm listening," she said.

"Okay, God. That word has exploded in meaning for me to the point that I am almost afraid to say it. Aristotle made his Prime Mover argument. The Buddha would not speculate about such weighty metaphysics and the Pali Canon relates only that he said he was neither God nor man but was enlightened. The ancient Jews dared not say the name but wrote it as the Tetragrammaton or YHWH. Even Jesus said *Hallowed be thy name* to his father in heaven. But, I have some idea of what that means."

Jake paused for a few seconds again.

"The reality of God terrifies me yet brings me peace, if that makes any sense. A simple, flawed person, a retarded one saying *I am safe* brought that home to me. We may not know God directly but God knows us intimately. When that happy little girl ran by me, the whole universe suddenly felt sane to me and I could let go in peace. God saves what is good. I really thought I was going to die playing cosmic baseball!"

Jake sighed before continuing his introspective narrative. It was hard work trying not to sound stupid.

"The little girl marked my moment of finding sanity—of healing," he reiterated. "She's a sign, a messenger, not a cause. She was the *amen* to my encounter with Master G."

After those words, a swirl of leaves flew around the park bench where they sat.

"See!" Jake tilted his head and winked at Alka. "Even the leaves dance to my insights!"

"Yes, I see the leaves whirling," she said, not impressed with the coincidence.

"Can I tell you my confession now?"

Jake leaned back on the bench. He turned to her and said, "I want to hear anything and everything you have to say, but I have one more question. That vision I had seemed to take a lot longer than the time I entered that room until the staff found me. I mean, it could not have been more than ten minutes."

"It may have taken mere seconds," Alka surmised. "Reconstructing the narrative that dream activity in the brain stimulates takes a lot longer than the dream. Think of seeing a picture of a social event and then trying to describe it."

"Is that what people mean when they see their entire lives pass by at the moment of a near death event?"

"Neurologically, it is in the same territory, I think. I'm still learning." Alka said.

Jake sighed again before he asked, "Without neurons, what is there?" He had nothing more. He wanted to hear Alka talk. With a slight lift of his eyebrows, he signaled her to let it out.

"Okay," Alka began. "When we were in New Mexico and later flew back in separate planes out of Albuquerque, I landed in Washington, missing you very much. I have been attracted to you since we met, but this feeling was very different for me. Marga helped me see you in ways I could not have without her confidence. She showed me all the work you did around the grounds. I saw that the Center remains a big part of you and will remain with you for life in some way. I want to say that, that lady truly cares for your well-being. She talked about the good times, but she also mentioned the abuse you guys suffered under the teacher. She talked about the severe whippings when Roshi was drunk. She said you have several scars on your back."

Jake smiled uneasily as she spoke. Someday he would have to explain those scars to her if Alka ever saw his back. Now she knew the story from someone else who could verify how real it all was. Marga actually took a load off his mind by betraying a confidence to this lovely woman sitting with him. He did not want to have to risk seeming like a whining man who sought sympathy. He wanted no sappy response from Alka. He wanted understanding and acceptance.

"Oh yeah, the scars. I don't see them so I rarely think about what my back looks like. They're not that bad—just a few thin streaks. But you're right. I can't run from my past even if I wanted to. The old man marked me for life, for sure, in more ways than one, but he taught us some good things—too bad for us and him that his behavior fell of the rails. It took me a while to jump off his bogus, Buddha-train ride."

"You had no way of knowing it was bogus, at least not at first. And it seems much healthier there now that Marga took over."

"If I only knew—I really respect Marga, but I don't see her improved Zen center going anywhere either for me. To me it is just one more intentional community for hopeful rebels in society. For me, the experiment is over. The data remains for analysis and edification."

"The data remains—hmmm. You've overcome a lot. The old man came at you like a parent or father figure. You let him plug a hole in your life. By breaking away from a fake father, I believe you reconnected with your real father, Jake." Alka paused, wishing to herself that she had not said what she just said. "Sorry if that sounded like I'm playing therapist again."

Jake ignored her apology. "Ziggy is back in my life. I had no idea how much I missed him or having him for a father even if he was a wounded man. We all need a father and a mother, don't you think?"

Alka did not answer. She only nodded silently.

"I was wondering," Jake continued, "do you think what happened to me at Psych Hall is explained by science? I mean, how can we be more than a brain function?"

Alka broke out in laughter. "Forgive me. I'm not laughing at you." She collected herself and cleared her throat as she noticed Jake glaring at her.

"We have these conversations at the lab—about consciousness, I mean. What is it really? In your case, if I may speculate, you experienced a powerful convergence of post-cult anxiety brought on by a nearly fatal accident. Then you had an unusual drug experience and all within a week. I looked up some things on yoga and kundalini. There are a host of anecdotes from both practicing and former meditators about strange somatic and mental reactions to what should be a relaxation and clarity of awareness technique. Panic disorder was one talked about by a few people. And then you had a fever from an infection and that can cause delirium. Your RBC or red blood cells were on the low side, causing slight anemia perhaps brought on by years of vegetarian diet. You should have been taking B-12 at least. Anyway, we can't explain why we have conscious self-awareness any more than we can describe what forms of life exist on other planets. Mystics may be better equipped than scientists to clue us in."

"So mystics are still relevant," he proclaimed. Then, to shift the topic from speculation about his psychotic experience, Jake lifted his hands and looked at the palms. "These two guys really helped bring my brain back to reality last year."

"What?" Alka said surprised by his tangential response. She stopped herself from asking for clarification.

As if reading her mind, he said, "Yep, it was quite a year." Jake slapped his thighs to indicate he was not saying any more about that. "I'm done; your turn to talk."

"Okay, my turn." Alka sat up straight and took a deep breath, as if she were about to recite a poem in class. Jake could not help noting her breasts lift under her jacket in the process. He clenched his teeth in an effort not to demean her story with thoughts about sex. She did not notice his expression. She was looking straight ahead. He focused on her face and concentrated.

"Let's see. We seem to be on about dads. I'm still trying to resolve my father issues. I mentioned his situation to you last year. He's still alive, of course, and basically a good man. Continues to work, has an occasional drink and, from what I can tell, remains faithful to mom. Like your dad, he's Polish but second generation American. His father and mother were political Progressives with leanings toward socialism in the 1930s. They were nominal Catholics who made my father go through Catholic grade school but that ended religion for him. He was baptized and confirmed and got his first communion. My mom has a similar background. She's half Polish."

"What's the other half?"

"Welsh. Grandpapa was a coal miner in Pennsylvania. He died of black lung when mom was fifteen. Anyway, they had me baptized in the Church for some reason but never followed up. So I was raised in a basically secular household. But dad was kind of a seeker, like you—I hope you don't mind the comparison. When I was a teenager, dad got into a Sufi stage studying the work of Pir Vilayat Khan. Have you heard of him?"

"I think there is a following in Albuquerque, but that's all I know."

"Okay, good. It's not important what group. But, he went overboard for a few years. Mom thought he was going to leave us—they argued a lot, so they separated for a year. That year marked me for life. After he tried living with his group for a month he apparently had second thoughts. Dad came back to us, took some time to reconcile with mom, and moved back in. He's one of those men who resigned himself to the task of being a husband and a father, yet I can tell he's not especially happy. When I first met you and read your case notes, I thought you were a connection to my father's world. But something happened to you that did not to him. He's unresolved. His religious life is anticlimactic. I'd say he is in a state of spiritual anomie. He says he's agnostic now. I feel you encountered something unique to you at Psych Hall yet fulfilling—something that he may have wanted and maybe still wants."

"Let me get this straight. Let *me* play shrink for a second."

Jake stroked his beardless chin with his left hand.

"You found your father's salvation in me. Hmmm, are you trying to save him as you once tried to save me? You know, I looked up the meaning of Alka. It comes from the Greek and means *defending men.*"

"It means what? Hey, I wasn't trying to save you!" Alka was matter of fact. "I was doing my job. I was treating you. But that's an interesting coincidence regarding my name. I never knew what it meant."

"Treat, save, salve, salvation, heal, forgive—whatever. Did you ever forgive him for leaving you?"

Jake felt like hugging her but he sat still with hands cupped over his knees.

Alka looked at him. "I never thought of it that way, but yes, I have come closer to letting it go since I met you—and especially after meeting your friends at the Center. I realize now that what he tried to do is not so easy. Wrong teacher, bad timing, and torn loyalties kept him from fulfillment. Maybe he gave up something for us when he came back. He gave up the search. Someday I want to talk to him to see how he still feels about it."

"A man in a divided house…cannot serve two masters. Let thine eye be single. Keep your eye on the ball, son!" Jake recalled his own separate reality struggles at Psych Hall and at the Center. "That's a big one. But I think he feels like he did the right thing. Dharma fulfilled is karma negated."

"What? Is that an aphorism of some kind?" Alka was curious about where he got that phrase from.

"It's the essence of the Bhagavad-Gita, as I recall," Jake answered. "I'd like to meet your dad someday, if you wish, and your mom."

Alka was pleased with his interest. She wanted him to meet them. She wondered about his parents. "And, are we still going to meet Monica and Neal?"

"Yes, they'll be home this evening. We're invited for dinner. I told Monica I will be bringing a guest. I described you to her. She's kind of…well, kind of anxious to meet you." Jake paused a moment before he said, "She's been worried. I haven't been dating anyone. She's afraid I'm going to go monk again."

"Are we on a date?" Alka laughed at how odd things felt just then between them. She knew that he knew that she was very interested in him. And she knew that he was hesitant to overestimate her interest.

"If it ain't, it'll do till the date comes along."

"That's from *No County for Old Men*, isn't it?"

They discussed the McCarthy book in their emails. She knew Jake was parodying an exchange in the story when a lawman and his assistant came upon the bodies of several men and drug dealers shot to death in the desert:

It's a mess, ain't it, sheriff.
If it ain't, it'll do till the mess gets here.

"You read it then, finally?" Jake wondered.

"No. I finally saw the movie with a colleague."

"A colleague?"

"Yea, with Nat."

Jake's heart rate rose slightly.

"Who is Nat?" He felt queasy.

"Doctor Natalia Kulik. She's an anthropologist. No, we're not dating if that's what you were worried about."

Alka enjoyed the tweak she gave him and she felt flattered by his anxious reaction. She thought to change the subject back to Jake's family.

"You said that Monica is a devout Catholic and Neal is agnostic. It seems they've worked it out okay. How about you? Are you a Catholic at all now?"

"If you mean going to church like Monica, no. Do I believe everything Catholics recite in the Creed? No. I did go to church with mom a few times since moving back here, you know, Christmas and Easter and maybe one other time. I'm not sure about the Church and if I fit anymore. I guess I could be a Catholic because I am, if that makes any sense. I've been branded since birth."

He continued after a pause. "Out of curiosity, before I left New Mexico, I approached a priest about confession, at that monastery I told you about. What he said made sense to me. The Church is lot more sophisticated than I thought. I almost confessed right there but he understood that I was not ready. He gave me a blessing anyway. And you, could you be a Catholic? You were branded as well."

"It would be a stretch. There are all kinds of Catholics! If you're asking about right now, then no."

"It was only a question. You said you were baptized in the Church too."

Then Jake asked a question that he was almost afraid to ask. "Have you been dating anyone lately?"

"Yes, but it has been more like a marriage."

Alka held back a smile when Jake raised his eyebrows.

"I've been married to my dissertation," she said.

Jake relaxed.

Alka noted his relief.

"I broke up with a guy nearly two years ago. And I'd rather not talk about it now. It's over. And you?"

"No. Not since Gigi! Since that outing, dating scares the hell out of me!"

Jake meant that as an exaggeration and Alka took it that way. He smiled exposing his crooked tooth. "I guess I'm really kind of a nerd, huh?"

"No less than I am," she said. Then Alka thought, "What a dumb thing to say."

A brown-speckled, city pigeon landed in front of their bench. It pecked at debris on the ground near their feet. Another pigeon, a common gray with black and white markings, joined in. The second pigeon fluffed its feathers and strutted around the first one as the first one continued pecking while moving to avoid the second one. When the birds arrived Alka stopped talking. She sat quietly with Jake as they let their thoughts settle. Both of them watched the bird ballet. Alka spoke up first. "Do you recall that line from a Woody Allen film: *I think people should mate for life like pigeons or Catholics?*"

"No. Which film was it?" Jake turned to look at Alka.

"*Manhattan.*"

Jake watched her as she kept her eyes on the pigeons. He tapped her on the shoulder.

"Hey, why did you say that?"

Alka looked at Jake quizzically.

"It just popped into my head." She paused a second. "Oh, I didn't mean, I mean, I meant it as a funny comment."

Jake laughed at her. "Come on. Let's walk some more."

She took his outstretched hand. She noted again how his hand felt rugged from working with stone. He noticed that she held his hand firmly.

Jake had a good run with work. Some jobs ran sixty to seventy hours a week. He returned the thousand dollars to Marga despite her protest. He made monthly payments to the hospitals. He arranged to pay a modest rent to Monica despite *her* protests. He saved a few thousand dollars, the most money he ever had at one time. At that moment it seemed like a million dollars. He invested in a vehicle that a co-worker sold to him at low cost. Harry helped him to get it back in good running shape. It was enough to know that he was making a go of it. He realized that his community at home was far more important than what he found out West.

"Your hands are rough. You worked hard this year, haven't you?"

"So did you."

"I mean physical work—it's different."

"Thousand of stones and bricks, one by bloody one—yeah, you can say that. Every stone was different though." Jake paused. "I mean, it never felt like a routine or boring."

"Why that? I mean, you could have done any number of things. Mechanic with your brother, sales, or even trained for something while working."

"Something about selecting and setting stone always brought me peace. It's the one good thing I found in New Mexico and I did not learn it from a guru. It's a connection to the earth—a practical penance. I needed to stay focused on something that I understood and that paid off the bills. I also wanted to be outside. I found more insight working in all kinds of weather, in sweating, freezing and hurting than sitting at a sesshin—than getting smacked with a stick—or swallowing some drug. An office cubicle, or what I imagine one to be, might have driven me over the edge. Then I might have needed that prescription for Xanax that Kelly gave me! I had a lot of sorting out to do."

Jake sighed. He glanced over at Alka who remained attentive.

"You, know, I understand why masons love their work as long as they can do it. They have to love it or it becomes torture. And I think I resolved something by doing the right thing."

"What was that?"

"The Buddhists call it right action. Christians say to get right with God. Something righted itself in the process. It may have started with the vision but it took time to set in, to become a part of me. I see now that Marga was right. Those panic attacks and all that happened soon after I left the place. I wasn't right."

"I think I know what you mean. So, do you think you will remain a stone mason?"

"Not really. I mean, I could. I have two part time employees now. In fact, they're running a job, so I'm making money right now. I have become a capitalist! I can even see how to make it grow as a business. I'm sure I could make it work if I took out a loan to buy equipment instead of renting stuff. But the work itself made me refocus my goals. So did you."

"Pourquoi moi, s'il vous plaît?" Alka spoke French with an American accent.

"Oui, you!" was all the French Jake could muster at the moment. "Not only have you been an inspiration to me to pursue an academic career but the stone work revealed something that I want to study more. Maybe my general science morphed into archeology. I want to trace why stone still has such a powerful effect on the human psych. In a way, we carry the Stone Age physically and culturally and we do not want to leave it behind. It dawned on me one morning when I was sizing rock for a stone wall at a new home. I watched one of the children playing a game outside on her laptop. She sat at a table by the family pool. The patio table top was a large slab of slate set on a solid rock base. Why are we still using rocks for our homes after hundreds of thousands of years of evolution? Why do we pray at the stone wall of an ancient temple? And why is Peter the rock of the Church?"

"Whoa. That was quite a jump to Peter, Jake! But I get your point, I think." Alka scrunched her face looking like she took a bite out of something sour. "And, what was your point?"

"The point? It's probably nothing more complex than having a specific career. Like you, for example, you have your dissertation about how the brain works. Forget religion. No matter what you investigate it will all filter through examining the brain and nervous system somehow. The brain is your rock. I'm being more literal. Rocks are my rock."

"Can I call you Rocky, then?"

"Huh? Oh."

Jake laughed out loud. He felt good. Even her dumb jokes were delightful to his ear. He stretched his arms out and cupped his hands together behind his head. He looked up into the sky. A cloud heavy with gray tones drifted overhead. As he stared into space he thought out loud, "Keep your eye on the ball, son."

Alka leaned back, stared up at the sky with Jake, and asked casually, "What is *the ball*?"

"Huh?" Jake snapped out of his trance.

"You're revisiting your vision. That ball means something."

"Okay, Mizz Freud. You really want me to answer that?" Jake turned his gaze to the last pigeon by his feet. The others had flown off toward a large city fountain.

"Yeah. Go for it."

Jake did his best imitation of a word association drill. "The ball is...round, smudged, spinning, coming at me dangerously fast, a challenge, a goal...confidence, fun, simplicity, the game is on, the ball is in play..."

Jake stopped suddenly as if he were struck by something.

Alka waited for Jake to go on.

Jake sat up straight. In measured words he said, "The...ball...is...in...play. That's it! The old man never let us play ball. He never really pitched anything across the plate. There was no way we could prove how good a pitcher he was if he would not play fair. The koans kept us off base. No one ever whacked *him* with the stick. He did not play *with* us. He was not one of us. He remained in another world, a world we imagined he came from, a world apart."

"That's good, Jake! I mean, that *is* good," Alka said trying to correct her enthusiasm. She refrained from directing Jake to say anything more. She regretted that she reintroduced her role as a therapist into the relationship. He sensed that she did but he continued anyway. A cork had popped in his brain. He wanted to air out the contents.

"Yes, it is good," he reiterated, "because I thought it was about my connection with my father, which it was. But there's more. Master G was like that, like the old man, but in an opposite way. He was also in a world apart yet he was from an inner world, one that was disconnected from the world of common sense. The ball in play means just that. There are common rules to this game, in any game. I didn't know the rules and he, the old man, was making up his own as he went. The Master G in my vision was trying to get me to make up all the rules as if it was up to me alone. You know, those days at the Center were like playing for a team with a coach but we were not part of a league—a wider field of competition—a wider frame of reference."

Jake stopped for a few seconds to reconsider the ball.

"I see Ziggy, my father in heaven, playing baseball the best way possible and asking me to do the same. He threw a mean slider or cutter at me. I had to be at my best to hit it. Buddhism has rules and a way to play well. The problem for me was to find the best game in town and play well. In my pride, my trust in my instincts, I settled for less."

Jake bit his lower lip while nodding his head. "We played a game of softball at Jim's but by Jim's rules and…"

Alka was puzzled so she interrupted. "And who is Jim?"

"Jim? Oh yea, that's where I was before the incident with Gigi that sent me to the hospital. At Jim's outdoor gathering. They have a tradition of playing softball there but according to Jim's rules—to make it fair or fairer for everyone. It's basically a slow pitch, three-inning game and everyone gets to bat three times. Anyway, it is what it is. Nobody has to play that way forever. It's like local theater—it's free, fun, and when play is over the game disappears until the next year. The old man set up a game under his rules too but he let on that it was the best game, the best way to play the game, everyday for life. I more or less bought into that—call it naïve pride. I was among the elite at the beginning of a great movement. By staying so long I basically gave him permission to manipulate me with his fucked up rules."

"So it wasn't Hamlet by the Royal Shakespeare Company?" Alka kidded.

"It was the old man's dumbed-down Buddhism. We were refining our roles endlessly for him instead of performing for the critical crowd. There was no way to get off his stupid stage—at least, no way to leave without feeling like a failure in his eyes. He got those of us who stayed to feel indebted to him—and we were—but for what? A lousy game of Zen."

Jake stopped to scratch his head with both hands in a gesture of frustration.

"What was I thinking? What was I doing? Aargh!"

"Easy, slugger, you're done with that and it's a new stage now."

Jake took a breath and exhaled with a long slow blow.

"Sorry—got carried away a bit there…and what do you mean by a *new stage*?"

"Could be a new stage in your life or it could be a new platform for a performance."

"And what might I be doing on a platform?"

"Good place to dance from my point of view," Alka teased. "Can you dance?"

"Dance? I thought I already was, you know, dancing around," Jake said with his words trailing off as Alka's intent sunk in. She meant dancing with her.

Alka was not worried about Jake's recovery from ten years as a pseudo-Buddhist. In her eyes he was better than good, and his effort to make sense of his past only made him a more interesting, more mature man. She sat in awe at how deeply she felt connected to this handsome fellow. He was more than his past could ever reveal.

Jake looked at her sheepishly, saying, "I suppose a gentleman should ask a lady first."

"Only if the gentleman pleases," Alka said theatrically.

"Does the gentleman please?" Jake asked smiling slightly.

Alka liked the pun.

"Please, please me, oh yea, like I please you…," she sang in her best Beatles voice which was not very good.

They laughed readily, ending their amusement with a silent moment. Barriers and cautions fell, rather collapsed between them during that silence. Jake sighed. He felt the openness. Yet, he wanted to switch the topic to her. He wanted to hear her say something about her ideas, her feelings—but about what? This was awkward for him not knowing how to charm, to say the appropriate thing, to take advantage of an open field.

All he could think of was to ask, "In your view, if everything we believe is linked to the brain, what's more sane? I mean, are we as races of people drifting toward one religion, more religions or no religion?"

This time Alka imitated Jake by scratching her head with both hands before saying, "Let's see…that discussion is ongoing in the academy. One academic calls mankind Homo religioso while another will say Homo sapiens and another, Homo aestheticus which only covers religion, reason and art. But brain science is primarily biological science with behavioral science as a matrix for assessing it. Religious behavior and the brain is my specialty but in that context I might use a comparison to answer your question. Asking what is sane about religion or religious behavior is like asking what is sane about race and racial behavior. There is no such thing as race from a purely biological view—we are all generated or degenerated from the same gene pool. Race, to me, is a superficial thing despite its power over human consciousness and identity. It's based on ethnicity, culture and color, yet, medically, we are not so different. Religion is like that. Religion comes from one source also, and from my point of view, leaving God out of it, religion comes from activity in the human brain responding to the environment. Now, I am not referring to the New Age nonsense about biology of belief when I say this, but I believe we produce our gods, superstitions and rituals out of the neurological interactions between us and what we experience. Our perceptions and emotions interact with the sun, planets, and stars and with nature and the elements, not to mention other people. I think we can test the interactions. How and why that works to produce religious ideas is full of mystery but that makes the work more exciting." Alka smiled with closed lips and with her head slightly tilted while shrugging her shoulders after she finished her mini-lecture. "Did I pass your test?"

"If I didn't know you better, I'd think you were utterly profound," Jake teased.

"Okay, I'm done expounding for you," she said with a mock sense of feeling hurt. "What do you want to do next?"

Jake looked up at the dark, ominous cloud creeping overhead. "It will be a miracle if the evidence leads to a resolution of why humans are so religious." He said this lazily as an afterthought, as if the statement had no importance whatsoever, as if he had no idea why he said it. Both of them knew that that topic was done and not the topic at all.

Lightning illuminated the cloud and thunder rolled over them immediately.

Alka looked up at the sky too.

"Looks like rain."

"Looks like we should get moving," Jake said as he stood up. "Come on." Jake grabbed Alka's hand to help her up from the bench.

They walked toward the Logan Square that contained the grand, circular Swann Fountain designed by Alexander Stirling Calder. It was installed in 1924. Water spouted from a circle of reclining bronze nudes with animals. The aging sculptures displayed a blue-green patina. Animal bronzes along the periphery shot water from their mouths into the fountain center. A few local people on lunch break ambled by. Tourists posed for pictures in front of a public statue near the fountain. A young, wiry skateboarder steered skillfully around them.

A short, black gentleman in a black beret played gentle jazz on his alto saxophone. He wore one gold earring in his left ear, simple black slacks and a colorful *Coogi jumper*, or sweater as they call them in America. Alka stopped in front of the jazz man. She smiled to acknowledge his skill. He responded with a flourish of notes a la Charlie Parker.

Alka enjoyed jazz and she told Jake she did. Jake pulled out a five dollar bill. As Jake dropped the fin into a brown cardboard donation box, the jazz man blew notes more like Bird again. He played well if not exactly for free. The noon sun broke through a large cumulus cloud instantly flooding the park with bright light. Bird's lingering legacy played on.

Pigeons flew overhead toward other pigeons already on the ground. They flew toward and landed around an old, raggedy man. Jake noticed the old man in a long tan trench coat sitting on the curved concrete ledge of the fountain. Cooing pigeons curiously surrounded the old man who casually tossed handfuls of seed for the birds.

He wore his trench coat over layers of clothing including a gray hooded sweatshirt and baggy tan slacks that crumpled over his scuffed white sneakers. The hood was not up. A navy-blue knit cap covered his long gray hair. His unkempt beard stuck out at a funny angle below his chin. He seemed familiar. He was talking in a low voice as if to the birds.

"Could that be Paul?" Jake wondered out loud.

"Paul who?" Alka quizzed.

"Paul, my Psych Hall roommate. I came down here twice this year hoping to see him. I promised him that I would feed his pigeons—once—so I did it once. I even bought the bloody cockatiel mix he requested for them."

As Alka and Jake approached the unkempt, old-looking man, the pigeons moved aside to let them pass. It was Paul. Jake did not want to startle him. He waited until Paul looked up to give him a chance to respond first. Paul did look up but did not appear to recognize the couple. Jake squatted down on his haunches.

"Hey, Paul! It's Jake from room 313. Good to see you again."

Paul stopped talking. A soft look came over him. He kept watching his birds, however, without openly acknowledging the pleasant intruders.

"I was hoping to see you here. Do you remember Alka, er, Miss Krol?"

Alka greeted Paul with a short "Hi" and a wave of her hand. She noticed a tiny bug crawling on his coffee-stained beard. She took one step back.

"How have you been?" Jake inquired reaching out to touch Paul's arm.

Paul said nothing, his eyes darting a few times left and right. Then he proffered a quick glance in Jake's direction. Jake suspected that Paul had regressed, that he was not taking medication, and that he was *responding to internal stimuli* as they would say in the clinic. Yet there was something vibrant about him, a glint in his eye. Paul was listening.

"Paul, what's going on? Is it about Tesla?"

"Yea, man, yea. You know. You are among the few," he said excitedly.

Mention of the eccentric genius triggered Paul to speak up.

"Here, see what I have."

Paul dug deep into one of his bags from which he pulled a blue plastic bag wrapped tightly around something the size of an average bottled drink. Paul quickly unsealed the object. When he lifted it up for Jake to see, Alka burst out laughing. The coincidental symbolism was too much for her. Jake merely stood there expressionless with his mouth partly open. They were looking at something that resembled a mushroom with a wide base. It was a gray plastic scale model of the 187 ft tall, steel grid Tesla Tower!

Also called the Wardenclyffe Tower, it was constructed around 1903 for wireless telephony. The tower was one of Tesla's grandest failed experiments, but for the Tesla cult, the tower continues to represent a viable, revolutionary way to collect and send electricity through the air. The actual tower on Long Island was razed in 1917.

Paul was not offended by Alka's laughter. He even joined her, laughing for another reason altogether. Paul expressed his joy with his treasure.

"It's Tesla's Tower. I got this from a bookstore owner at the Reading Market. He gave it to me!" Paul beamed. "The real thing was over 180 feet tall!"

At that revelation, Jake joined Alka in her laughter. At first he was astounded that Paul may have made a psychic connection with his last name. "Right, Paul. It's Tesla's Tower. You had me wondering there, pal."

The good humor coming from Alka and Jake brought Paul to life. Paul recalled the kind young man who made paper birds for him. The sparkling champagne of Paul's bottled up ego poured forth. He launched into his fixed delusions regarding Tesla and the government. One twist in his testament, one unfamiliar to Jake, featured the city and, more specifically, Swann Fountain.

Paul stood, standing a few feet away from his tiny audience of attentive people and wary pigeons. He was animated in happy agitation with his hands pointing and his unbuttoned, dirty tan coat flailing about as he turned and bent to accent his story. He was completely absorbed in the details, reciting every one from the script etched in his brain.

Paul's movements were not lost on the jazz man who moved a few steps closer to Paul while not missing a note. His quirkily improvised riffs complimented Paul's every move. Paul was jazzed. This was jazz in plain surreal performance. A pleasantly amazed Alka and a delighted Jake had a front row seat as they settled down on the fountain's stone ledge to enjoy a form of street theater never to occur again.

"Look, look up there," Paul motioned.

He pointed to City Hall with the notable statue of William Penn on top. The alto sax released a trill of high notes.

"An ion condenser marshals quantum fields and it sorts out the relevant waves. Look! Can't see it now but they embedded the condenser under Billy Penn's hat in days gone by when that was the highest point in the city in the 1960s, before all this, these skyscraper barriers built by the corporate clowns shot up."

The sax man played with deeper tones as he bowed toward the ground.

Paul was right. The impressive 37 ft tall bronze statue of William Penn atop City Hall was the limit at one time for any tall building in the city. The Penn statue stands above the forty stories level. Philadelphia thus achieved a kind of boring flattop feel to its skyline. By 2007 the new skyscrapers reached up to 58 stories. And a new one in planning stage would tower even higher.

"Look at them, high enough to prevent Tesla's free energy from reaching the people. That one, Liberty One, the spire, it captures the beam and recycles it through the Schumann Cavity into their ion condenser and they sell it. Just like the others. Thieves, looters, all of them! The new one, Comcast, does the same thing. Look how they ruined the plan, Tesla's plan. It's unfair. There's not much left but this one, this one here that is safe with the water. Here the water distributes the telluric energy. The circle is squared here."

Paul spun around pointing to the corners of the plaza and the circle of the fountain. He spun around twice more for the simple enjoyment of the feeling. The jazz man repeated a cycle of scales. The unlikely whirling dervish got dizzy from the effort and had to collect himself by leaning on the fountain's edge before going on. The jazzman shifted to a short burst of soft riffs over and over imitating someone catching his breath until Paul refocused and continued.

"This water, right there and there, is specially treated by a hidden ion transformer

384

built by the company where I worked. I was an engineer. They arranged agents to spy on us, and they took over the company and changed anyone who would not go along. They used Reich's orgone accumulator box and psychotronics to change our brains so we would not remember. But I remember!"

Paul lifted his knit cap and pointed to his head.

"You think I'm nuts, don't you, man?" he exclaimed while smiling broadly. "I know it sounds crazy. They will never let me work again. Everywhere I go they keep sending the mind controls so I can no longer concentrate. That company where we worked crashed. It will never, never again release Tesla's free energy except here. They don't know how it works here at the fountain but we do."

Paul waggled his fingers at the pigeons. As if grasping his point several pigeons looked up at him.

The jazz man blew high notes. The fountain continued to serve up the sound of rushing water. Gusts of air drew yellow and orange leaves into swirling patterns around Paul's feet. A pigeon held its place by leaning into the flurry. That bird spotted a small green caterpillar that came off a tree on a leaf. The bird promptly ate its prize catch. A few feet away, Paul continued.

"The birds redirect the forces. They take it far and away to the people. These are Tesla's birds. Without them many would lose energy and die."

Paul seemed to run out of energy when moving back toward the birds. The birds stood back watching every move of his hands as if bird seed was about to fly. Paul bowed graciously to the jazzman who reciprocated as his notes trailed off into a soft riff.

"You play very well, man," Paul said in a most gracious tone. "We should do it again some other time!"

The sax laughed out loud. So did Paul. Then the smiling jazzman pointed to Paul and said, "You're the man and thanks for the ride."

Part of Paul appeared to recognize his unusual antics as just that—as play, as theatrical. Nevertheless, another bizarre reality in his mind compelled him to remain faithful to Tesla's dreams. Paul waved his appreciation to the jazzman again before sitting down on the fountain edge a few feet from Alka. He reached into the bag in his pocket and sprinkled seed among the frantic birds.

Shortly after leaving Paul a year earlier at Psych Hall, Jake did some research on Nikola Tesla. He read that Tesla, toward the end of his long life in 1943, actually kept pigeons, fed them in Central Park in New York and sustained a quirky relationship with them, even recognizing one as his soul mate. Jake learned to better appreciate Paul's separate reality as a mirror of the fringes of Tesla's sanity. There was a historical basis for Paul's thought process.

Tesla was prone to an illness that caused hallucinations. He was a kind of synesthete with a photographic memory, seeing visions associated with ideas he had for his inventions, including his invention of alternating current. In the early 20th century, Tesla actually proposed a wireless way to transmit electricity with a machine or large electric oscillator through the atmosphere. Jake surmised that Paul was one devotee of a loose cult of conspiracy-minded people who believe that cheap or "free" energy inventions are mysteriously quashed by shadow forces in the government. Jake discovered that the author of the once popular *Celestine Prophecy* promoted the conspiracy against Tesla's *free* electricity machine in that book. Jake recalled a similar magical invention to create energy in *Atlas Shrugged* by Ayn Rand. Paul never mentioned those books but he was clearly within the cult devoted to unhinged aspects of Tesla's genius.

Whenever the city cut off the water supply to the fountain for cleaning or for conserving water, Paul became more disturbed. He expressed his agitation directly to certain local business owners or city officials. When inspired, he randomly voiced his complaints to tourists who would invariably shrink away from the wild-eyed nut that stunk at close range.

The local business folk were familiar enough with Logan Square's squatters to know what to expect. For example, Paul would verbally assault a banker or menace a street meter reader accusing them of working with the FBI or worse, with the psychiatrists. After repeated complaints, police would have to take him into custody.

Paul was notorious among the beat cops. As a matter of routine, they called Paul's brother in Chester County and the brother would come to get him. Police officers rarely charged Paul with any crime. They knew that his intentions were not criminal. They knew that Paul was fighting for human welfare in a parallel universe. Paul was certain that people would get sick and die without the ion beam. He also claimed that keeping the pigeons alive would please Tesla thus ensuring that Tesla's operatives would not cut-off the secret beam. Tesla depended on Paul. Tesla spoke to Paul every day. Paul had an important job to do.

Jake moved closer to Paul who held a nearly empty bag of pigeon feed.

"Yo, can we buy you some more bird seed?"

Paul nodded.

"Paul, we're going to get some lunch. Would you like to join us?"

Alka froze inside at the image of sitting in a restaurant with smelly Paul, his bugs, and all his bags, but Paul had other ideas that mercifully rescued her from the unwanted experience.

"Hey, man, can I have two hotdogs and a Coke?" Paul pointed to a hotdog vendor across the street.

"Done. Let's eat," Jake said as he and Alka waited for Paul to gather himself and his shabby belongings.

Alka noticed the pigeons closest to Paul. Among them she recognized the pair they met earlier and the gray male was again cooing and circling the brown female.

The raggedy man retrieved four, plastic shopping bags of stuff with both hands and he followed his hosts. They crossed the street with Alka in the lead and Paul lagging behind Jake. Paul did not like anyone following him. The kiosk offered a variety of drinks, snacks, hotdogs, and other sandwiches. They all ordered hotdogs. Alka bought a bottle of water. Paul and Jake had Cokes.

Paul truly stunk from weeks if not months of not cleaning up while sleeping on the streets. Alka stood apart casually while Jake sat with Paul on a bench. Paul ate hastily, finishing both his dogs and the drink before Alka chewed and swallowed two bites. Jake reminisced about rooming in Psych Hall with Paul. When Jake asked Paul about the paper birds, Paul became agitated.

"What happened to them, Paul?"

Paul simply pointed to one of his bags that contained other bags that held numerous small, wrapped items and foodstuffs that were obviously compacted. Paul horded items of personal significance. Every time he was committed for treatment, either the police or the hospital workers would go through the stuff. Much of it would be contaminated with mold or bacteria and had to be thrown out. Paul's physical burdens were significantly reduced every time he left a hospital, but his disease insured that within a few months he could be carrying around fifty or more pounds of stuff. Before answering Jake's question Paul looked around to be sure no one else could hear him. In low, soft tones he said, "Do not tell anyone." Jake surmised that the paper birds, if they were in the bag at all, were most likely crushed and possibly moldy.

"Hey, how about I make three more?"

Paul smiled as he stared at the ground.

Jake turned to Alka. "I need some paper. Maybe we can get something from a bank or the library. As if on cue, Alka spotted someone, a college-aged girl, standing a half-block away handing out flyers. Alka ran over to her and asked her for several flyers. The young lady was passing out notices for a new show opening at a nearby art school. The flyers were printed on a shade of green card stock. Jake immediately went to work on three more origami birds for Paul. Paul and Alka cheered and clapped after each bird magically appeared. Jake handed them to Paul who held them as if they were alive. The mentally ill man seemed slightly guarded, not wanting to put them away while anyone was looking. Then he turned to Alka as he pointed to a green paper bird.

"You wore a green shirt, remember, at Psych Hall?"

Alka scrambled through her memory. She recalled that Paul would have seen her only once or twice in the clinic. "I have a green shirt—maybe."

Jake chimed in, "I recall clearly it was a green shirt. I made it a point to study your chest."

Alka frowned. "I hope you found the effort worth your while."

"I reserve judgment. I shall require more evidence," Jake opined in a professorial manner.

"I'll send you the shirt," she quipped playfully.

Alka took another bite of her hot dog and tossed the remainder in a trash can. Her smile went unnoticed by Jake.

"That's very kind of you," Jake retorted sustaining his professional air. Then he faced the raggedy man. "Paul, will you be okay? We're going to move along."

"Sure, man, I'm fine right here. And thanks for the hotdogs. They were very good."

"Do you want me to take you somewhere to get birdseed?"

"I buy that at Reading Market. I always buy there," Paul said directly.

"How about I give you ten bucks so you can get it yourself? Would that be better?"

"Yes."

Paul preferred to do things alone. Jake understood. Jake handed him a twenty.

"Paul, do you realize that now I made one, then three and then three more birds for you. 313 was our room number."

Paul responded with a wide grin. He especially enjoyed connections between events and numbers, connections that may or may not seem bizarre to others.

Jake touched his shoulder and said, "Good-bye. Good to see you again."

"Time to split, eh, man? Thanks for the money, man."

Alka did not touch Paul but she wished the deluded man well. In the background, the jazzman blew the distinct melody from *Over the Rainbow*. Paul remained on the bench putting his things in order in special places in his bags and pockets.

"Well, that was auspicious," Alka noted. "I really never expected to see him again. It brought back the first day I laid eyes on you." She hummed the beginning of *Over the Rainbow* and sang the words *bluebirds fly*. "That was sweet of you to make birds for him—you're a good guy. But don't you think you fed into his disease with that 313 connection?"

"One thing useful I learned from the old man," Jake reminded himself out loud about the origami. "Fed into his disease? Wow, never thought about that. How so?"

"Paul's inner world has set him apart, split him off from useful, normal communication. He can't easily separate what is real from the imaginary. To have schizophrenia means to be split off from reality. It's like you added more fuel to his confusion."

"What's one more facet in his already fractured picture of the world? He thinks like a cubist painting. He's at least trying to arrange the pieces into a kind of symmetry. Now he has a piece of kindness to work with too."

Alka smiled, satisfied with Jake's answer. Then, as if out of the blue, she said, "Do you believe in fate?"

"What?" The question surprised him. "Well, I already knew Paul hung out here—but do you mean us?"

Alka nodded.

Her nod caught Jake off guard. He was not expecting her to be that direct. Instead of reacting directly or instinctively, he offered a tangential rationalization.

"If fate exists it acts either by compulsion or attraction or both. I don't know. At best the Fates bait us. Do we take the bait? But I do not think that fate arranges our lives because we are too good at rearranging fate." Jake hesitated. "Where did that come from?" He sighed after his response. He looked down at his feet as he turned his attention to Alka's intent about their first encounter.

"When we first met, or sort of met, I was in a fog, wasn't right. I recall being quite struck by you. You were an apparition that pierced the fog when you said you *saw* me—or something to that effect. You were so close yet impossibly far away. I… I was ashamed…I was confused."

"Well, it never entered my mind then that I'd be sitting here with you now," Alka said softly. "You impressed me the second time we met at Psych Hall. It shocked me how different you were—how completely alive. You seemed dead to the world just two days before. My immediate attraction for you surprised me. It violated everything in my professional bones. Handing you my card was a way for me to tempt fate even if the research was real. Fate to me is another word for circumstances we find ourselves in. I think it gets wrongly identified with destiny. I like what you said that we're too good at rearranging fate. Predicting it is hogwash. I felt that meeting you was special but I had no idea why."

Alka looked into Jake's eyes. "Do you feel something happening?" She watched his eyes for a reaction.

Jake could hardly contain himself. His eyes opened wider. "Yes, like I am about to leap over Niagara Falls and live—what do you think of that?"

Alka smiled broadly, realizing full well how insane that sounded yet grasping his intent. He trusted her and he wanted to be with her. She squeezed his hand. They walked toward the Cathedral Basilica of Saints Peter and Paul. The massive church is perhaps the most impressive one in the city. Built in the mid-19th Century, the spacious interior has magnificent proportions reminiscent of old Roman churches. It comfortably accommodates two thousand parishioners. They were perhaps within two blocks of the entrance when a stiff wind heralded the quickly darkening sky they saw above. They picked up their pace.

"Where're we going?" shouted Alka through the din of wind and coming rain.

"We can duck into the cathedral. I wanted to go in anyway to light a candle."

"Light a candle for what?" Large raindrops began to hit hard around and on them.

"My dad. I'll explain later. Let's go."

They broke into a run as the rain burst from the thundering sky above. Within the short minute it took to cover the distance both of them were dripping wet but laughing at the cathedral's side entrance along Race Street. As they shook and swiped the rainwater off their hair and clothes, Alka glanced at the *Kopernik* monument across the street. Despite the driving rain, two pigeons perched on a safe location under the slanting, twelve foot diameter stainless steel circles mounted on a red granite base.

Years before, Alka studied the stainless steel sculpture when she was a student at Penn. It represented the solar system by a flat circle within a circle with a triangle shape connecting the two circles on one side. The outer circle symbolized the orbit of the earth. The inner circle was the sun with its rays extending out into infinity. The triangle shape that supported the celestial circles symbolized the home-made instruments that Copernicus used in his calculations. Copernicus did not need the Bible as a reference for his view of the heavens. His science unsettled some churchmen of the day.

Alka was about to enter the abode of the very powers that once resisted evidence of a universe very different than the one expressed by the ancient Biblical writers. The irony was not lost on her. Jake took no notice of the Kopernik monument as he stomped his feet before opening the door. He was only interested in the warm, dry lobby out of the wind.

They stepped further inside. Alka looked for a ladies' room while Jake went to the nearby men's room. He relieved himself at a pine-scented urinal. He used the paper towels to dry off his head, face and hands. Jake stepped out into the aisle to wait for Alka. It was early afternoon. He saw few people inside the building. Some of them were tourists. Two parishioners prayed separately at side chapels. One was a middle-aged woman with too much make-up and a haggard expression. Jake surmised that she had a hard life. "Could be an alcoholic," he thought. Behind her he saw a slim custodian in a dark blue work uniform quietly cleaning around the pews. Down the aisle, an elderly Asian couple took pictures of a marble relief of a Station of the Cross. There would be no services in the church until early that evening.

Jake looked past the couple to the artwork on the walls. He looked at the walls themselves lined with fine polished marble. He thought of the exterior brownstone walls cut most likely from quarries in Connecticut. He felt connected to the quarrymen and the masons as well as the architects and engineers and their hands and tools. In their honor, he took out some bills from his wallet and stuffed them into a donation box for the poor. Although he stopped here twice in the past year to light candles, it had been eighteen years since he was here with his family to attend a service. He stopped going to church altogether as a senior in high school.

Alka reappeared. "So, Mister Buddhist, why are we here, in a Catholic Church?"

"Months before Ziggy died we all came here for Christmas Eve mass. My mother wanted to attend church here in this grand setting at least once, so we went with her. It was quite a production, easily worth the price of admission. Even as kids, Harry and I were impressed with the space, the music, and the choir. That was the last time Ziggy went to church, as far as I know. Since we were close by, I thought I'd light one more candle for him. Maybe we can do it together."

"Sure."

"Do you know why Catholics do this?" Jake asked her.

"Isn't it a form of prayer? Why are *you* doing it anyway?"

"Could be a form of prayer. Let's go to the votive stand over there. Don't worry about a donation—I gave at the office!" Jake teased. "Why am I doing it? That's a good question."

They were near one of several votive stands where many of the candles glowed in red glass casings.

"These aren't candles," Alka whispered with a hint of sarcasm in her delivery. "I was expecting real flames. Do these bulbs work as well as real flames?"

"Better."

"Better?"

"Hey, the Church is with it these days—the latest in science. If Paul is right, these candles are hooked into Tesla's free energy source. No big buildings in the way between Swann Fountain and here."

Alka poked Jake in the ribs. "Aren't you afraid of burning for blasphemy?"

Jake pointed to an electric candle and Alka flicked the switch. It lit up like a red Christmas bulb. Jake continued talking with more seriousness.

"Catholics believe that you can help souls not yet in heaven, or if they are in heaven, we can ask that they pray for us. The burning, er, glowing candle is a form of prayer. It's similar to hanging a Tibetan prayer flag in the wind."

"Well, no wind will blow out these puppies. Do we say a prayer to make it work?" she asked.

"I don't know if saying anything makes it work any better. I don't believe this works like magic. I want to believe the ritual is a way of acknowledging that dad's with us and with God." Jake noticed that Alka scrunched up her face. "What's the face for?" he asked her.

"There's God again. What do you mean by God?"

"You really want me to answer that?"

"Yep."

"If you killed me I might be able to tell you."

"Well if you're going to be that way about it, maybe I'll pass. I'm not looking for a relationship with a talking ghost."

"I would quote the catechism if I could remember it."

"Take a shot, Mr. Catholic!" Alka challenged with a giggle.

"You asked for it." Jake made a quick sign of the cross. "Here goes: Um, God is an infinite being, um, being infinite, inscrutable, ineffable, all-powerful, all-knowing, all-merciful, and a guy whose relations with a young Jewish woman instigated the religion that built this basilica."

Alka whispered with urgency, "You are going to burn, Master Jake, you know that don't you?"

"Father forgives me for I know not what I am talking about."

"I am sure he does," Alka whispered close to Jake's ear, "because his candle is still on. See."

"Your whispering is turning me on," Jake said softly.

Alka elbowed him hard in the ribs. "We're in church, Rocky. Show some respect," she whispered.

Jake winced, reminded suddenly of his cracked ribs at Psych Hall. "Well, you are," he said in a low voice. "Here, come with me. I want to offer a prayer for Ziggy." Jake walked over to the center altar area with Alka following. Jake assumed a prayerful pose with his head bowed. Alka did likewise. They stood facing the main sanctuary with its ornate cupola.

Lightning flashed and thunder rolled softly through the building. The effect of sudden illumination through stained glass drew Alka's attention toward the empty marble slab of the main altar. She felt oddly moved as she held her breath in momentary trance, taking in the sacred space. The grand dome above mocked a heaven hovering over something theatrical and mystical that occurred on that slab of marble erected for the incomprehensibly eternal sacrifice of the Christian God. She imagined lines of people all over the world taking and eating the white wafers and sipping from goblets of wine. She also saw a place for a man and a woman to stand, to vow to sacrifice for one another through a life of selfless love.

Jake remained bowed in his silence. He did this to honor his father though his thoughts wandered from how damp he felt to the humor of the faux candle to the woman standing silently next to him. Alka noticed his silence. She waited for him to raise his head. When he did she touched his hand. At the touch of her hand he turned to face her, slid his arms around her waist and embraced her gently. The warmth of their bodies quickly penetrated the cool chill of wet clothing between them. Her heart rate increased with his as he held her and she held him. He drew back a bit, far enough to look deep into her blue eyes and then, for the first time, he kissed her and he kissed her full on her open lips. Alka swooned, astonished by a joy that bordered on ecstasy. Jake felt her graceful, supple reaction at every point of body contact. He felt in his bones then, at that moment, that he could die for this woman.

Waylon was right. He was a dead man. He was a dead man because of her and he would live because of her. Their lips parted and Alka rested her head on his shoulder, remaining in his embrace.

If the Buddhist dharma meant anything more to Jake after all his effort, it meant this: to dissolve in love for another. Maybe this was what Professor Pedersen the nun meant by seeking *communion* during her meditation.

A second peal of thunder drummed through the building. The raw, sacred presence of the structure's intention hovered around them. Every brownstone block shouted a silent hallelujah. Subtle energies filled the holy emptiness forged by forces beyond understanding after the storm.

Somewhere in New Mexico, a playful raven waits on a rock. Another droplet falls from a storm-soaked pine needle, toward the pond below.